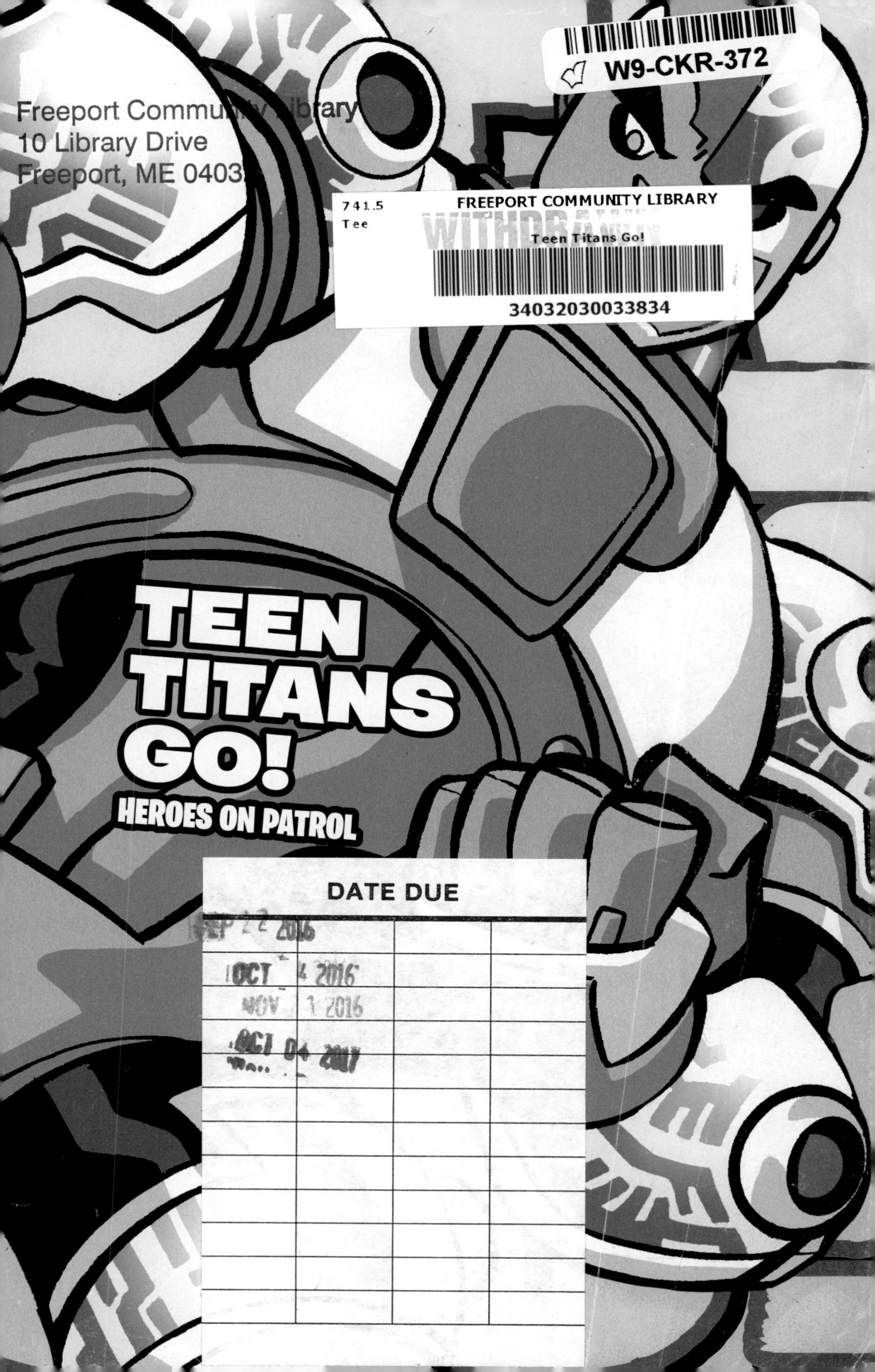
TEEN TITANS GO!
HEROES ON PATROL

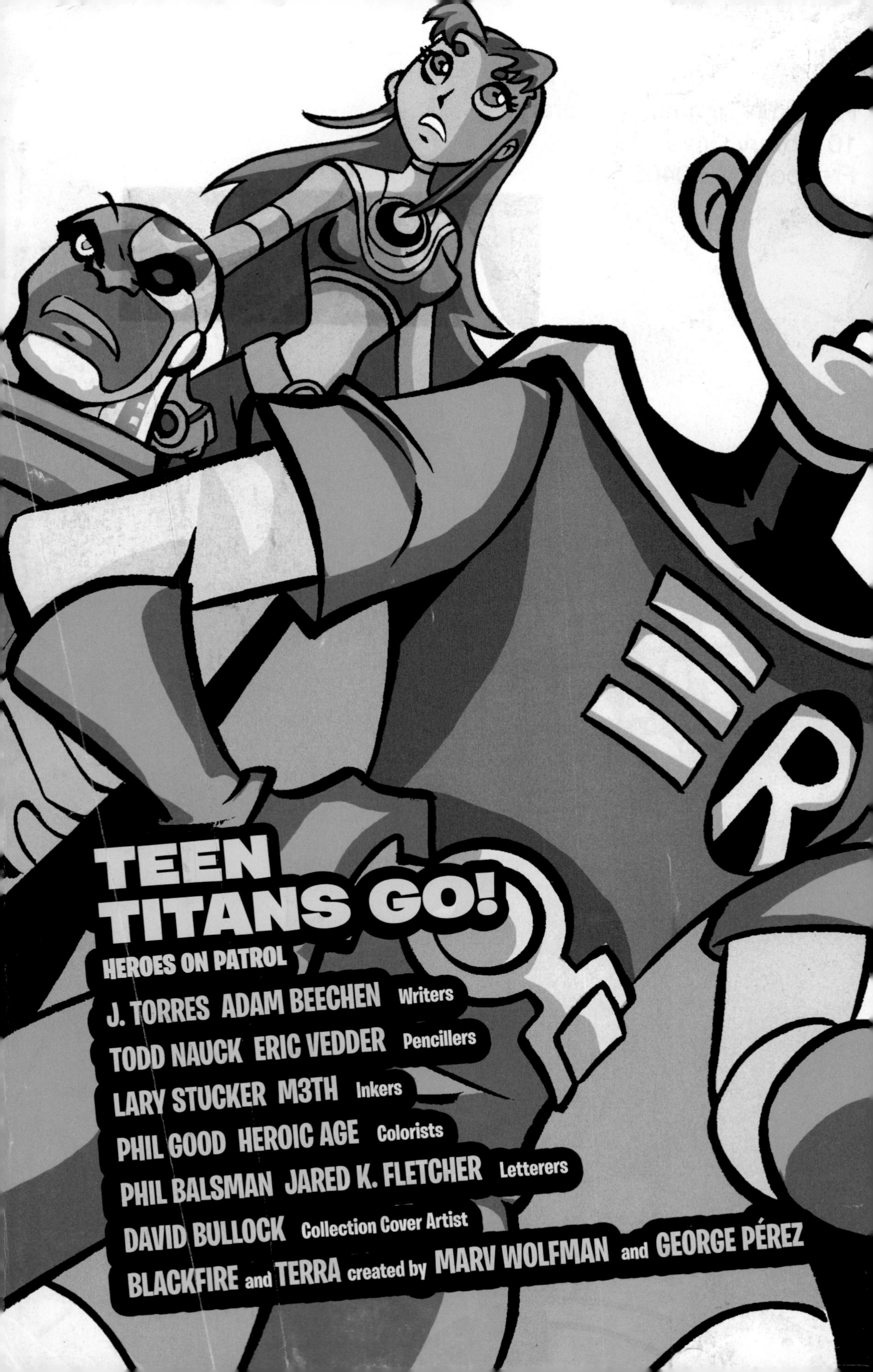

TEEN TITANS GO!

HEROES ON PATROL

J. TORRES ADAM BEECHEN Writers

TODD NAUCK ERIC VEDDER Pencillers

LARY STUCKER M3TH Inkers

PHIL GOOD HEROIC AGE Colorists

PHIL BALSMAN JARED K. FLETCHER Letterers

DAVID BULLOCK Collection Cover Artist

BLACKFIRE and TERRA created by MARV WOLFMAN and GEORGE PÉREZ

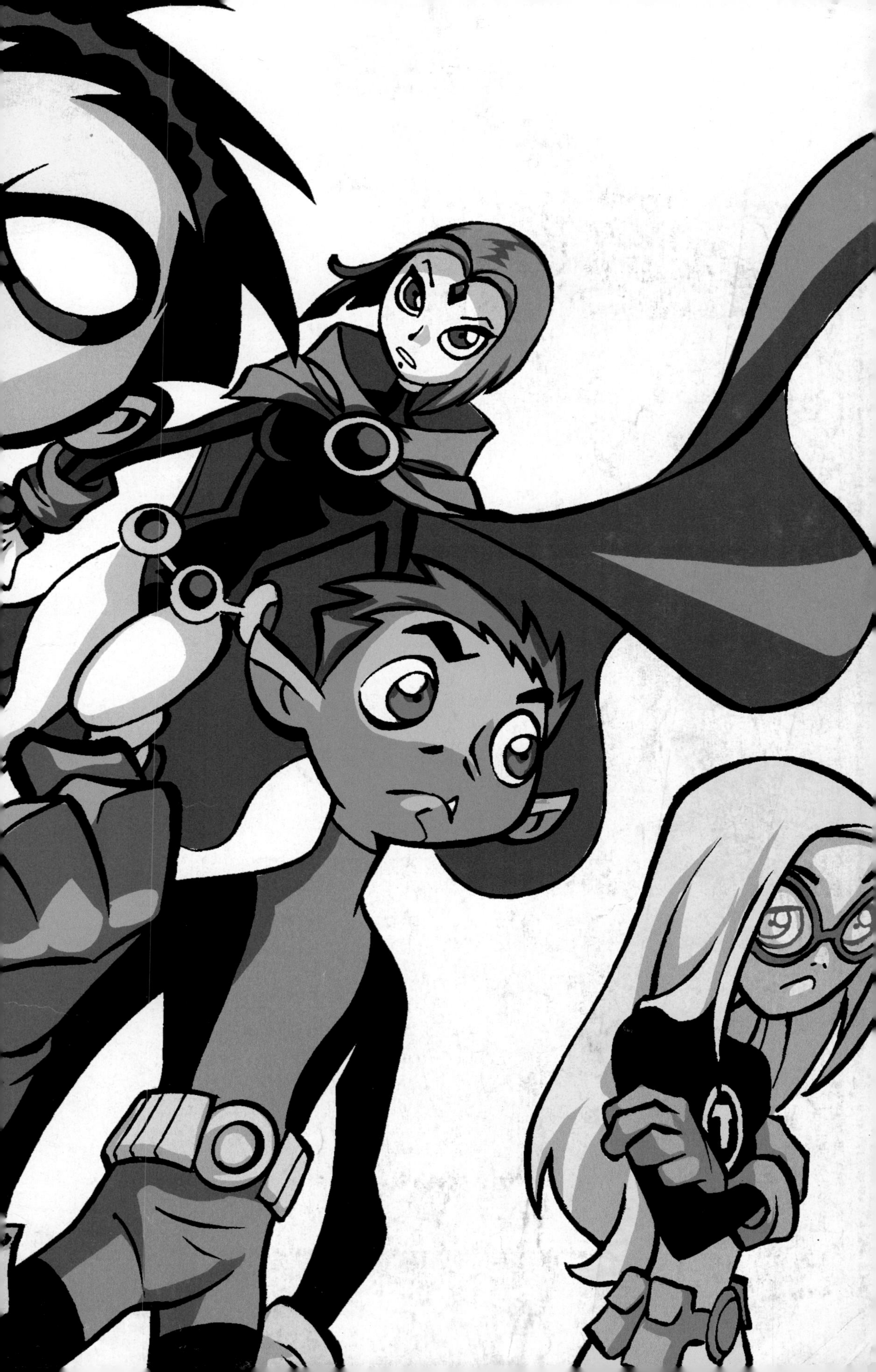

Lysa Hawkins, Tom Palmer Jr. Editors – Original Series
Jeanine Schaefer Assistant Editor – Original Series
Jeb Woodard Group Editor – Collected Editions
Seve Cook Design Director – Books
Louis Prandi Publication Design

Bob Harras Senior VP – Editor-in-Chief, DC Comics

Diane Nelson President
Dan DiDio and **Jim Lee** Co-Publishers
Geoff Johns Chief Creative Officer
Amit Desai Senior VP – Marketing & Global Franchise Management
Nairi Gardiner Senior VP – Finance
Sam Ades VP – Digital Marketing
Bobbie Chase VP – Talent Development
Mark Chiarello Senior VP – Art, Design & Collected Editions
John Cunningham VP – Content Strategy
Anne DePies VP – Strategy Planning & Reporting
Don Falletti VP – Manufacturing Operations
Lawrence Ganem VP – Editorial Administration & Talent Relations
Alison Gill Senior VP – Manufacturing & Operations
Hank Kanalz Senior VP – Editorial Strategy & Administration
Jay Kogan VP – Legal Affairs
Derek Maddalena Senior VP – Sales & Business Development
Jack Mahan VP – Business Affairs
Dan Miron VP – Sales Planning & Trade Development
Nick Napolitano VP – Manufacturing Administration
Carol Roeder VP – Marketing
Eddie Scannell VP – Mass Account & Digital Sales
Courtney Simmons Senior VP – Publicity & Communications
Jim (Ski) Sokolowski VP – Comic Book Specialty & Newsstand Sales
Sandy Yi Senior VP – Global Franchise Management

TEEN TITANS GO!: HEROES ON PATROL

DC Comics, 2900 West Alameda Ave., Burbank, CA 91505
Printed by RR Donnelley, Salem, VA, USA. 4/22/16 First Printing.
ISBN: 978-1-4012-6638-7

Library of Congress Cataloging-in-Publication Data

Names: Torres, J., 1969- author. | Beechen, Adam, author. | Nauck, Todd,
illustrator. | Vedder, Eric, illustrator. | Stucker, Lary, illustrator. |
M3th, illustrator. | Good, Phil (Colorist) illustrator | Balsman, Phil,
illustrator. | Fletcher, Jared K., illustrator. | Bullock, David, 1971-
illustrator. | Heroic Age Studios, illustrator.
Title: Teen Titans Go! Volume 2, Heroes on patrol / J. Torres, Adam Beechen,
writers ; Todd Nauck, Eric Vedder, pencillers ; Lary Stucker, M3th, inkers
; Phil Good, Heroic Age, colorists ; Phil Balsman, Jared K. Fletcher,
letterers ; Dave Bullock, collection cover artist.
Other titles: Heroes on patrol
Description: Burbank, CA : DC Comics, [2016] | "Originally published in
single magazine form in TEEN TITANS GO! 7-13."
Identifiers: LCCN 2015050934 | ISBN 9781401266387
Subjects: LCSH: Graphic novels. | Superhero comic books, strips, etc.
Classification: LCC PN6728.T34 T53 2016 | DDC 741.5/973–dc23
LC record available at http://lccn.loc.gov/2015050934

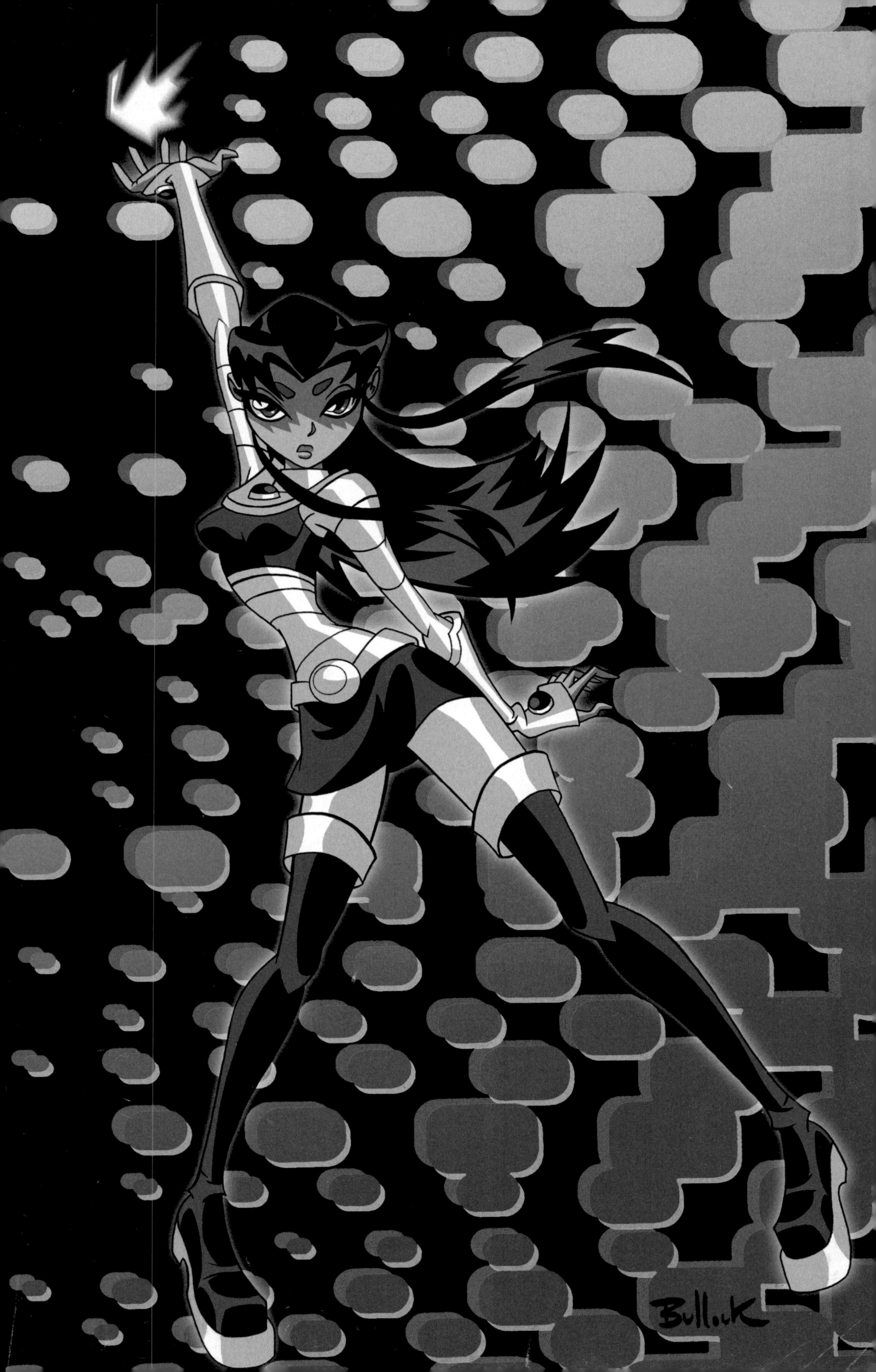
Bullock

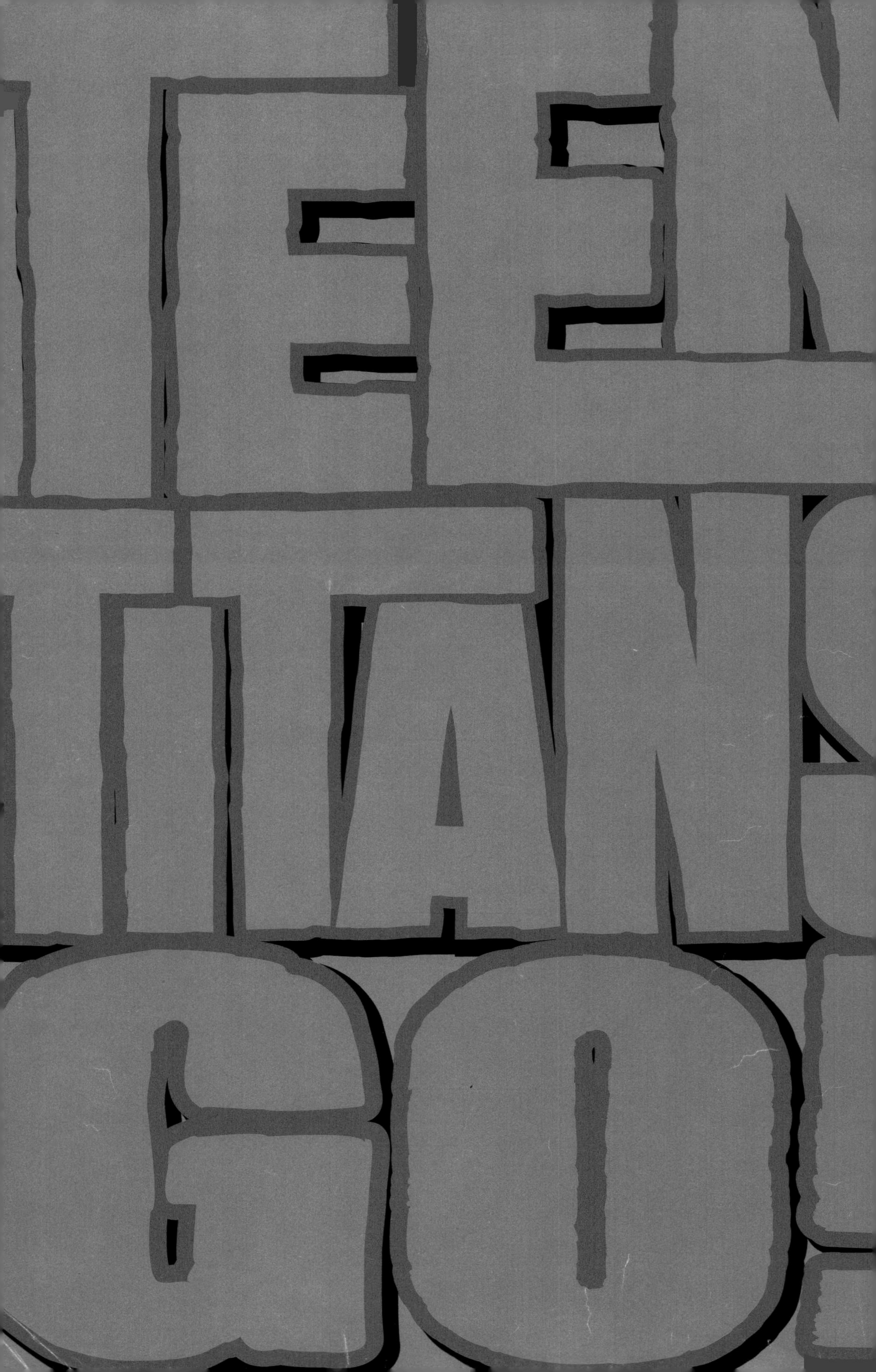

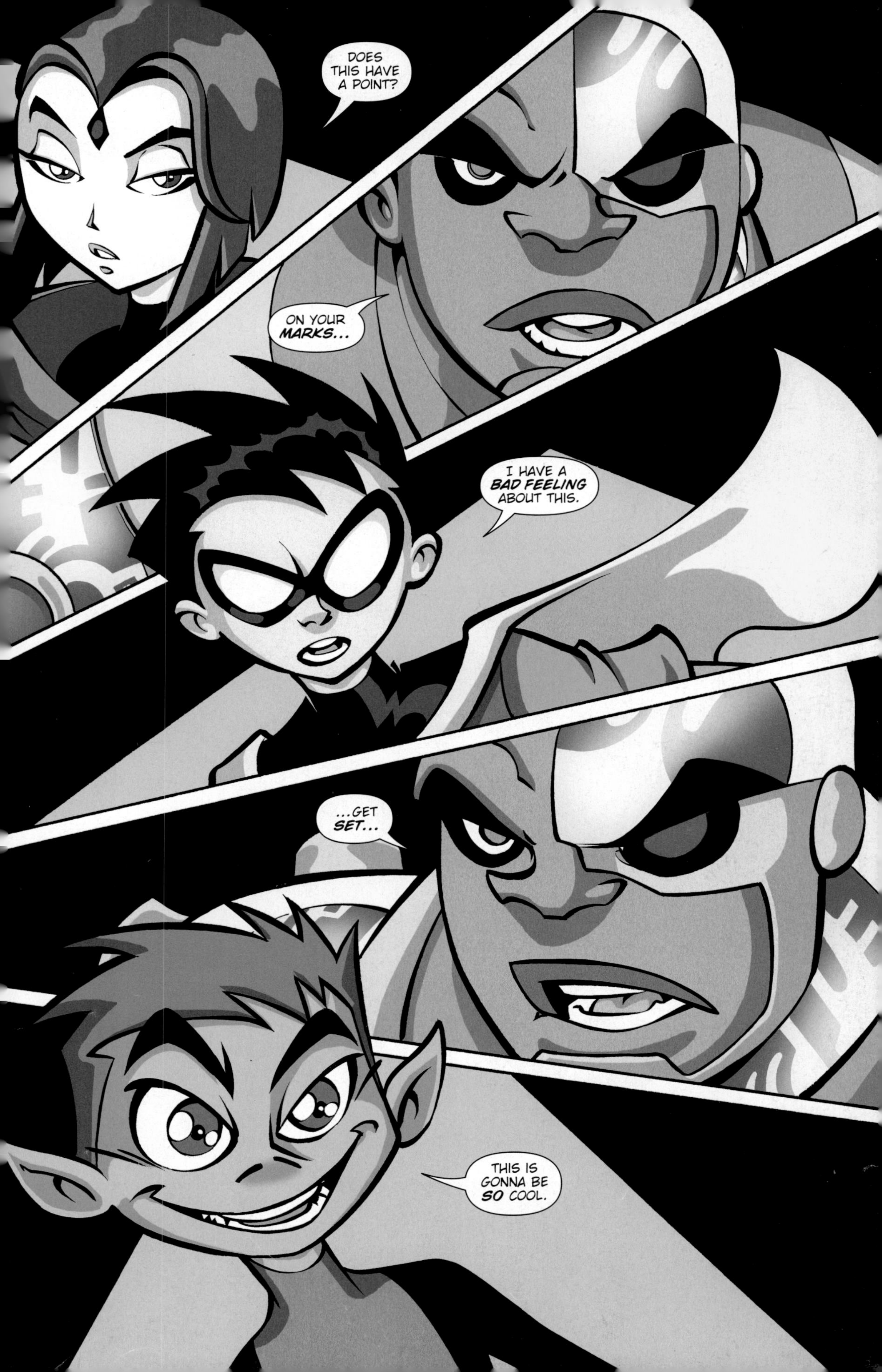
DOES THIS HAVE A POINT?
ON YOUR MARKS...
I HAVE A BAD FEELING ABOUT THIS.
...GET SET...
THIS IS GONNA BE SO COOL.

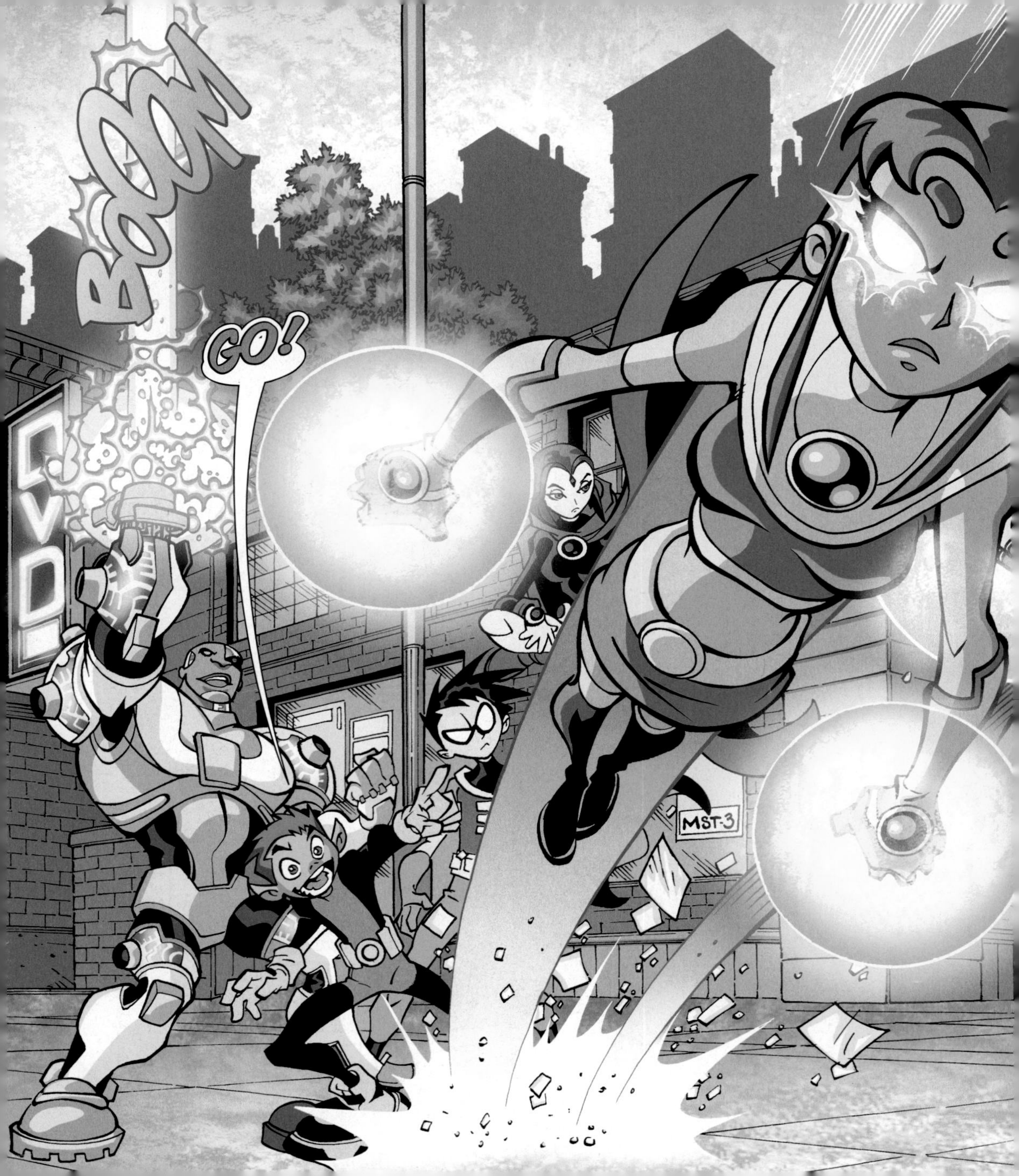
BOOOM
GO!
DVD
MST-3

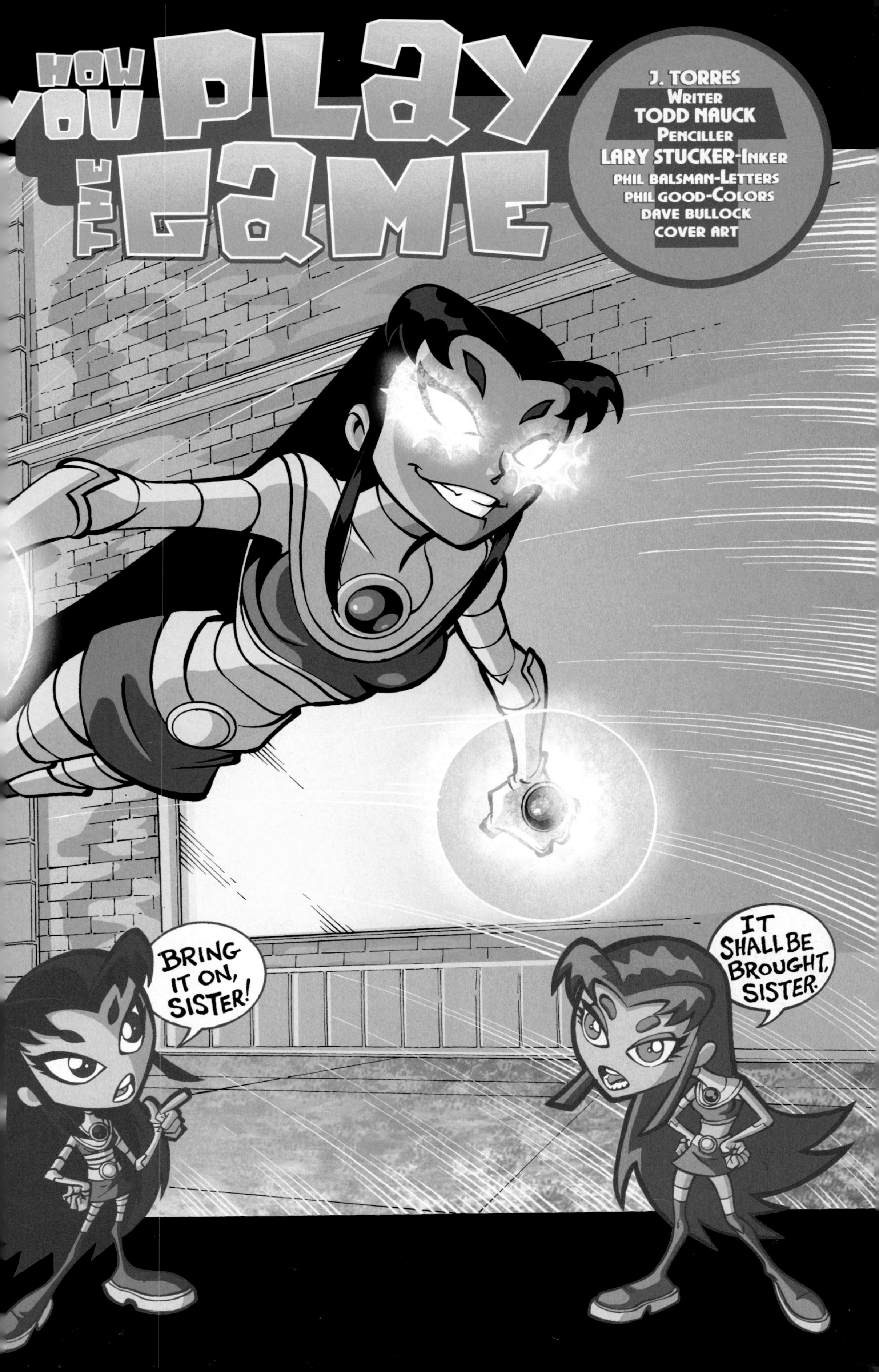
HOW YOU PLAY THE GAME
J. TORRES
WRITER
TODD NAUCK
PENCILLER
LARY STUCKER-INKER
PHIL BALSMAN-LETTERS
PHIL GOOD-COLORS
DAVE BULLOCK
COVER ART
BRING IT ON, SISTER!
IT SHALL BE BROUGHT, SISTER.

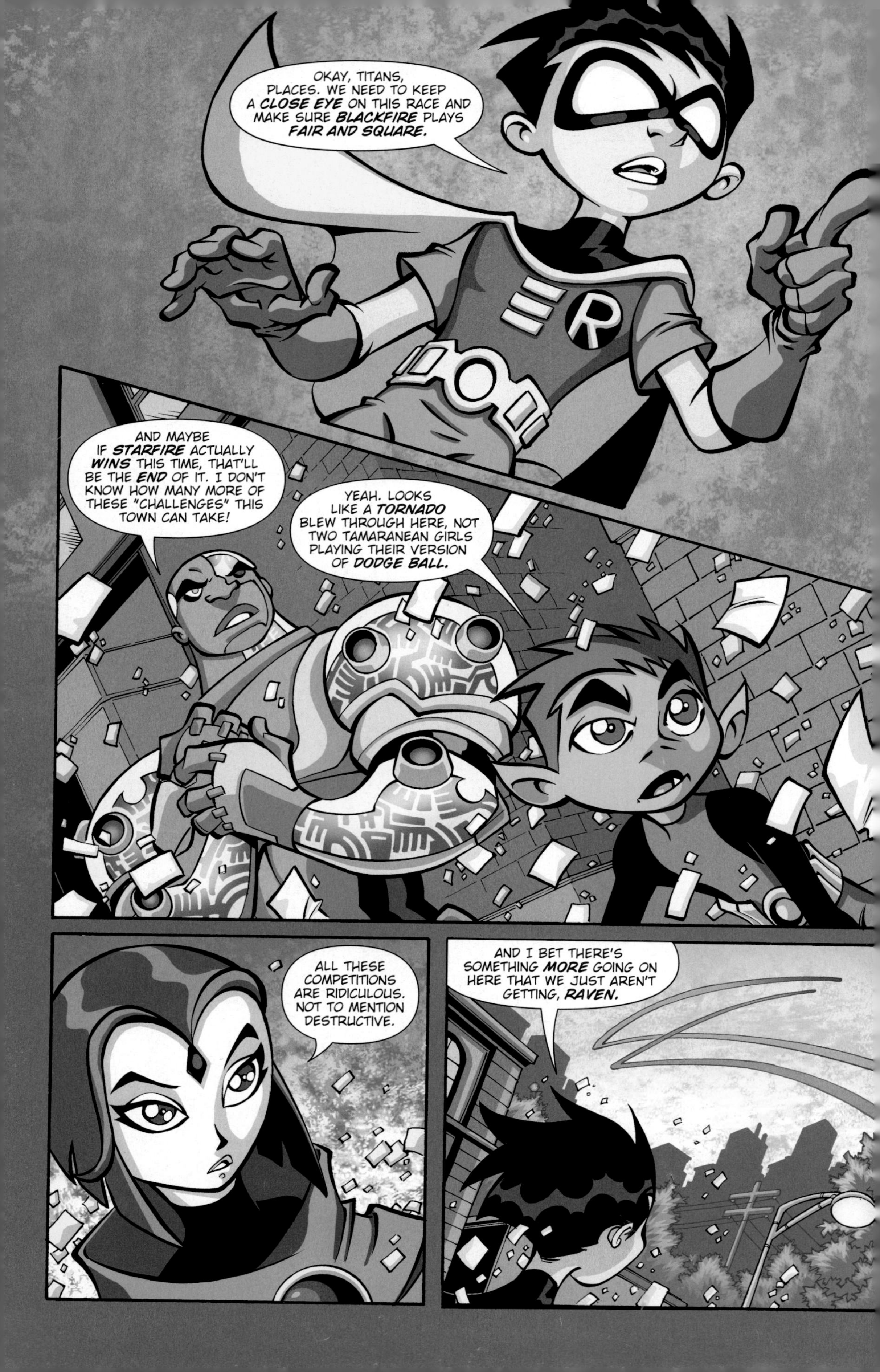
OKAY, TITANS, PLACES. WE NEED TO KEEP A CLOSE EYE ON THIS RACE AND MAKE SURE BLACKFIRE PLAYS FAIR AND SQUARE.
AND MAYBE IF STARFIRE ACTUALLY WINS THIS TIME, THAT'LL BE THE END OF IT. I DON'T KNOW HOW MANY MORE OF THESE "CHALLENGES" THIS TOWN CAN TAKE!
YEAH. LOOKS LIKE A TORNADO BLEW THROUGH HERE, NOT TWO TAMARANEAN GIRLS PLAYING THEIR VERSION OF DODGE BALL.
ALL THESE COMPETITIONS ARE RIDICULOUS. NOT TO MENTION DESTRUCTIVE.
AND I BET THERE'S SOMETHING MORE GOING ON HERE THAT WE JUST AREN'T GETTING, RAVEN.

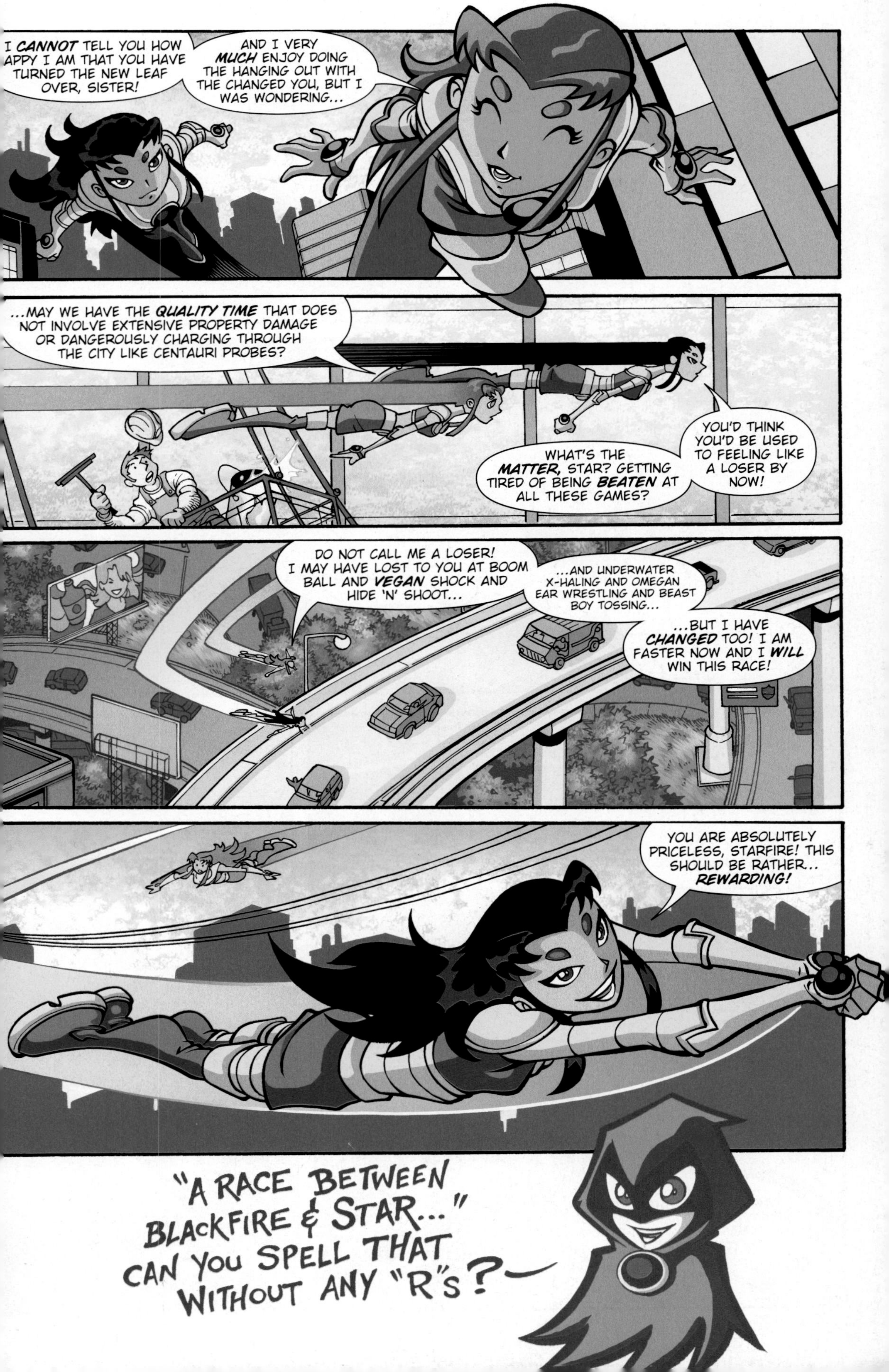
I CANNOT TELL YOU HOW APPY I AM THAT YOU HAVE TURNED THE NEW LEAF OVER, SISTER!
AND I VERY MUCH ENJOY DOING THE HANGING OUT WITH THE CHANGED YOU, BUT I WAS WONDERING...
...MAY WE HAVE THE QUALITY TIME THAT DOES NOT INVOLVE EXTENSIVE PROPERTY DAMAGE OR DANGEROUSLY CHARGING THROUGH THE CITY LIKE CENTAURI PROBES?
WHAT'S THE MATTER, STAR? GETTING TIRED OF BEING BEATEN AT ALL THESE GAMES?
YOU'D THINK YOU'D BE USED TO FEELING LIKE A LOSER BY NOW!
DO NOT CALL ME A LOSER! I MAY HAVE LOST TO YOU AT BOOM BALL AND VEGAN SHOCK AND HIDE 'N' SHOOT...
...AND UNDERWATER X-HALING AND OMEGAN EAR WRESTLING AND BEAST BOY TOSSING...
...BUT I HAVE CHANGED TOO! I AM FASTER NOW AND I WILL WIN THIS RACE!
YOU ARE ABSOLUTELY PRICELESS, STARFIRE! THIS SHOULD BE RATHER... REWARDING!
"A RACE BETWEEN BLACKFIRE & STAR..." CAN YOU SPELL THAT WITHOUT ANY "R"S?

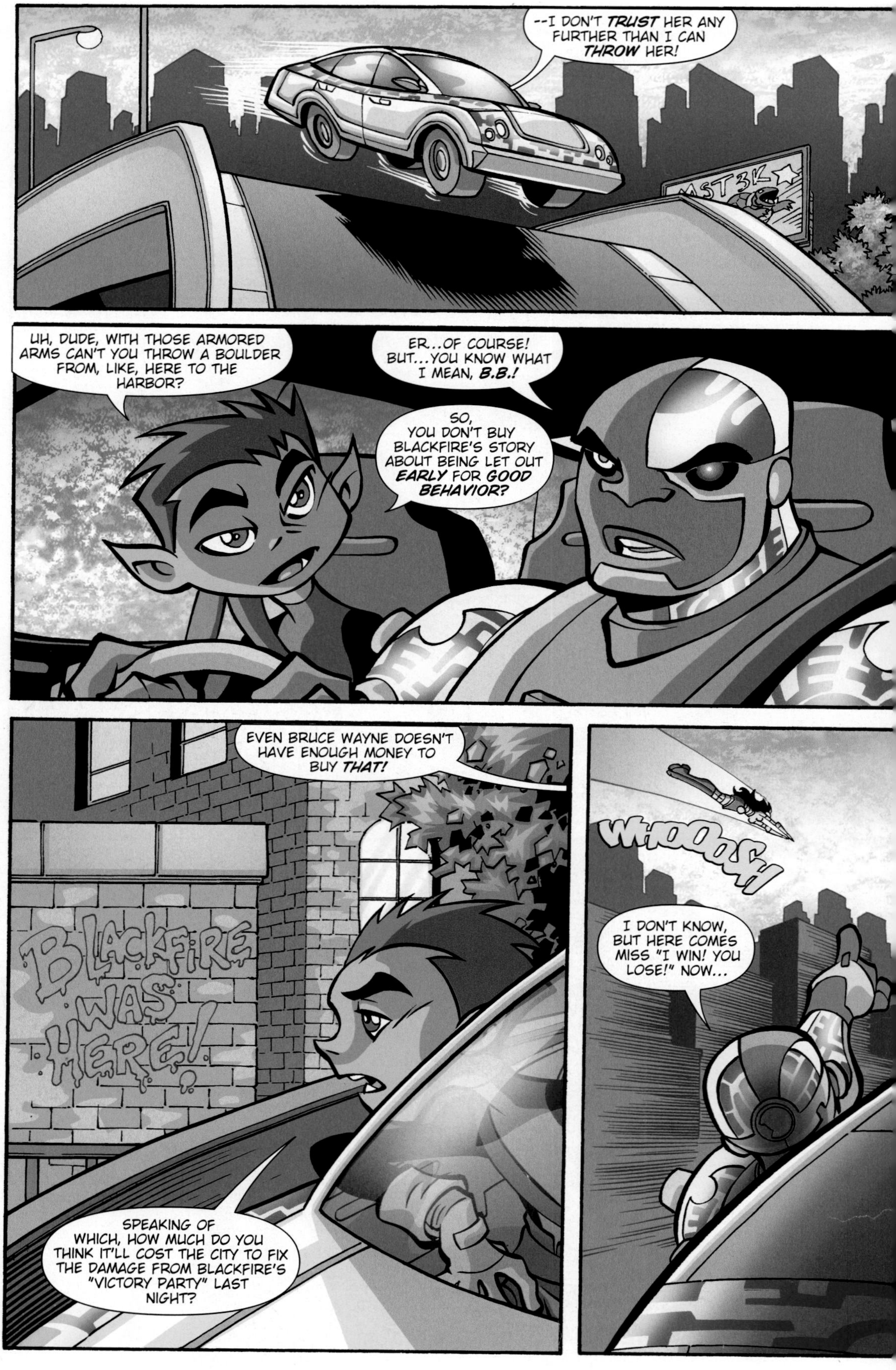

--I DON'T TRUST HER ANY FURTHER THAN I CAN THROW HER!
UH, DUDE, WITH THOSE ARMORED ARMS CAN'T YOU THROW A BOULDER FROM, LIKE, HERE TO THE HARBOR?
ER...OF COURSE! BUT...YOU KNOW WHAT I MEAN, B.B.!
SO, YOU DON'T BUY BLACKFIRE'S STORY ABOUT BEING LET OUT EARLY FOR GOOD BEHAVIOR?
BLACKFIRE WAS HERE!
SPEAKING OF WHICH, HOW MUCH DO YOU THINK IT'LL COST THE CITY TO FIX THE DAMAGE FROM BLACKFIRE'S "VICTORY PARTY" LAST NIGHT?
EVEN BRUCE WAYNE DOESN'T HAVE ENOUGH MONEY TO BUY THAT!
WHOOOSH
I DON'T KNOW, BUT HERE COMES MISS "I WIN! YOU LOSE!" NOW...

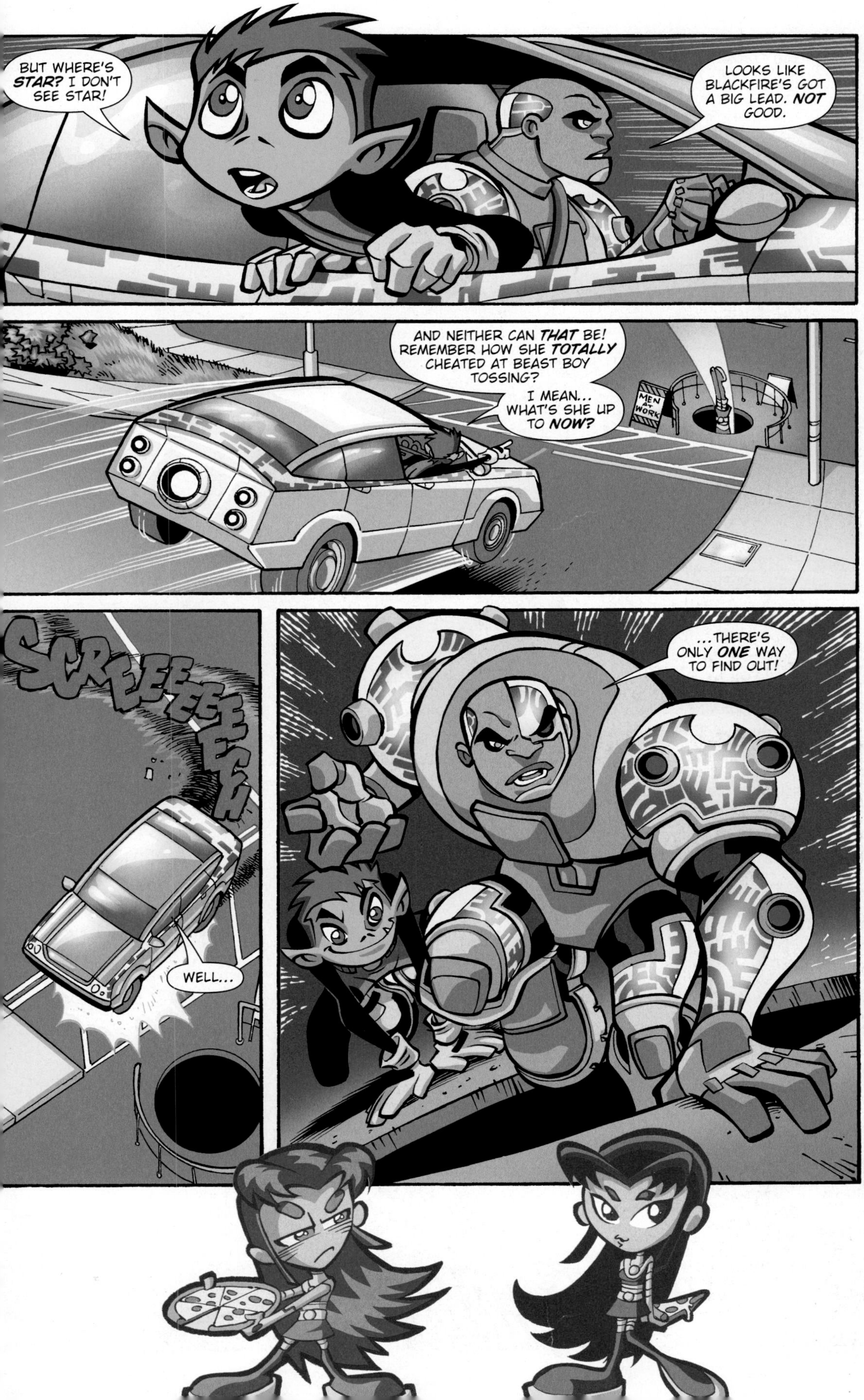
BUT WHERE'S STAR? I DON'T SEE STAR!
LOOKS LIKE BLACKFIRE'S GOT A BIG LEAD. NOT GOOD.
AND NEITHER CAN THAT BE! REMEMBER HOW SHE TOTALLY CHEATED AT BEAST BOY TOSSING?
I MEAN... WHAT'S SHE UP TO NOW?
MEN AT WORK
SCREEEEEEECH
WELL...
...THERE'S ONLY ONE WAY TO FIND OUT!

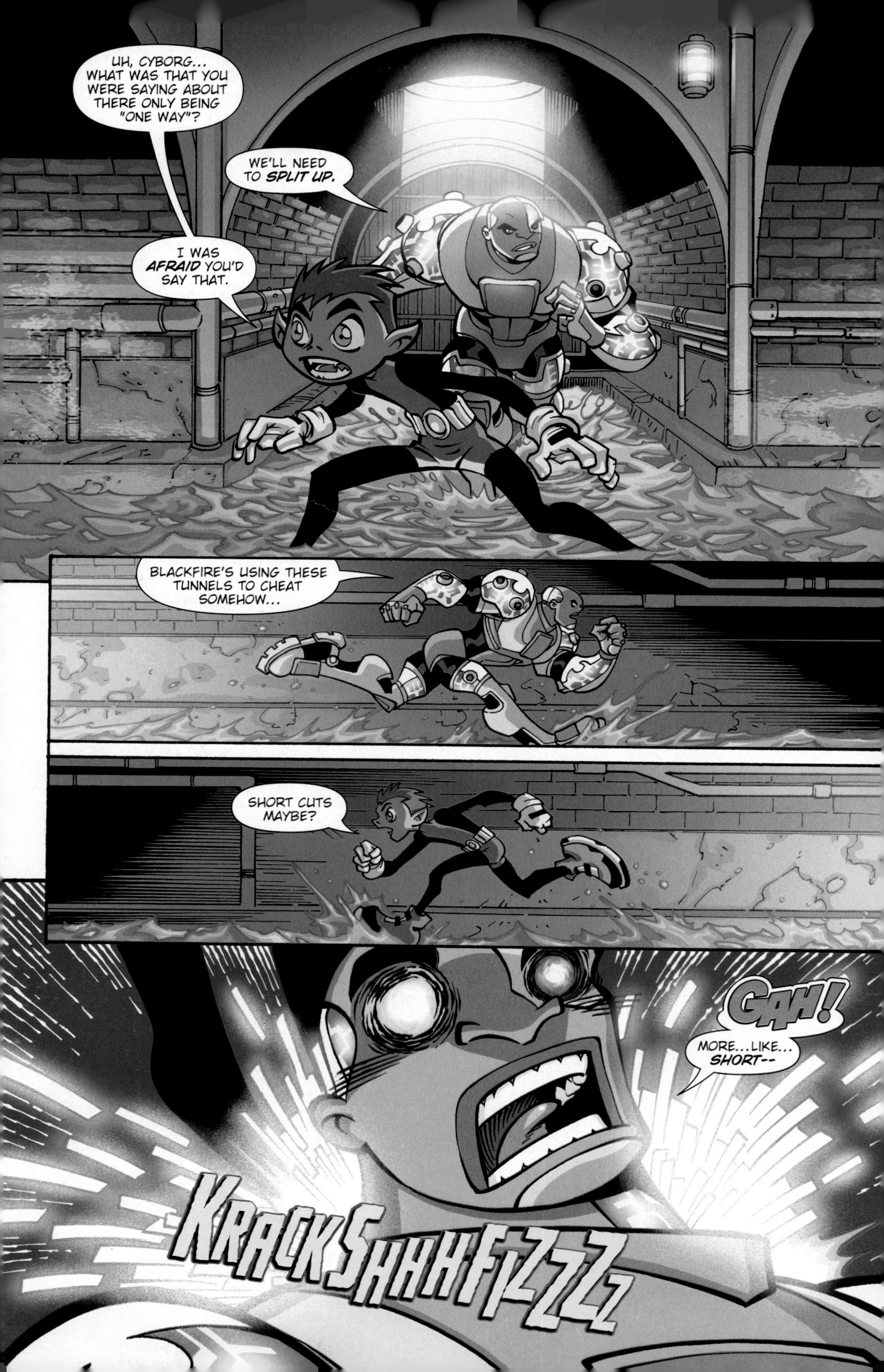
UH, CYBORG... WHAT WAS THAT YOU WERE SAYING ABOUT THERE ONLY BEING "ONE WAY"?
WE'LL NEED TO SPLIT UP.
I WAS AFRAID YOU'D SAY THAT.
BLACKFIRE'S USING THESE TUNNELS TO CHEAT SOMEHOW...
SHORT CUTS MAYBE?
GAH!
MORE...LIKE... SHORT--
KRACKSHHHFIZZZZ

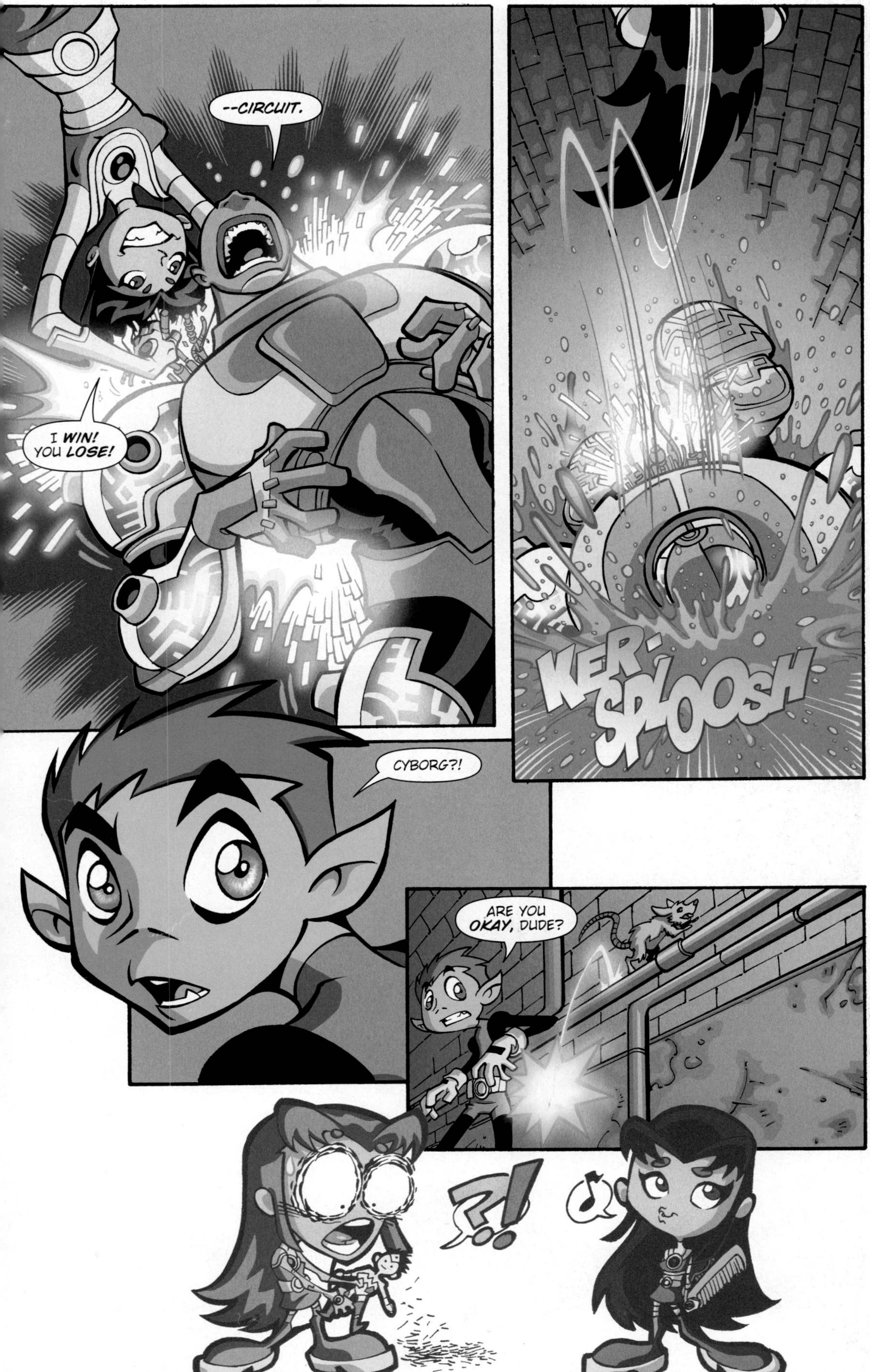
--CIRCUIT.
I WIN! YOU LOSE!
KER-SPLOOSH
CYBORG?!
ARE YOU OKAY, DUDE?
?!

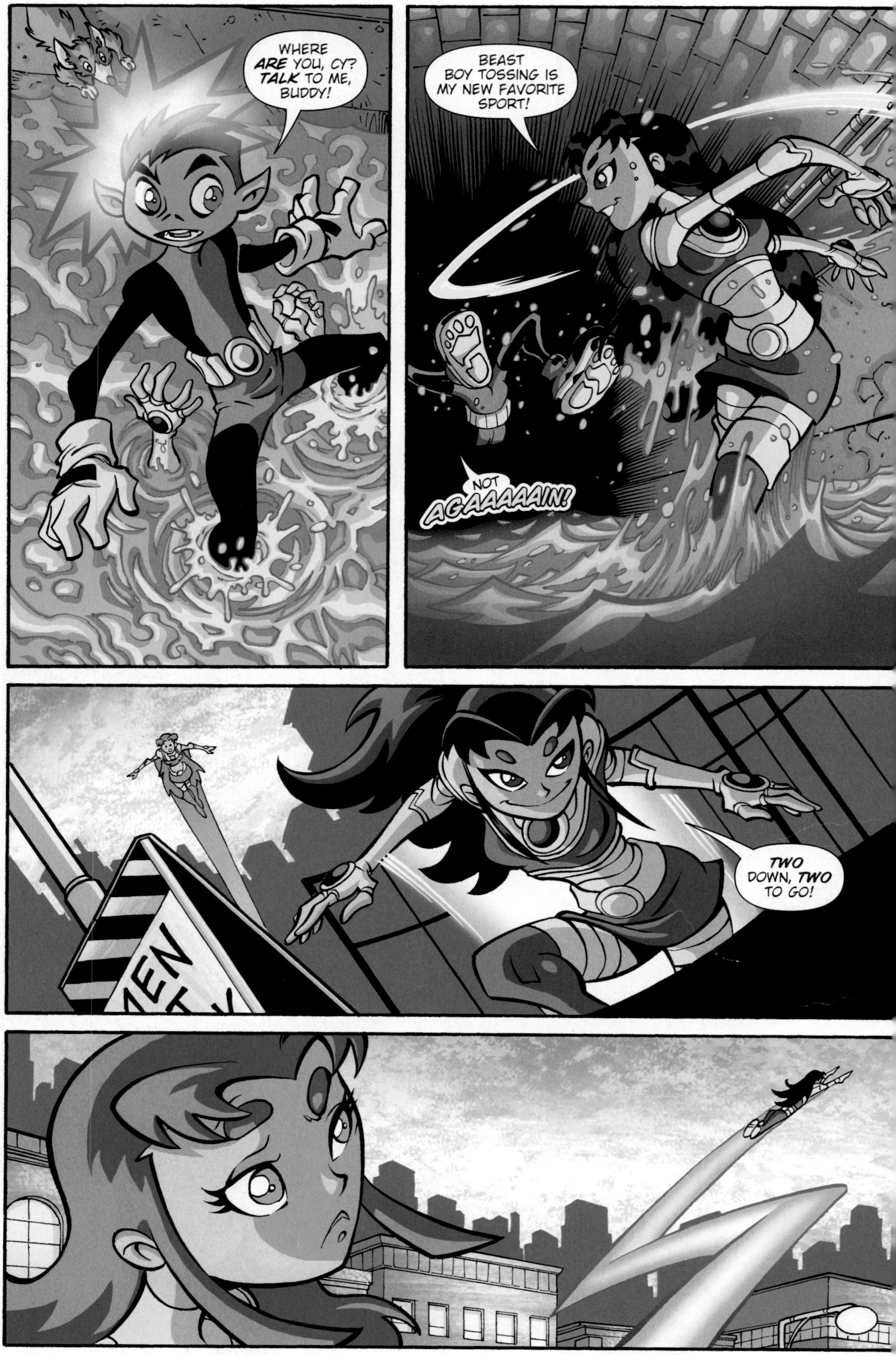
WHERE ARE YOU, CY? TALK TO ME, BUDDY!
BEAST BOY TOSSING IS MY NEW FAVORITE SPORT!
NOT AGAAAAAIN!
TWO DOWN, TWO TO GO!

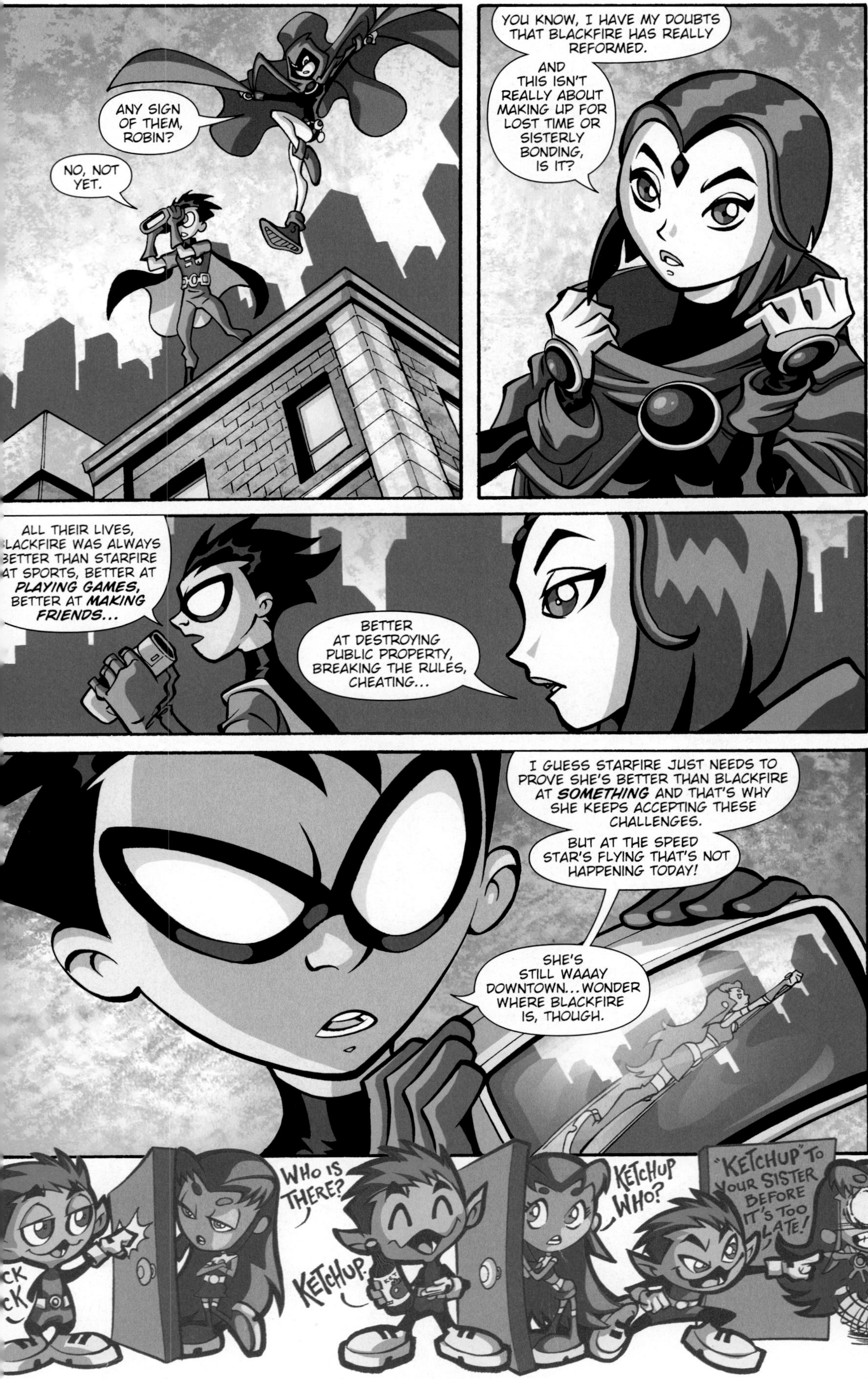
ANY SIGN OF THEM, ROBIN?
NO, NOT YET.
YOU KNOW, I HAVE MY DOUBTS THAT BLACKFIRE HAS REALLY REFORMED.
AND THIS ISN'T REALLY ABOUT MAKING UP FOR LOST TIME OR SISTERLY BONDING, IS IT?
ALL THEIR LIVES, BLACKFIRE WAS ALWAYS BETTER THAN STARFIRE AT SPORTS, BETTER AT *PLAYING GAMES*, BETTER AT *MAKING FRIENDS...*
BETTER AT DESTROYING PUBLIC PROPERTY, BREAKING THE RULES, CHEATING...
I GUESS STARFIRE JUST NEEDS TO PROVE SHE'S BETTER THAN BLACKFIRE AT *SOMETHING* AND THAT'S WHY SHE KEEPS ACCEPTING THESE CHALLENGES.
BUT AT THE SPEED STAR'S FLYING THAT'S NOT HAPPENING TODAY!
SHE'S STILL WAAAY DOWNTOWN... WONDER WHERE BLACKFIRE IS, THOUGH.
WHO IS THERE?
KETCHUP.
KETCHUP WHO?
"KETCHUP" TO YOUR SISTER BEFORE IT'S TOO LATE!

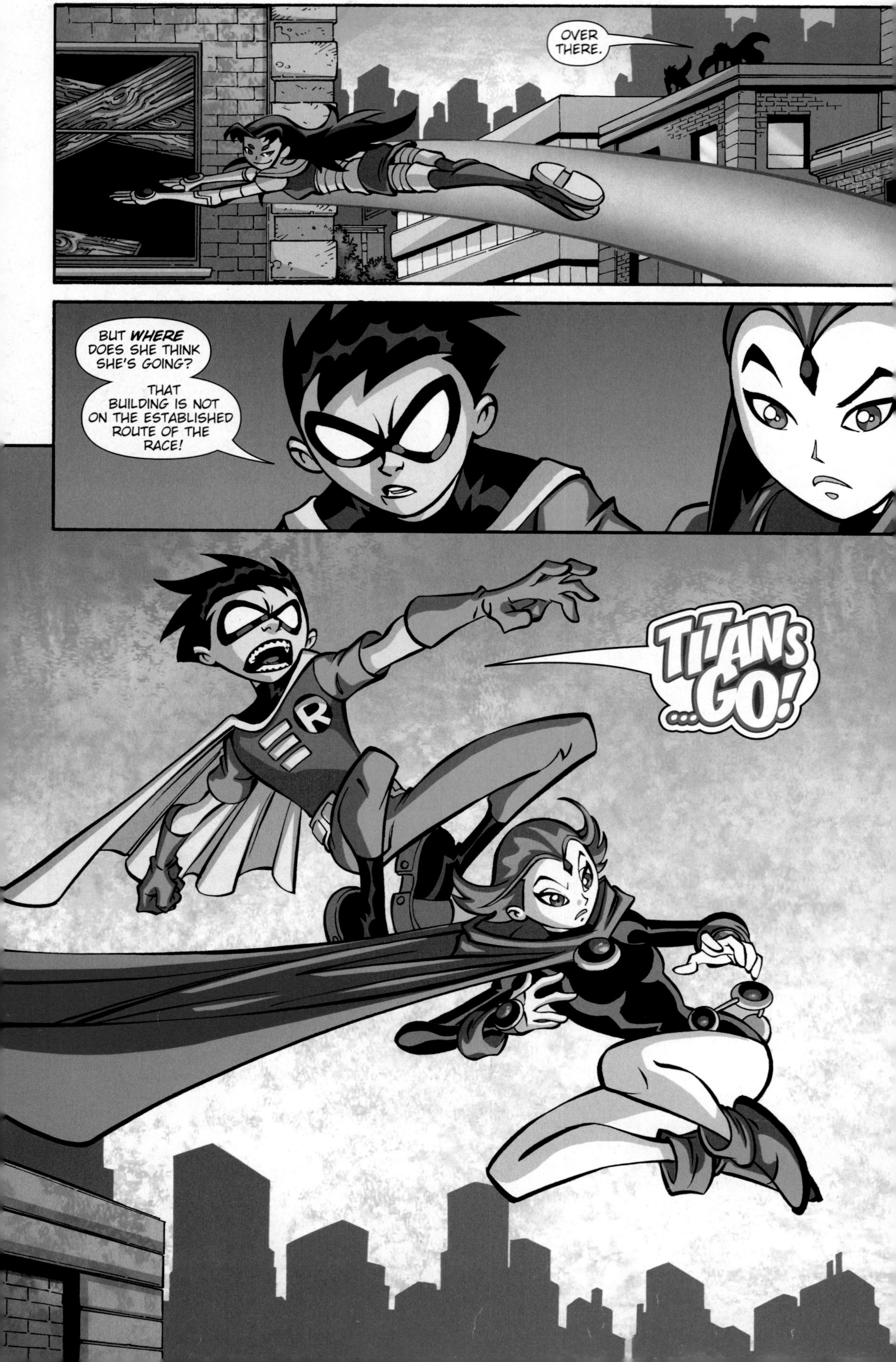
OVER THERE.
BUT *WHERE* DOES SHE THINK SHE'S GOING?
THAT BUILDING IS NOT ON THE ESTABLISHED ROUTE OF THE RACE!
TITANS ...GO!

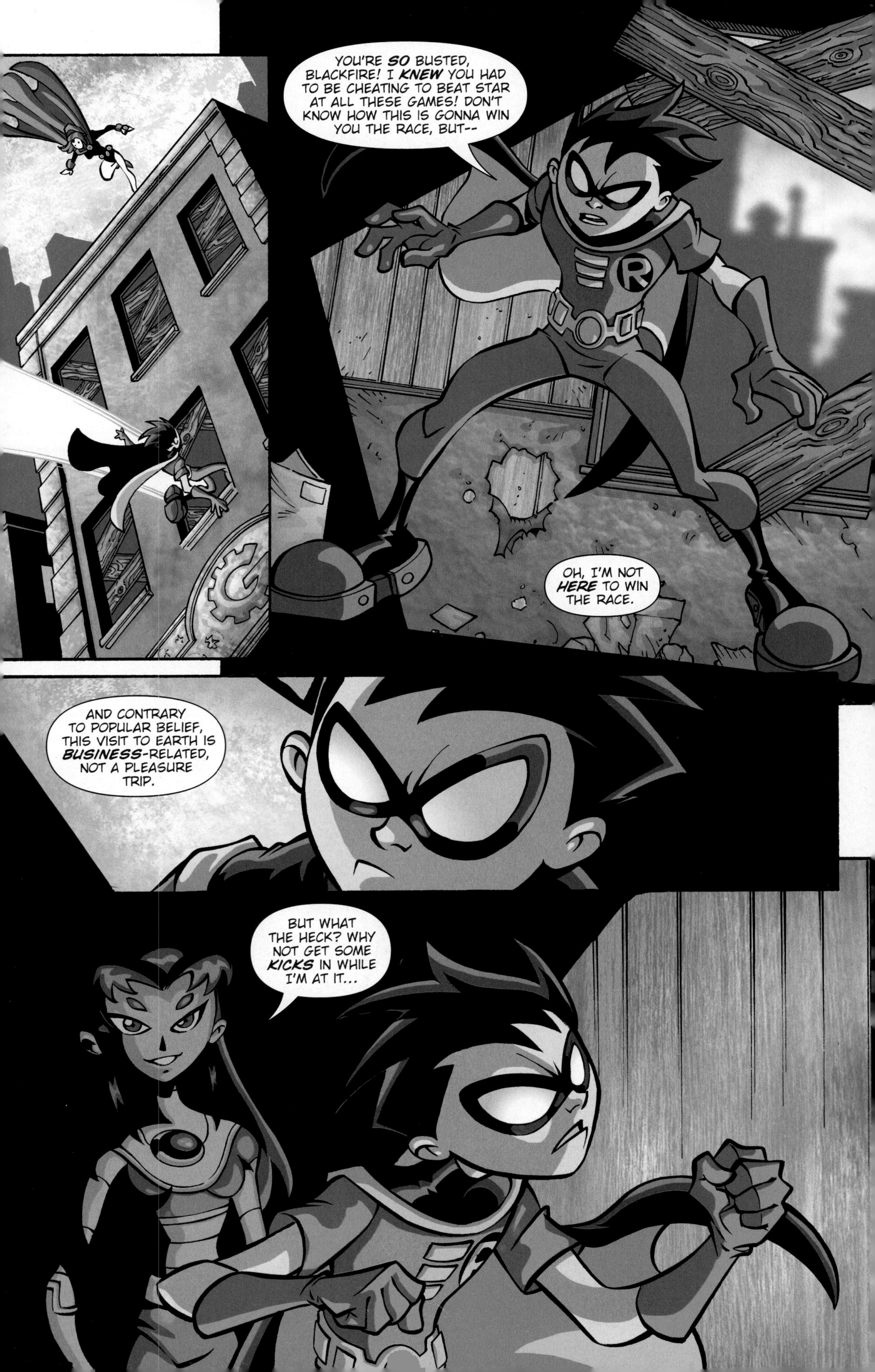
YOU'RE SO BUSTED, BLACKFIRE! I KNEW YOU HAD TO BE CHEATING TO BEAT STAR AT ALL THESE GAMES! DON'T KNOW HOW THIS IS GONNA WIN YOU THE RACE, BUT--
OH, I'M NOT HERE TO WIN THE RACE.
AND CONTRARY TO POPULAR BELIEF, THIS VISIT TO EARTH IS BUSINESS-RELATED, NOT A PLEASURE TRIP.
BUT WHAT THE HECK? WHY NOT GET SOME KICKS IN WHILE I'M AT IT...

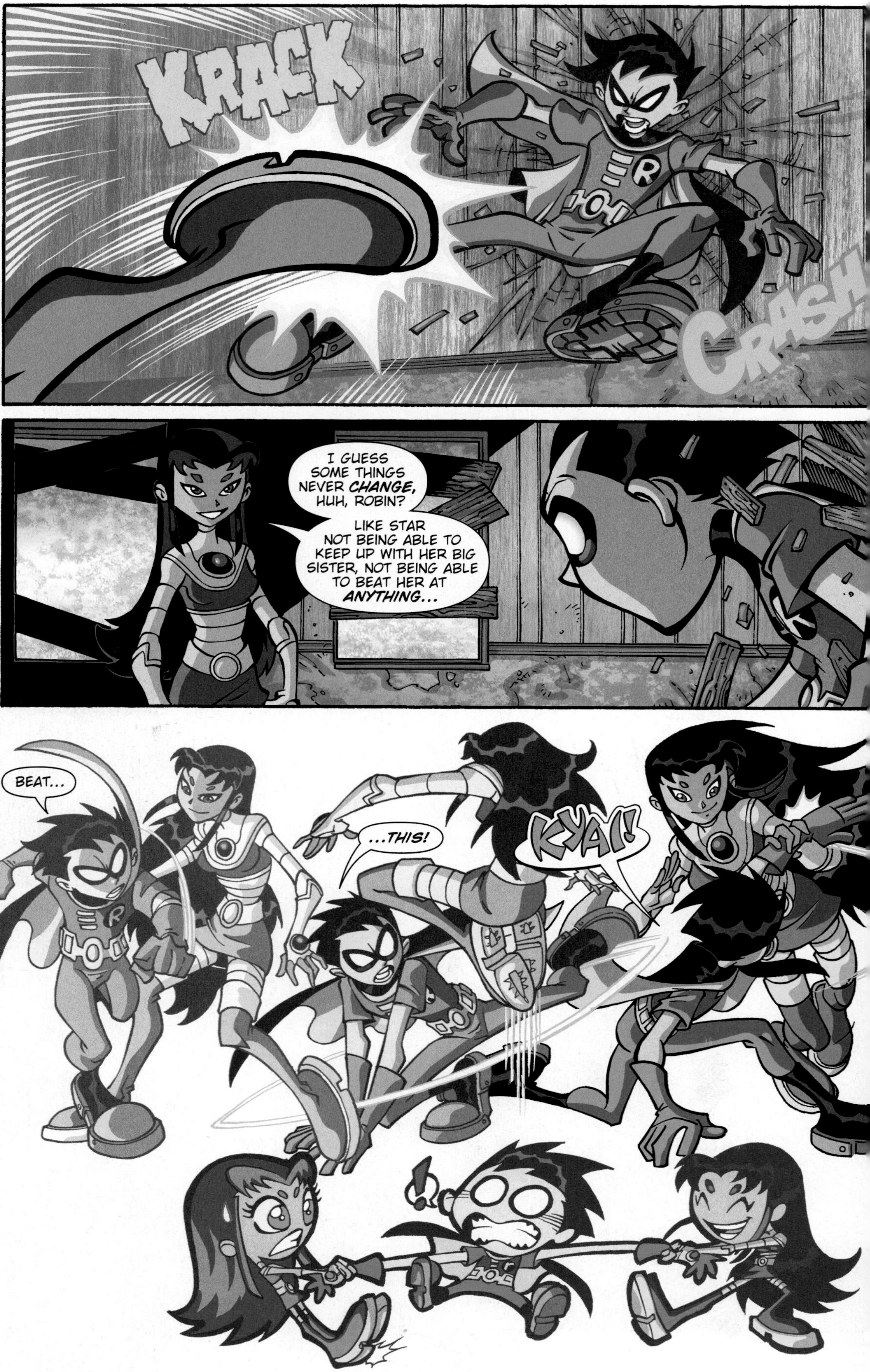

KRACK
CRASH
I GUESS SOME THINGS NEVER CHANGE, HUH, ROBIN?
LIKE STAR NOT BEING ABLE TO KEEP UP WITH HER BIG SISTER, NOT BEING ABLE TO BEAT HER AT ANYTHING...
BEAT...
...THIS!
KYAI!

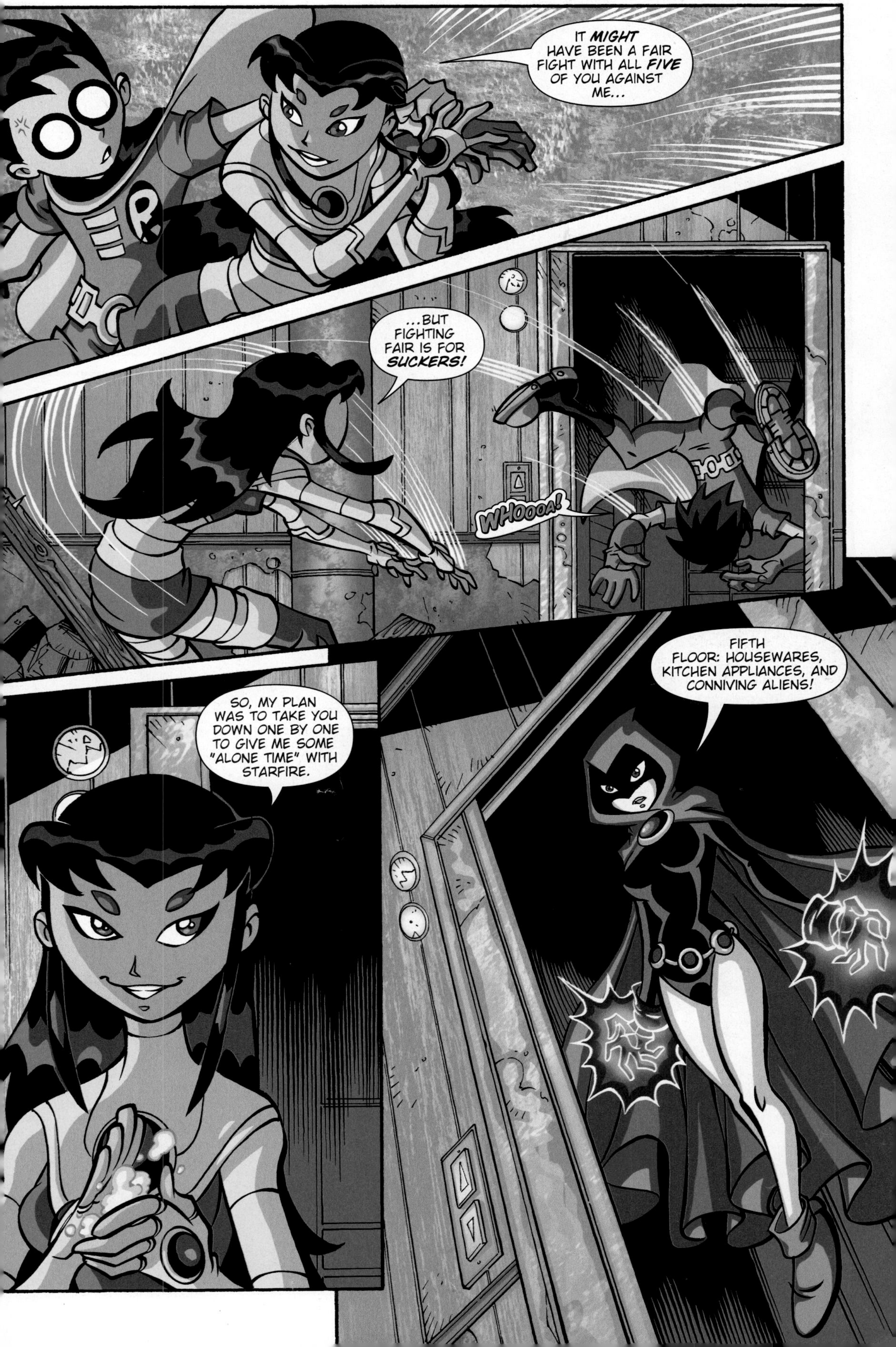
IT MIGHT HAVE BEEN A FAIR FIGHT WITH ALL FIVE OF YOU AGAINST ME...
...BUT FIGHTING FAIR IS FOR SUCKERS!
WHOOOA!
SO, MY PLAN WAS TO TAKE YOU DOWN ONE BY ONE TO GIVE ME SOME "ALONE TIME" WITH STARFIRE.
FIFTH FLOOR: HOUSEWARES, KITCHEN APPLIANCES, AND CONNIVING ALIENS!

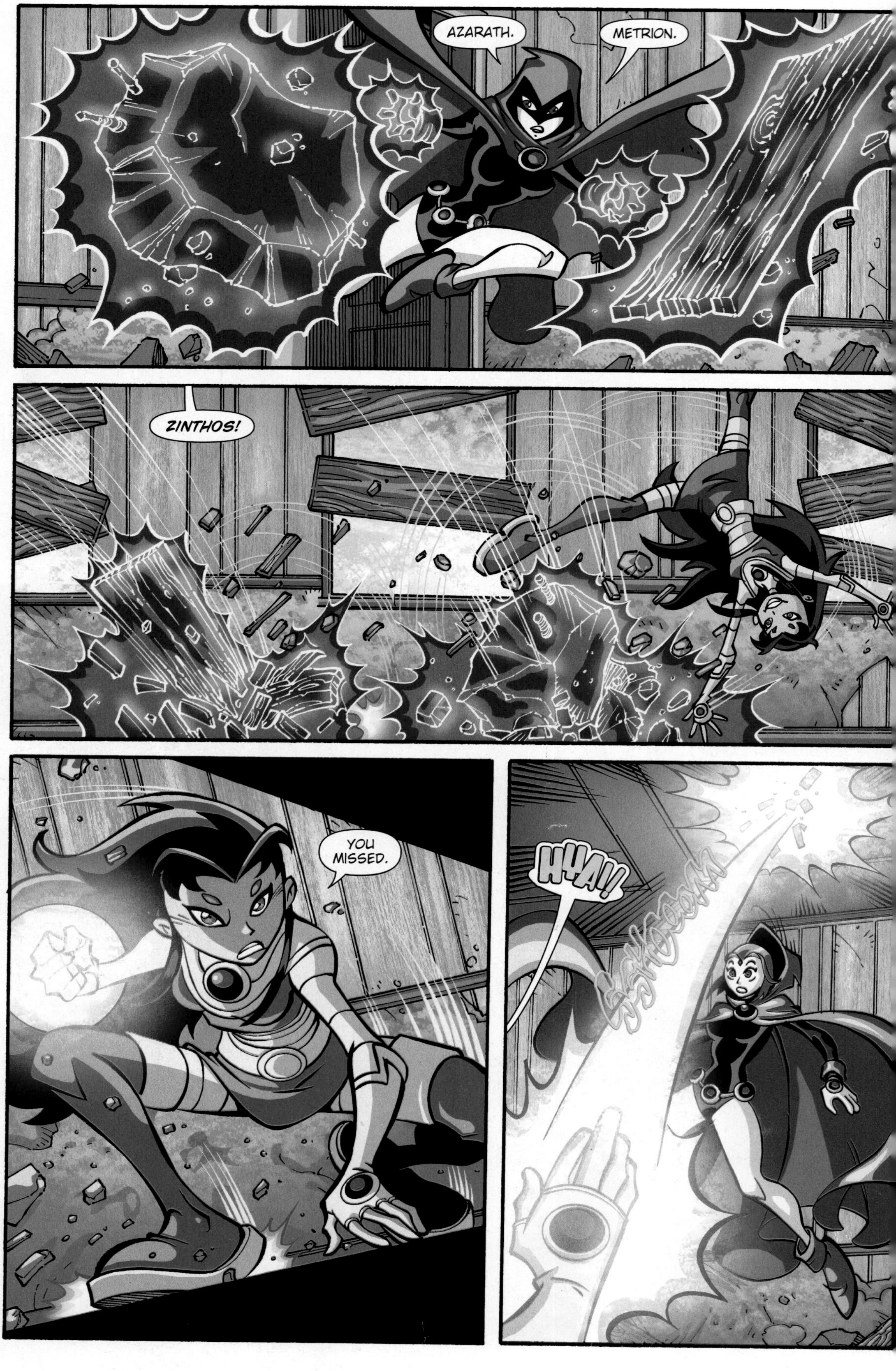
AZARATH.
METRION.
ZINTHOS!
YOU MISSED.
HYA!!

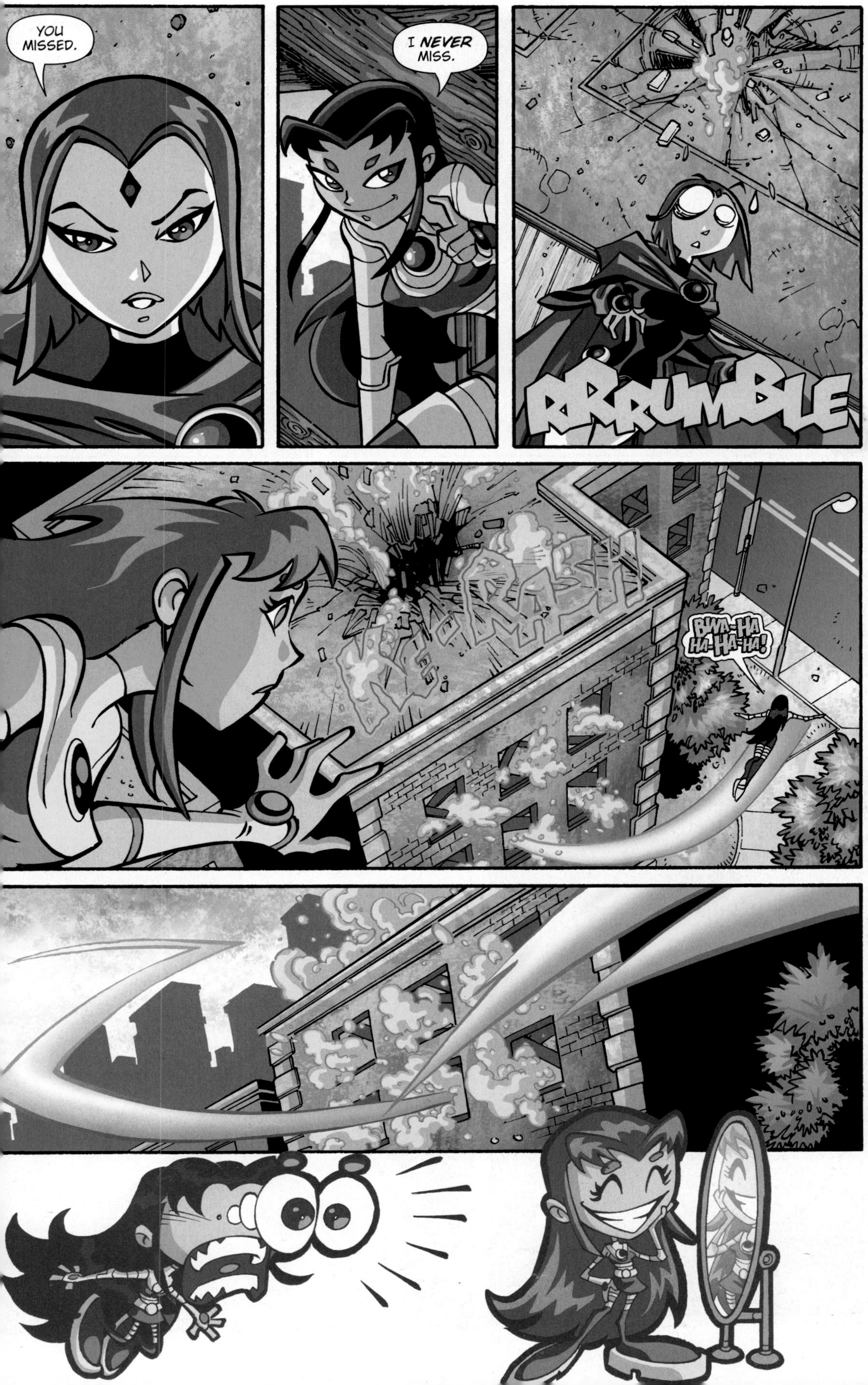
YOU MISSED.
I NEVER MISS.
RRRUMBLE
KRASH
BWA-HA HA-HA-HA!

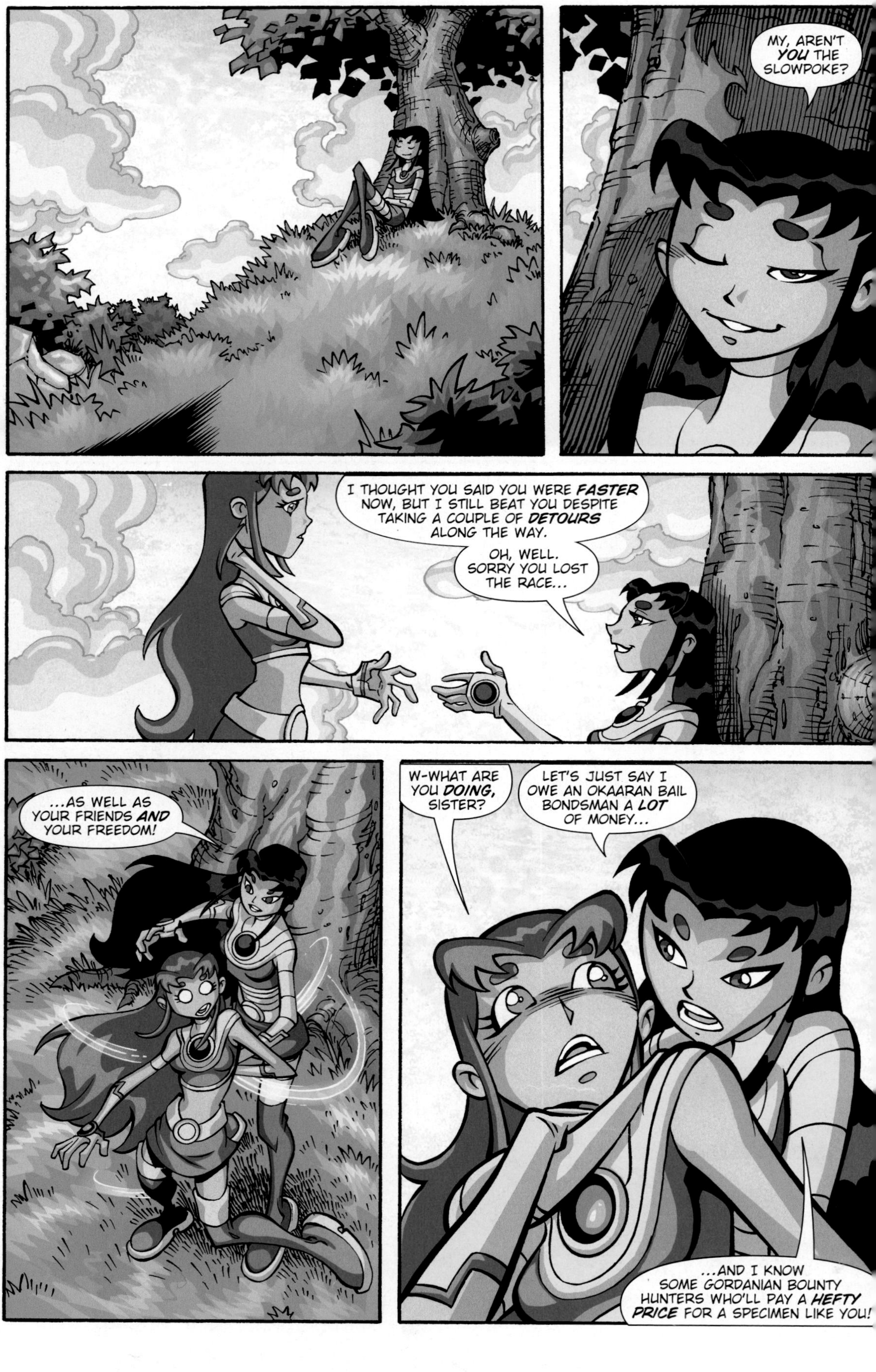
MY, AREN'T YOU THE SLOWPOKE?
I THOUGHT YOU SAID YOU WERE FASTER NOW, BUT I STILL BEAT YOU DESPITE TAKING A COUPLE OF DETOURS ALONG THE WAY.
OH, WELL. SORRY YOU LOST THE RACE...
...AS WELL AS YOUR FRIENDS AND YOUR FREEDOM!
W-WHAT ARE YOU DOING, SISTER?
LET'S JUST SAY I OWE AN OKAARAN BAIL BONDSMAN A LOT OF MONEY...
...AND I KNOW SOME GORDANIAN BOUNTY HUNTERS WHO'LL PAY A HEFTY PRICE FOR A SPECIMEN LIKE YOU!

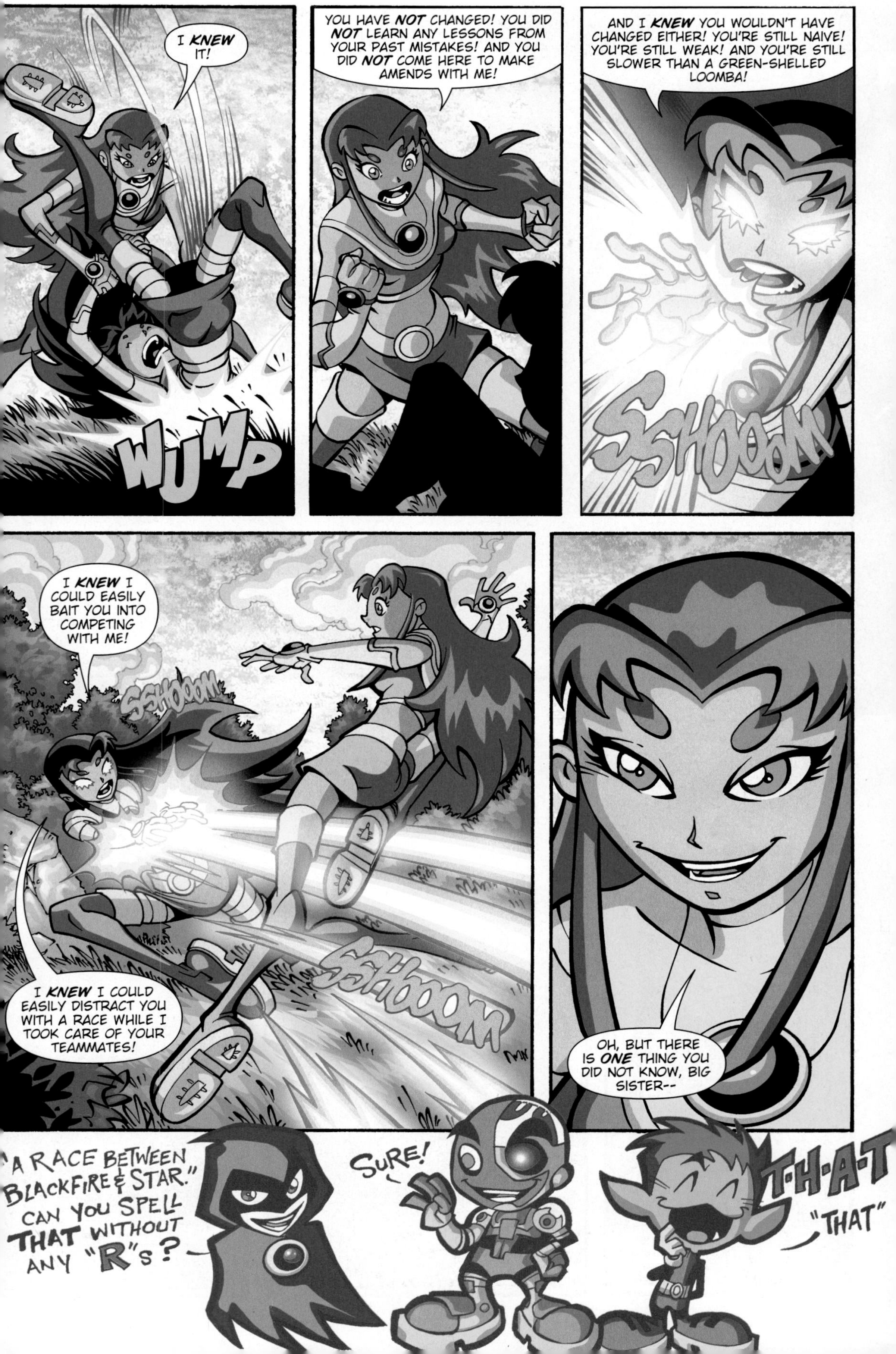
I KNEW IT!
WUMP
YOU HAVE NOT CHANGED! YOU DID NOT LEARN ANY LESSONS FROM YOUR PAST MISTAKES! AND YOU DID NOT COME HERE TO MAKE AMENDS WITH ME!
AND I KNEW YOU WOULDN'T HAVE CHANGED EITHER! YOU'RE STILL NAIVE! YOU'RE STILL WEAK! AND YOU'RE STILL SLOWER THAN A GREEN-SHELLED LOOMBA!
SSHOOOM
I KNEW I COULD EASILY BAIT YOU INTO COMPETING WITH ME!
SSHOOOM
I KNEW I COULD EASILY DISTRACT YOU WITH A RACE WHILE I TOOK CARE OF YOUR TEAMMATES!
SSHOOOM
OH, BUT THERE IS ONE THING YOU DID NOT KNOW, BIG SISTER--
"A RACE BETWEEN BLACKFIRE & STAR." CAN YOU SPELL THAT WITHOUT ANY "R"s?
SURE!
T-H-A-T
"THAT"

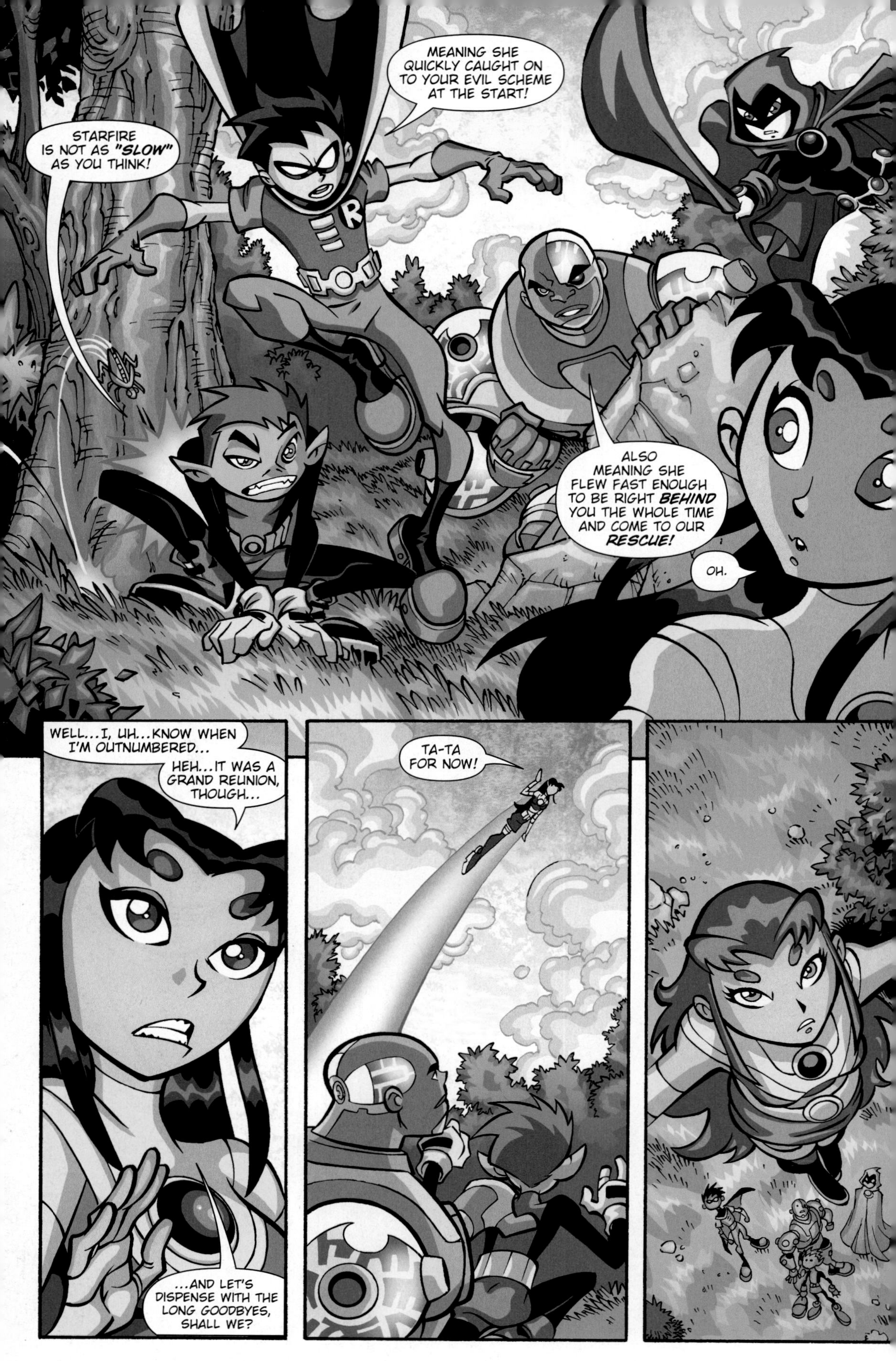
STARFIRE IS NOT AS "SLOW" AS YOU THINK!
MEANING SHE QUICKLY CAUGHT ON TO YOUR EVIL SCHEME AT THE START!
ALSO MEANING SHE FLEW FAST ENOUGH TO BE RIGHT BEHIND YOU THE WHOLE TIME AND COME TO OUR RESCUE!
OH.
WELL...I, UH...KNOW WHEN I'M OUTNUMBERED...
HEH...IT WAS A GRAND REUNION, THOUGH...
...AND LET'S DISPENSE WITH THE LONG GOODBYES, SHALL WE?
TA-TA FOR NOW!

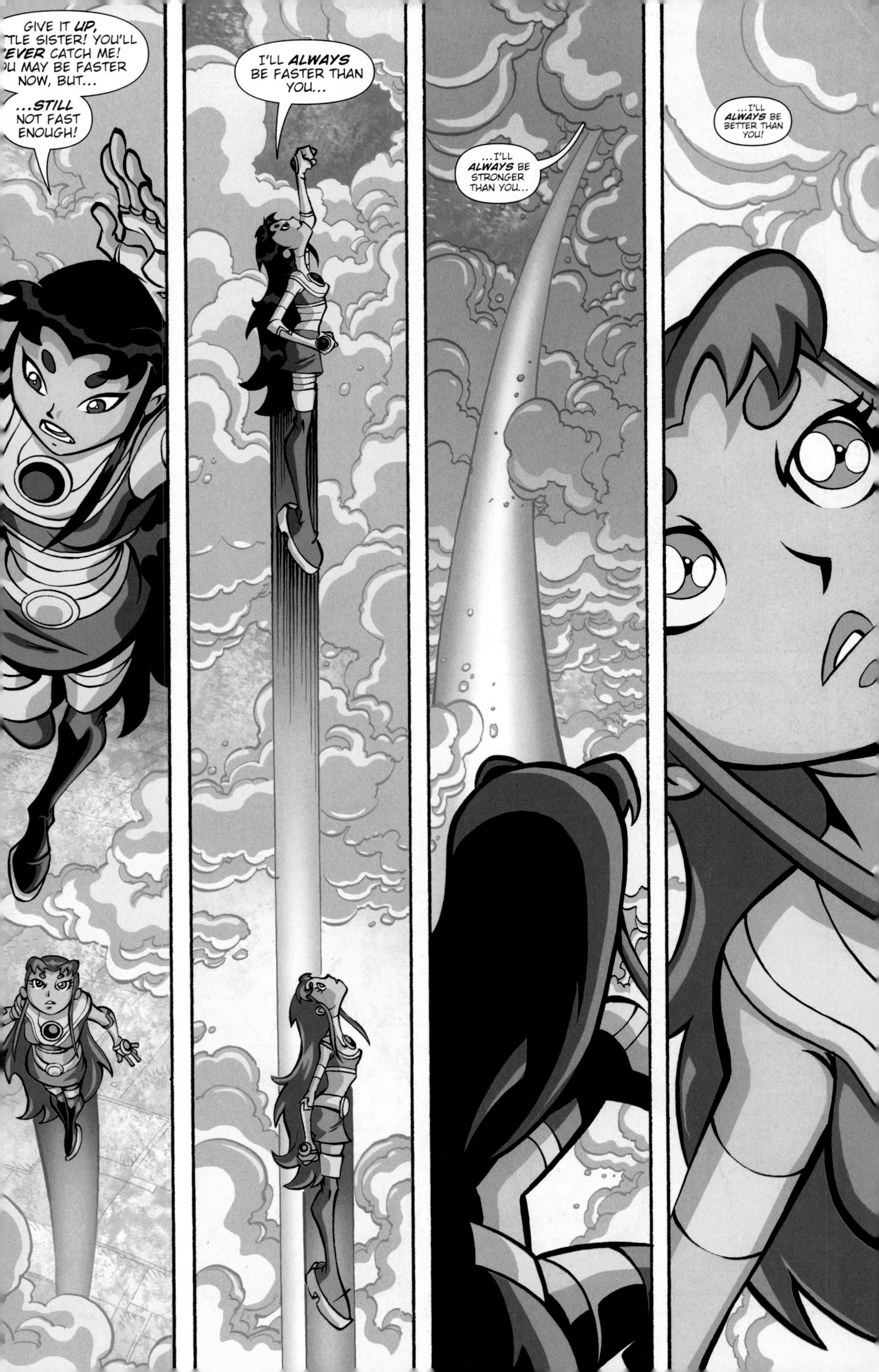

GIVE IT UP, TLE SISTER! YOU'LL EVER CATCH ME! U MAY BE FASTER NOW, BUT...
...STILL NOT FAST ENOUGH!
I'LL ALWAYS BE FASTER THAN YOU...
...I'LL ALWAYS BE STRONGER THAN YOU...
...I'LL ALWAYS BE BETTER THAN YOU!

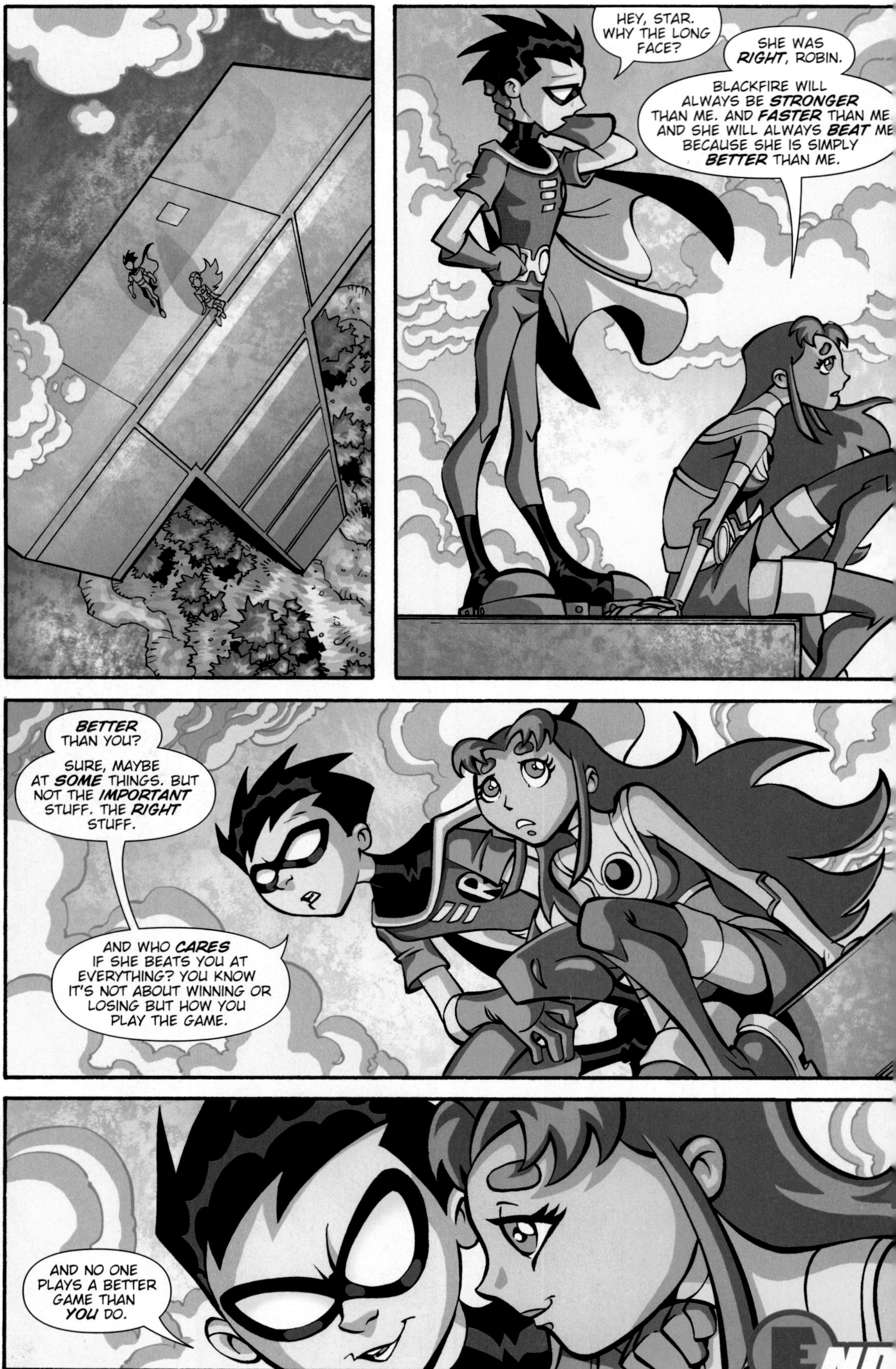
HEY, STAR. WHY THE LONG FACE?
SHE WAS RIGHT, ROBIN.
BLACKFIRE WILL ALWAYS BE STRONGER THAN ME. AND FASTER THAN ME AND SHE WILL ALWAYS BEAT ME BECAUSE SHE IS SIMPLY BETTER THAN ME.
BETTER THAN YOU?
SURE, MAYBE AT SOME THINGS. BUT NOT THE IMPORTANT STUFF. THE RIGHT STUFF.
AND WHO CARES IF SHE BEATS YOU AT EVERYTHING? YOU KNOW IT'S NOT ABOUT WINNING OR LOSING BUT HOW YOU PLAY THE GAME.
AND NO ONE PLAYS A BETTER GAME THAN YOU DO.
END

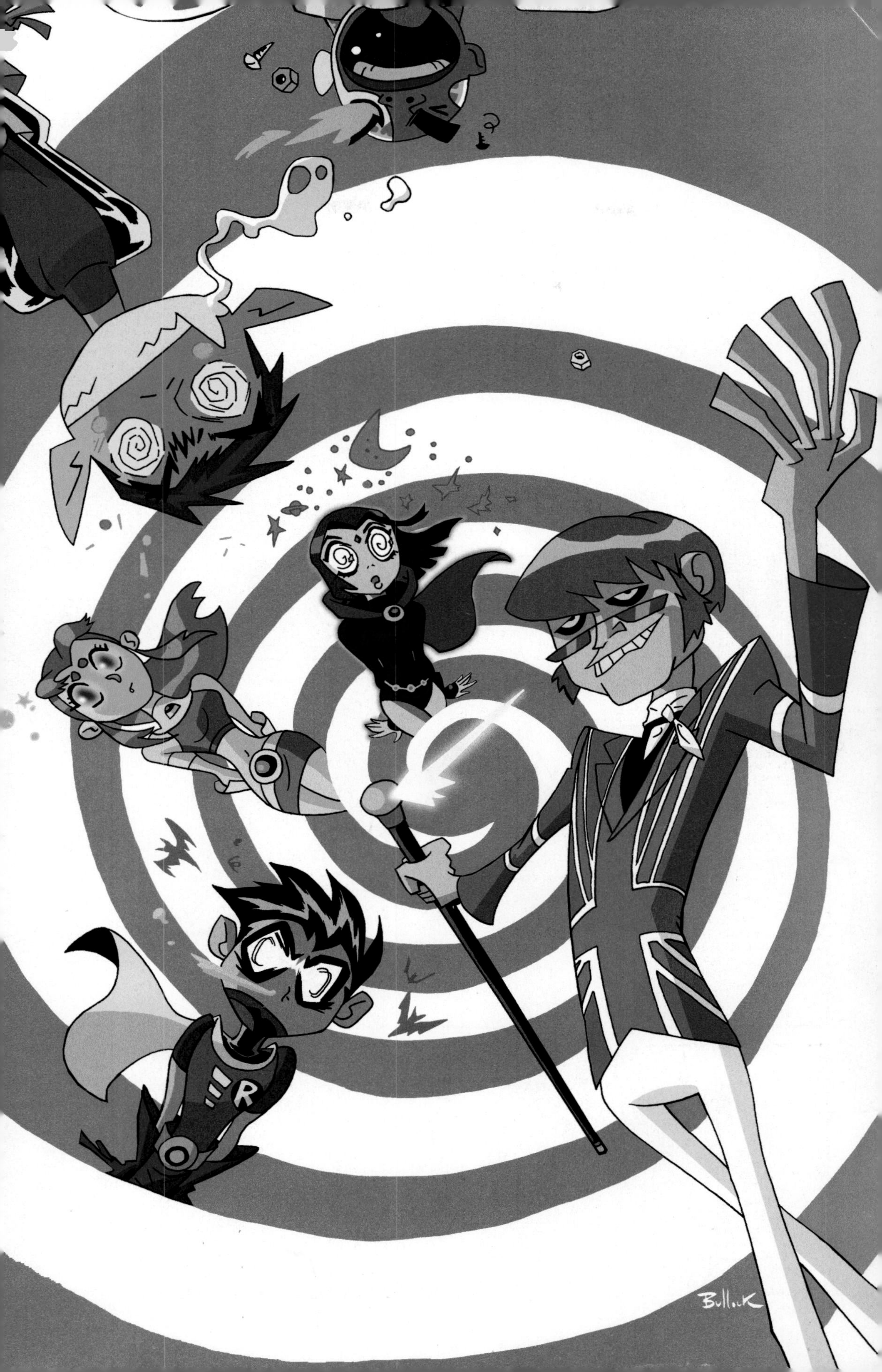
Bullock

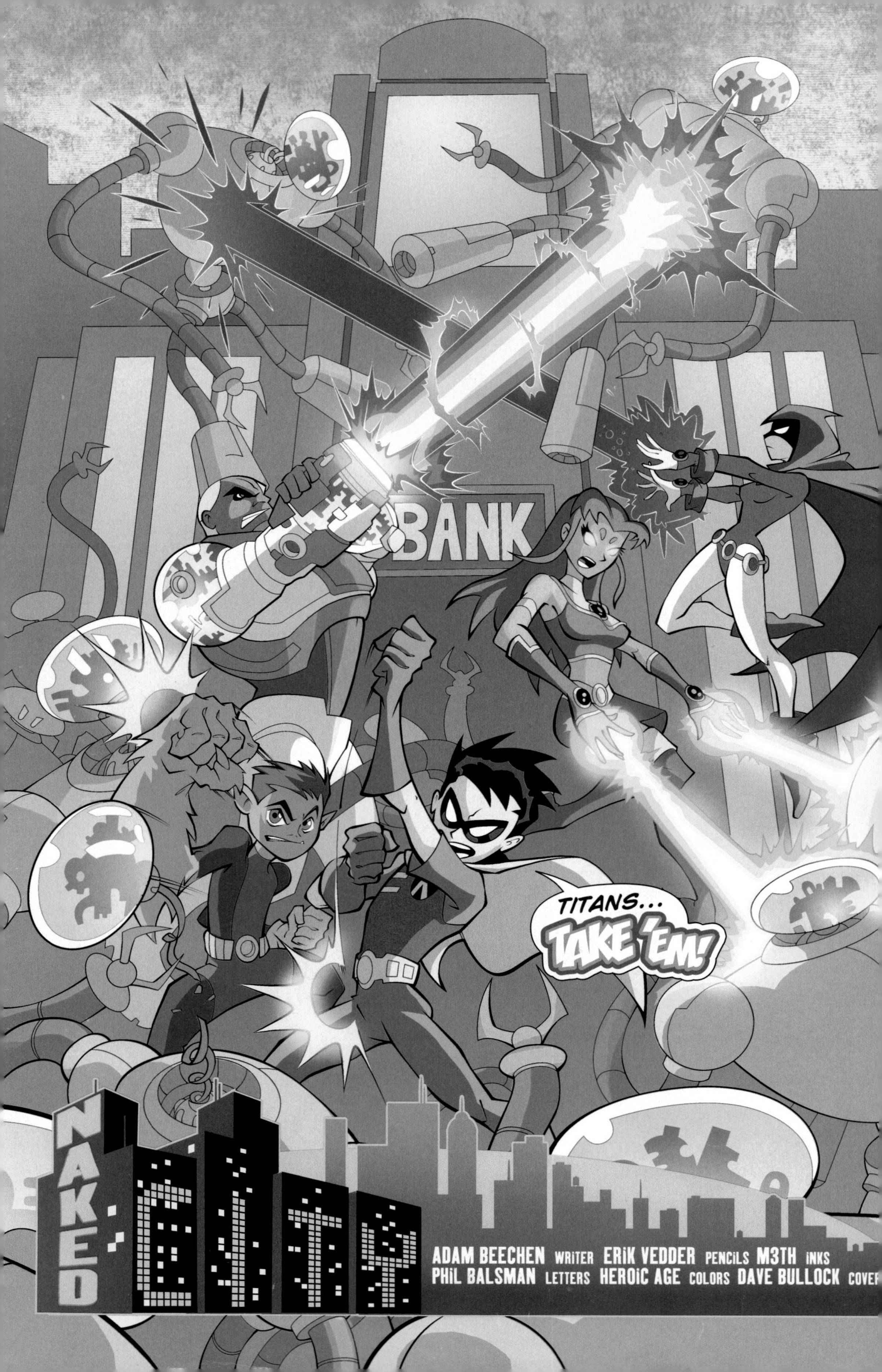
BANK
TITANS... TAKE 'EM!
NAKED CITY
ADAM BEECHEN WRITER ERIK VEDDER PENCILS M3TH INKS
PHIL BALSMAN LETTERS HEROIC AGE COLORS DAVE BULLOCK COVER

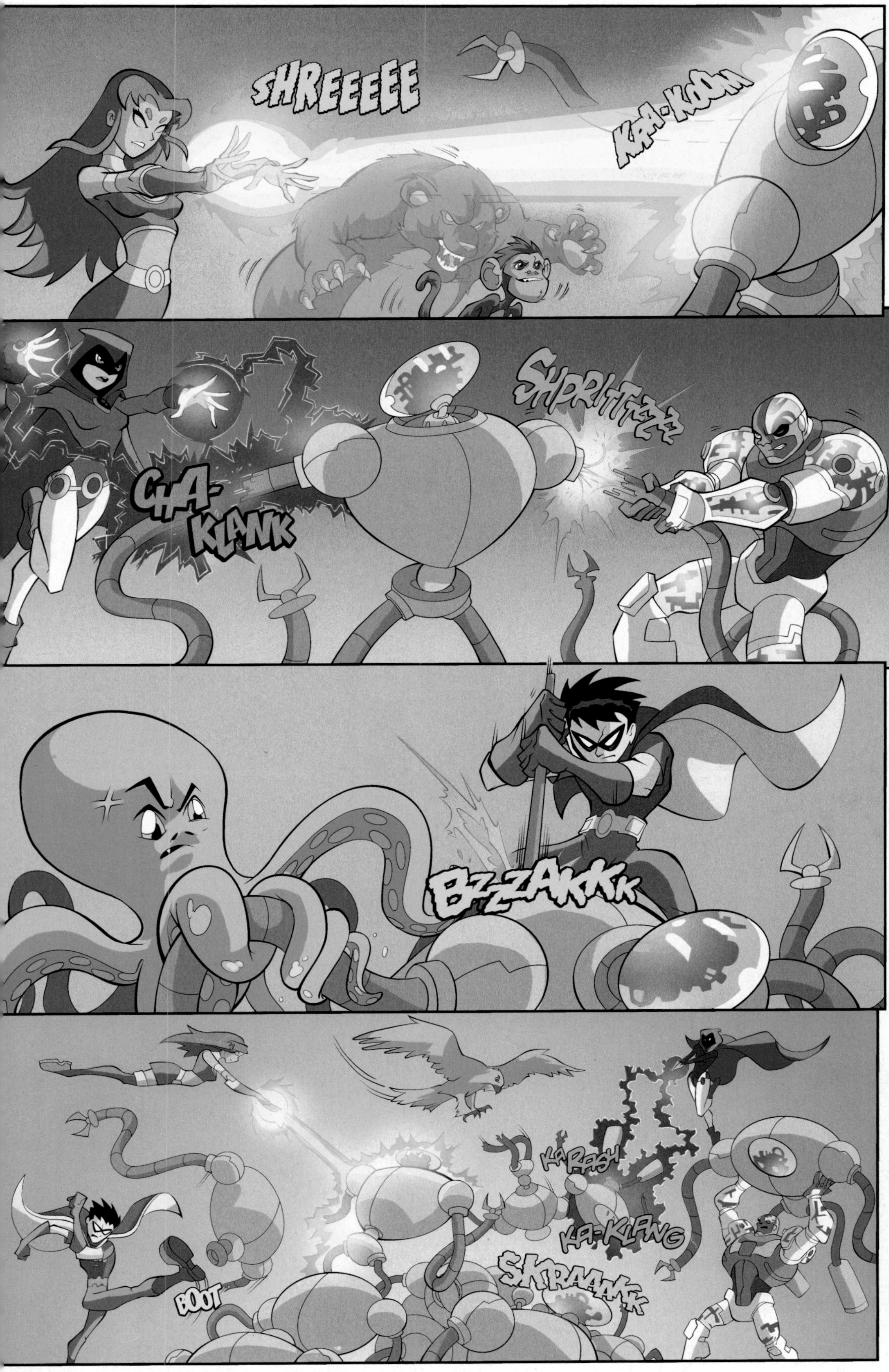
SHREEEEE
KA-KOOM
SHRITTZZZ
CHA-KLANK
BZZZAKKKK
KA-RASH
KA-KLANG
SKRAAAKKK
BOOT

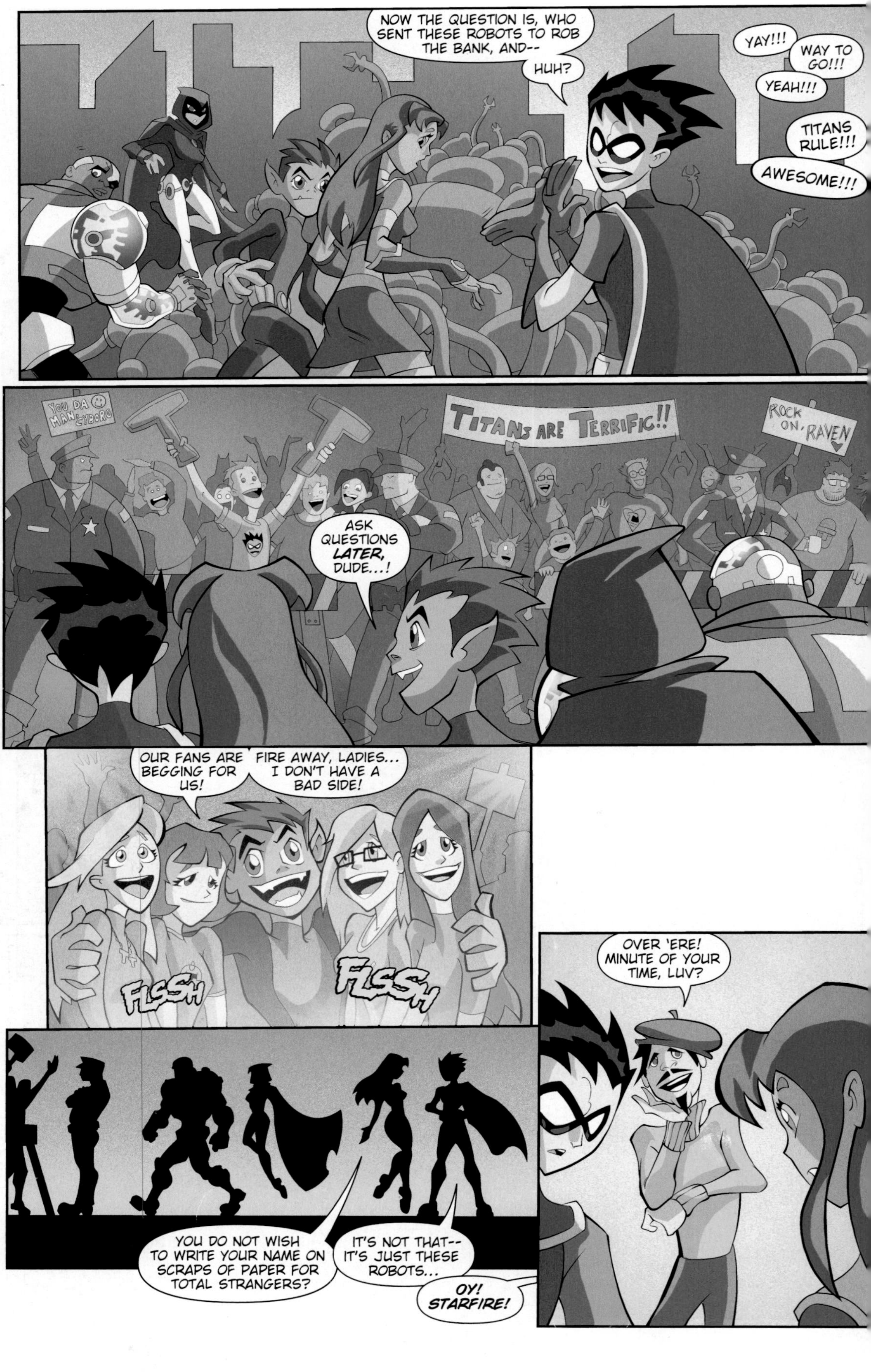

NOW THE QUESTION IS, WHO SENT THESE ROBOTS TO ROB THE BANK, AND--
HUH?
YAY!!!
WAY TO GO!!!
YEAH!!!
TITANS RULE!!!
AWESOME!!!
YOU DA MAN, CYBORG
TITANS ARE TERRIFIC!!
ROCK ON, RAVEN
ASK QUESTIONS LATER, DUDE...!
OUR FANS ARE BEGGING FOR US!
FIRE AWAY, LADIES... I DON'T HAVE A BAD SIDE!
FLSSH
FLSSH
OVER 'ERE! MINUTE OF YOUR TIME, LUV?
YOU DO NOT WISH TO WRITE YOUR NAME ON SCRAPS OF PAPER FOR TOTAL STRANGERS?
IT'S NOT THAT-- IT'S JUST THESE ROBOTS...
OY! STARFIRE!

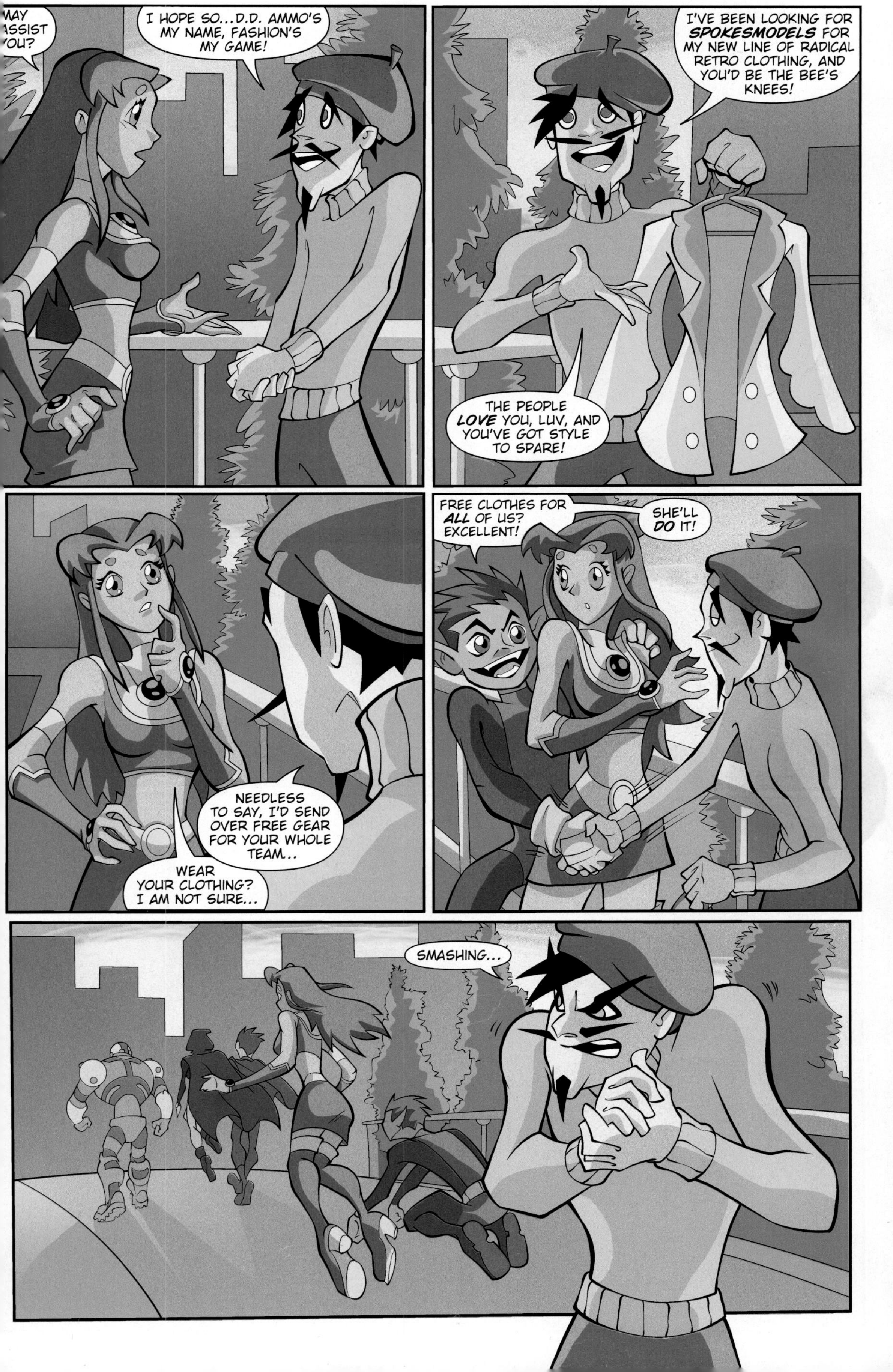
MAY ASSIST YOU?
I HOPE SO...D.D. AMMO'S MY NAME, FASHION'S MY GAME!
I'VE BEEN LOOKING FOR SPOKESMODELS FOR MY NEW LINE OF RADICAL RETRO CLOTHING, AND YOU'D BE THE BEE'S KNEES!
THE PEOPLE LOVE YOU, LUV, AND YOU'VE GOT STYLE TO SPARE!
NEEDLESS TO SAY, I'D SEND OVER FREE GEAR FOR YOUR WHOLE TEAM...
WEAR YOUR CLOTHING? I AM NOT SURE...
FREE CLOTHES FOR ALL OF US? EXCELLENT!
SHE'LL DO IT!
SMASHING...

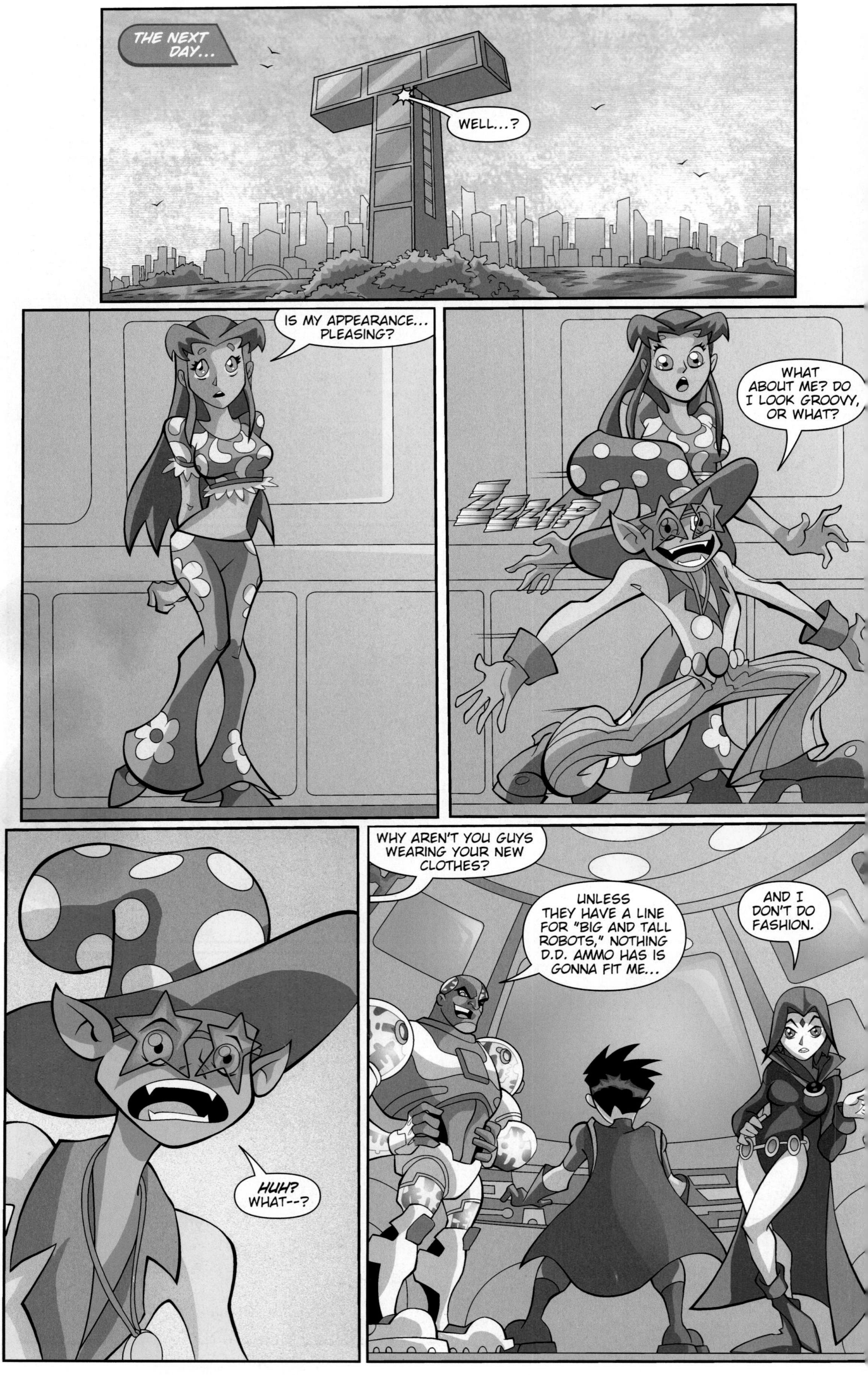
THE NEXT DAY...
WELL...?
IS MY APPEARANCE... PLEASING?
WHAT ABOUT ME? DO I LOOK GROOVY, OR WHAT?
ZZZIP
HUH? WHAT--?
WHY AREN'T YOU GUYS WEARING YOUR NEW CLOTHES?
UNLESS THEY HAVE A LINE FOR "BIG AND TALL ROBOTS," NOTHING D.D. AMMO HAS IS GONNA FIT ME...
AND I DON'T DO FASHION.

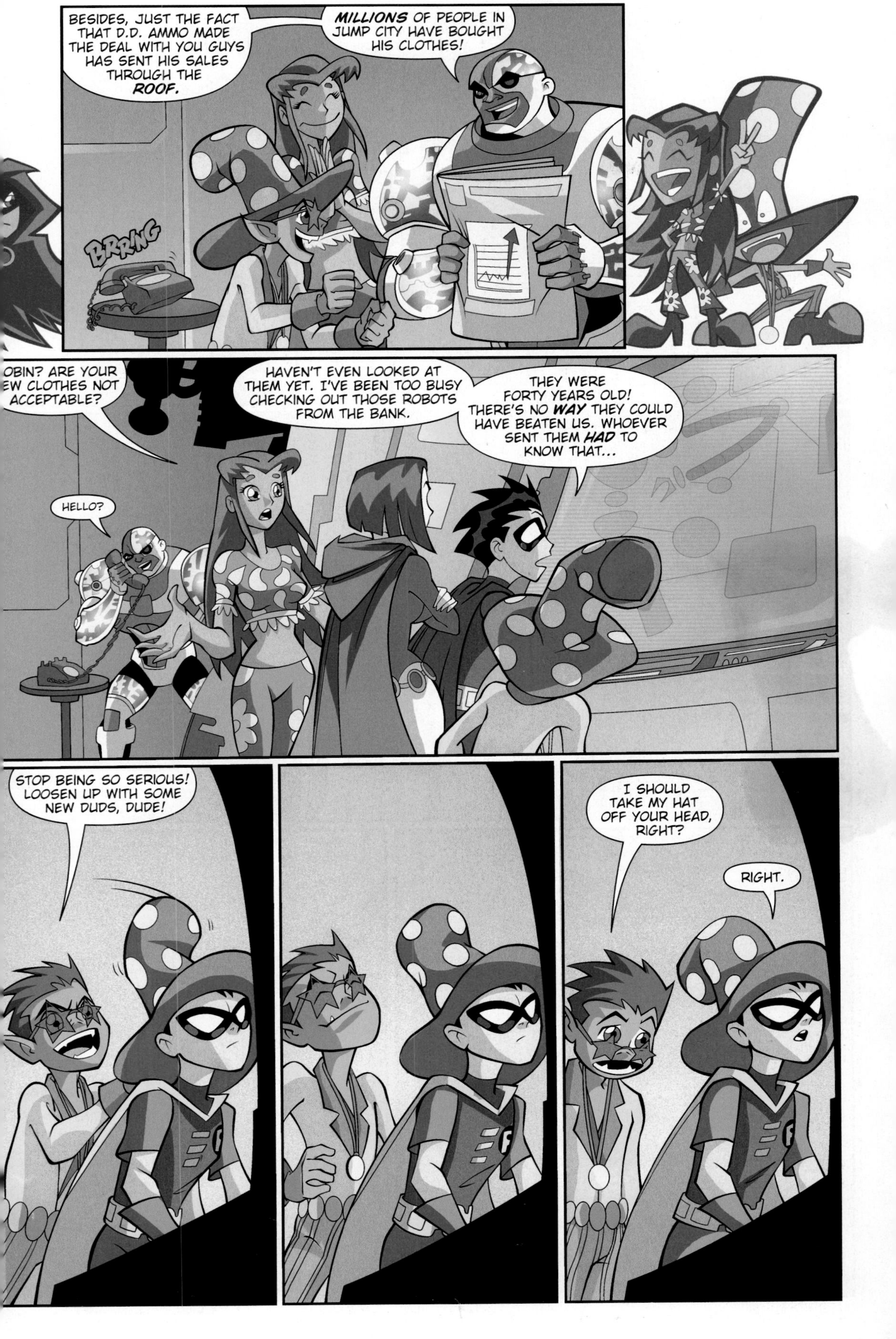

BESIDES, JUST THE FACT THAT D.D. AMMO MADE THE DEAL WITH YOU GUYS HAS SENT HIS SALES THROUGH THE ROOF.
MILLIONS OF PEOPLE IN JUMP CITY HAVE BOUGHT HIS CLOTHES!
BRRING
OBIN? ARE YOUR EW CLOTHES NOT ACCEPTABLE?
HAVEN'T EVEN LOOKED AT THEM YET. I'VE BEEN TOO BUSY CHECKING OUT THOSE ROBOTS FROM THE BANK.
THEY WERE FORTY YEARS OLD! THERE'S NO WAY THEY COULD HAVE BEATEN US. WHOEVER SENT THEM HAD TO KNOW THAT...
HELLO?
STOP BEING SO SERIOUS! LOOSEN UP WITH SOME NEW DUDS, DUDE!
I SHOULD TAKE MY HAT OFF YOUR HEAD, RIGHT?
RIGHT.

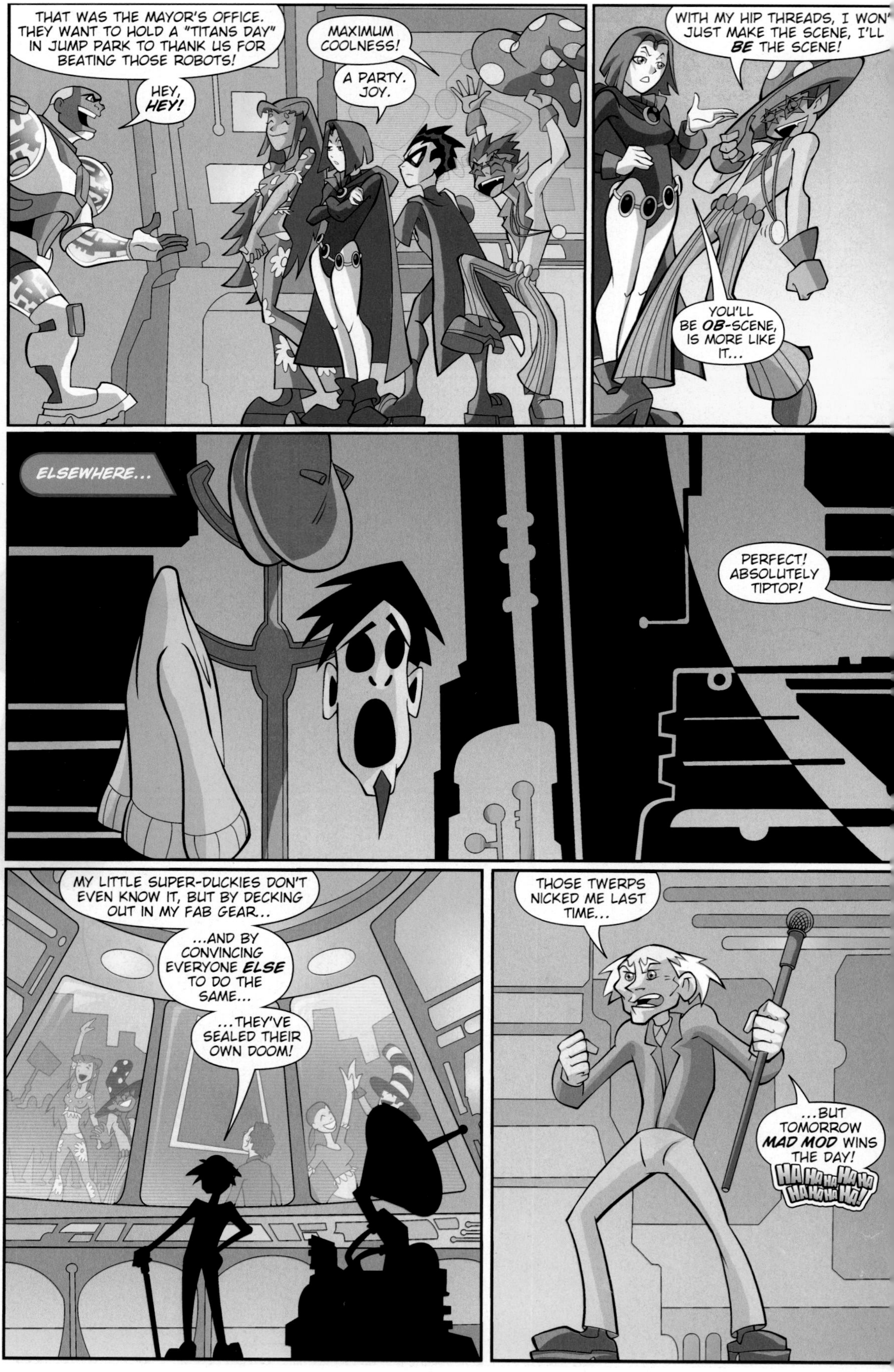
THAT WAS THE MAYOR'S OFFICE. THEY WANT TO HOLD A "TITANS DAY" IN JUMP PARK TO THANK US FOR BEATING THOSE ROBOTS!
HEY, HEY!
MAXIMUM COOLNESS!
A PARTY. JOY.
WITH MY HIP THREADS, I WON' JUST MAKE THE SCENE, I'LL BE THE SCENE!
YOU'LL BE OB-SCENE, IS MORE LIKE IT...
ELSEWHERE...
PERFECT! ABSOLUTELY TIPTOP!
MY LITTLE SUPER-DUCKIES DON'T EVEN KNOW IT, BUT BY DECKING OUT IN MY FAB GEAR...
...AND BY CONVINCING EVERYONE ELSE TO DO THE SAME...
...THEY'VE SEALED THEIR OWN DOOM!
THOSE TWERPS NICKED ME LAST TIME...
...BUT TOMORROW MAD MOD WINS THE DAY!
HA HA HA HA HA HA HA HA HA!

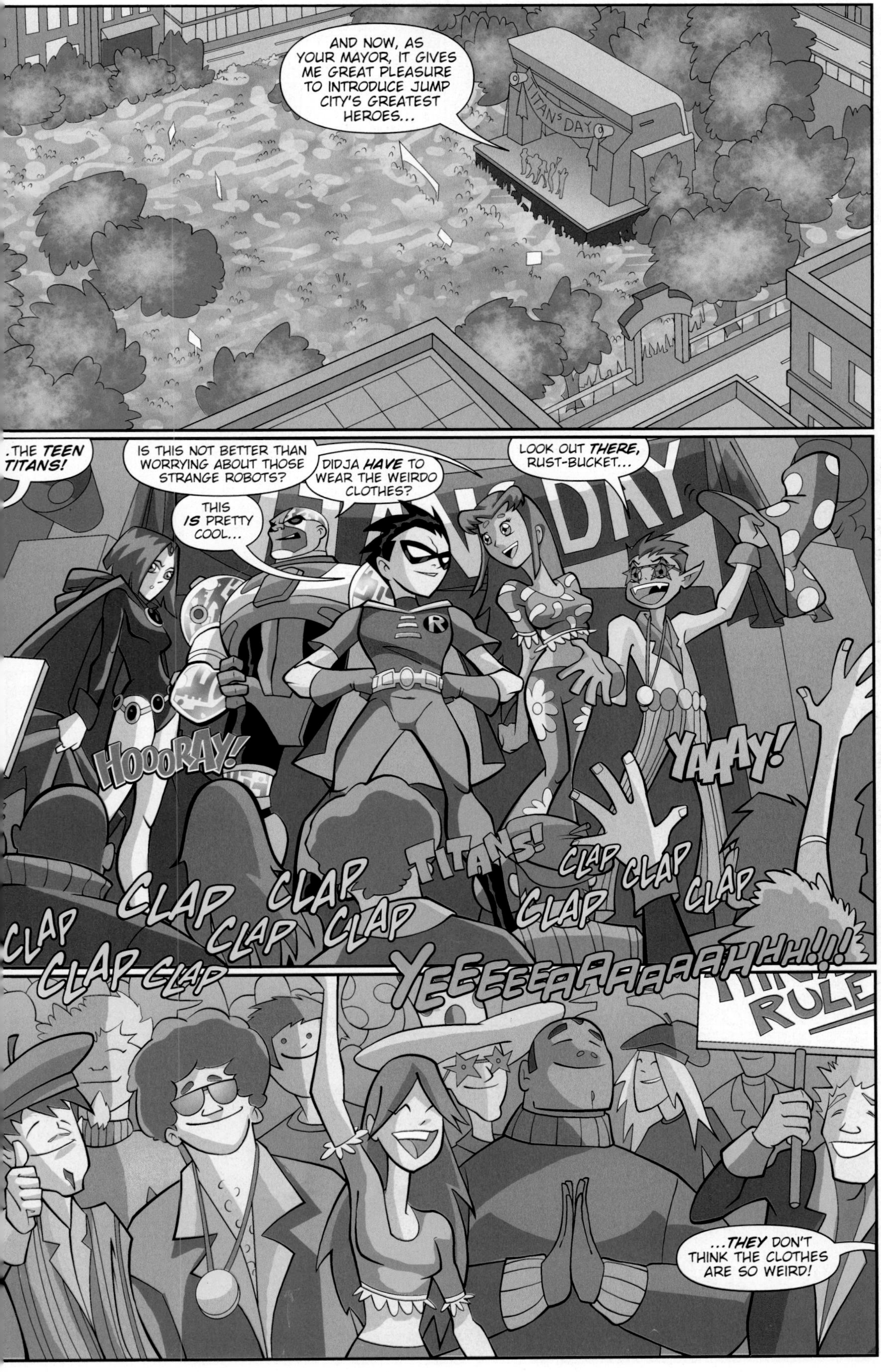
TITANS DAY
AND NOW, AS YOUR MAYOR, IT GIVES ME GREAT PLEASURE TO INTRODUCE JUMP CITY'S GREATEST HEROES...
...THE TEEN TITANS!
IS THIS NOT BETTER THAN WORRYING ABOUT THOSE STRANGE ROBOTS?
THIS IS PRETTY COOL...
DIDJA HAVE TO WEAR THE WEIRDO CLOTHES?
LOOK OUT THERE, RUST-BUCKET...
HOOORAY!
YAAAY!
TITANS!
CLAP CLAP CLAP CLAP CLAP CLAP CLAP CLAP CLAP CLAP CLAP CLAP
YEEEEEEAAAAAAAHHHH!!!
RULE
...THEY DON'T THINK THE CLOTHES ARE SO WEIRD!

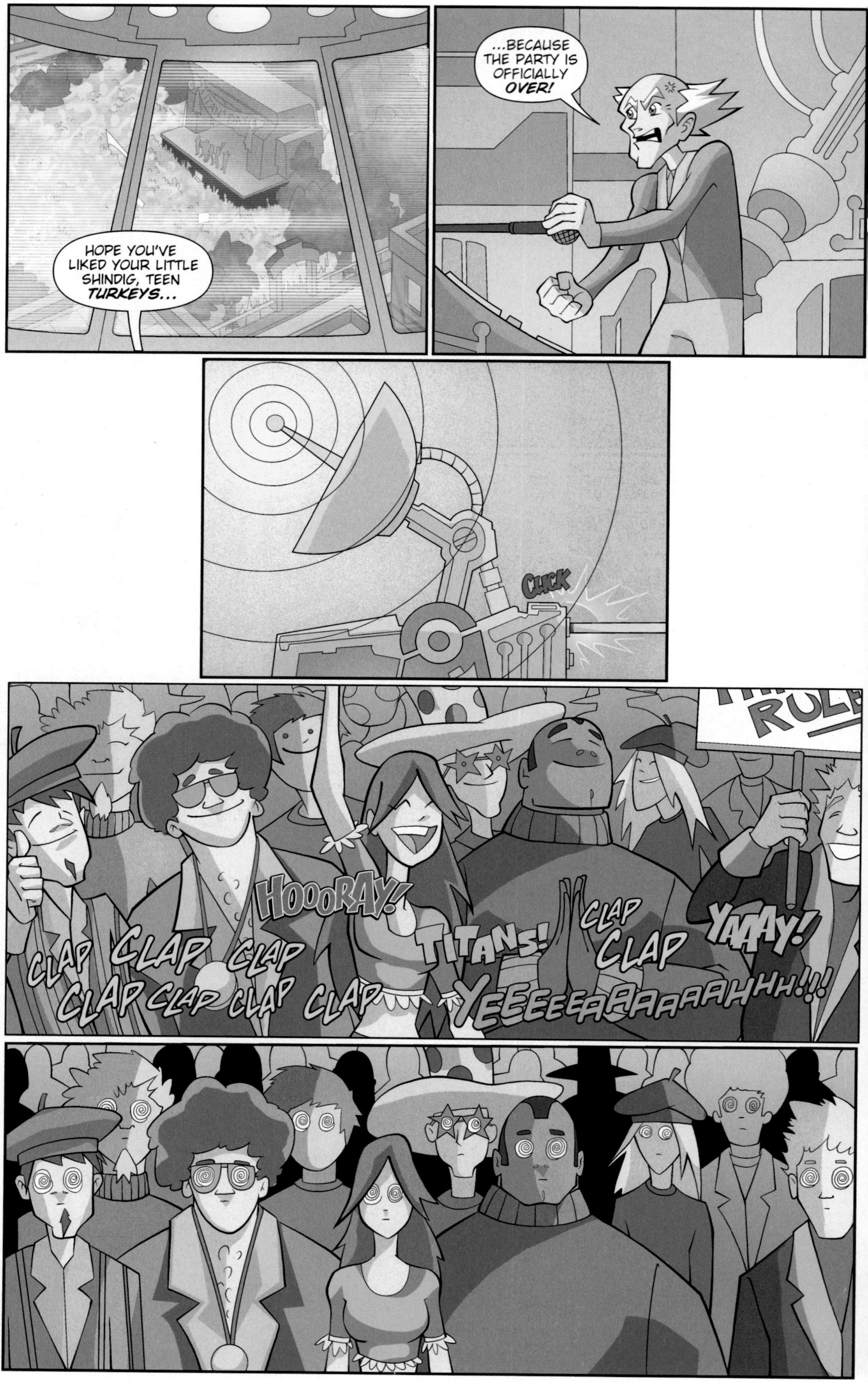
HOPE YOU'VE LIKED YOUR LITTLE SHINDIG, TEEN TURKEYS...
...BECAUSE THE PARTY IS OFFICIALLY OVER!
CLICK
HOOORAY!
CLAP CLAP CLAP
CLAP CLAP CLAP CLAP
TITANS!
CLAP CLAP
YAAAY!
YEEEEEAAAAAAAHHH!!!
RULE

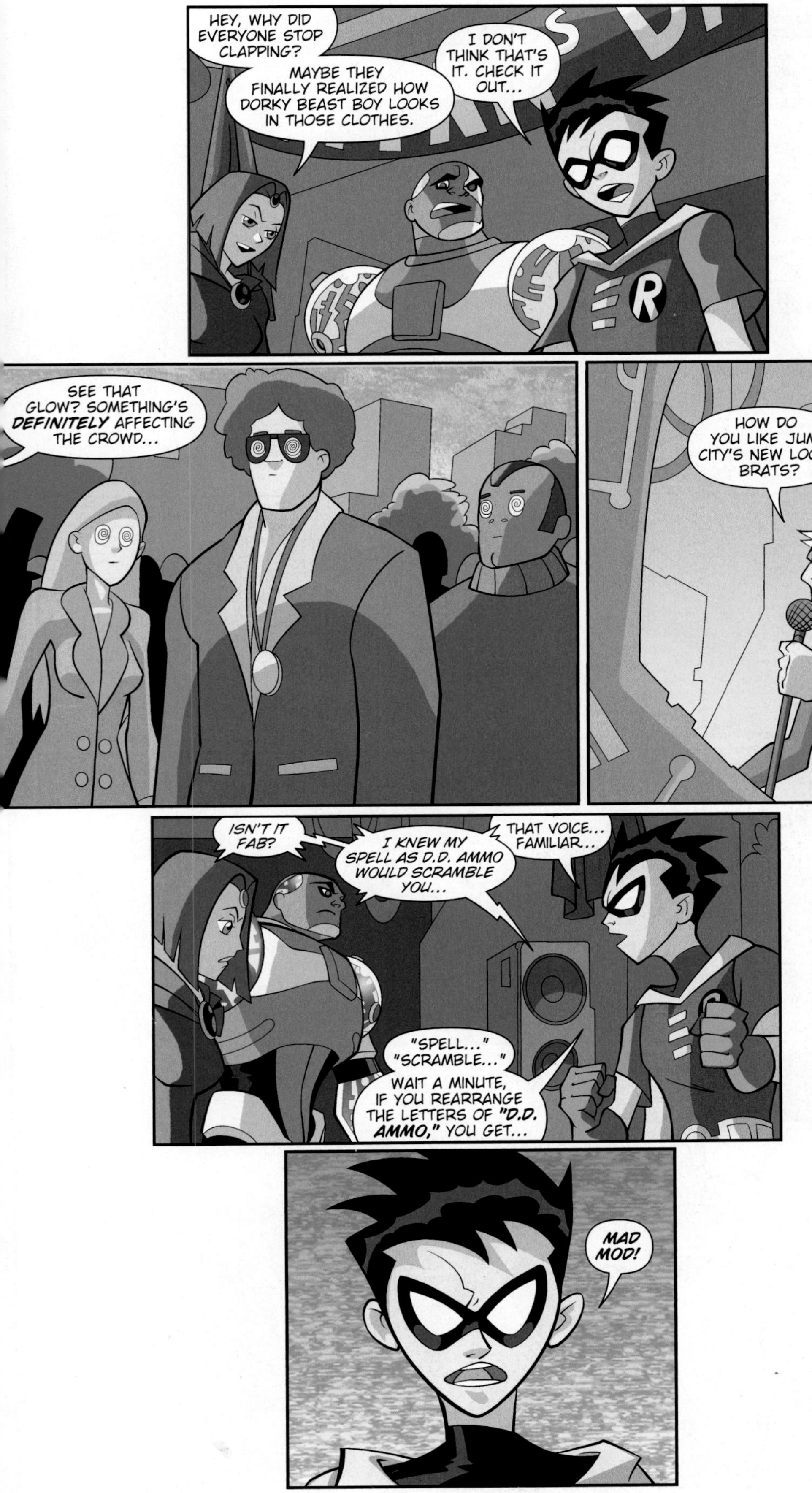
HEY, WHY DID EVERYONE STOP CLAPPING?
MAYBE THEY FINALLY REALIZED HOW DORKY BEAST BOY LOOKS IN THOSE CLOTHES.
I DON'T THINK THAT'S IT. CHECK IT OUT...
SEE THAT GLOW? SOMETHING'S DEFINITELY AFFECTING THE CROWD...
HOW DO YOU LIKE JUMP CITY'S NEW LOOK, BRATS?
ISN'T IT FAB?
I KNEW MY SPELL AS D.D. AMMO WOULD SCRAMBLE YOU...
THAT VOICE... FAMILIAR...
"SPELL..." "SCRAMBLE..." WAIT A MINUTE, IF YOU REARRANGE THE LETTERS OF "D.D. AMMO," YOU GET...
MAD MOD!

RIGHT YOU ARE, TEEN *TWIT!* AND I MUST SAY, YOU'VE HELPED MY PLAN SPLENDIDLY!

FIRST YOU FOUGHT MY GROOVY ROBOTS WHERE EVERYONE COULD SEE YOU...

...SO THAT WHEN YOU AGREED TO WEAR MY SPECIAL CLOTHES, THE REST OF JUMP CITY WAS ONLY TOO TICKLED TO GO ALONG!

OF COURSE, YOU THREE WERE SUPPOSED TO GEAR UP IN MY GEAR TOO, SO I COULD HYPNOTIZE **ALL** OF YOU...

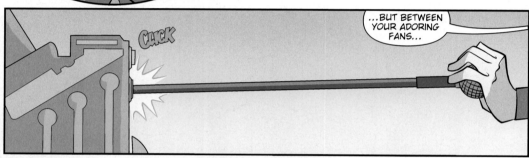

CLACK

...BUT BETWEEN YOUR ADORING FANS...

...WHO ARE NOW A SMIDGE LESS ADORING...

...AND YOUR EXCEPTIONALLY WELL-DRESSED TEAMMATES...

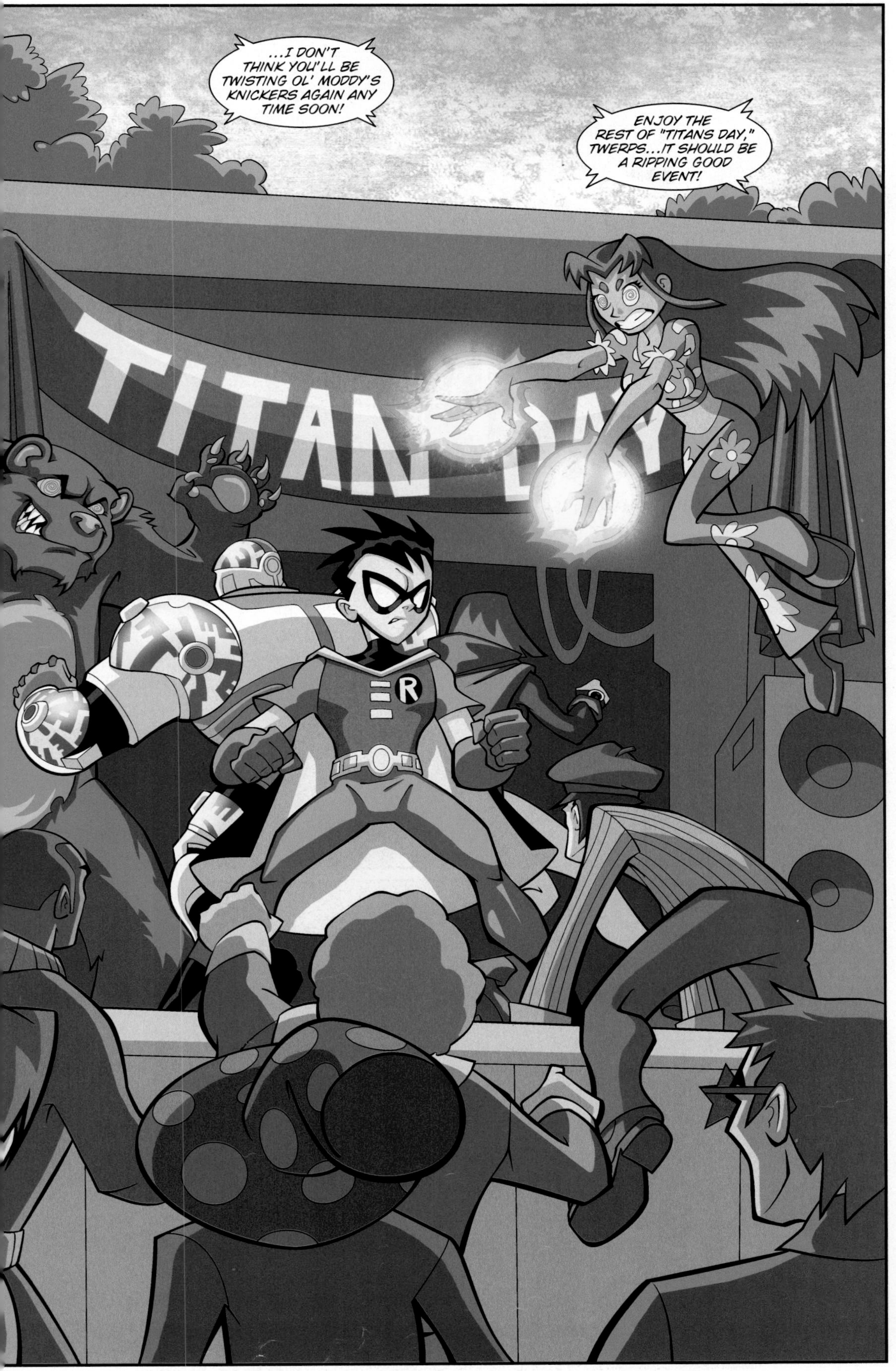
...I DON'T THINK YOU'LL BE TWISTING OL' MODDY'S KNICKERS AGAIN ANY TIME SOON!
ENJOY THE REST OF "TITANS DAY," TWERPS...IT SHOULD BE A RIPPING GOOD EVENT!
TITAN DAY

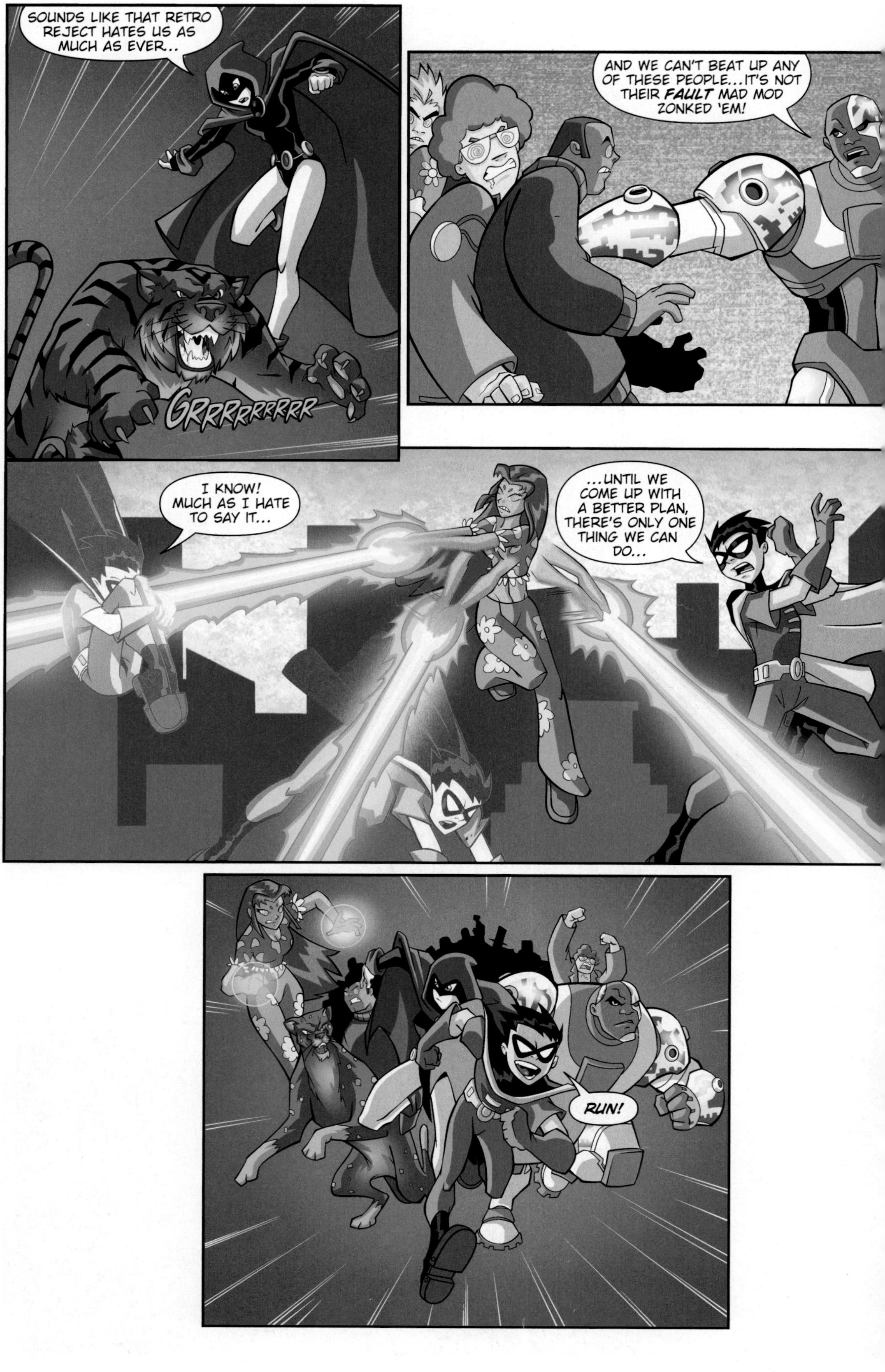
SOUNDS LIKE THAT RETRO REJECT HATES US AS MUCH AS EVER...
GRRRRRRRRR
AND WE CAN'T BEAT UP ANY OF THESE PEOPLE...IT'S NOT THEIR **FAULT** MAD MOD ZONKED 'EM!
I KNOW! MUCH AS I HATE TO SAY IT...
...UNTIL WE COME UP WITH A BETTER PLAN, THERE'S ONLY ONE THING WE CAN DO...
RUN!

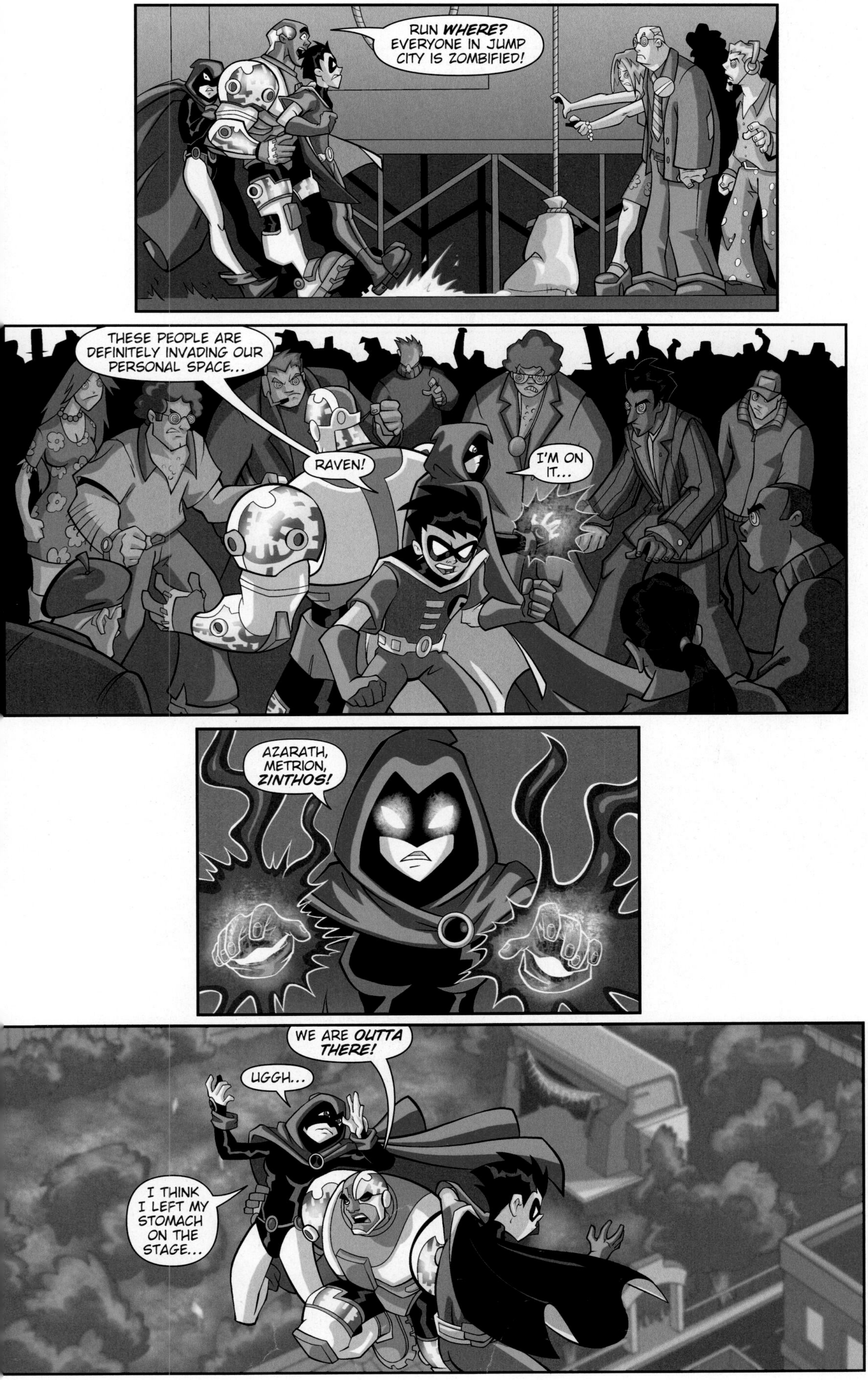
RUN WHERE? EVERYONE IN JUMP CITY IS ZOMBIFIED!
THESE PEOPLE ARE DEFINITELY INVADING OUR PERSONAL SPACE...
RAVEN!
I'M ON IT...
AZARATH, METRION, ZINTHOS!
WE ARE OUTTA THERE!
UGGH...
I THINK I LEFT MY STOMACH ON THE STAGE...

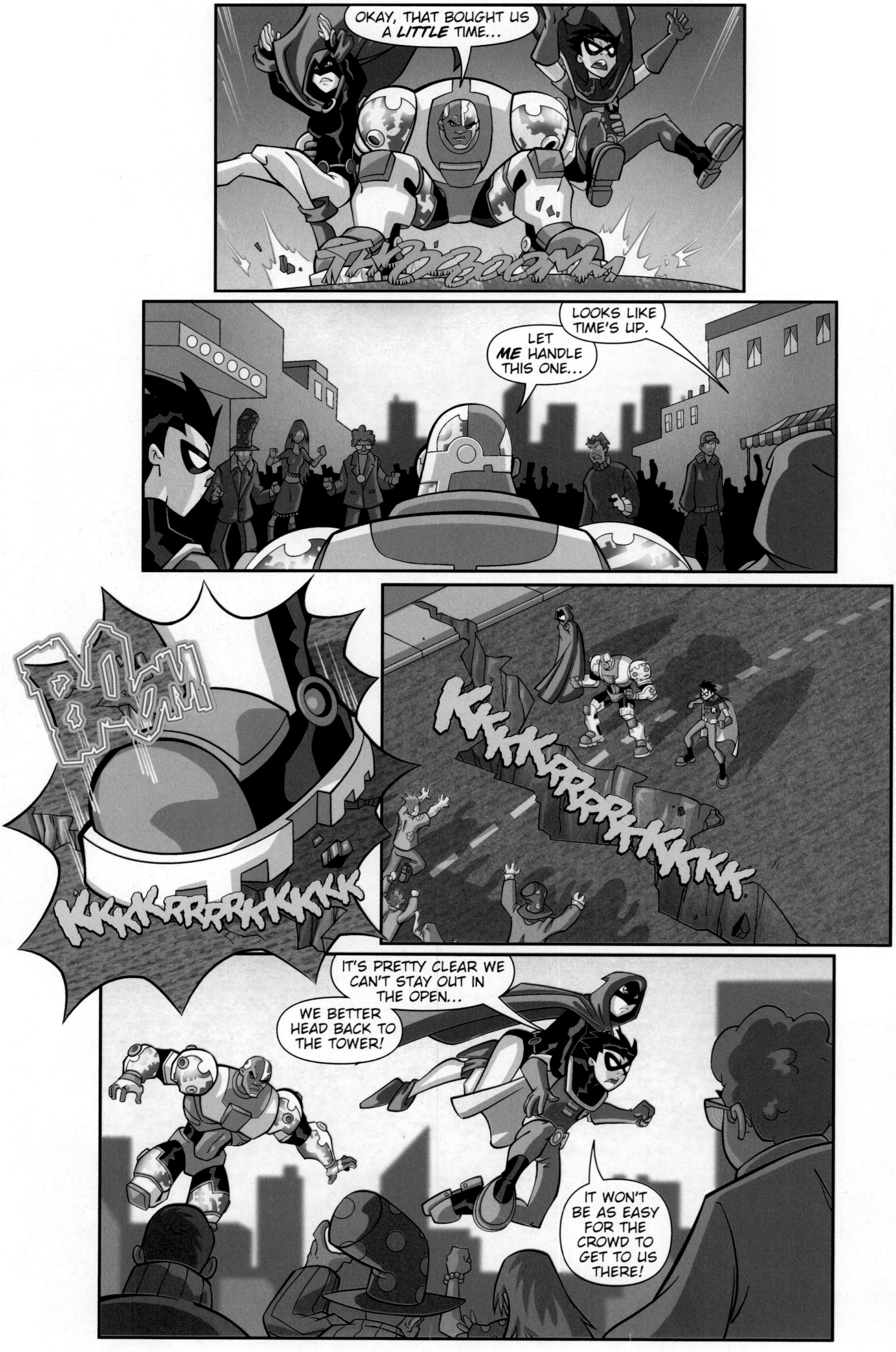
OKAY, THAT BOUGHT US A LITTLE TIME...
THOOOOOOMMM
LOOKS LIKE TIME'S UP.
LET ME HANDLE THIS ONE...
BOOM
KKKKRRRRKKKKK
KKKKRRRRKKKKK
IT'S PRETTY CLEAR WE CAN'T STAY OUT IN THE OPEN...
WE BETTER HEAD BACK TO THE TOWER!
IT WON'T BE AS EASY FOR THE CROWD TO GET TO US THERE!

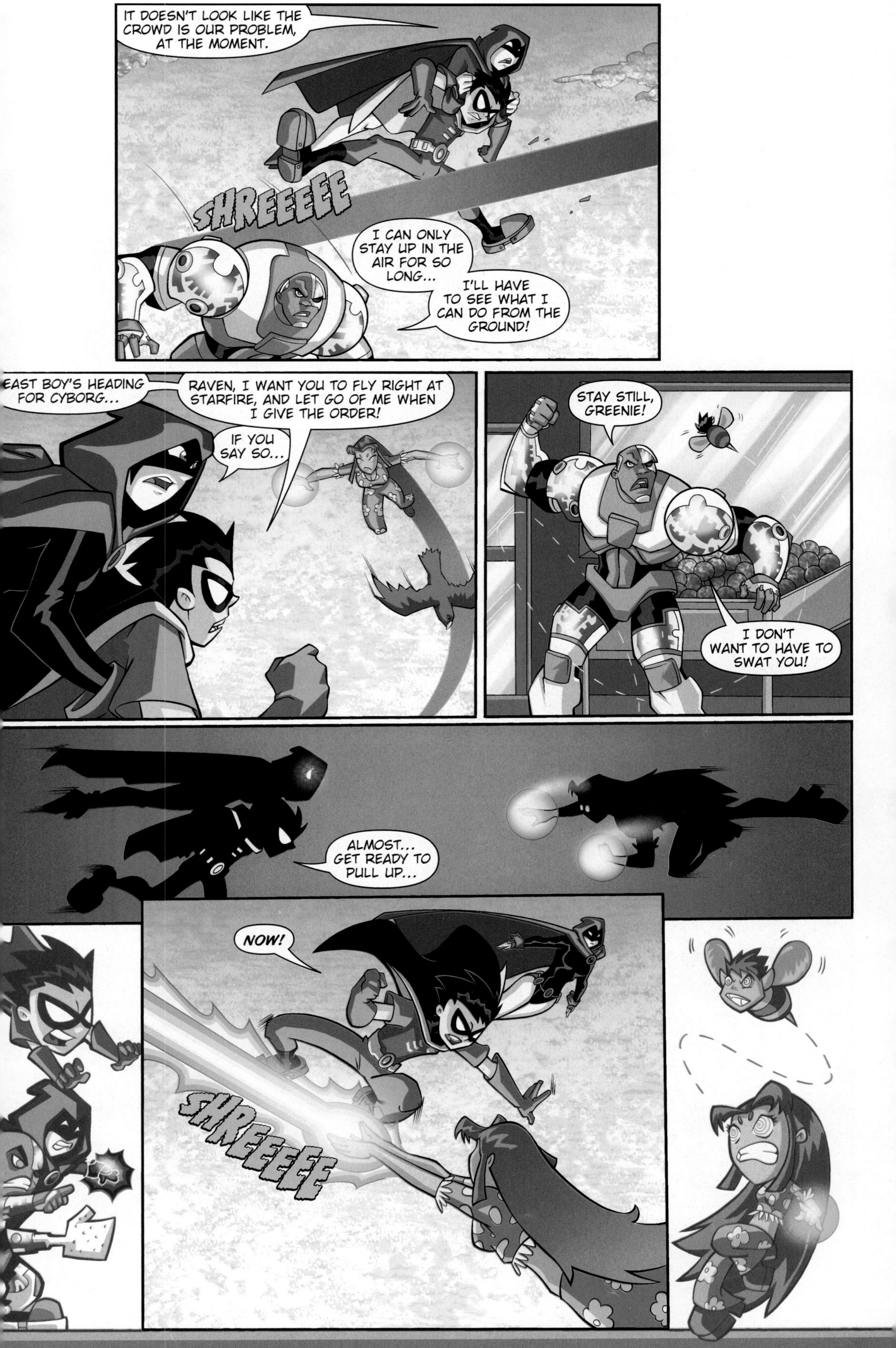
IT DOESN'T LOOK LIKE THE CROWD IS OUR PROBLEM, AT THE MOMENT.
SHREEEEE
I CAN ONLY STAY UP IN THE AIR FOR SO LONG...
I'LL HAVE TO SEE WHAT I CAN DO FROM THE GROUND!
EAST BOY'S HEADING FOR CYBORG...
RAVEN, I WANT YOU TO FLY RIGHT AT STARFIRE, AND LET GO OF ME WHEN I GIVE THE ORDER!
IF YOU SAY SO...
STAY STILL, GREENIE!
I DON'T WANT TO HAVE TO SWAT YOU!
ALMOST... GET READY TO PULL UP...
NOW!
SHREEEEEE

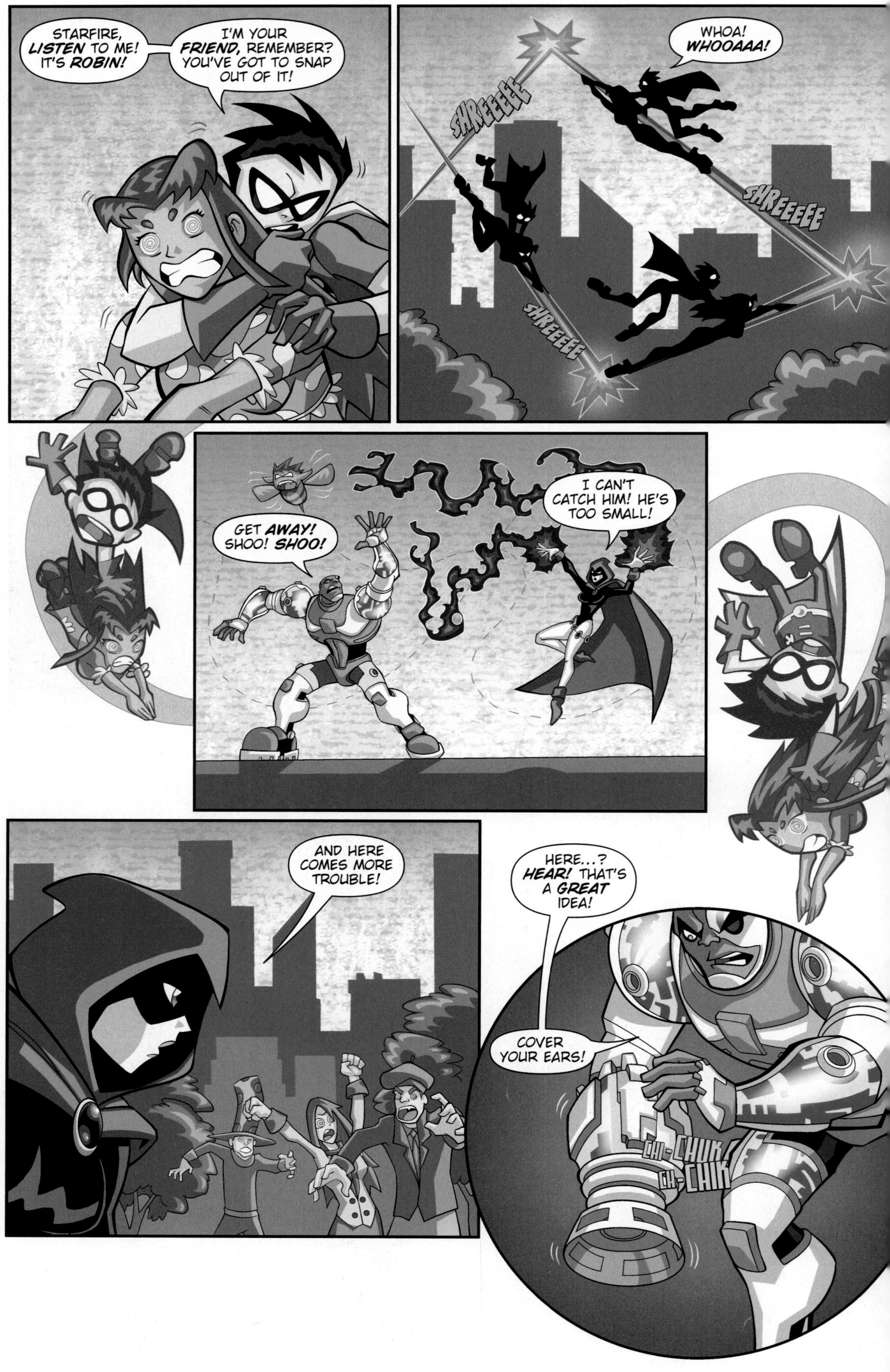
STARFIRE, LISTEN TO ME! IT'S ROBIN!
I'M YOUR FRIEND, REMEMBER? YOU'VE GOT TO SNAP OUT OF IT!
WHOA! WHOOAAA!
SHREEEEE
SHREEEEE
SHREEEEE
GET AWAY! SHOO! SHOO!
I CAN'T CATCH HIM! HE'S TOO SMALL!
AND HERE COMES MORE TROUBLE!
HERE...? HEAR! THAT'S A GREAT IDEA!
COVER YOUR EARS!
CH-CHUK! CH-CHIK

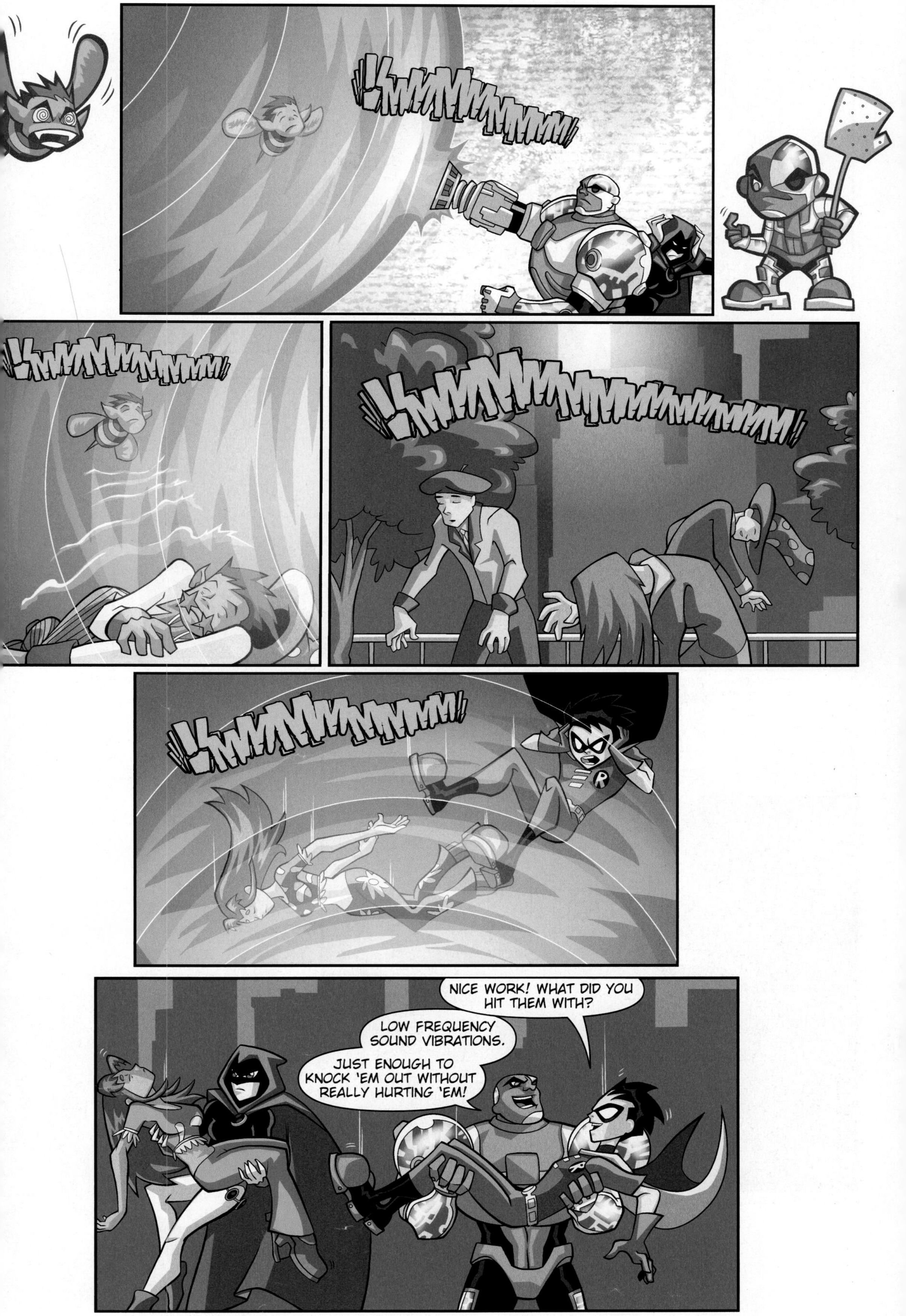
NICE WORK! WHAT DID YOU HIT THEM WITH?
LOW FREQUENCY SOUND VIBRATIONS.
JUST ENOUGH TO KNOCK 'EM OUT WITHOUT REALLY HURTING 'EM!

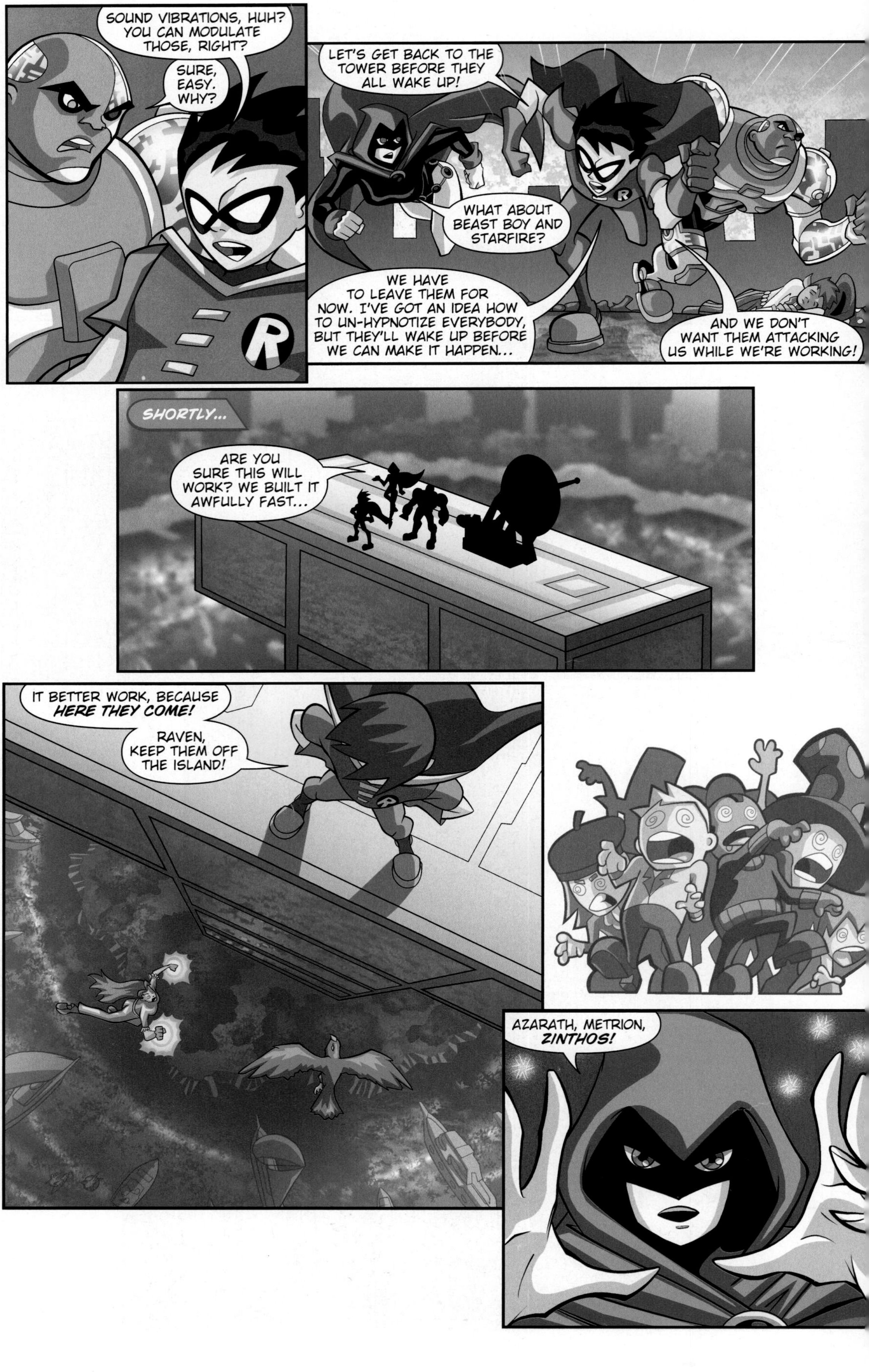
SOUND VIBRATIONS, HUH? YOU CAN MODULATE THOSE, RIGHT?
SURE, EASY. WHY?
LET'S GET BACK TO THE TOWER BEFORE THEY ALL WAKE UP!
WHAT ABOUT BEAST BOY AND STARFIRE?
WE HAVE TO LEAVE THEM FOR NOW. I'VE GOT AN IDEA HOW TO UN-HYPNOTIZE EVERYBODY, BUT THEY'LL WAKE UP BEFORE WE CAN MAKE IT HAPPEN...
AND WE DON'T WANT THEM ATTACKING US WHILE WE'RE WORKING!
SHORTLY...
ARE YOU SURE THIS WILL WORK? WE BUILT IT AWFULLY FAST...
IT BETTER WORK, BECAUSE HERE THEY COME!
RAVEN, KEEP THEM OFF THE ISLAND!
AZARATH, METRION, ZINTHOS!

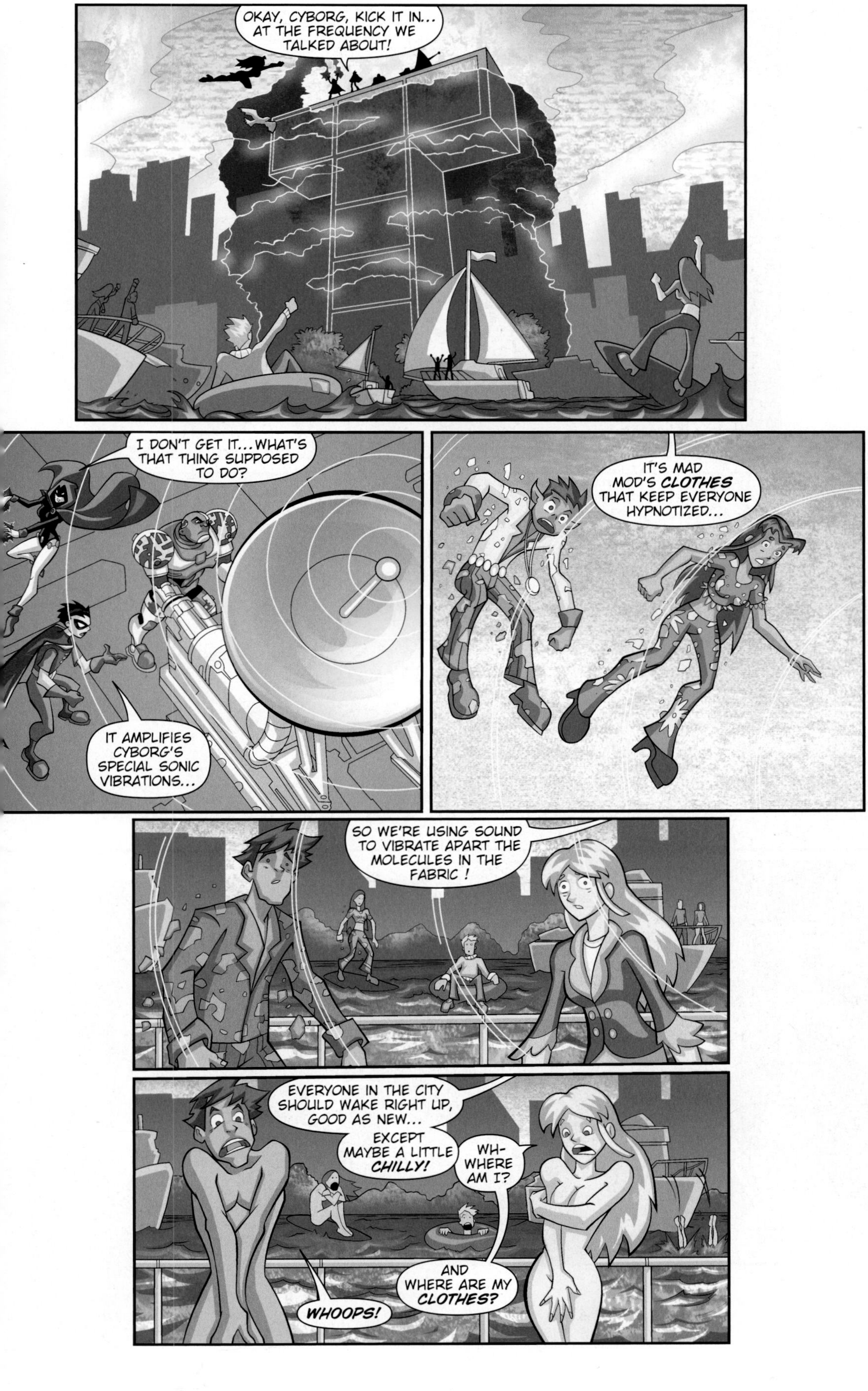
OKAY, CYBORG, KICK IT IN... AT THE FREQUENCY WE TALKED ABOUT!
I DON'T GET IT...WHAT'S THAT THING SUPPOSED TO DO?
IT AMPLIFIES CYBORG'S SPECIAL SONIC VIBRATIONS...
IT'S MAD MOD'S **CLOTHES** THAT KEEP EVERYONE HYPNOTIZED...
SO WE'RE USING SOUND TO VIBRATE APART THE MOLECULES IN THE FABRIC !
EVERYONE IN THE CITY SHOULD WAKE RIGHT UP, GOOD AS NEW...
EXCEPT MAYBE A LITTLE **CHILLY!**
WH- WHERE AM I?
AND WHERE ARE MY **CLOTHES?**
WHOOPS!

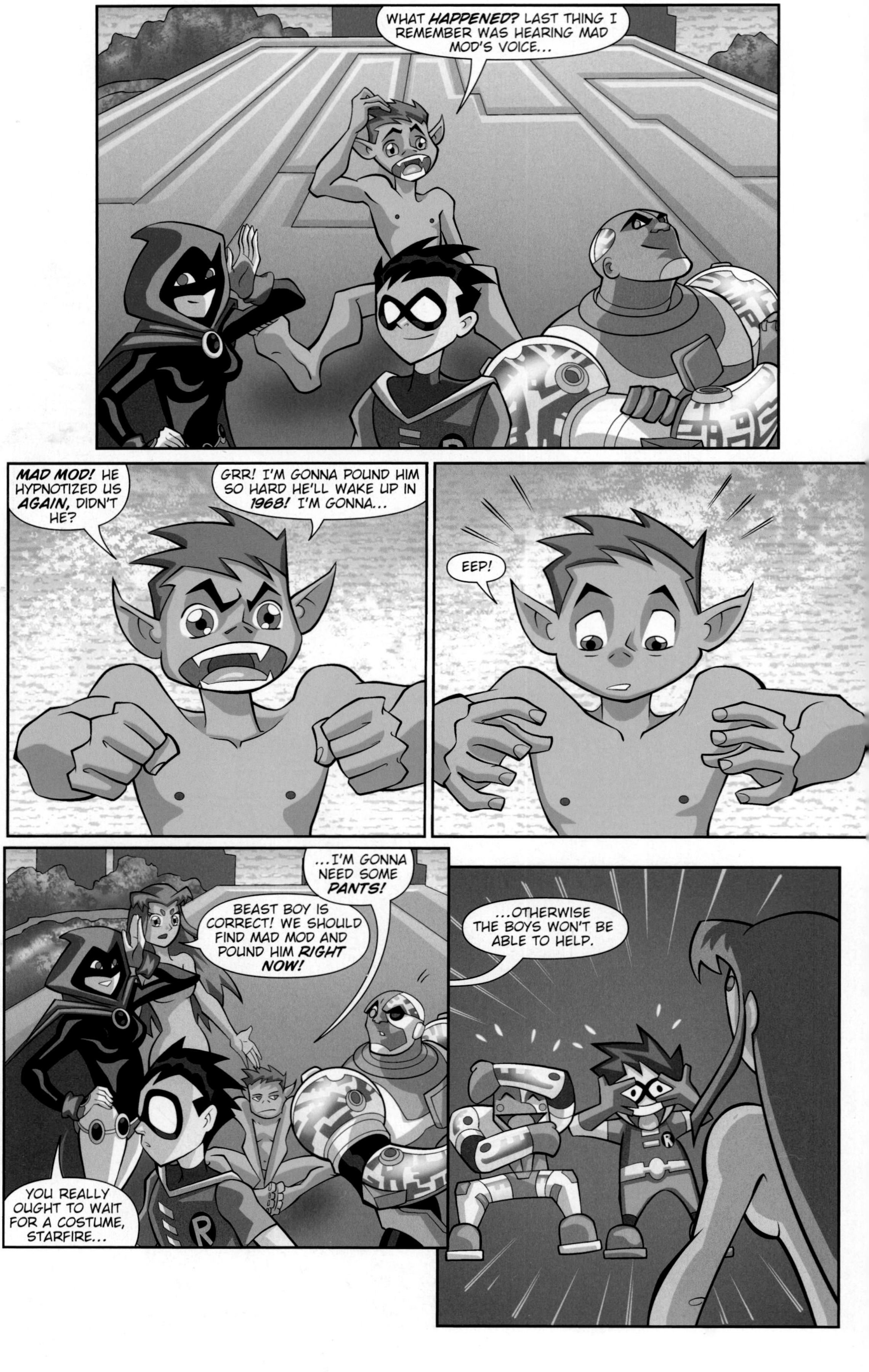
WHAT HAPPENED? LAST THING I REMEMBER WAS HEARING MAD MOD'S VOICE...
MAD MOD! HE HYPNOTIZED US AGAIN, DIDN'T HE?
GRR! I'M GONNA POUND HIM SO HARD HE'LL WAKE UP IN 1968! I'M GONNA...
EEP!
...I'M GONNA NEED SOME PANTS!
BEAST BOY IS CORRECT! WE SHOULD FIND MAD MOD AND POUND HIM RIGHT NOW!
YOU REALLY OUGHT TO WAIT FOR A COSTUME, STARFIRE...
...OTHERWISE THE BOYS WON'T BE ABLE TO HELP.

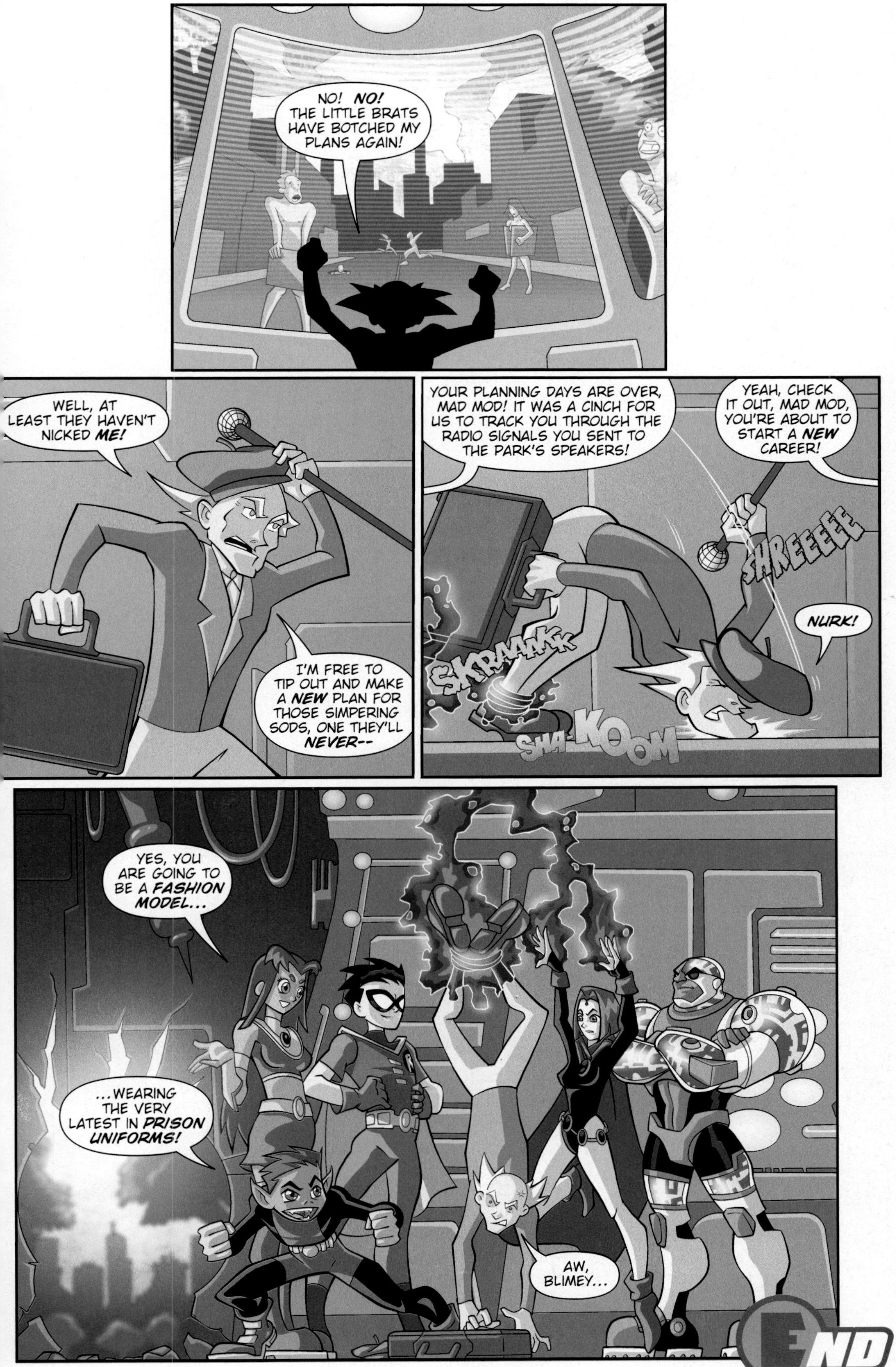
NO! NO! THE LITTLE BRATS HAVE BOTCHED MY PLANS AGAIN!
WELL, AT LEAST THEY HAVEN'T NICKED ME!
I'M FREE TO TIP OUT AND MAKE A NEW PLAN FOR THOSE SIMPERING SODS, ONE THEY'LL NEVER--
YOUR PLANNING DAYS ARE OVER, MAD MOD! IT WAS A CINCH FOR US TO TRACK YOU THROUGH THE RADIO SIGNALS YOU SENT TO THE PARK'S SPEAKERS!
YEAH, CHECK IT OUT, MAD MOD, YOU'RE ABOUT TO START A NEW CAREER!
SHREEEEE
NURK!
SKRAAAKK
SHA-KOOM
YES, YOU ARE GOING TO BE A FASHION MODEL...
...WEARING THE VERY LATEST IN PRISON UNIFORMS!
AW, BLIMEY...
END

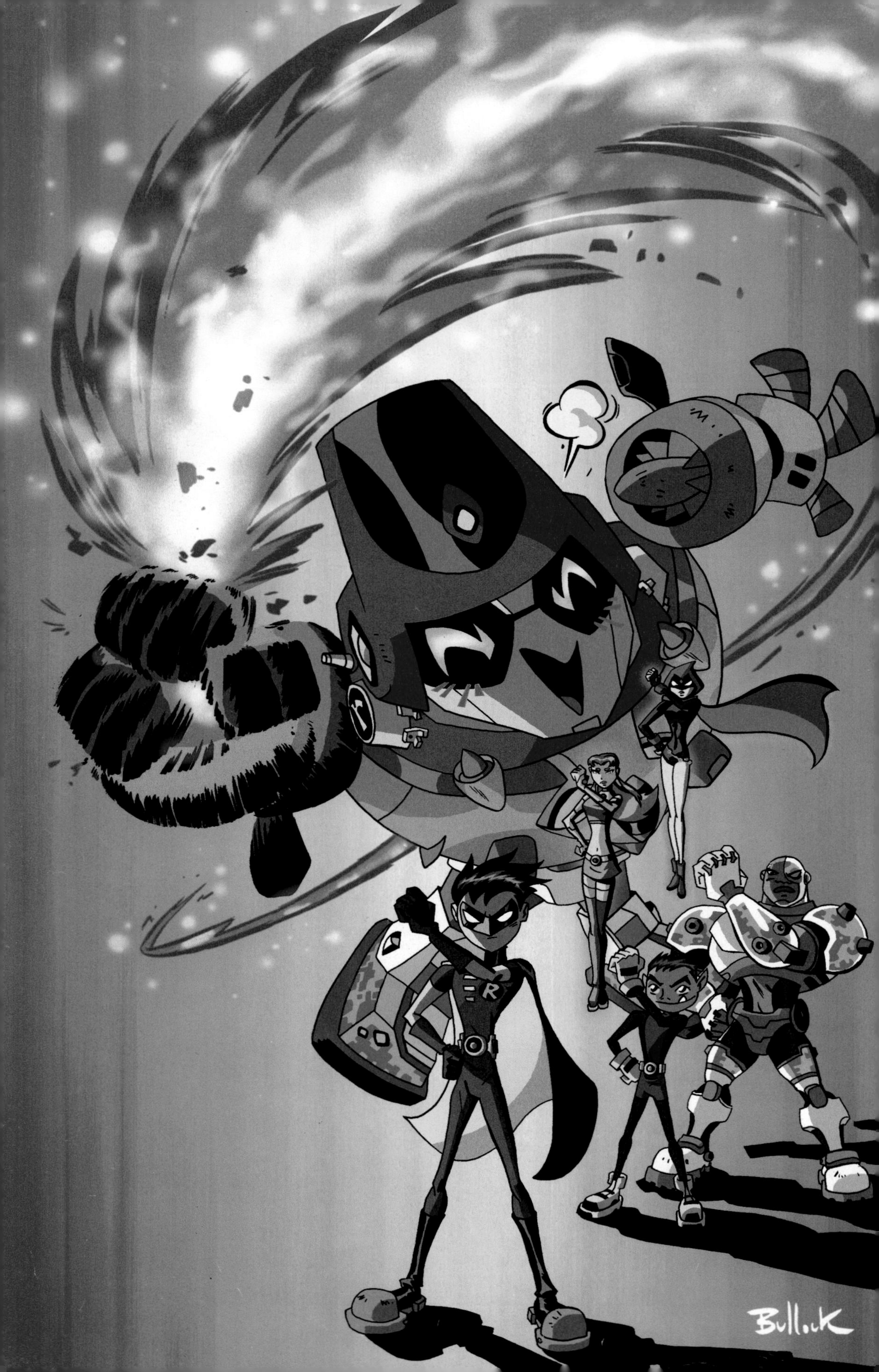
BullocK

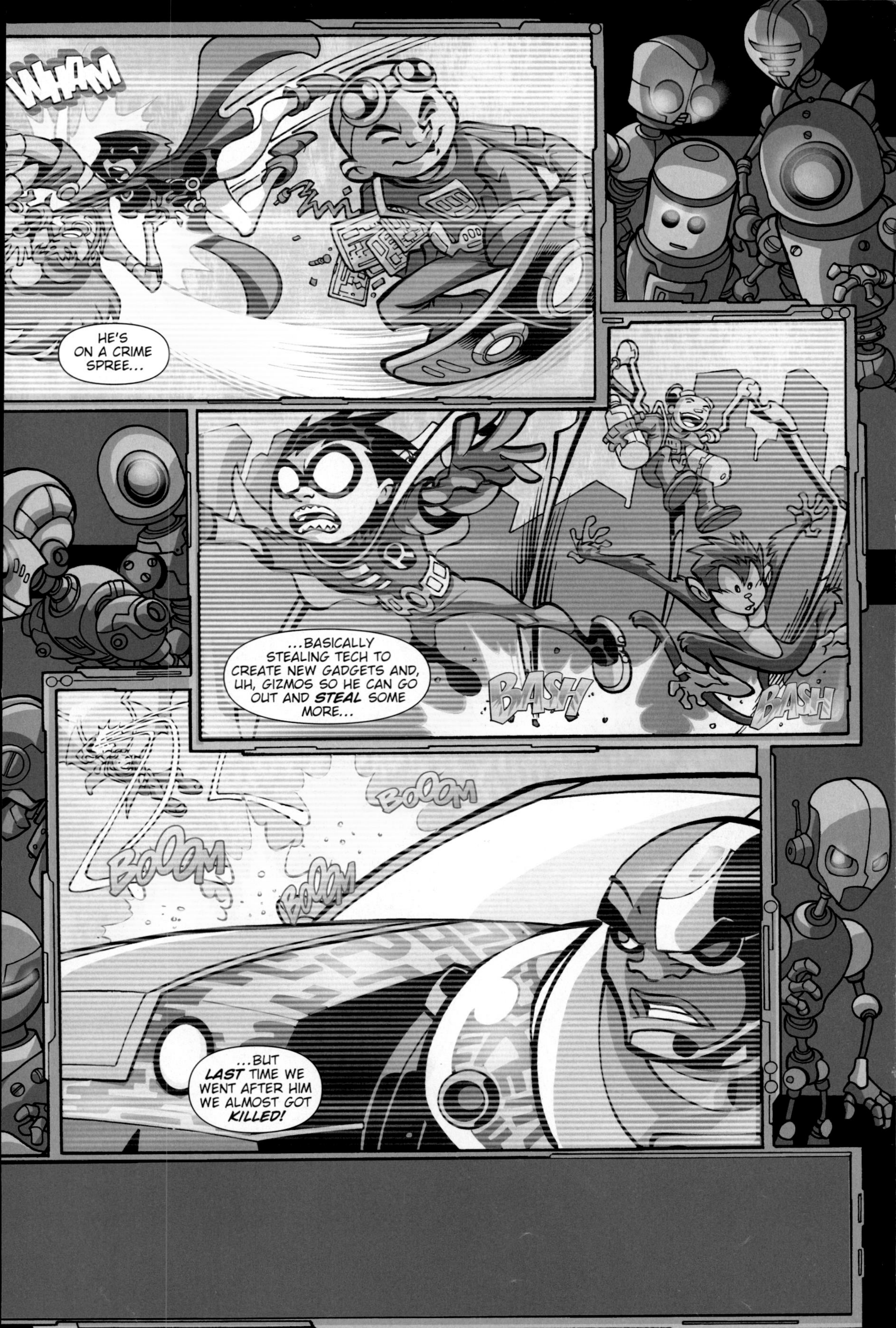
WHAM
HE'S ON A CRIME SPREE...
...BASICALLY STEALING TECH TO CREATE NEW GADGETS AND, UH, GIZMOS SO HE CAN GO OUT AND STEAL SOME MORE...
BASH
BASH
BOOOM
BOOOM
BOOOM
...BUT LAST TIME WE WENT AFTER HIM WE ALMOST GOT KILLED!

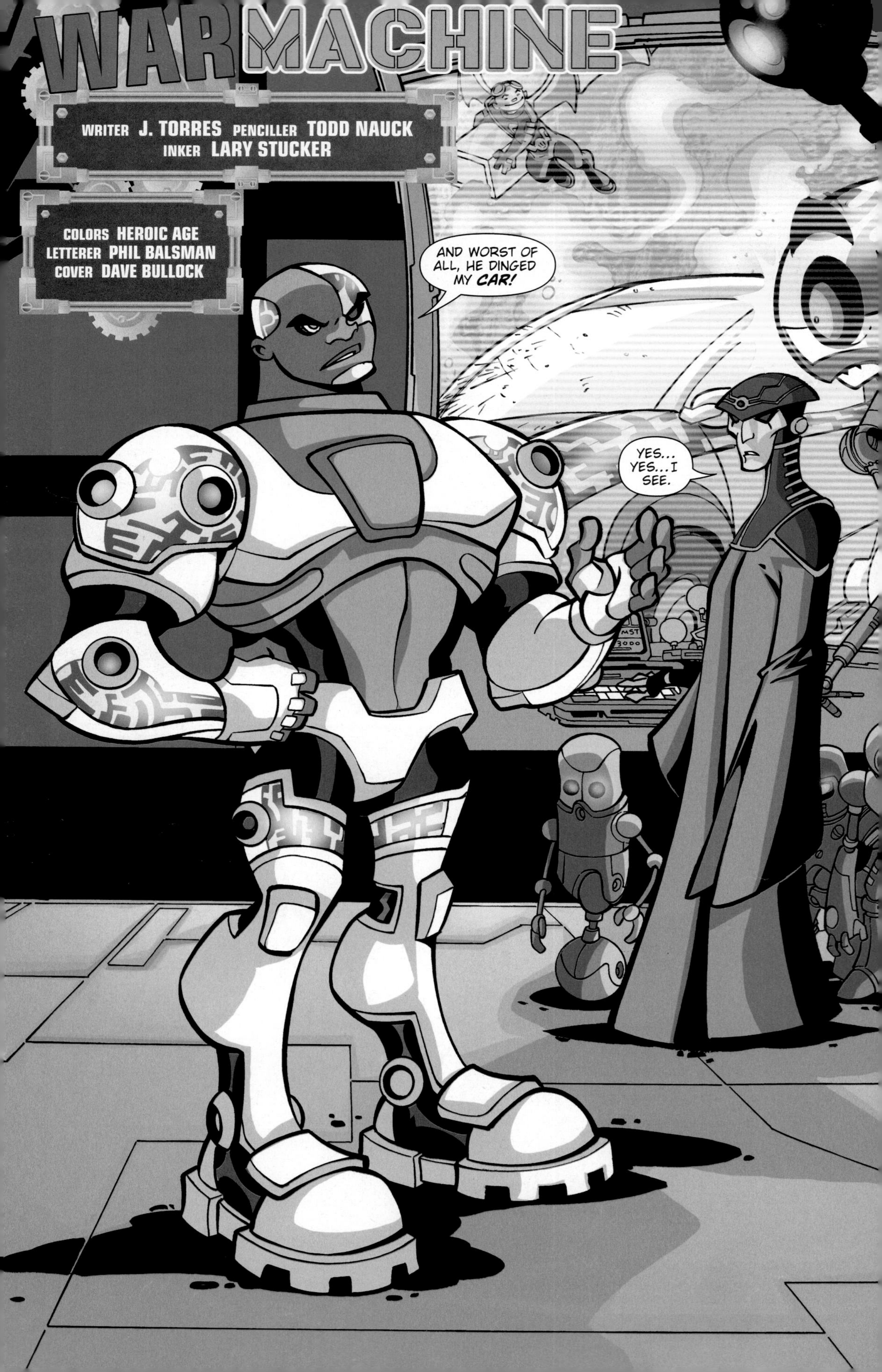
WAR MACHINE
WRITER J. TORRES PENCILLER TODD NAUCK
INKER LARY STUCKER
COLORS HEROIC AGE
LETTERER PHIL BALSMAN
COVER DAVE BULLOCK
AND WORST OF ALL, HE DINGED MY CAR!
YES... YES...I SEE.
MST 3000

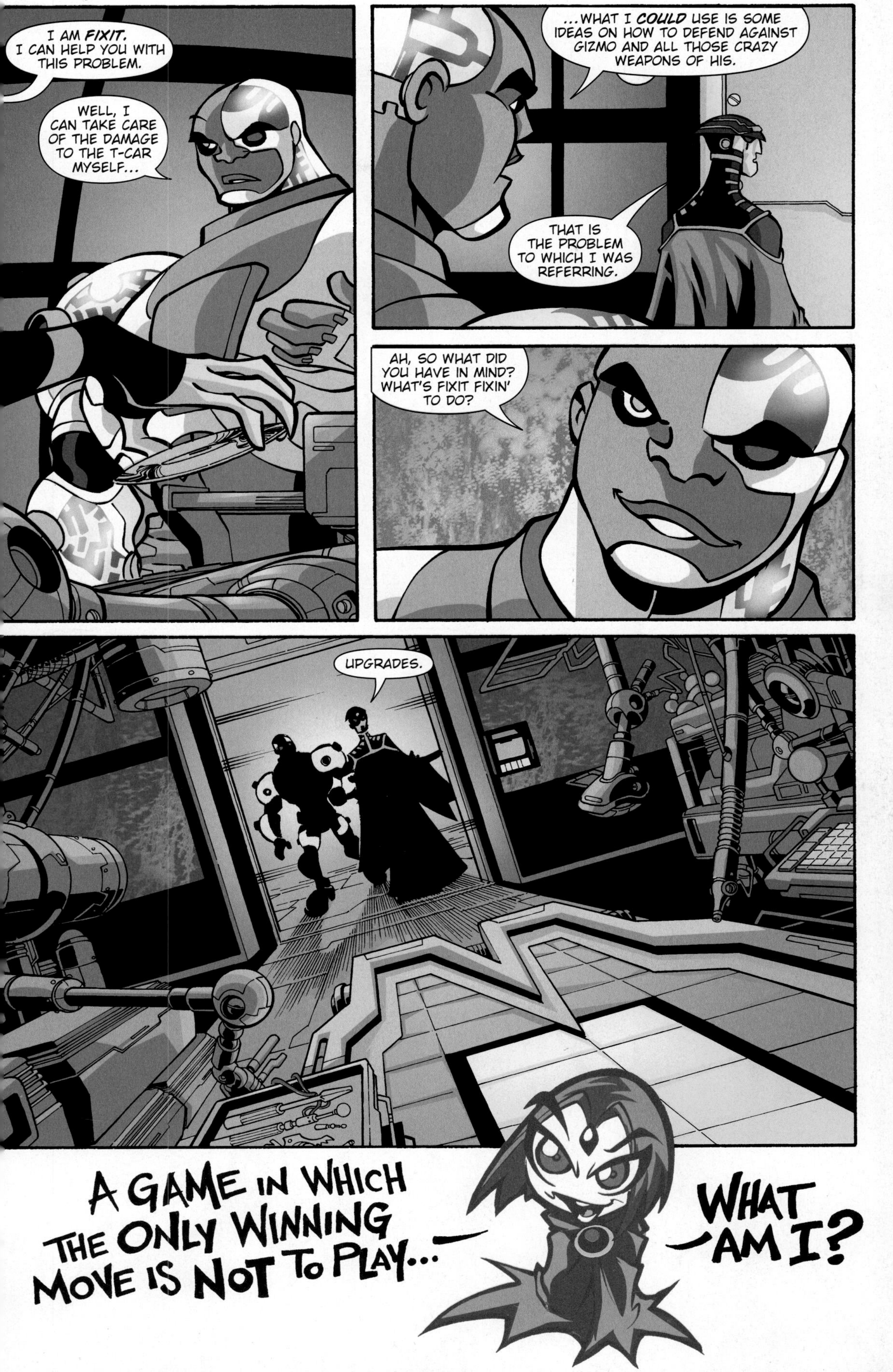
I AM FIXIT. I CAN HELP YOU WITH THIS PROBLEM.
WELL, I CAN TAKE CARE OF THE DAMAGE TO THE T-CAR MYSELF...
...WHAT I COULD USE IS SOME IDEAS ON HOW TO DEFEND AGAINST GIZMO AND ALL THOSE CRAZY WEAPONS OF HIS.
THAT IS THE PROBLEM TO WHICH I WAS REFERRING.
AH, SO WHAT DID YOU HAVE IN MIND? WHAT'S FIXIT FIXIN' TO DO?
UPGRADES.
A GAME IN WHICH THE ONLY WINNING MOVE IS NOT TO PLAY...
WHAT AM I?

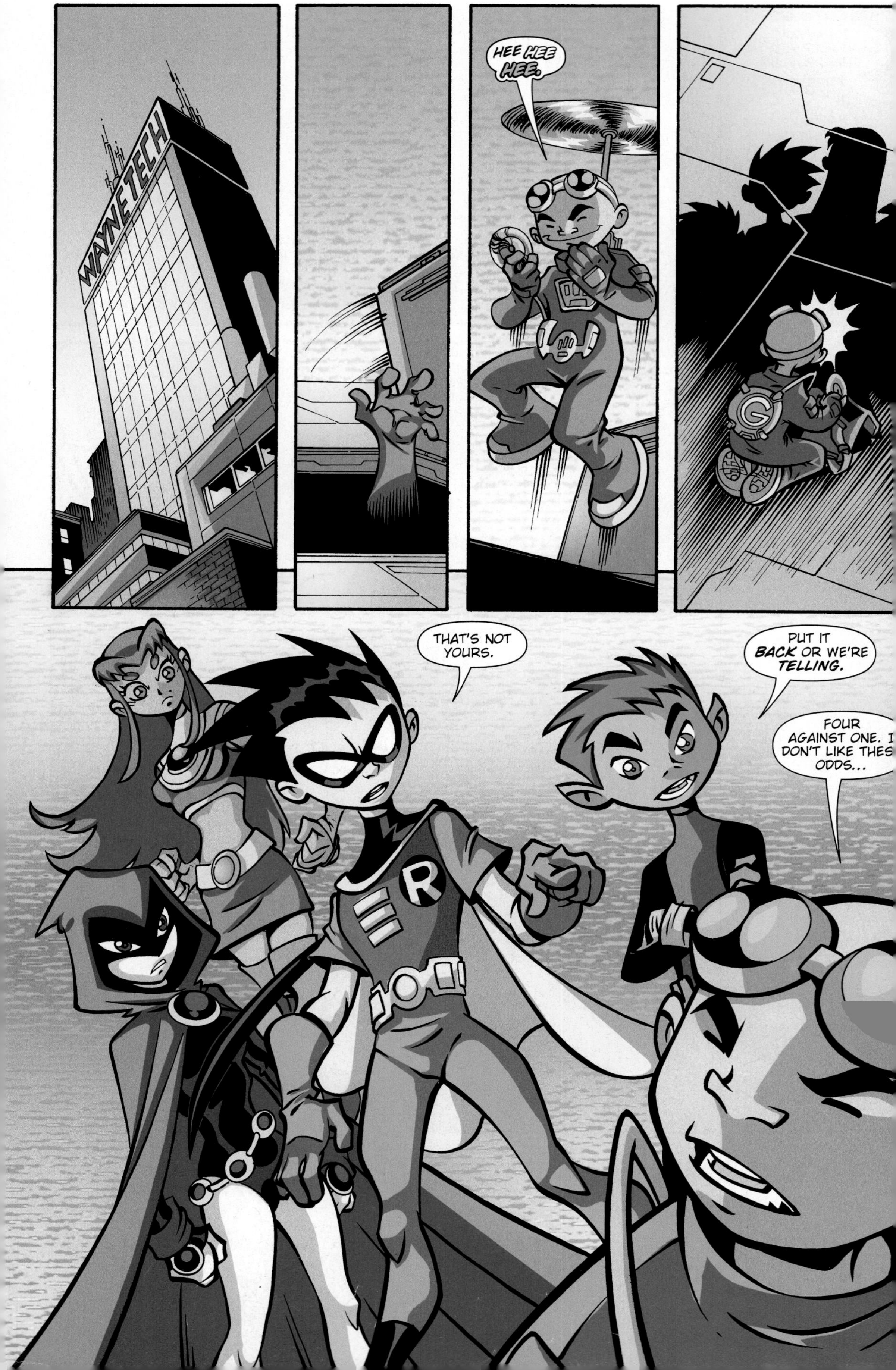
HEE HEE HEE.
THAT'S NOT YOURS.
PUT IT BACK OR WE'RE TELLING.
FOUR AGAINST ONE. I DON'T LIKE THES ODDS...

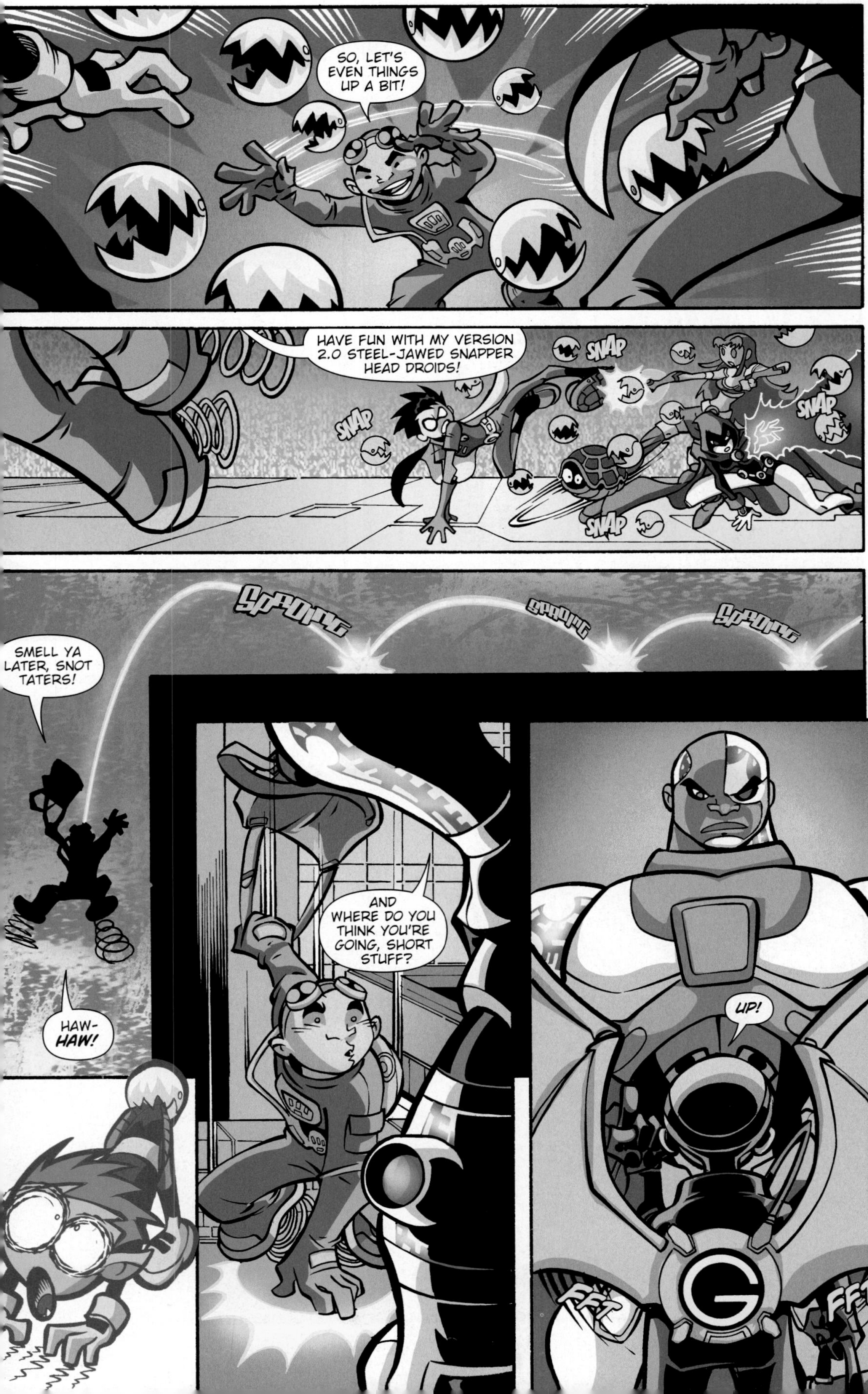
SO, LET'S EVEN THINGS UP A BIT!
HAVE FUN WITH MY VERSION 2.0 STEEL-JAWED SNAPPER HEAD DROIDS!
SNAP
SNAP
SNAP
SNAP
SPROING
SPROING
SPROING
SMELL YA LATER, SNOT TATERS!
HAW-HAW!
AND WHERE DO YOU THINK YOU'RE GOING, SHORT STUFF?
UP!
FFT
FFT

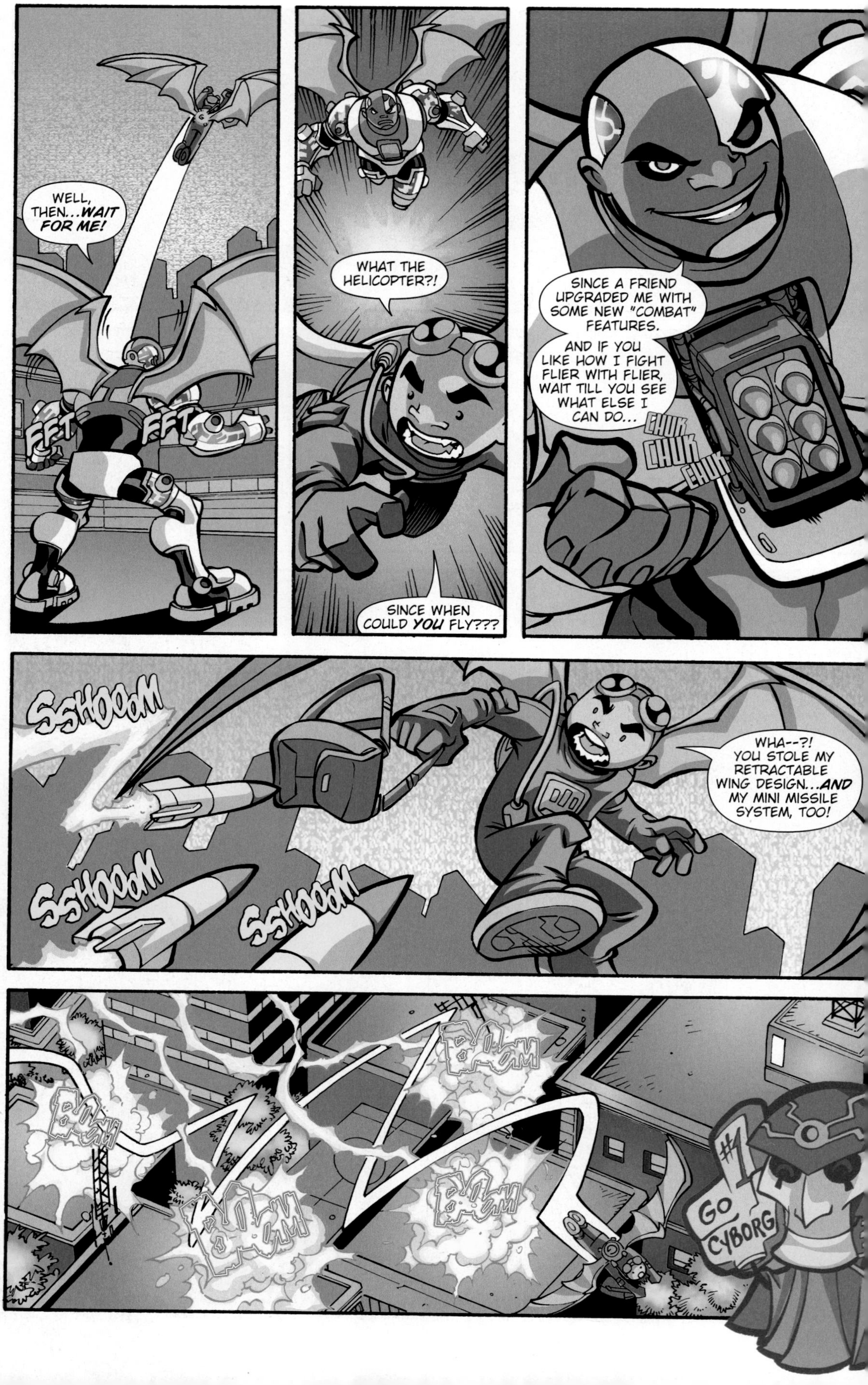

WELL, THEN...WAIT FOR ME!
FFT
FFT
WHAT THE HELICOPTER?!
SINCE WHEN COULD YOU FLY???
SINCE A FRIEND UPGRADED ME WITH SOME NEW "COMBAT" FEATURES.
AND IF YOU LIKE HOW I FIGHT FLIER WITH FLIER, WAIT TILL YOU SEE WHAT ELSE I CAN DO...
CHUK
CHUK
CHUK
SSHOOOM
SSHOOOM
SSHOOOM
WHA--?! YOU STOLE MY RETRACTABLE WING DESIGN...AND MY MINI MISSILE SYSTEM, TOO!
BOOM
BOOM
BOOM
BOOM
#1
GO CYBORG

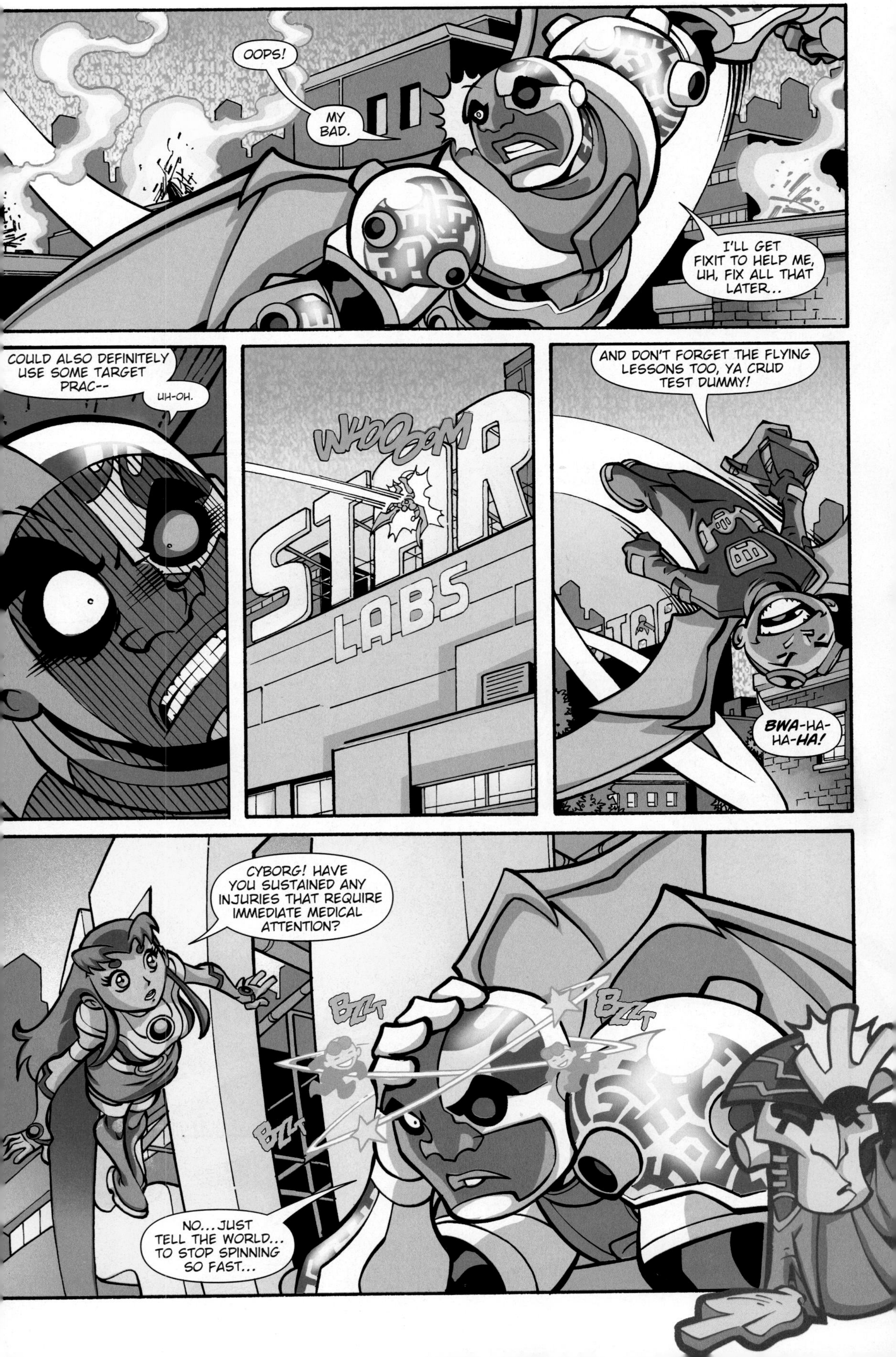
OOPS!
MY BAD.
I'LL GET FIXIT TO HELP ME, UH, FIX ALL THAT LATER..
COULD ALSO DEFINITELY USE SOME TARGET PRAC--
UH-OH.
WHOOOOM
STAR LABS
AND DON'T FORGET THE FLYING LESSONS TOO, YA CRUD TEST DUMMY!
BWA-HA-HA-HA!
CYBORG! HAVE YOU SUSTAINED ANY INJURIES THAT REQUIRE IMMEDIATE MEDICAL ATTENTION?
BZZT
BZZT
BZZT
NO... JUST TELL THE WORLD... TO STOP SPINNING SO FAST...

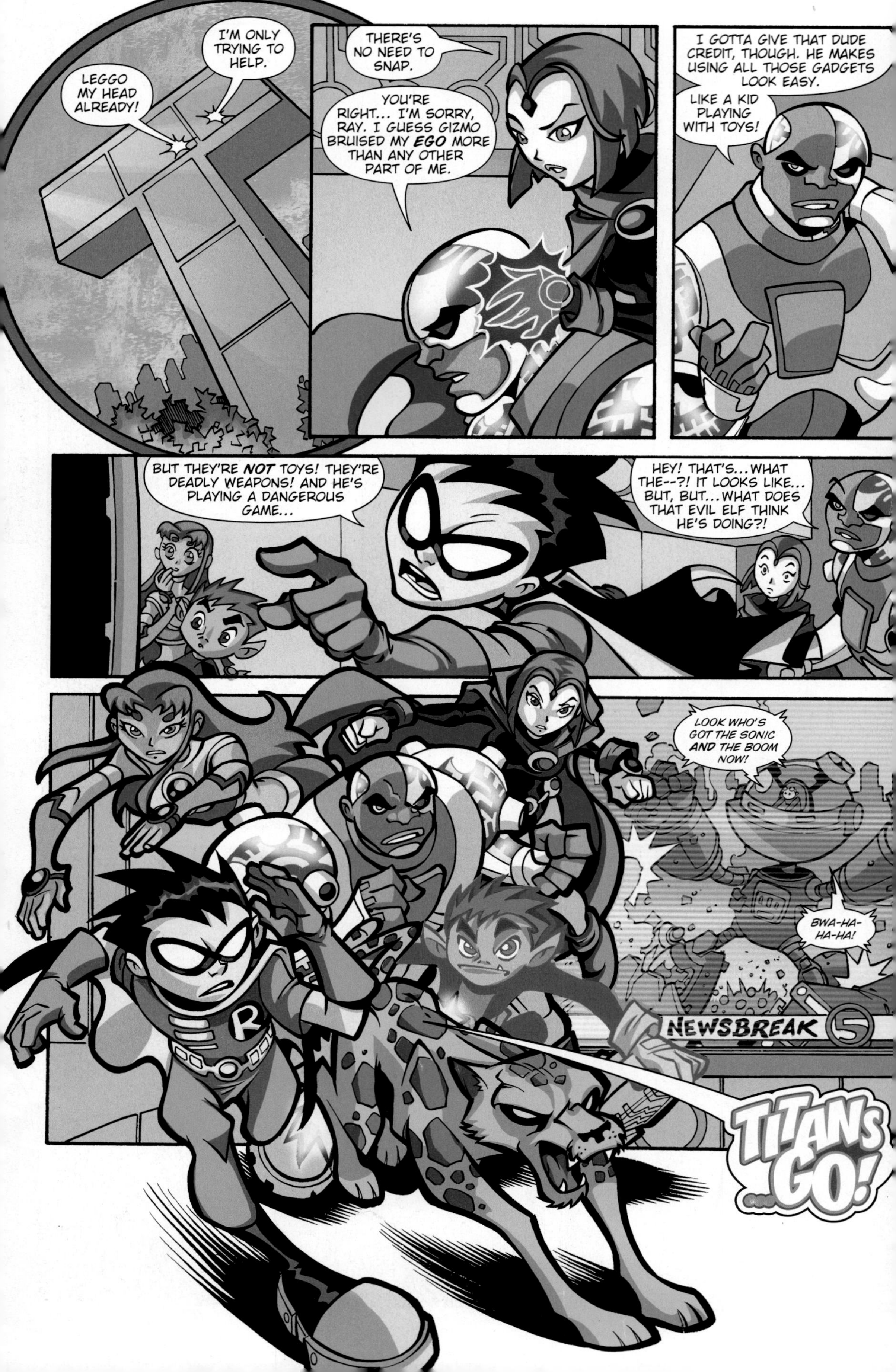
LEGGO MY HEAD ALREADY!
I'M ONLY TRYING TO HELP.
THERE'S NO NEED TO SNAP.
YOU'RE RIGHT... I'M SORRY, RAY. I GUESS GIZMO BRUISED MY EGO MORE THAN ANY OTHER PART OF ME.
I GOTTA GIVE THAT DUDE CREDIT, THOUGH. HE MAKES USING ALL THOSE GADGETS LOOK EASY.
LIKE A KID PLAYING WITH TOYS!
BUT THEY'RE NOT TOYS! THEY'RE DEADLY WEAPONS! AND HE'S PLAYING A DANGEROUS GAME...
HEY! THAT'S...WHAT THE--?! IT LOOKS LIKE... BUT, BUT...WHAT DOES THAT EVIL ELF THINK HE'S DOING?!
LOOK WHO'S GOT THE SONIC AND THE BOOM NOW!
BWA-HA-HA-HA!
NEWSBREAK 5
TITANS GO!

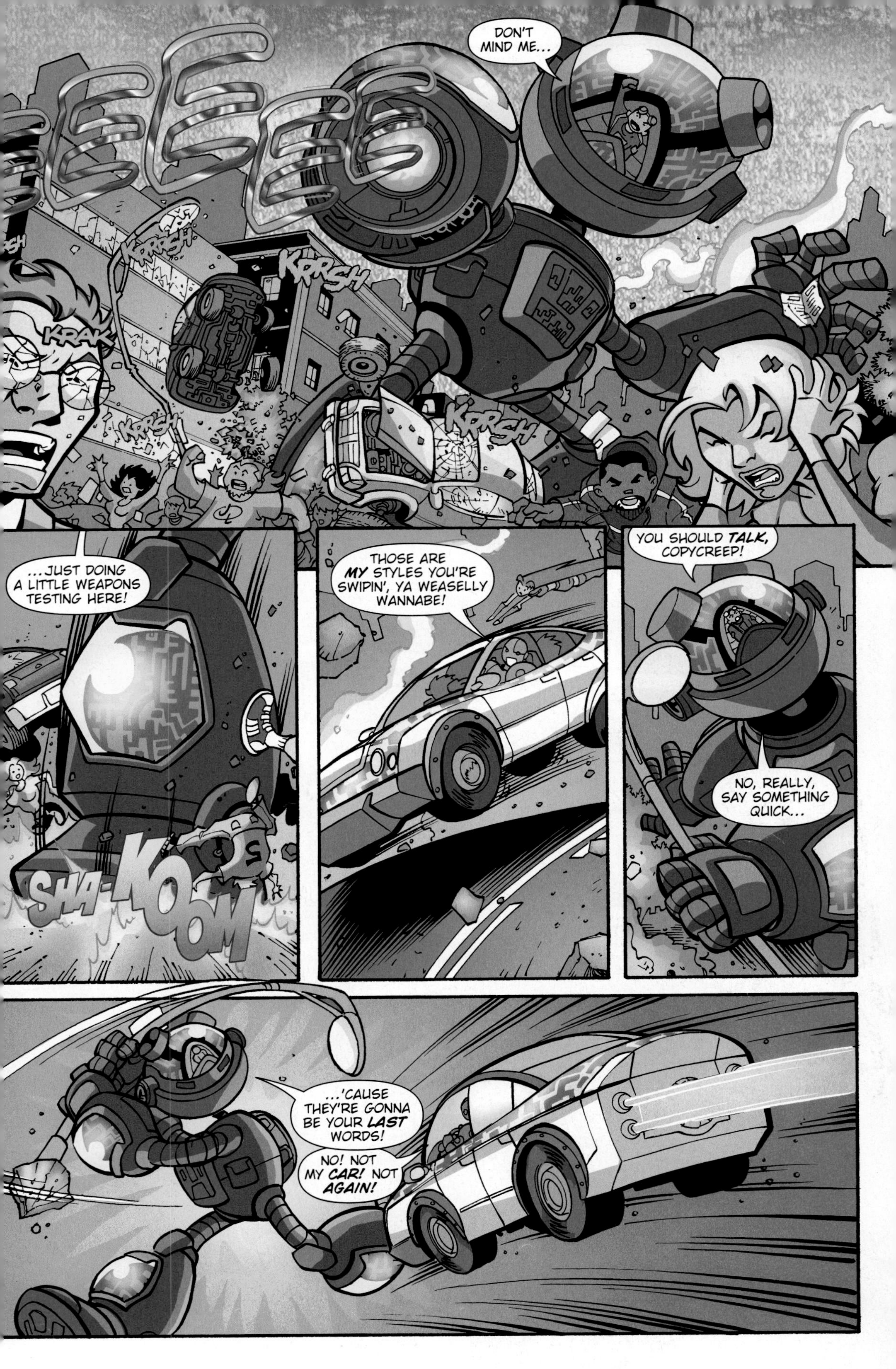
EEEEEE
KRSH
KRRSH
KRRSH
KRAK
KRRSH
KRRSH
DON'T MIND ME...
...JUST DOING A LITTLE WEAPONS TESTING HERE!
SHA-KOOOM
THOSE ARE MY STYLES YOU'RE SWIPIN', YA WEASELLY WANNABE!
YOU SHOULD TALK, COPYCREEP!
NO, REALLY, SAY SOMETHING QUICK...
...'CAUSE THEY'RE GONNA BE YOUR LAST WORDS!
NO! NOT MY CAR! NOT AGAIN!

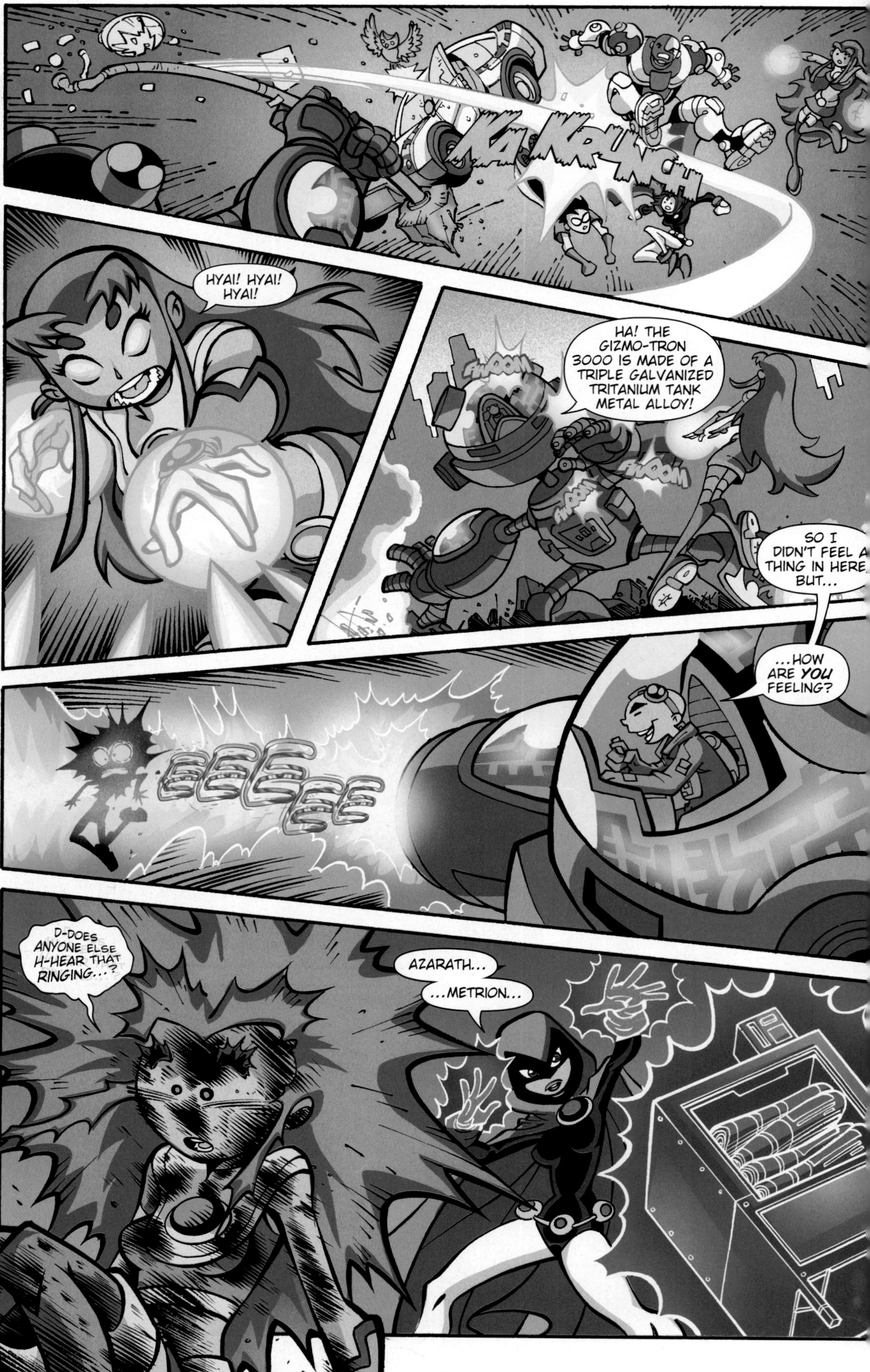

KA-KRUNCH
HYAI! HYAI! HYAI!
HA! THE GIZMO-TRON 3000 IS MADE OF A TRIPLE GALVANIZED TRITANIUM TANK METAL ALLOY!
FWOOM
FWOOM
FWOOM
FWOOM
SO I DIDN'T FEEL A THING IN HERE BUT...
...HOW ARE YOU FEELING?
EEEEEEE
D-DOES ANYONE ELSE H-HEAR THAT RINGING...?
AZARATH...
...METRION...

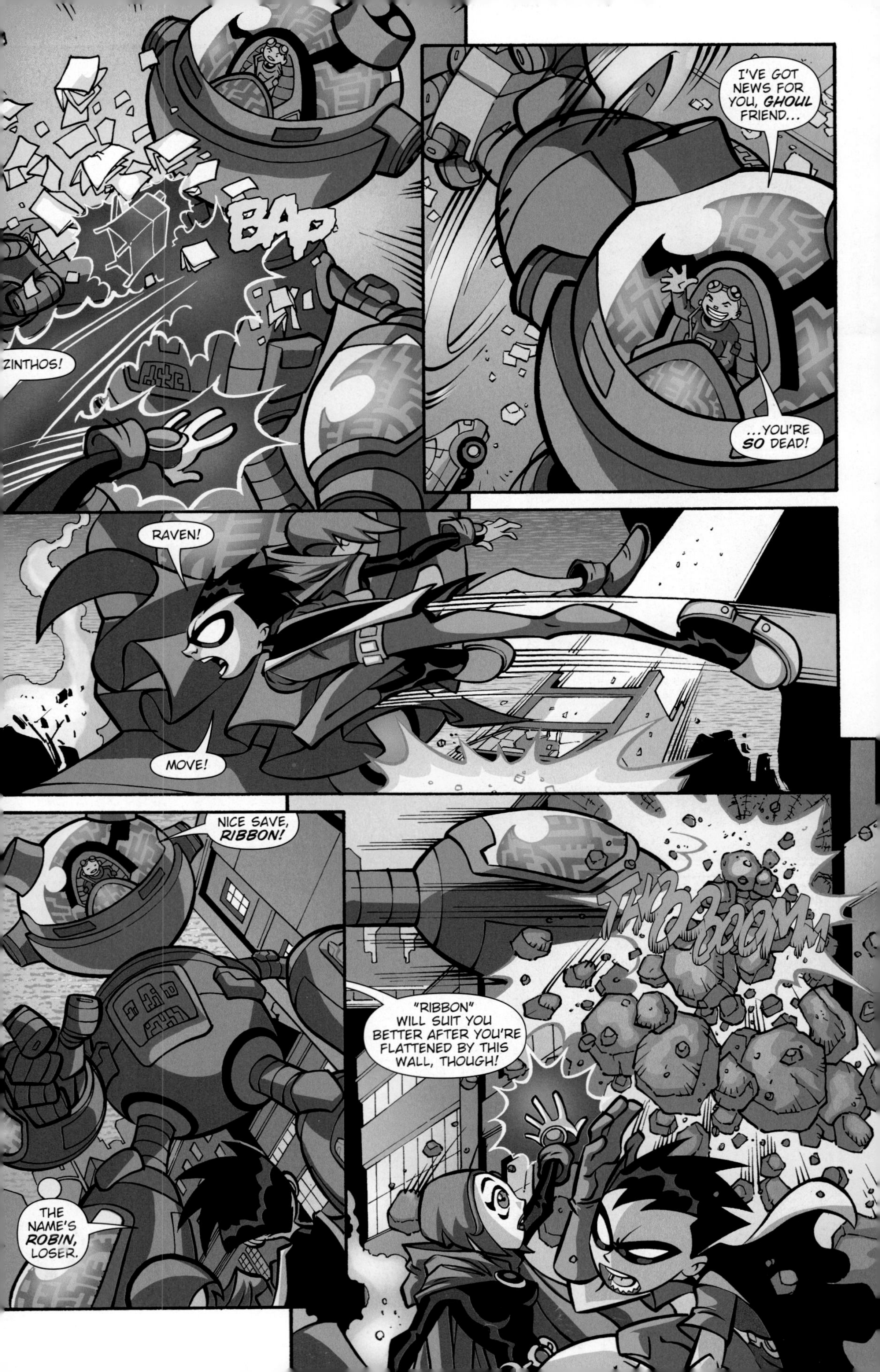
BAP
ZINTHOS!
I'VE GOT NEWS FOR YOU, GHOUL FRIEND...
...YOU'RE SO DEAD!
RAVEN!
MOVE!
NICE SAVE, RIBBON!
THE NAME'S ROBIN, LOSER.
"RIBBON" WILL SUIT YOU BETTER AFTER YOU'RE FLATTENED BY THIS WALL, THOUGH!

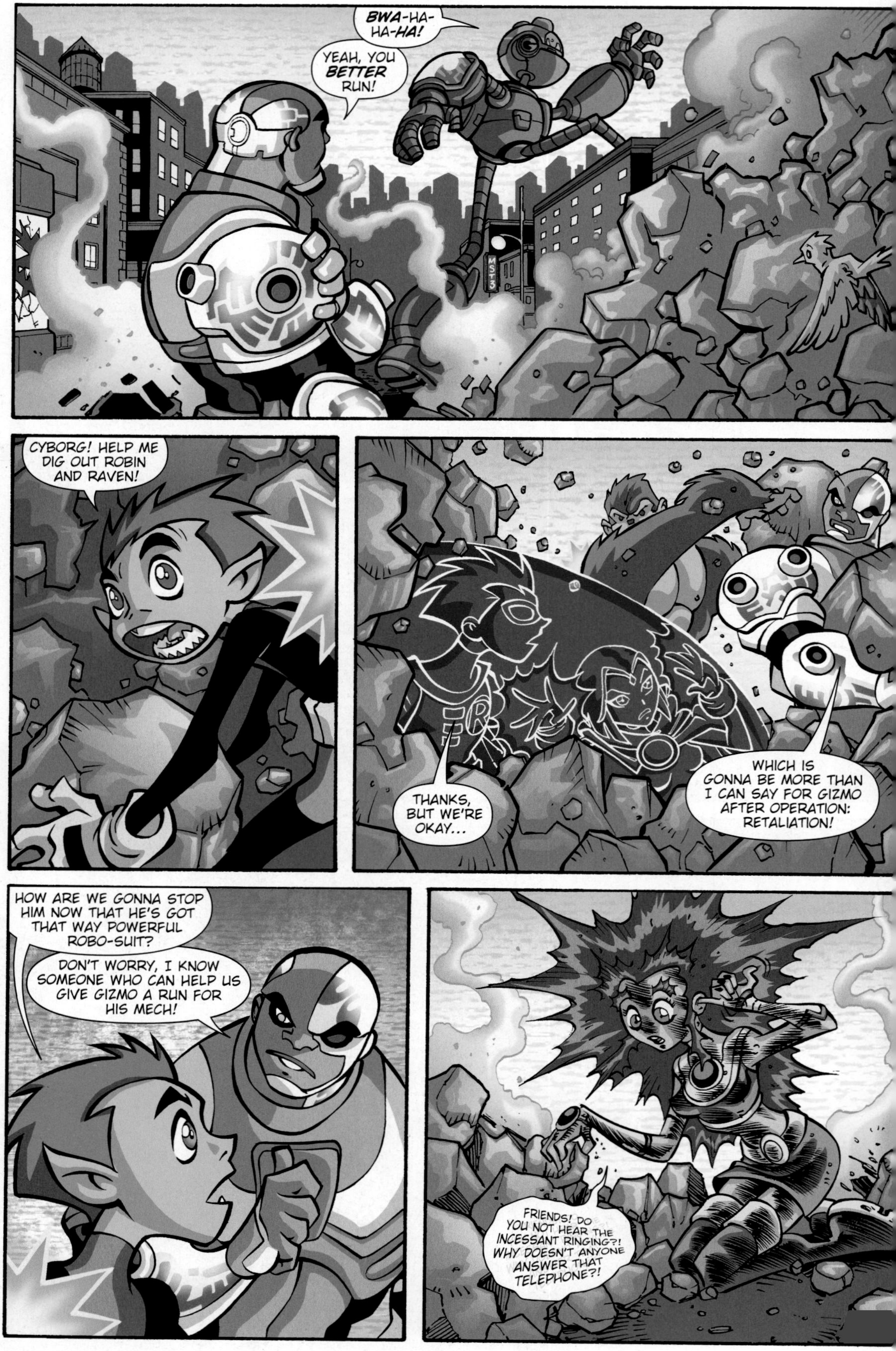
BWA-HA-HA-HA!
YEAH, YOU BETTER RUN!
MST3
CYBORG! HELP ME DIG OUT ROBIN AND RAVEN!
THANKS, BUT WE'RE OKAY...
WHICH IS GONNA BE MORE THAN I CAN SAY FOR GIZMO AFTER OPERATION: RETALIATION!
HOW ARE WE GONNA STOP HIM NOW THAT HE'S GOT THAT WAY POWERFUL ROBO-SUIT?
DON'T WORRY, I KNOW SOMEONE WHO CAN HELP US GIVE GIZMO A RUN FOR HIS MECH!
FRIENDS! DO YOU NOT HEAR THE INCESSANT RINGING?! WHY DOESN'T ANYONE ANSWER THAT TELEPHONE?!

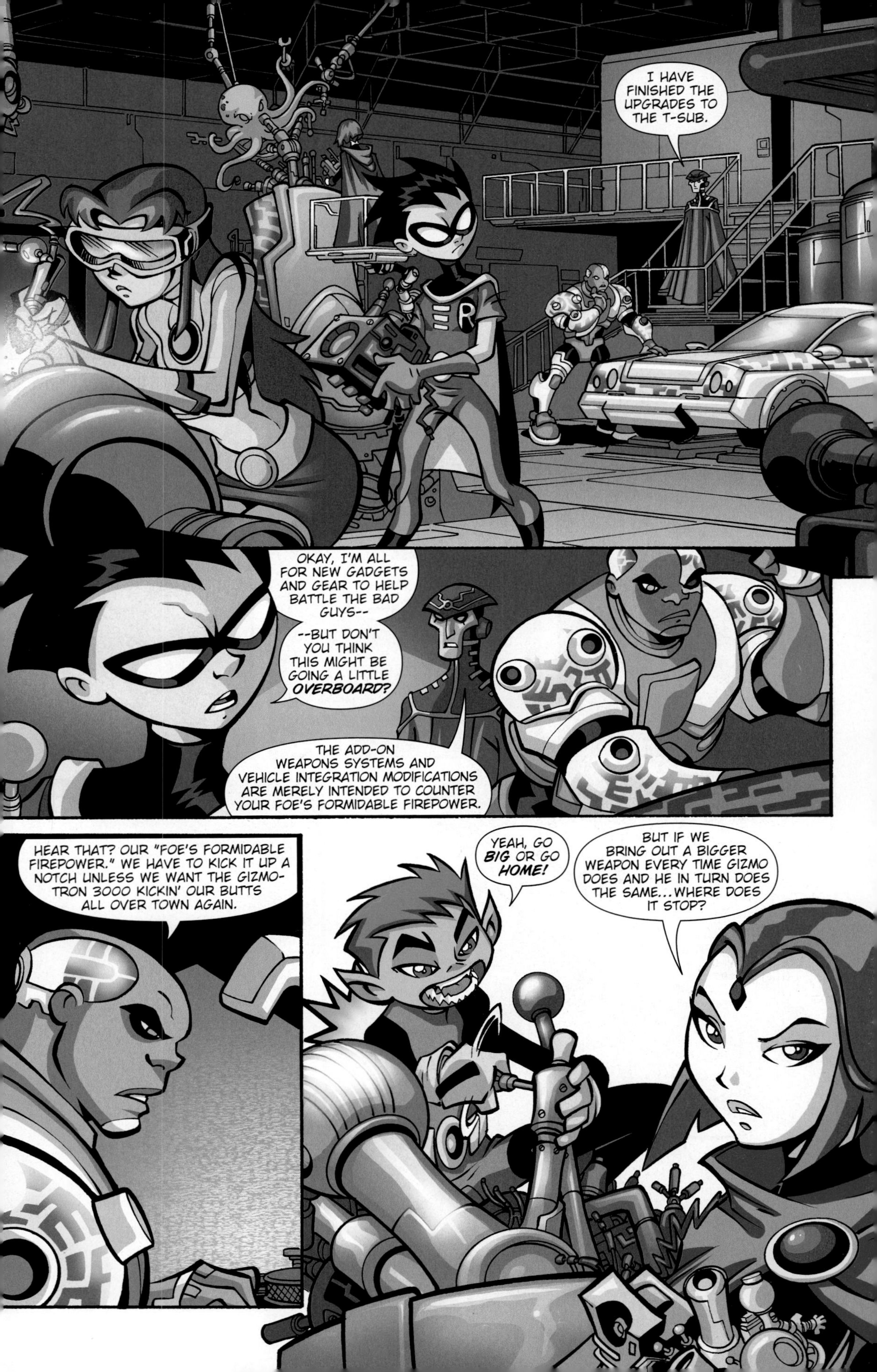
I HAVE FINISHED THE UPGRADES TO THE T-SUB.
OKAY, I'M ALL FOR NEW GADGETS AND GEAR TO HELP BATTLE THE BAD GUYS--
--BUT DON'T YOU THINK THIS MIGHT BE GOING A LITTLE OVERBOARD?
THE ADD-ON WEAPONS SYSTEMS AND VEHICLE INTEGRATION MODIFICATIONS ARE MERELY INTENDED TO COUNTER YOUR FOE'S FORMIDABLE FIREPOWER.
HEAR THAT? OUR "FOE'S FORMIDABLE FIREPOWER." WE HAVE TO KICK IT UP A NOTCH UNLESS WE WANT THE GIZMO-TRON 3000 KICKIN' OUR BUTTS ALL OVER TOWN AGAIN.
YEAH, GO BIG OR GO HOME!
BUT IF WE BRING OUT A BIGGER WEAPON EVERY TIME GIZMO DOES AND HE IN TURN DOES THE SAME...WHERE DOES IT STOP?

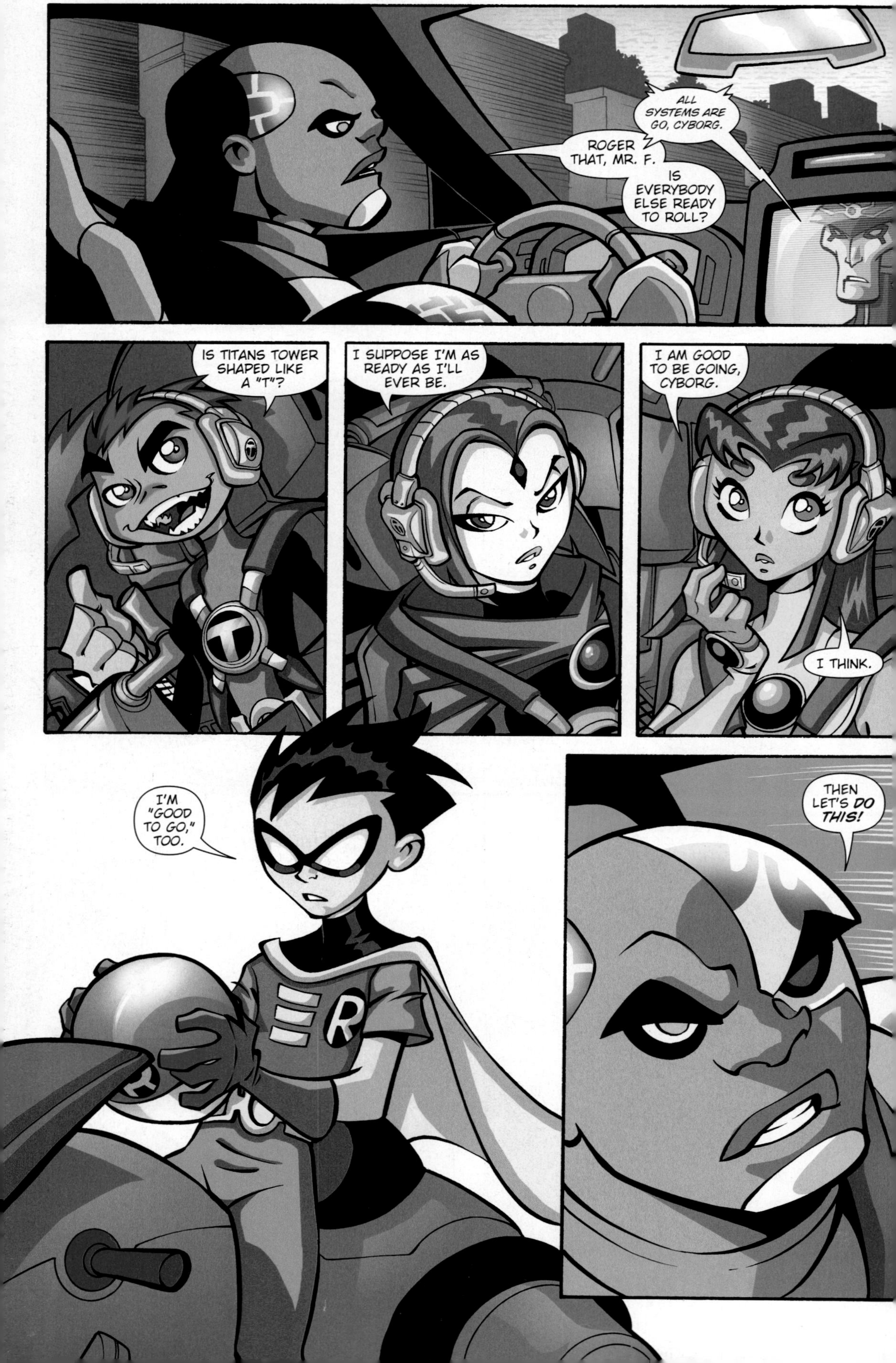
ALL SYSTEMS ARE GO, CYBORG.
ROGER THAT, MR. F.
IS EVERYBODY ELSE READY TO ROLL?
IS TITANS TOWER SHAPED LIKE A "T"?
I SUPPOSE I'M AS READY AS I'LL EVER BE.
I AM GOOD TO BE GOING, CYBORG.
I THINK.
I'M "GOOD TO GO," TOO.
THEN LET'S *DO THIS!*

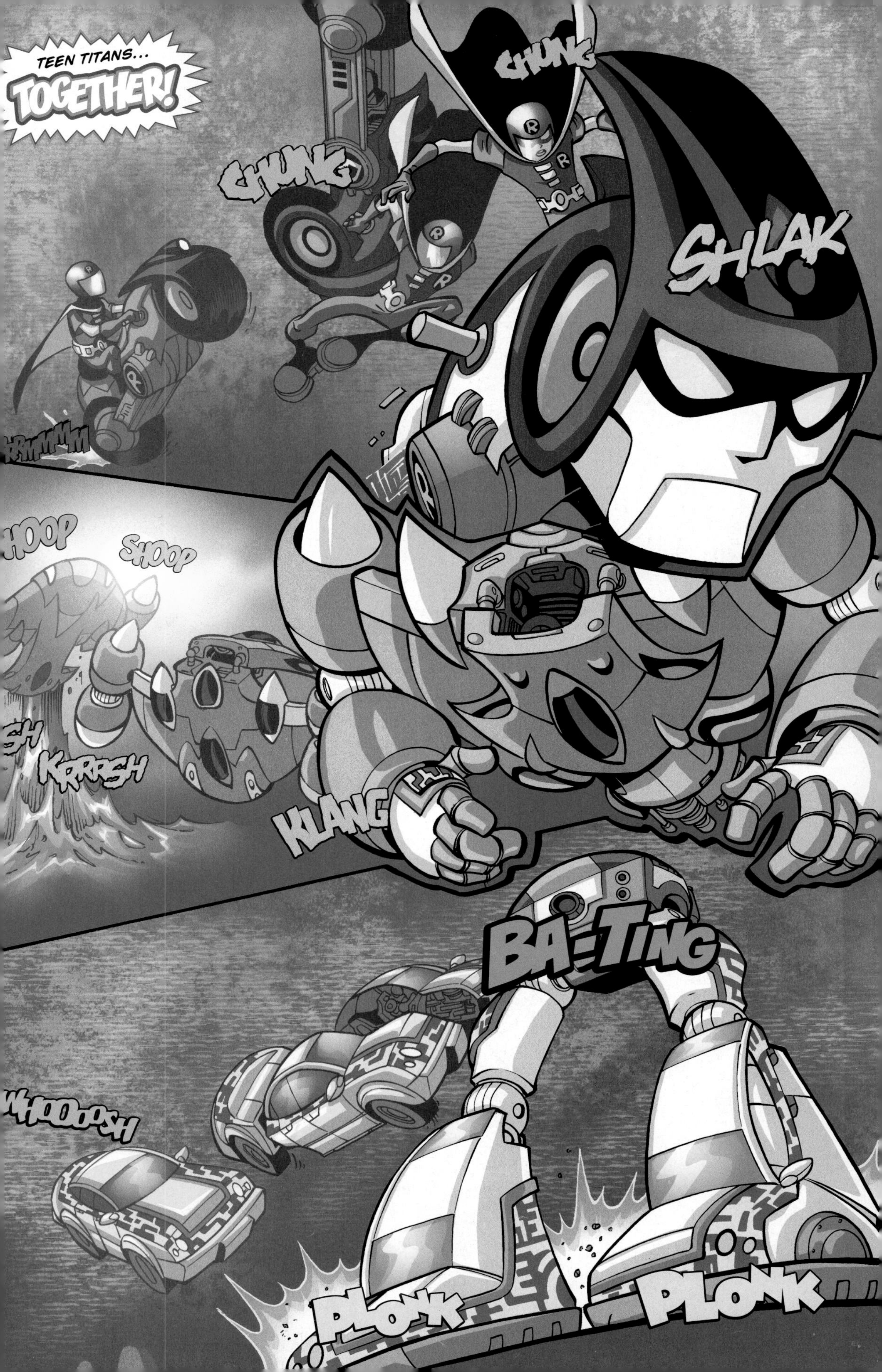

TEEN TITANS...
TOGETHER!
CHUNG
CHUNG
SHLAK
KRMMMM
SHOOP
SHOOP
KRRRSH
KLANG
BA-TING
WHOOOOOSH
PLONK
PLONK

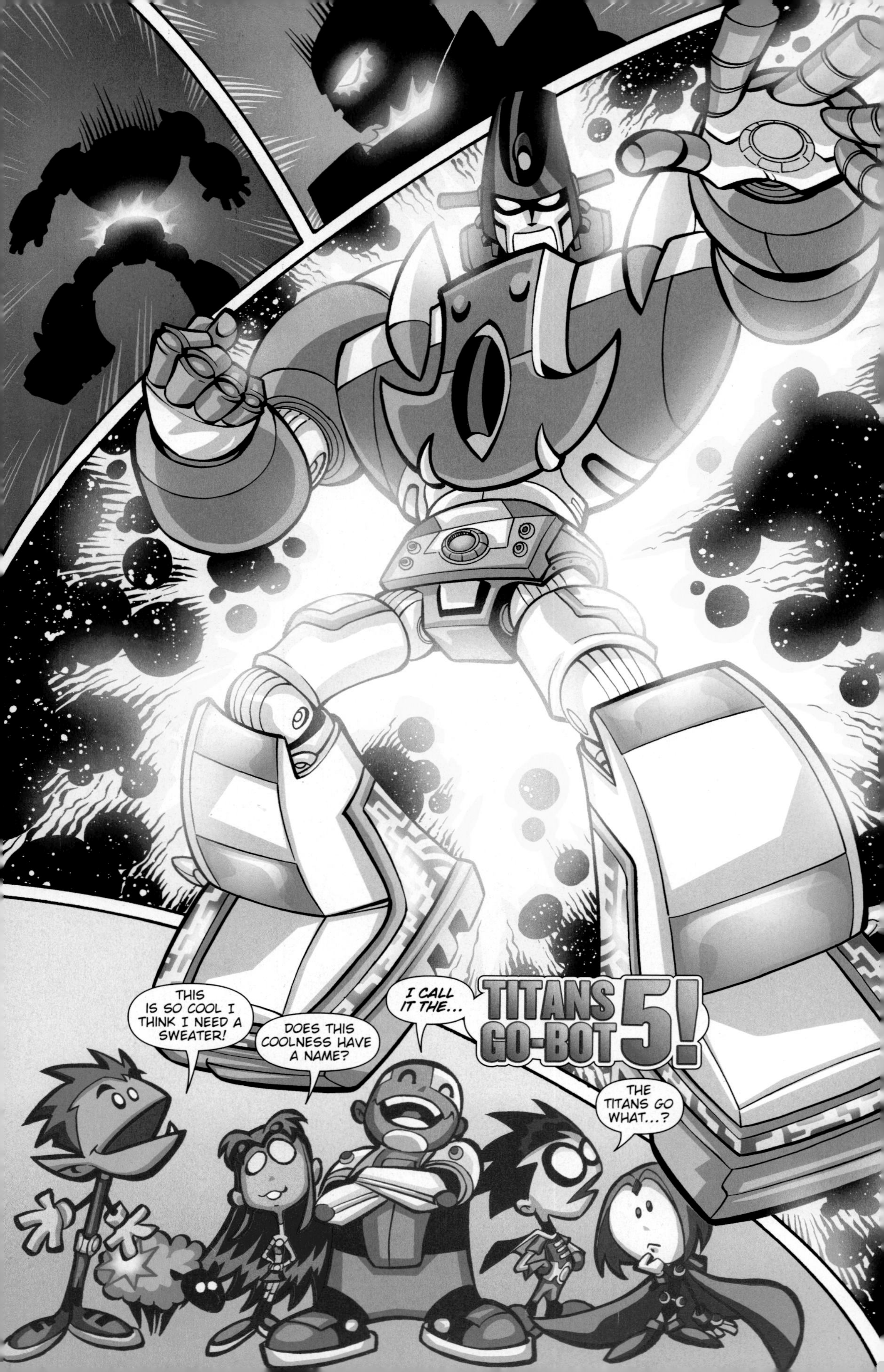
THIS IS SO COOL I THINK I NEED A SWEATER!
DOES THIS COOLNESS HAVE A NAME?
I CALL IT THE...
TITANS GO-BOT 5!
THE TITANS GO WHAT...?

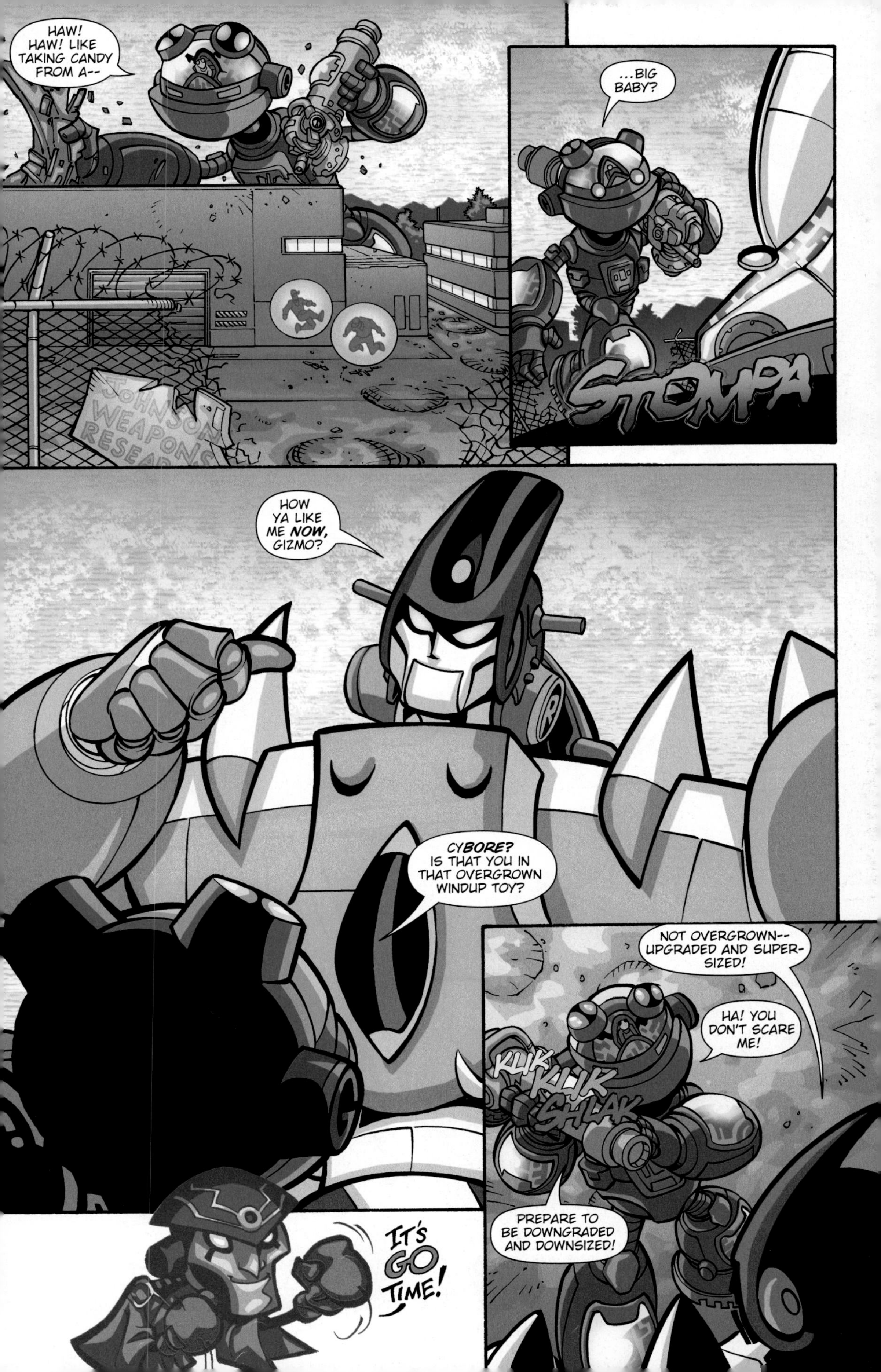
HAW! HAW! LIKE TAKING CANDY FROM A--
JOHNSON WEAPONS RESEAR
...BIG BABY?
STOMPA
HOW YA LIKE ME NOW, GIZMO?
CYBORE? IS THAT YOU IN THAT OVERGROWN WINDUP TOY?
NOT OVERGROWN-- UPGRADED AND SUPER-SIZED!
HA! YOU DON'T SCARE ME!
KLIK KLIK SHLAK
PREPARE TO BE DOWNGRADED AND DOWNSIZED!
IT'S GO TIME!

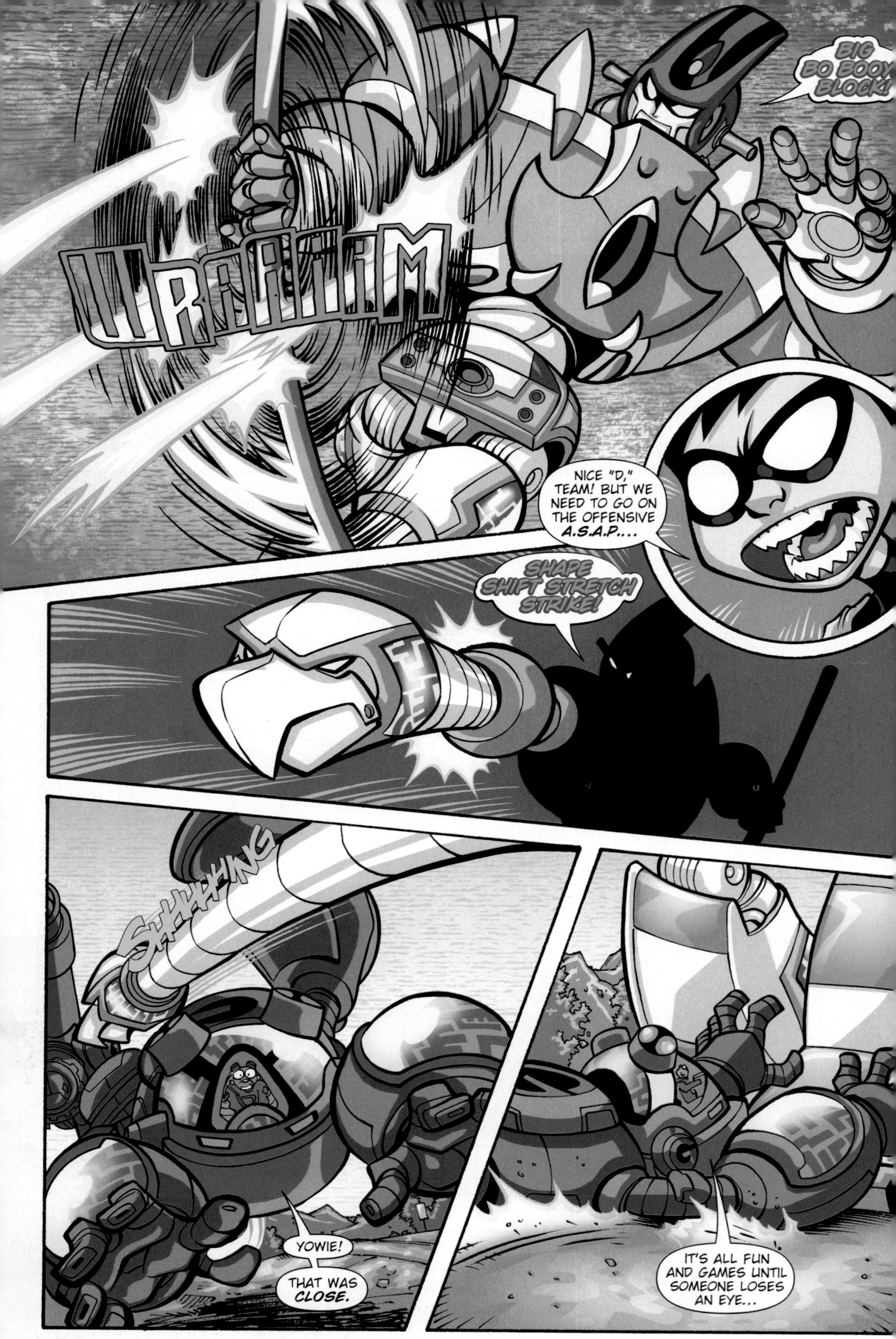
BIG BO BOOY BLOCK!
VRAAAAM
NICE "D," TEAM! BUT WE NEED TO GO ON THE OFFENSIVE A.S.A.P....
SHAPE SHIFT STRETCH STRIKE!
SHHHHING
YOWIE!
THAT WAS CLOSE.
IT'S ALL FUN AND GAMES UNTIL SOMEONE LOSES AN EYE...

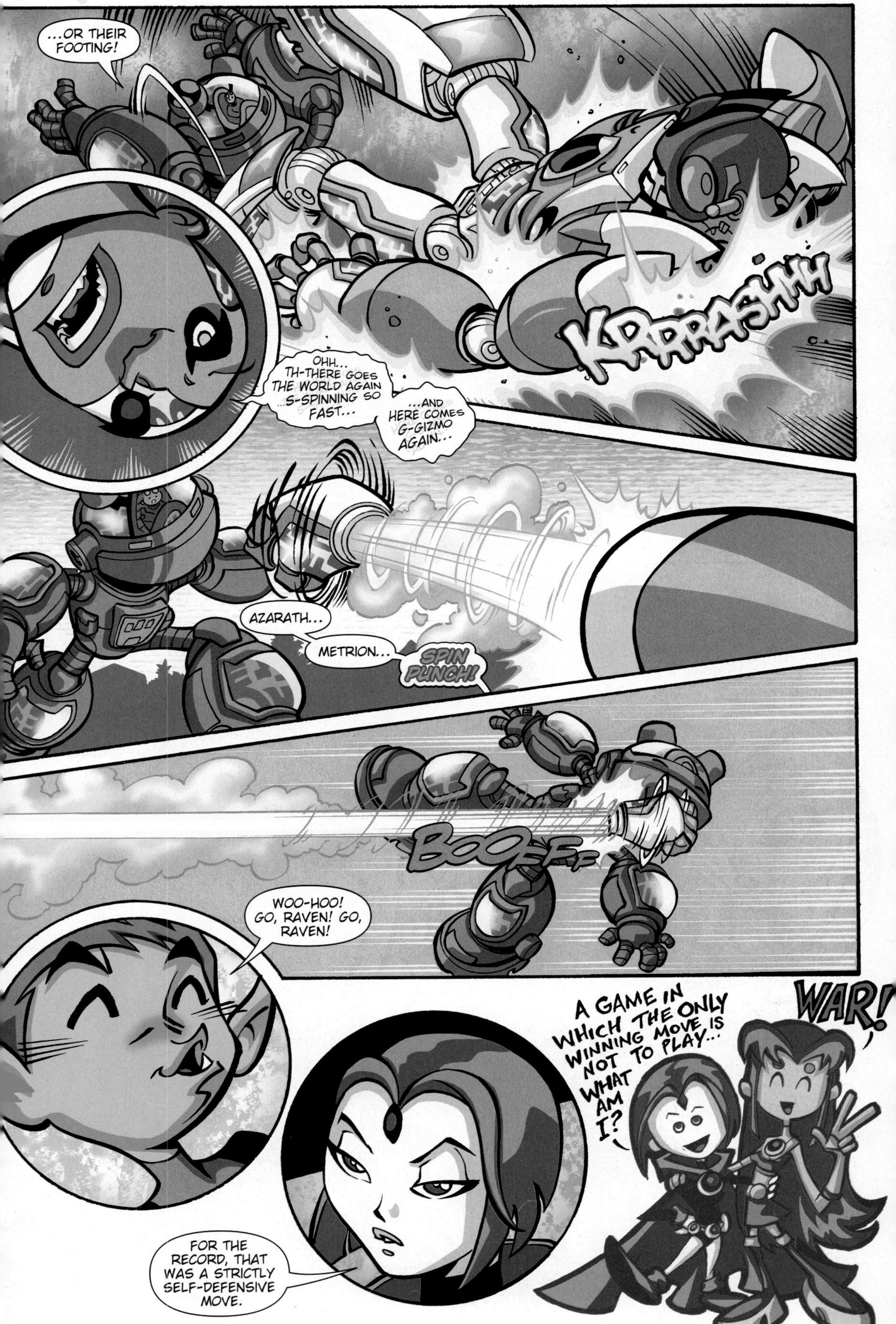
...OR THEIR FOOTING!
KRRRASHHH
OHH... TH-THERE GOES THE WORLD AGAIN ...S-SPINNING SO FAST...
...AND HERE COMES G-GIZMO AGAIN...
AZARATH...
METRION...
SPIN PUNCH!
BOOFFF
WOO-HOO! GO, RAVEN! GO, RAVEN!
FOR THE RECORD, THAT WAS A STRICTLY SELF-DEFENSIVE MOVE.
A GAME IN WHICH THE ONLY WINNING MOVE IS NOT TO PLAY... WHAT AM I?
WAR!

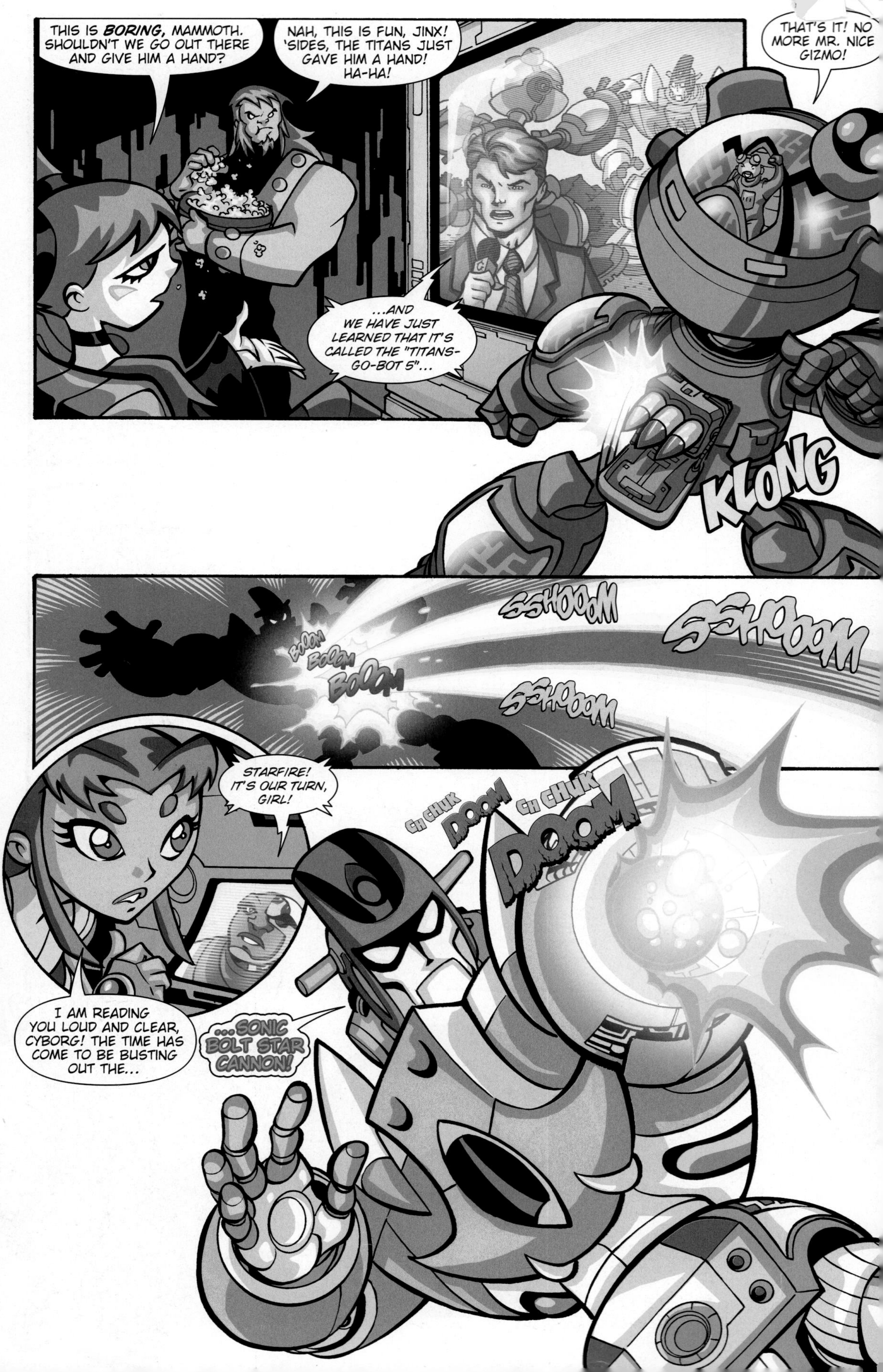
THIS IS BORING, MAMMOTH. SHOULDN'T WE GO OUT THERE AND GIVE HIM A HAND?
NAH, THIS IS FUN, JINX! 'SIDES, THE TITANS JUST GAVE HIM A HAND! HA-HA!
...AND WE HAVE JUST LEARNED THAT IT'S CALLED THE "TITANS-GO-BOT 5"...
THAT'S IT! NO MORE MR. NICE GIZMO!
KLONG
SSHOOOM
SSHOOOM
BOOOM BOOOM BOOOM
SSHOOOM
STARFIRE! IT'S OUR TURN, GIRL!
CH CHUK DOOOM
CH CHUK DOOOM
I AM READING YOU LOUD AND CLEAR, CYBORG! THE TIME HAS COME TO BE BUSTING OUT THE...
...SONIC BOLT STAR CANNON!

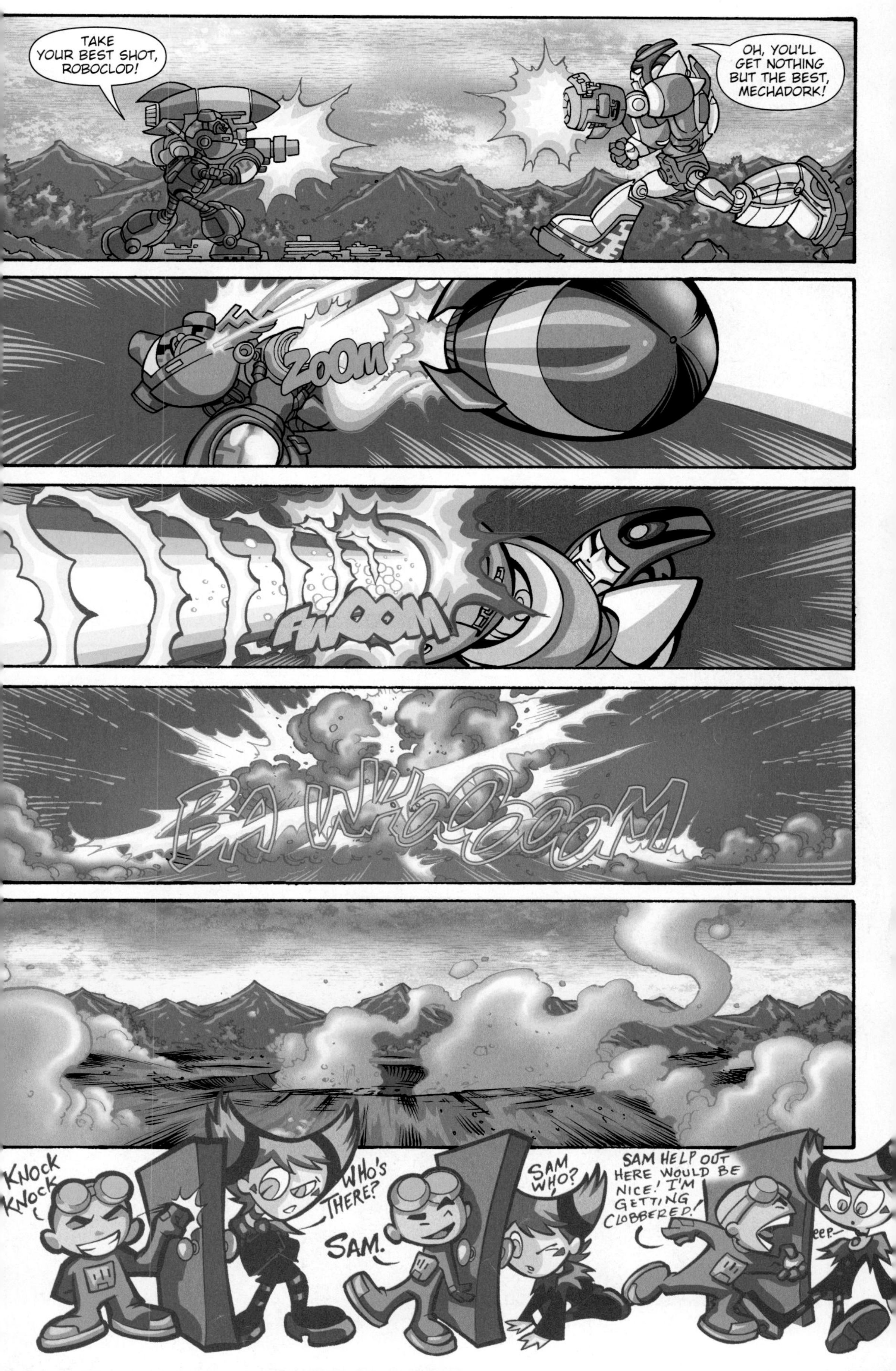
TAKE YOUR BEST SHOT, ROBOCLOD!
OH, YOU'LL GET NOTHING BUT THE BEST, MECHADORK!
ZOOM
FWOOM
BA WHOOOOOM
KNOCK KNOCK
WHO'S THERE?
SAM.
SAM WHO?
SAM HELP OUT HERE WOULD BE NICE! I'M GETTING CLOBBERED!
EEP.

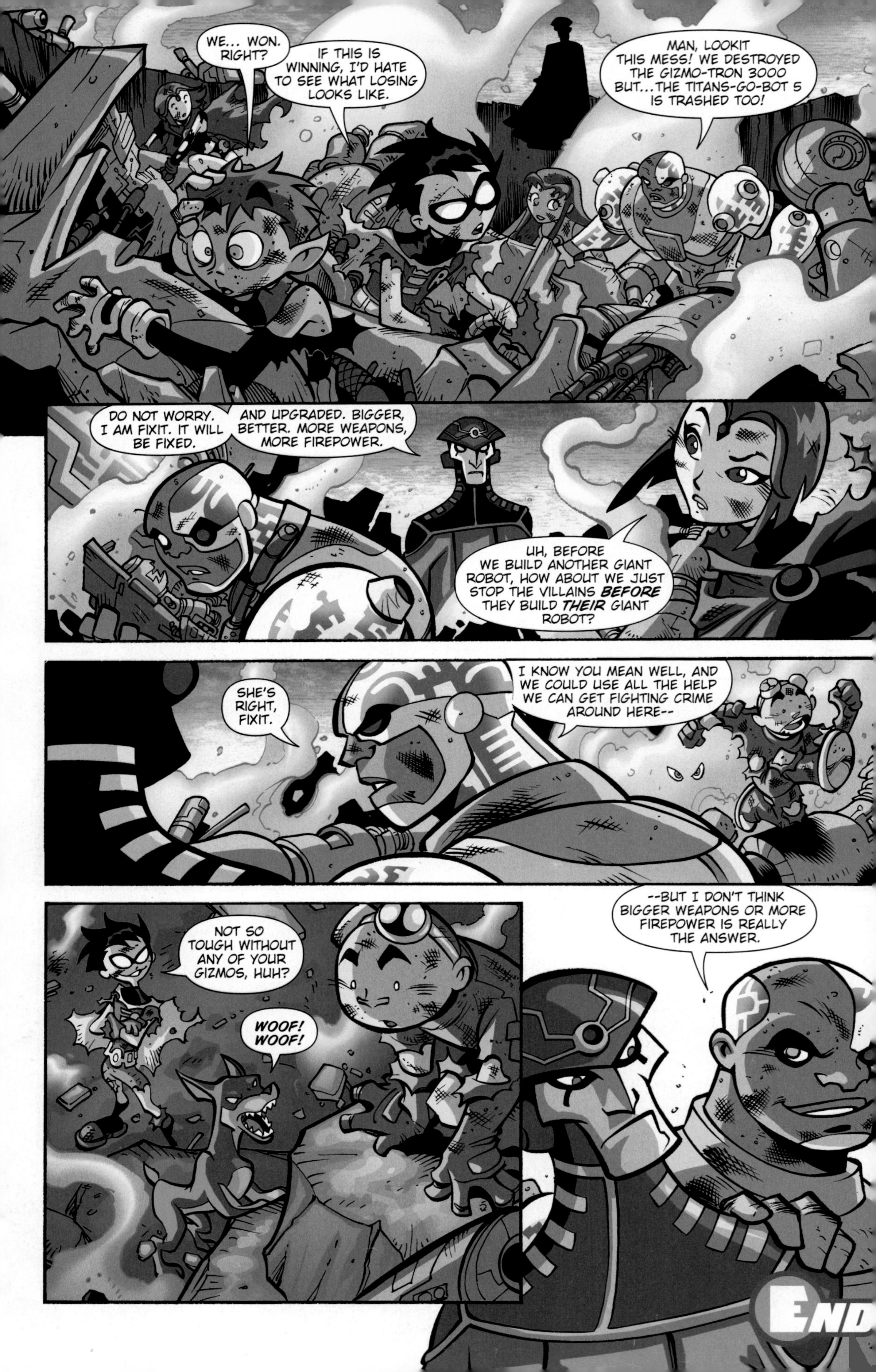
WE... WON. RIGHT?
IF THIS IS WINNING, I'D HATE TO SEE WHAT LOSING LOOKS LIKE.
MAN, LOOKIT THIS MESS! WE DESTROYED THE GIZMO-TRON 3000 BUT...THE TITANS-GO-BOT 5 IS TRASHED TOO!
DO NOT WORRY. I AM FIXIT. IT WILL BE FIXED.
AND UPGRADED. BIGGER, BETTER. MORE WEAPONS, MORE FIREPOWER.
UH, BEFORE WE BUILD ANOTHER GIANT ROBOT, HOW ABOUT WE JUST STOP THE VILLAINS *BEFORE* THEY BUILD *THEIR* GIANT ROBOT?
SHE'S RIGHT, FIXIT.
I KNOW YOU MEAN WELL, AND WE COULD USE ALL THE HELP WE CAN GET FIGHTING CRIME AROUND HERE--
NOT SO TOUGH WITHOUT ANY OF YOUR GIZMOS, HUH?
WOOF! WOOF!
--BUT I DON'T THINK BIGGER WEAPONS OR MORE FIREPOWER IS REALLY THE ANSWER.
END

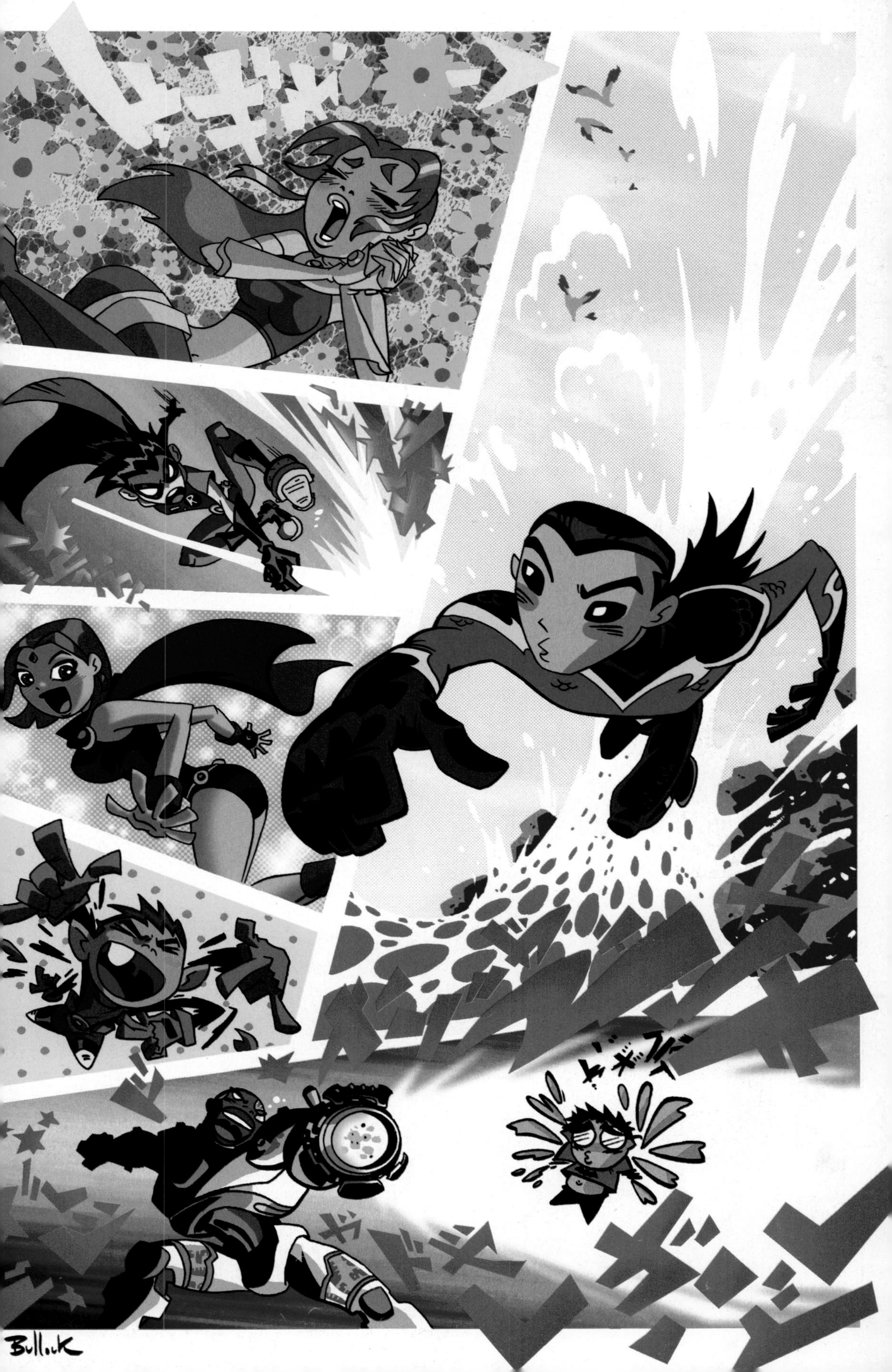
Bullock

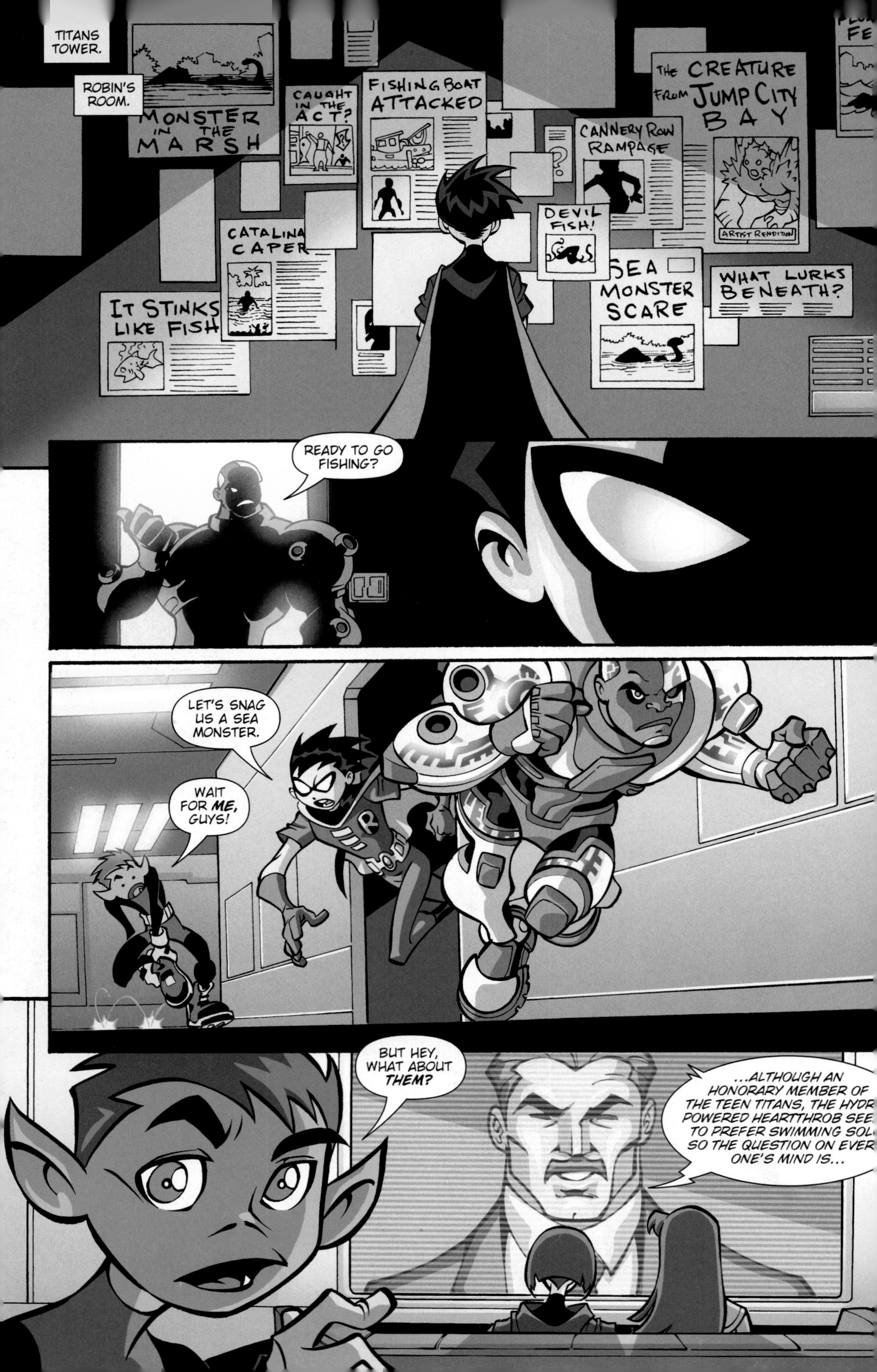

TITANS TOWER.
ROBIN'S ROOM.
MONSTER IN THE MARSH
CAUGHT IN THE ACT?
FISHING BOAT ATTACKED
THE CREATURE FROM JUMP CITY BAY
CANNERY ROW RAMPAGE
CATALINA CAPER
DEVIL FISH!
ARTIST RENDITION
SEA MONSTER SCARE
WHAT LURKS BENEATH?
IT STINKS LIKE FISH
READY TO GO FISHING?
LET'S SNAG US A SEA MONSTER.
WAIT FOR *ME*, GUYS!
BUT HEY, WHAT ABOUT *THEM*?
...ALTHOUGH AN HONORARY MEMBER OF THE TEEN TITANS, THE HYDR POWERED HEARTTHROB SEE TO PREFER SWIMMING SOL SO THE QUESTION ON EVER ONE'S MIND IS...

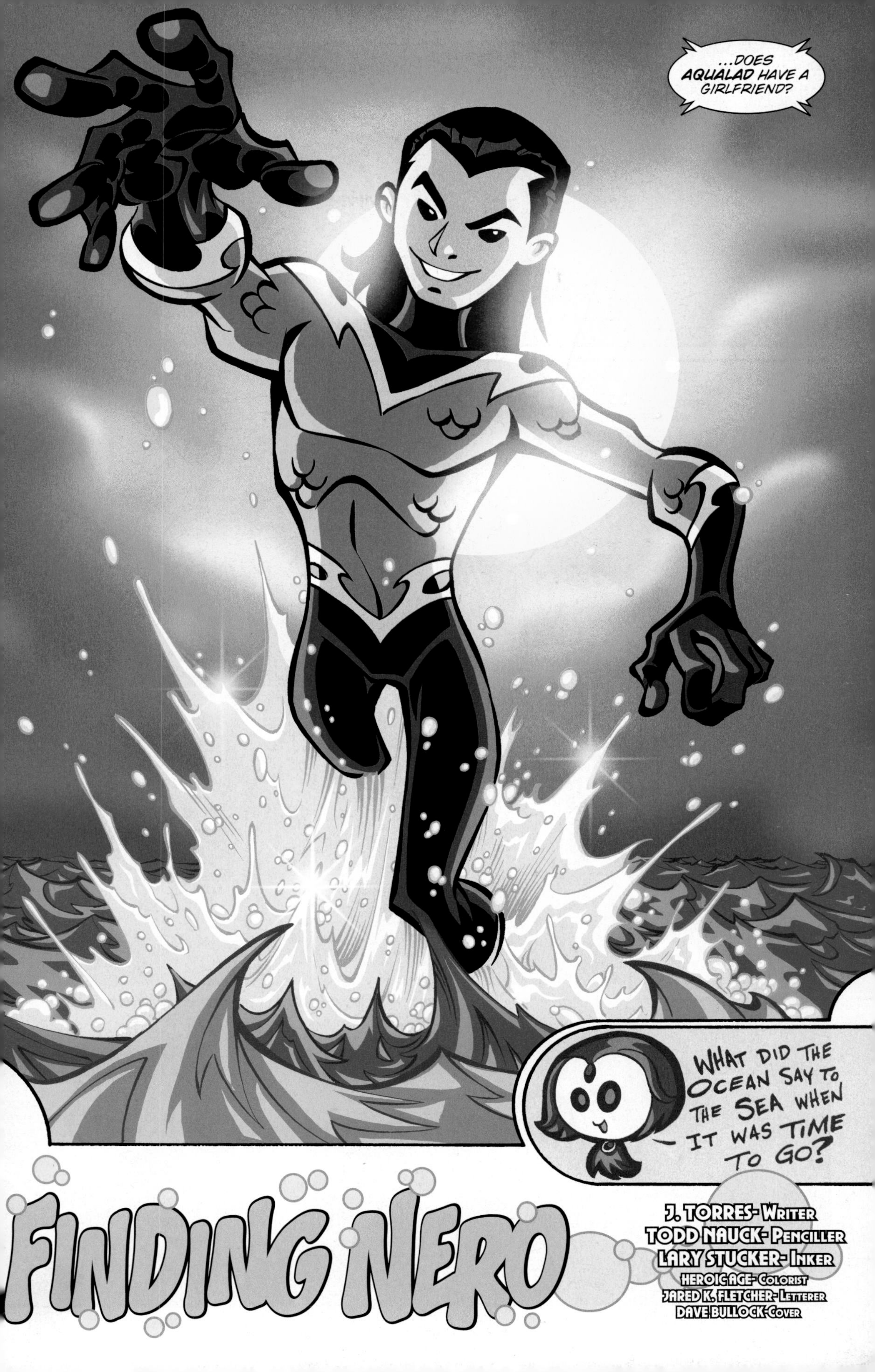
...DOES AQUALAD HAVE A GIRLFRIEND?
WHAT DID THE OCEAN SAY TO THE SEA WHEN IT WAS TIME TO GO?
FINDING NERO
J. TORRES- WRITER
TODD NAUCK- PENCILLER
LARY STUCKER- INKER
HEROIC AGE- COLORIST
JARED K. FLETCHER- LETTERER
DAVE BULLOCK- COVER

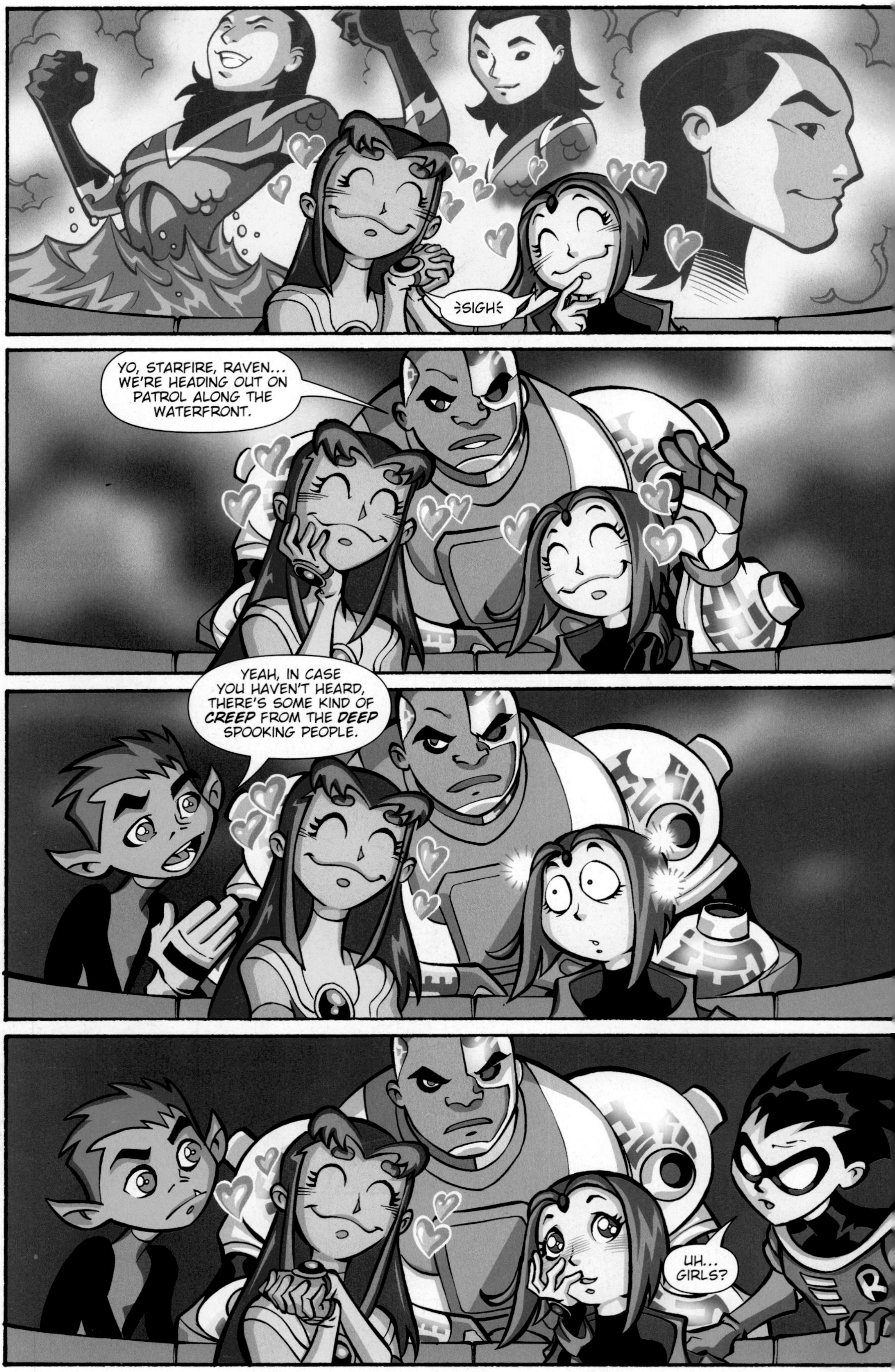

SIGH
YO, STARFIRE, RAVEN... WE'RE HEADING OUT ON PATROL ALONG THE WATERFRONT.
YEAH, IN CASE YOU HAVEN'T HEARD, THERE'S SOME KIND OF CREEP FROM THE DEEP SPOOKING PEOPLE.
UH... GIRLS?

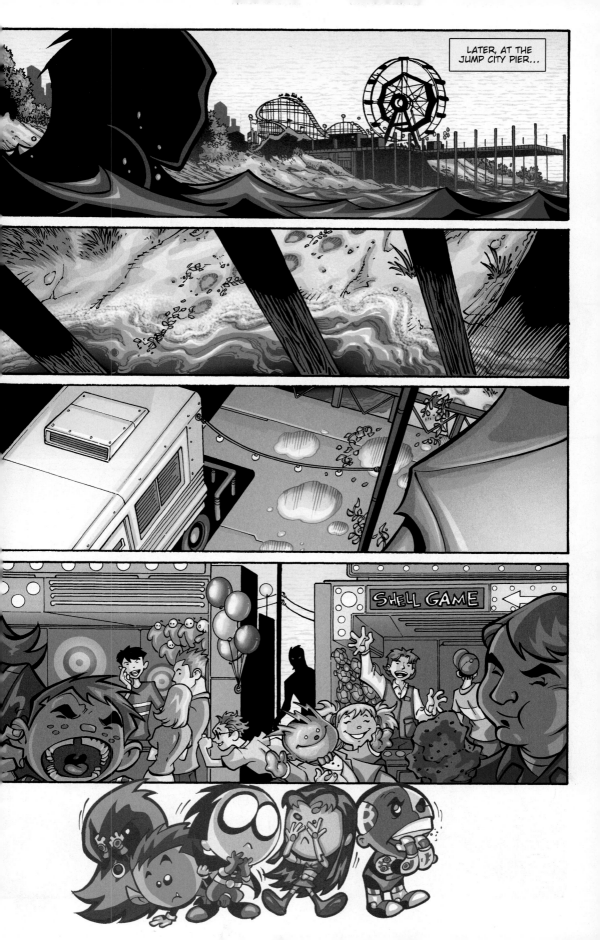

LATER, AT THE JUMP CITY PIER...

SHELL GAME

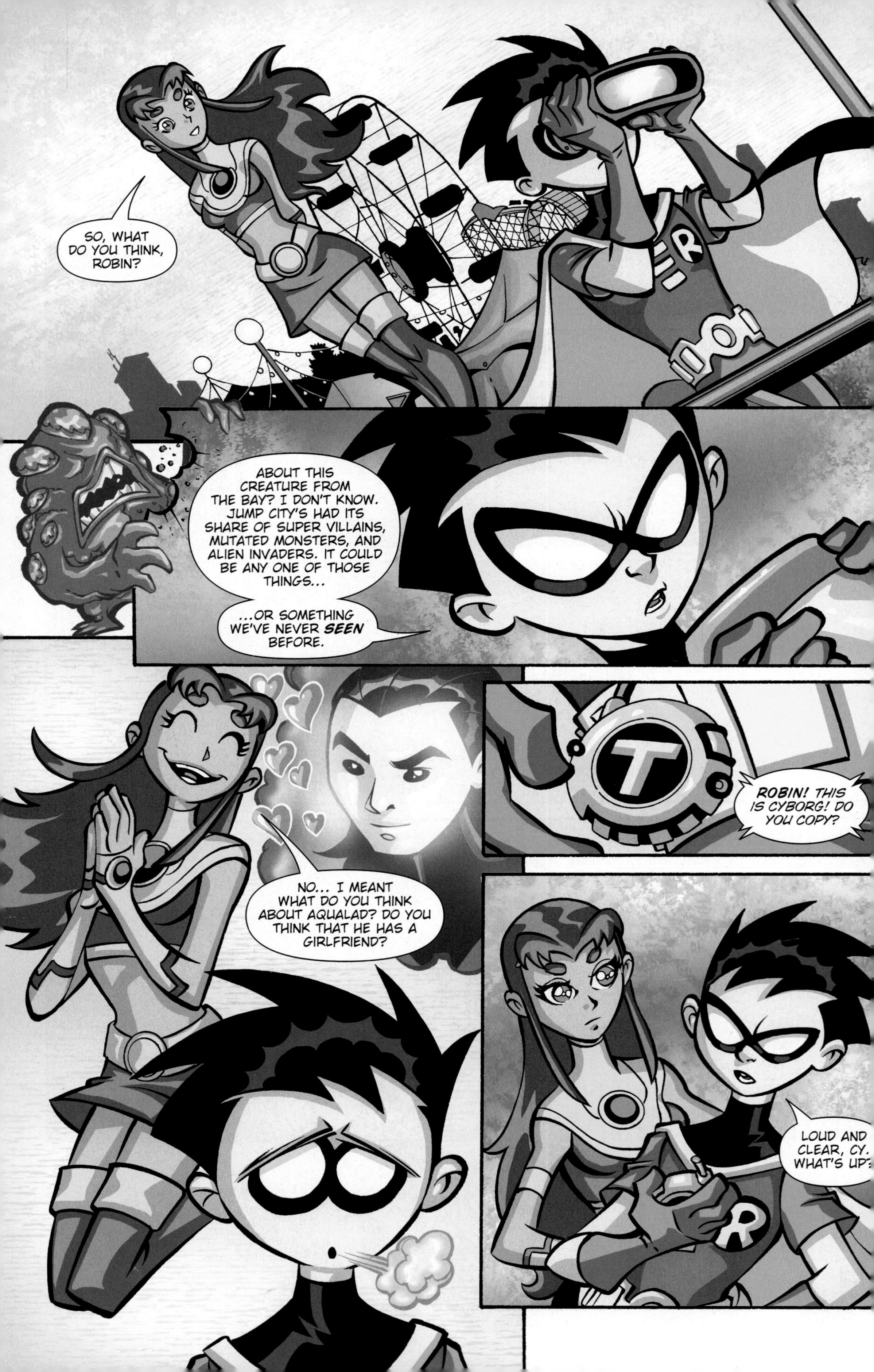
SO, WHAT DO YOU THINK, ROBIN?
ABOUT THIS CREATURE FROM THE BAY? I DON'T KNOW. JUMP CITY'S HAD ITS SHARE OF SUPER VILLAINS, MUTATED MONSTERS, AND ALIEN INVADERS. IT COULD BE ANY ONE OF THOSE THINGS...
...OR SOMETHING WE'VE NEVER SEEN BEFORE.
NO... I MEANT WHAT DO YOU THINK ABOUT AQUALAD? DO YOU THINK THAT HE HAS A GIRLFRIEND?
ROBIN! THIS IS CYBORG! DO YOU COPY?
LOUD AND CLEAR, CY. WHAT'S UP?

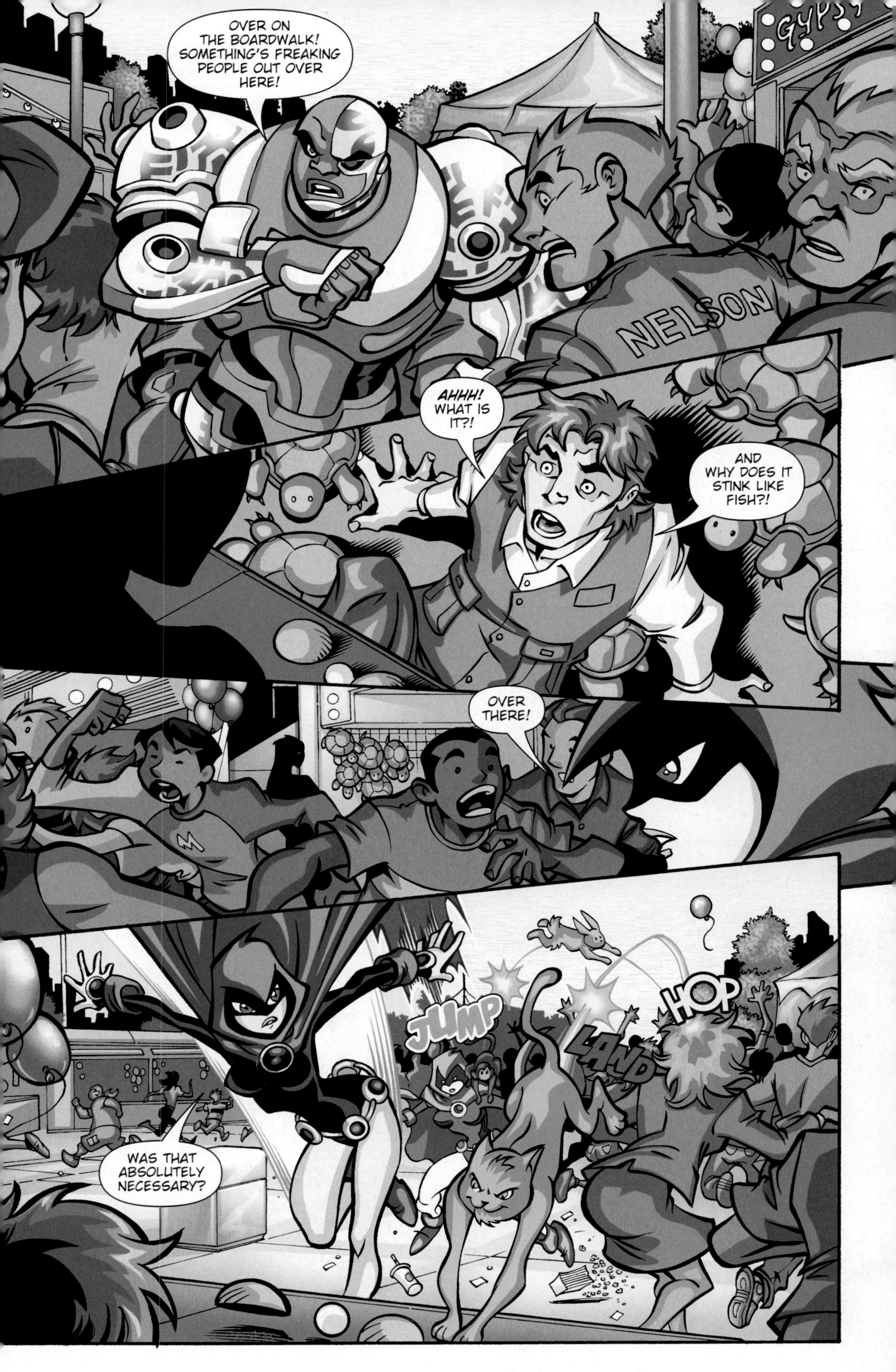

GYPSY
OVER ON THE BOARDWALK! SOMETHING'S FREAKING PEOPLE OUT OVER HERE!
NELSON
AHHH! WHAT IS IT?!
AND WHY DOES IT STINK LIKE FISH?!
OVER THERE!
JUMP
LAND
HOP
WAS THAT ABSOLUTELY NECESSARY?

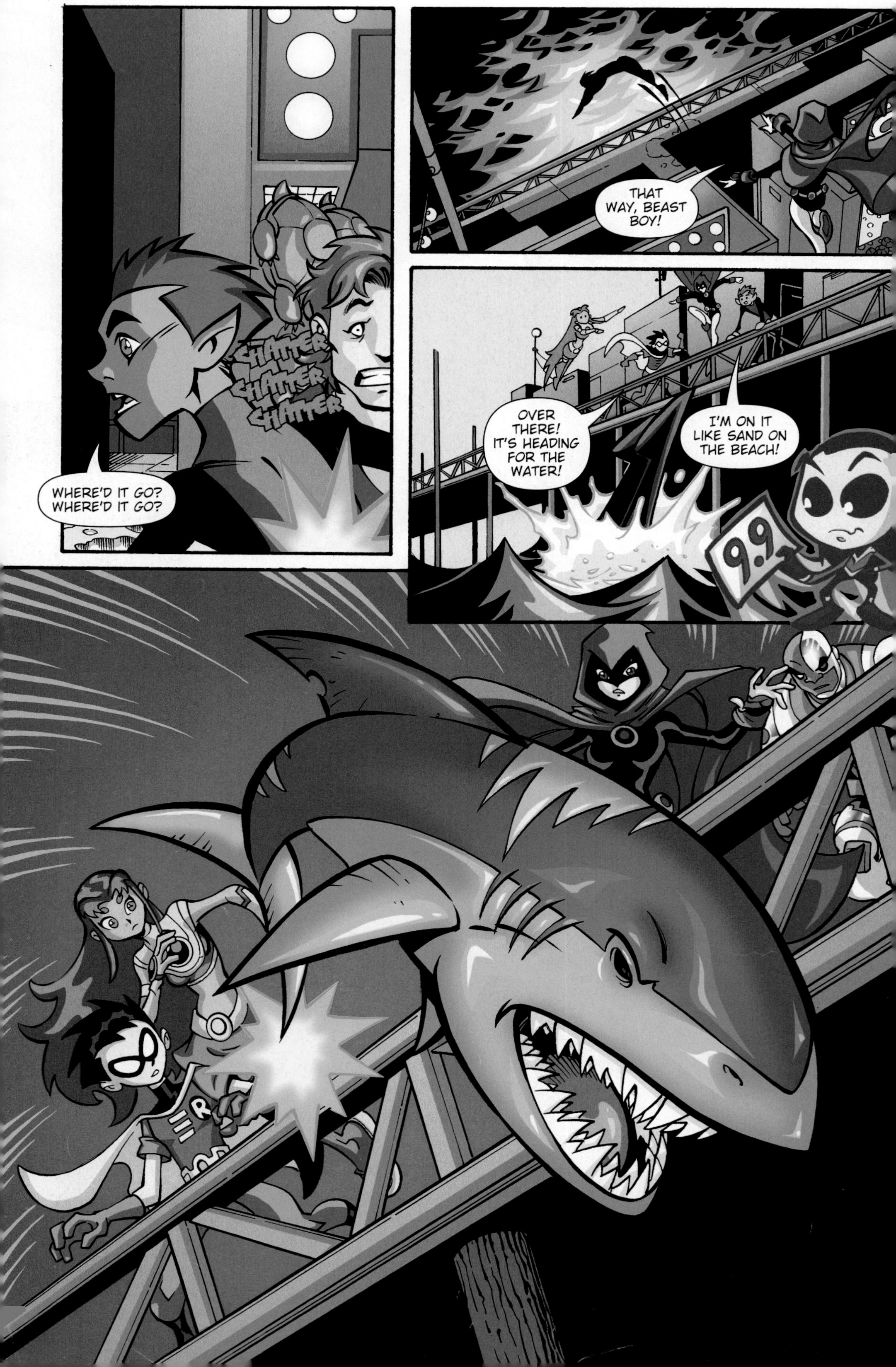
CHATTER CHATTER CHATTER
WHERE'D IT GO? WHERE'D IT GO?
THAT WAY, BEAST BOY!
OVER THERE! IT'S HEADING FOR THE WATER!
I'M ON IT LIKE SAND ON THE BEACH!
9.9

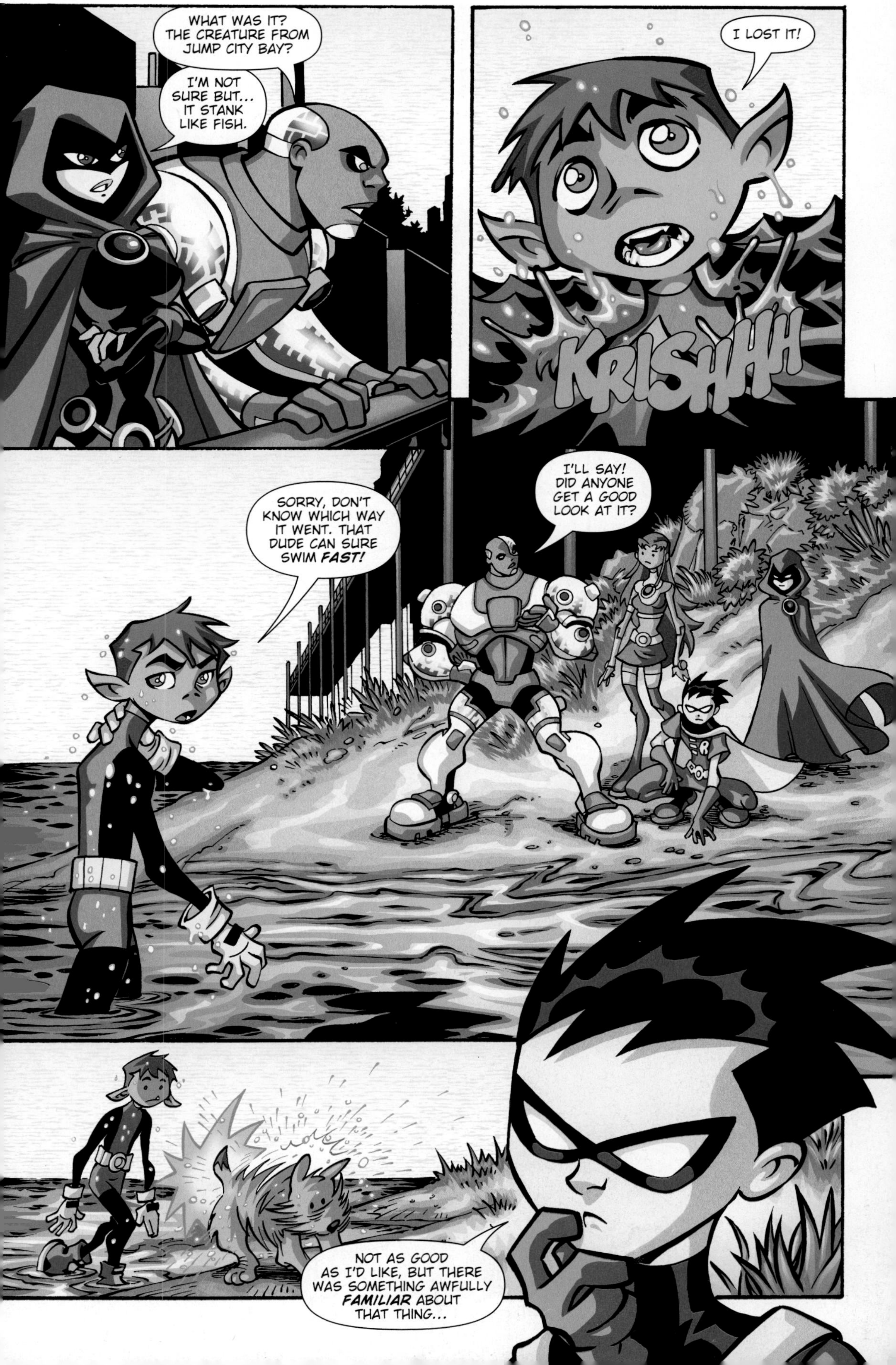
WHAT WAS IT? THE CREATURE FROM JUMP CITY BAY?
I'M NOT SURE BUT... IT STANK LIKE FISH.
I LOST IT!
KRISHHH
SORRY, DON'T KNOW WHICH WAY IT WENT. THAT DUDE CAN SURE SWIM FAST!
I'LL SAY! DID ANYONE GET A GOOD LOOK AT IT?
NOT AS GOOD AS I'D LIKE, BUT THERE WAS SOMETHING AWFULLY FAMILIAR ABOUT THAT THING...

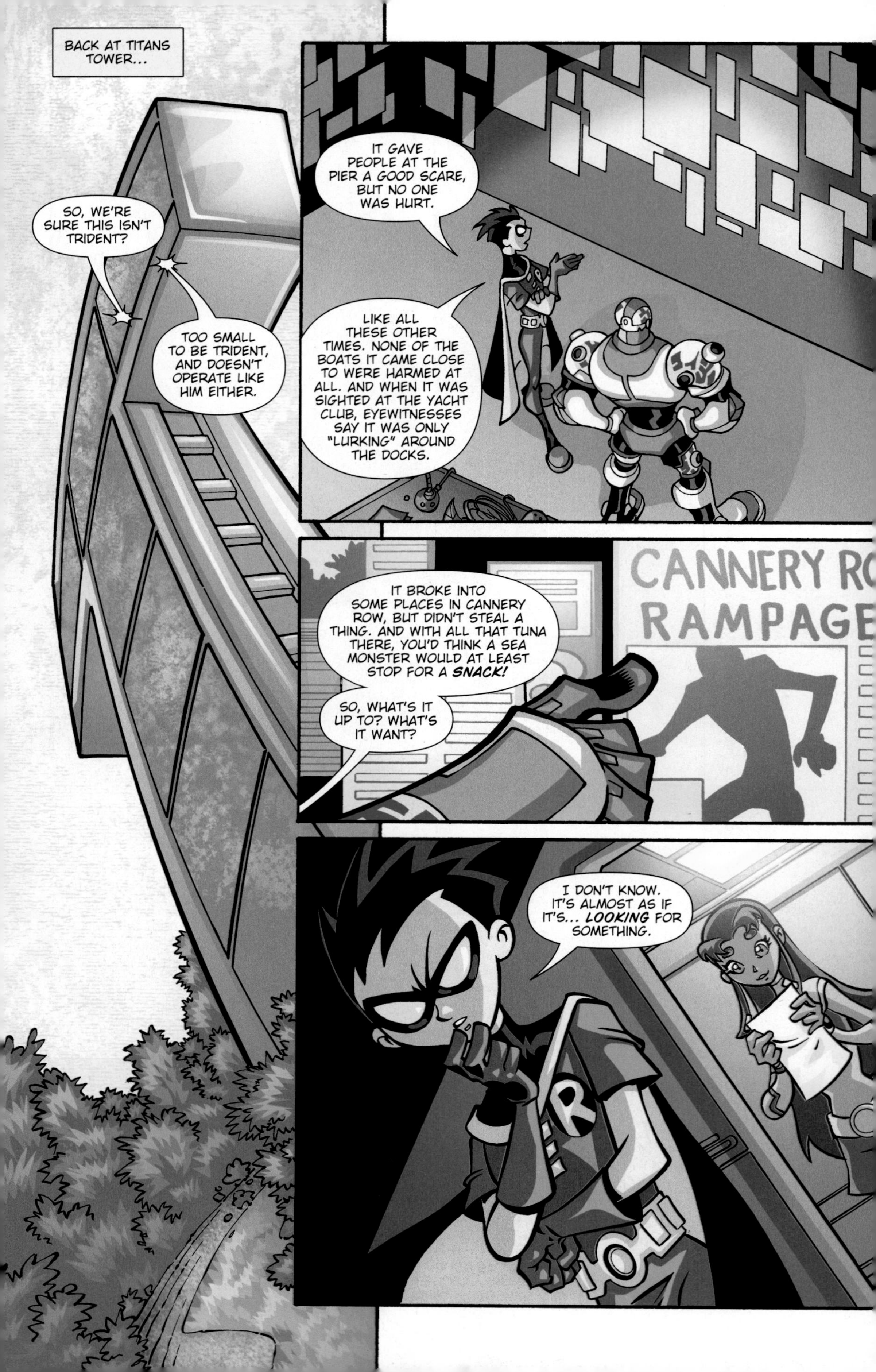
BACK AT TITANS TOWER...
SO, WE'RE SURE THIS ISN'T TRIDENT?
TOO SMALL TO BE TRIDENT, AND DOESN'T OPERATE LIKE HIM EITHER.
IT GAVE PEOPLE AT THE PIER A GOOD SCARE, BUT NO ONE WAS HURT.
LIKE ALL THESE OTHER TIMES. NONE OF THE BOATS IT CAME CLOSE TO WERE HARMED AT ALL. AND WHEN IT WAS SIGHTED AT THE YACHT CLUB, EYEWITNESSES SAY IT WAS ONLY "LURKING" AROUND THE DOCKS.
CANNERY RO
RAMPAGE
IT BROKE INTO SOME PLACES IN CANNERY ROW, BUT DIDN'T STEAL A THING. AND WITH ALL THAT TUNA THERE, YOU'D THINK A SEA MONSTER WOULD AT LEAST STOP FOR A *SNACK!*
SO, WHAT'S IT UP TO? WHAT'S IT WANT?
I DON'T KNOW. IT'S ALMOST AS IF IT'S... *LOOKING* FOR SOMETHING.

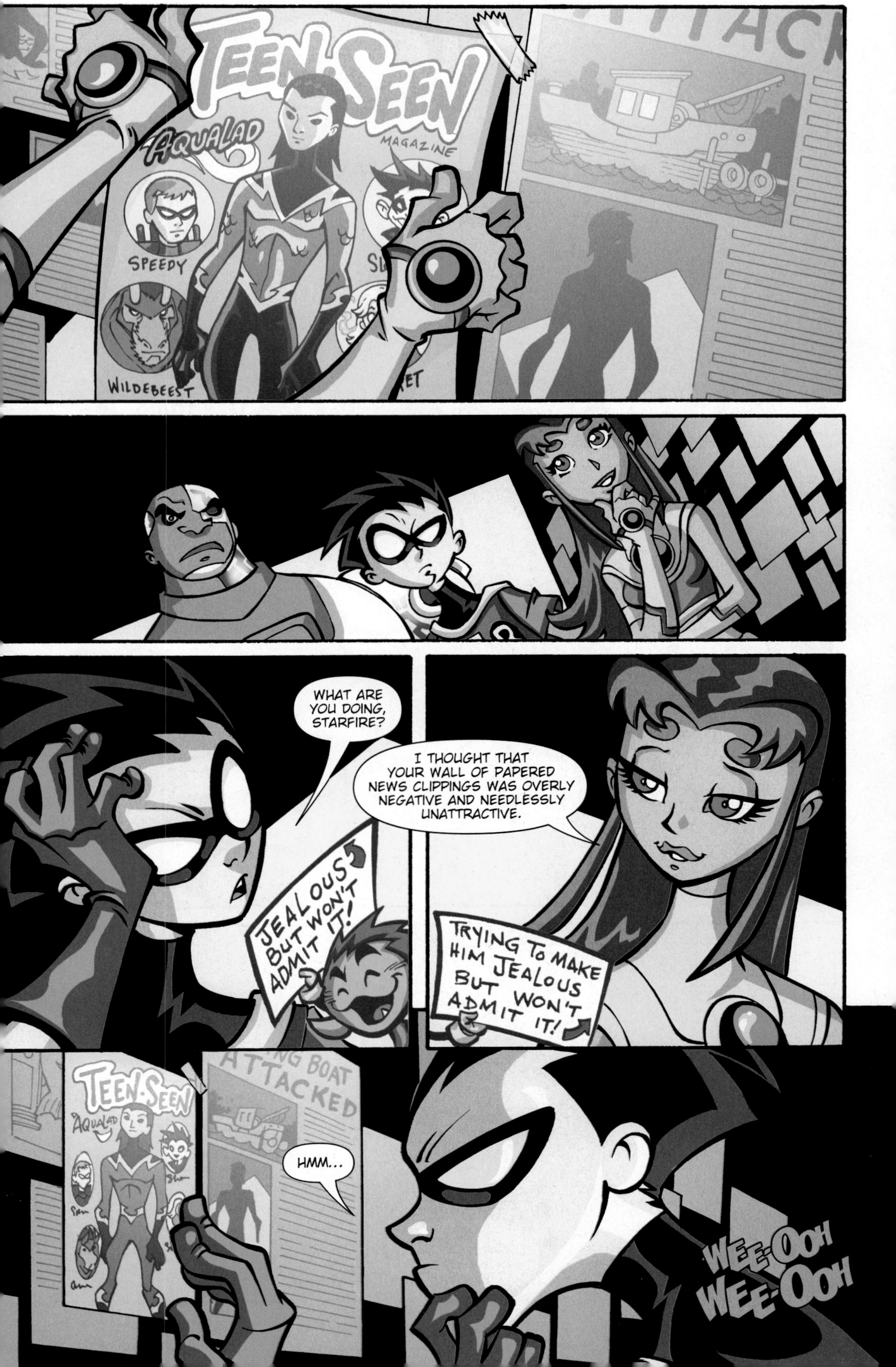
TEEN SEEN
MAGAZINE
AQUALAD
SPEEDY
WILDEBEEST
WHAT ARE YOU DOING, STARFIRE?
I THOUGHT THAT YOUR WALL OF PAPERED NEWS CLIPPINGS WAS OVERLY NEGATIVE AND NEEDLESSLY UNATTRACTIVE.
JEALOUS BUT WON'T ADMIT IT!
TRYING TO MAKE HIM JEALOUS BUT WON'T ADMIT IT!
TEEN SEEN
AQUALAD
ATTACKED
HMM...
WEE-OOH WEE-OOH

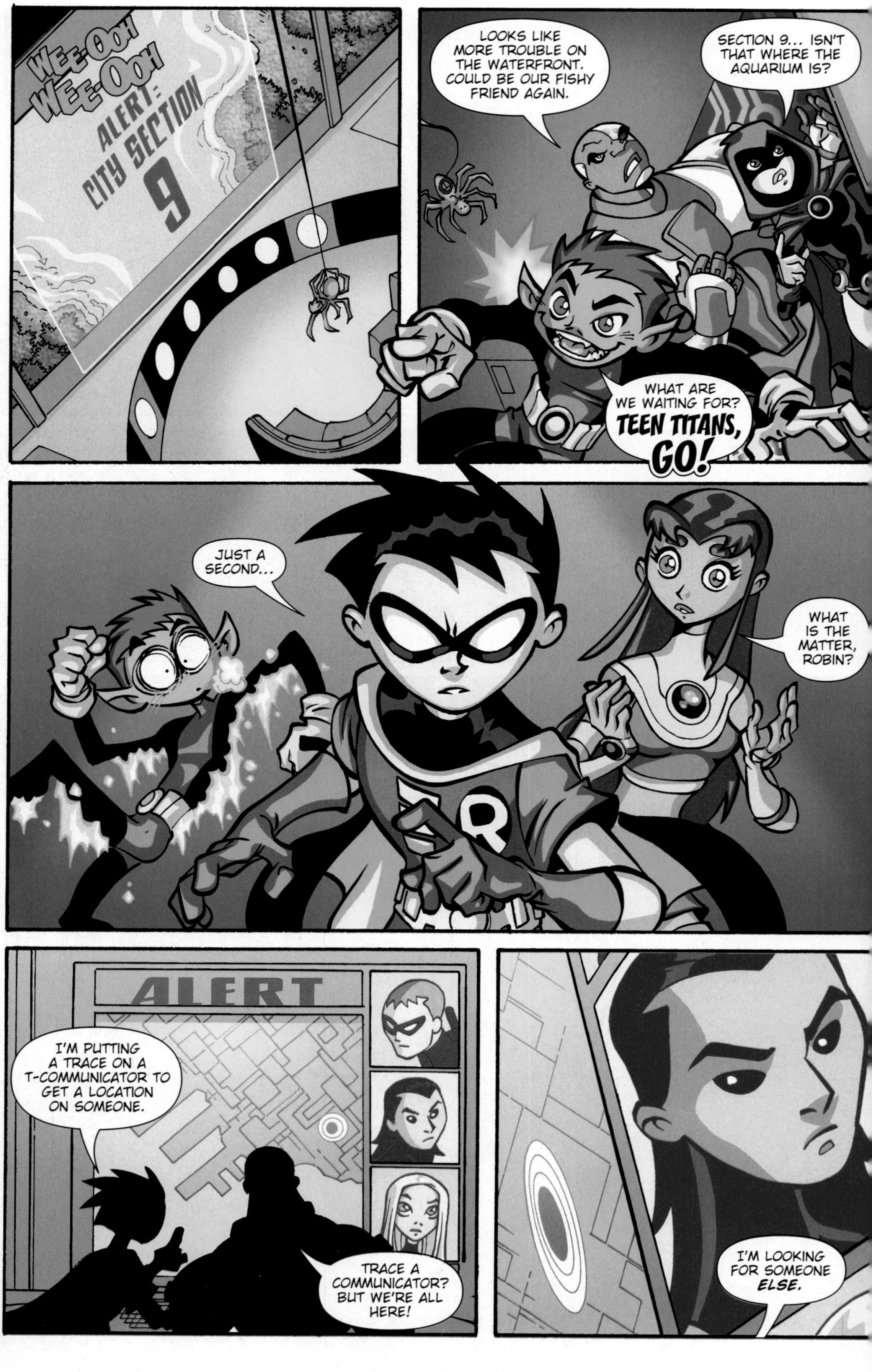
WEE-OOH
WEE-OOH
ALERT:
CITY SECTION
9
LOOKS LIKE MORE TROUBLE ON THE WATERFRONT. COULD BE OUR FISHY FRIEND AGAIN.
SECTION 9... ISN'T THAT WHERE THE AQUARIUM IS?
WHAT ARE WE WAITING FOR? TEEN TITANS, GO!
JUST A SECOND...
WHAT IS THE MATTER, ROBIN?
ALERT
I'M PUTTING A TRACE ON A T-COMMUNICATOR TO GET A LOCATION ON SOMEONE.
TRACE A COMMUNICATOR? BUT WE'RE ALL HERE!
I'M LOOKING FOR SOMEONE *ELSE.*

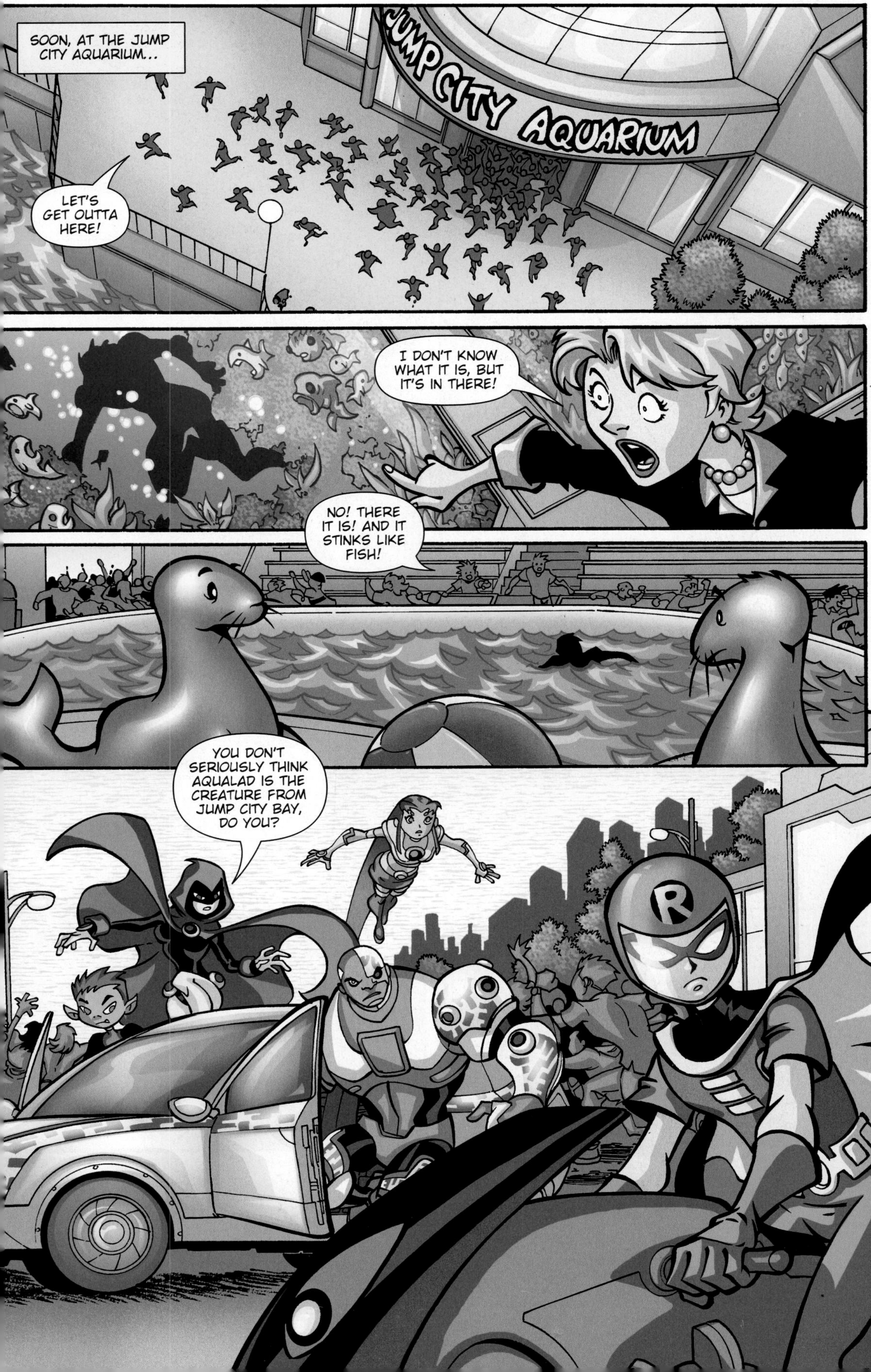
SOON, AT THE JUMP CITY AQUARIUM...
JUMP CITY AQUARIUM
LET'S GET OUTTA HERE!
I DON'T KNOW WHAT IT IS, BUT IT'S IN THERE!
NO! THERE IT IS! AND IT STINKS LIKE FISH!
YOU DON'T SERIOUSLY THINK AQUALAD IS THE CREATURE FROM JUMP CITY BAY, DO YOU?

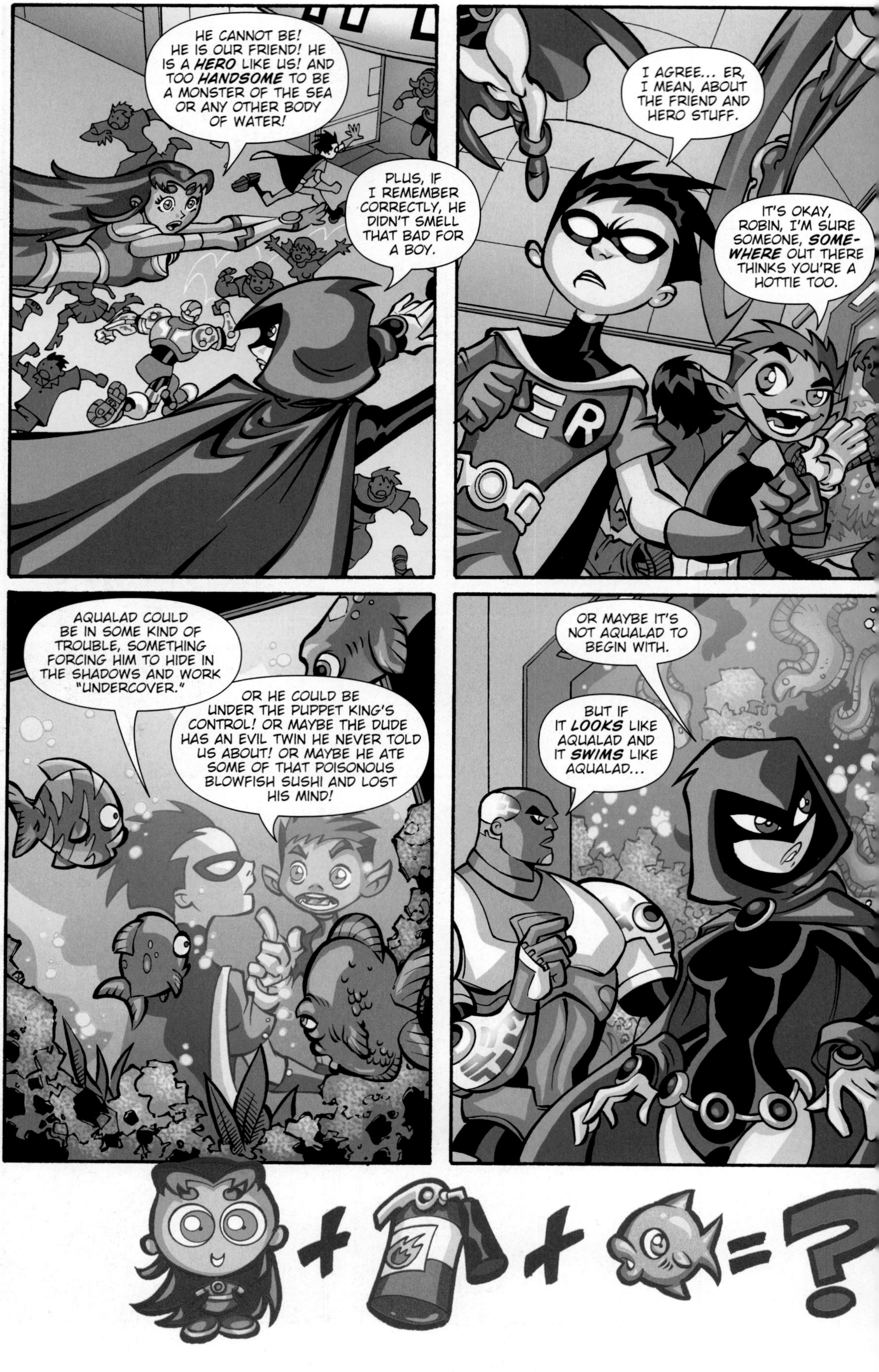
HE CANNOT BE! HE IS OUR FRIEND! HE IS A HERO LIKE US! AND TOO HANDSOME TO BE A MONSTER OF THE SEA OR ANY OTHER BODY OF WATER!
PLUS, IF I REMEMBER CORRECTLY, HE DIDN'T SMELL THAT BAD FOR A BOY.
I AGREE... ER, I MEAN, ABOUT THE FRIEND AND HERO STUFF.
IT'S OKAY, ROBIN, I'M SURE SOMEONE, SOME-WHERE OUT THERE THINKS YOU'RE A HOTTIE TOO.
AQUALAD COULD BE IN SOME KIND OF TROUBLE, SOMETHING FORCING HIM TO HIDE IN THE SHADOWS AND WORK "UNDERCOVER."
OR HE COULD BE UNDER THE PUPPET KING'S CONTROL! OR MAYBE THE DUDE HAS AN EVIL TWIN HE NEVER TOLD US ABOUT! OR MAYBE HE ATE SOME OF THAT POISONOUS BLOWFISH SUSHI AND LOST HIS MIND!
OR MAYBE IT'S NOT AQUALAD TO BEGIN WITH.
BUT IF IT LOOKS LIKE AQUALAD AND IT SWIMS LIKE AQUALAD...

DON'T KNOW WHAT HE'S LOOKING FOR IN HERE, BUT YOU *GO THAT* WAY! WE'LL HEAD HIM OFF IN THIS DIRECTION!

I'M ON IT LIKE SEA ON SHORE!

KER-SPLASH!

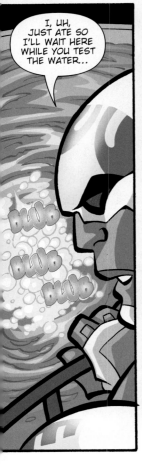

I, UH, JUST ATE SO I'LL WAIT HERE WHILE YOU TEST THE WATER...

BLUB BLUB BLUB

B.B.!

SPROOSH!

YOU OKAY, LI'L BUDDY?

LOOK AT ALL THE PURDY BIRDIES...

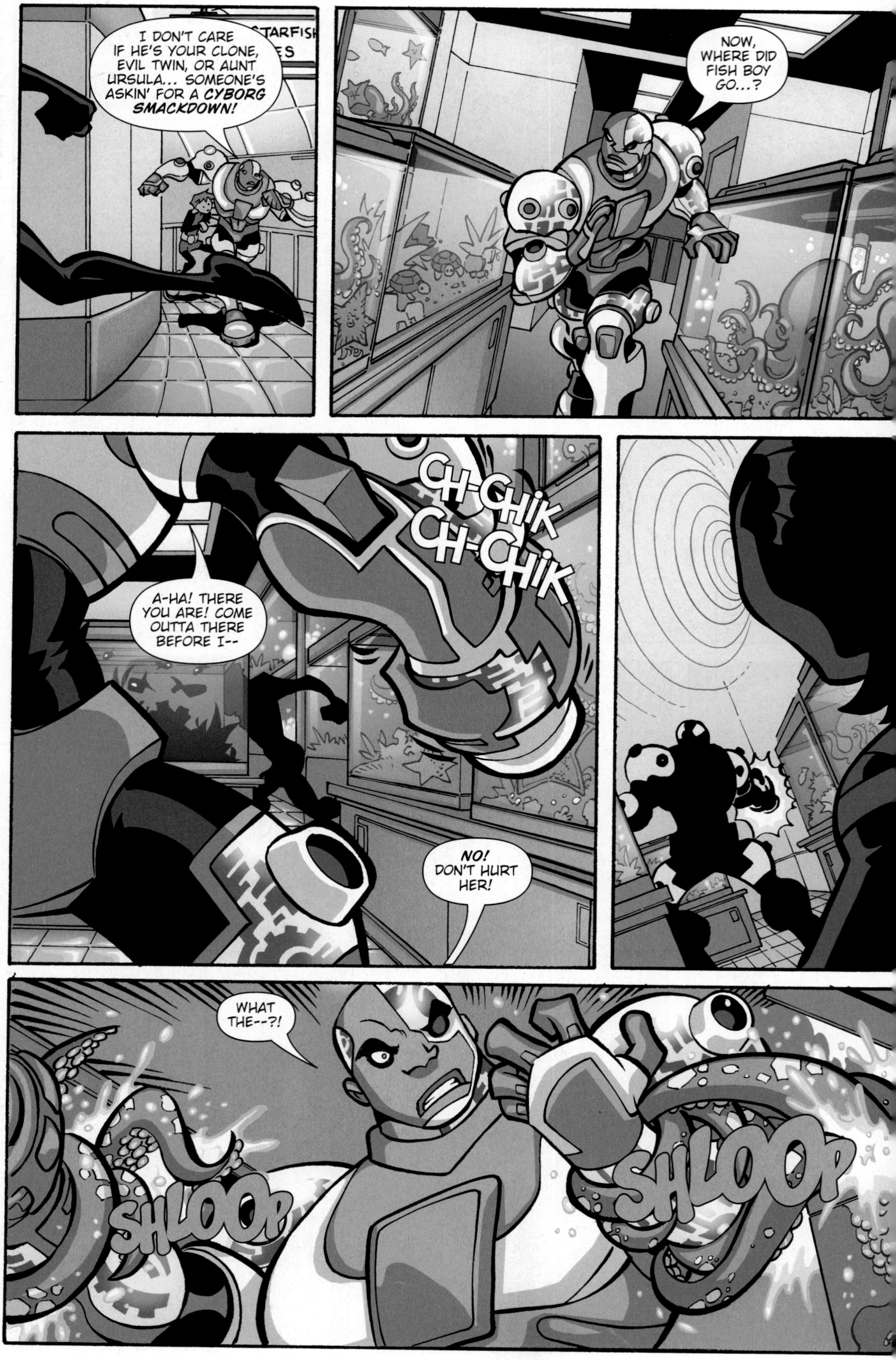
STARFISH
I DON'T CARE IF HE'S YOUR CLONE, EVIL TWIN, OR AUNT URSULA... SOMEONE'S ASKIN' FOR A CYBORG SMACKDOWN!
NOW, WHERE DID FISH BOY GO...?
CH-CHIK CH-CHIK
A-HA! THERE YOU ARE! COME OUTTA THERE BEFORE I--
NO! DON'T HURT HER!
WHAT THE--?!
SHLOOP
SHLOOP

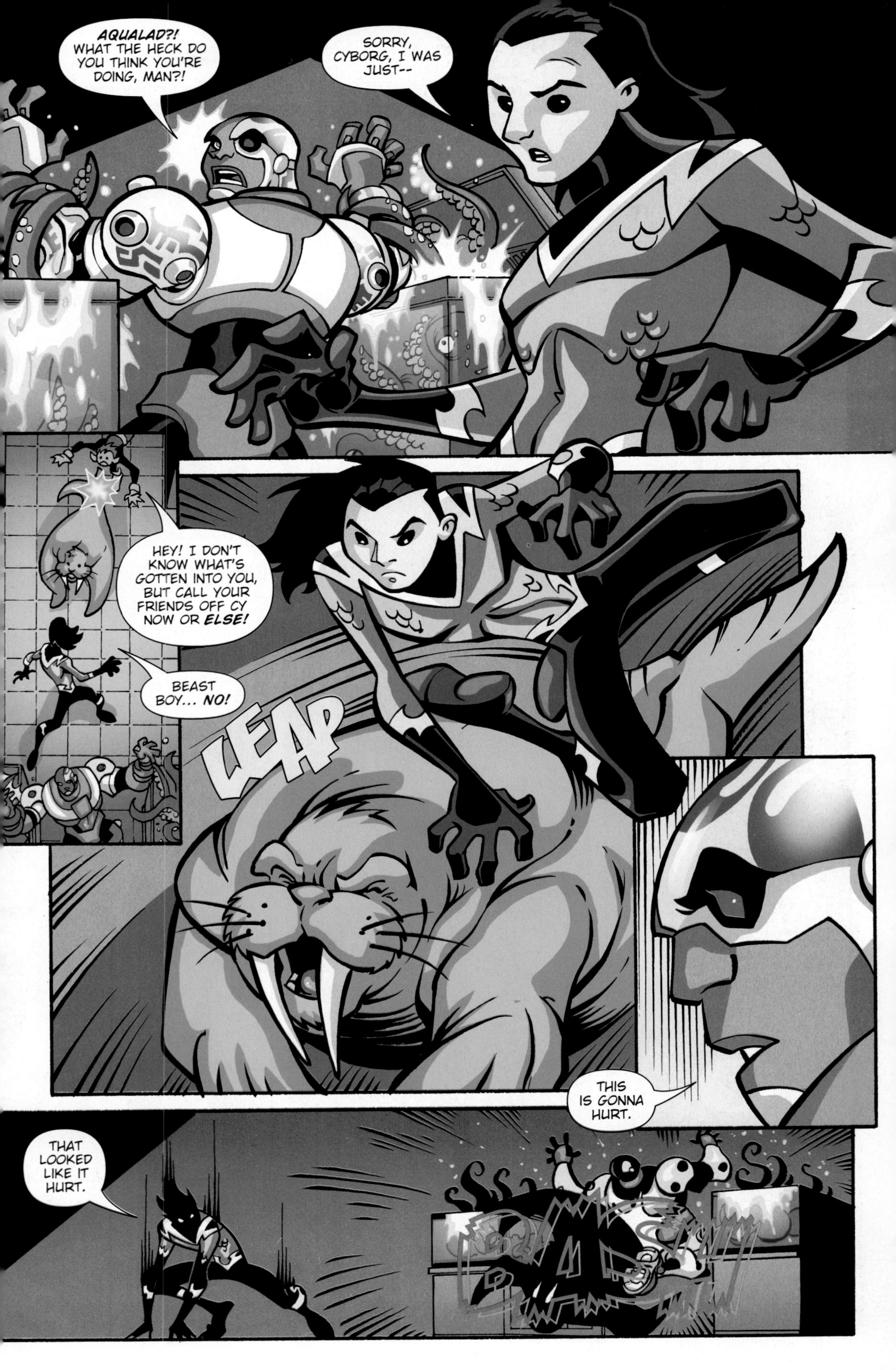
AQUALAD?! WHAT THE HECK DO YOU THINK YOU'RE DOING, MAN?!
SORRY, CYBORG, I WAS JUST--
HEY! I DON'T KNOW WHAT'S GOTTEN INTO YOU, BUT CALL YOUR FRIENDS OFF CY NOW OR ELSE!
BEAST BOY... NO!
LEAP
THIS IS GONNA HURT.
THAT LOOKED LIKE IT HURT.

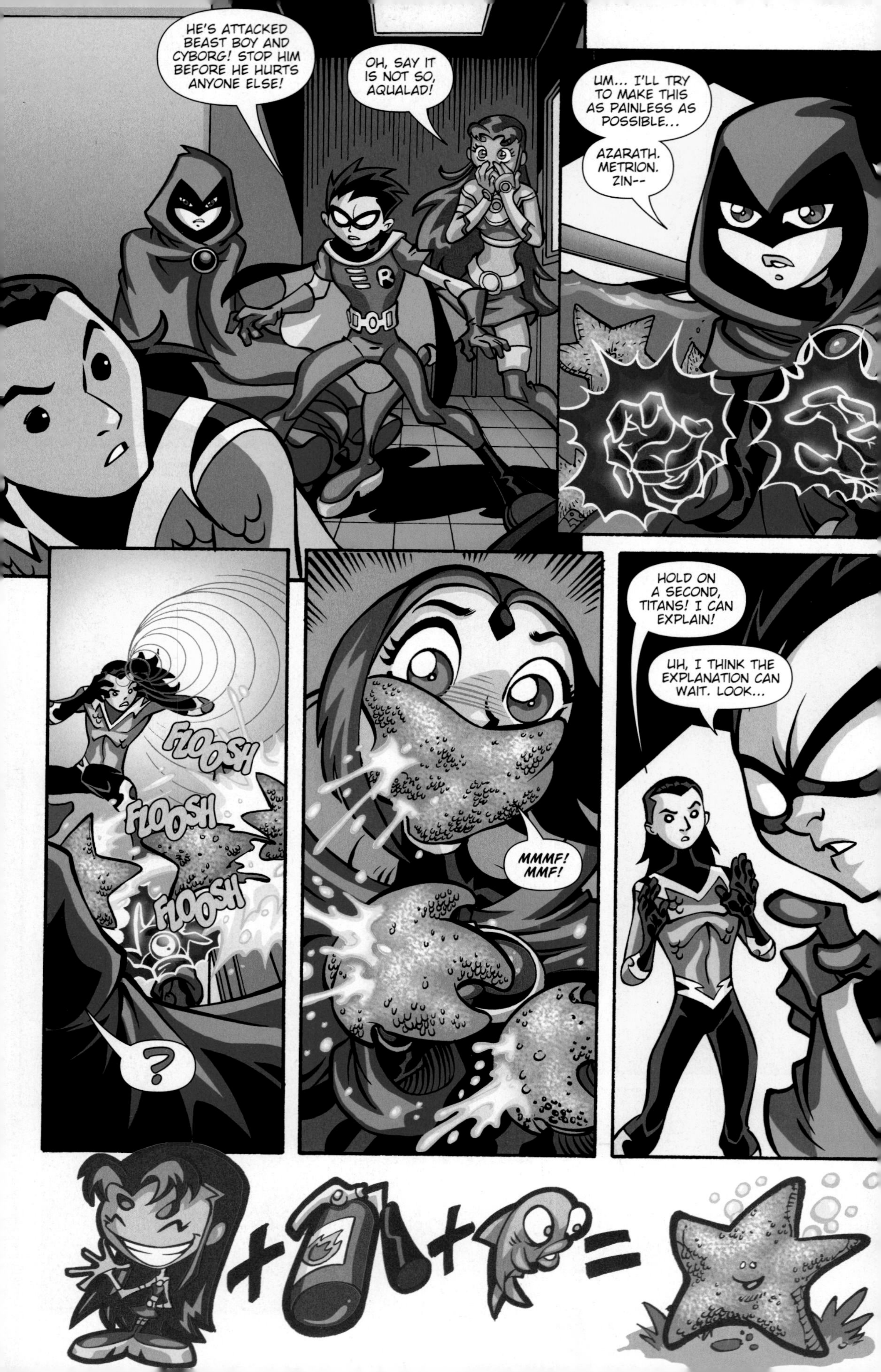
HE'S ATTACKED BEAST BOY AND CYBORG! STOP HIM BEFORE HE HURTS ANYONE ELSE!
OH, SAY IT IS NOT SO, AQUALAD!
UM... I'LL TRY TO MAKE THIS AS PAINLESS AS POSSIBLE...
AZARATH. METRION. ZIN--
FLOOSH
FLOOSH
FLOOSH
?
MMMF! MMF!
HOLD ON A SECOND, TITANS! I CAN EXPLAIN!
UH, I THINK THE EXPLANATION CAN WAIT. LOOK...

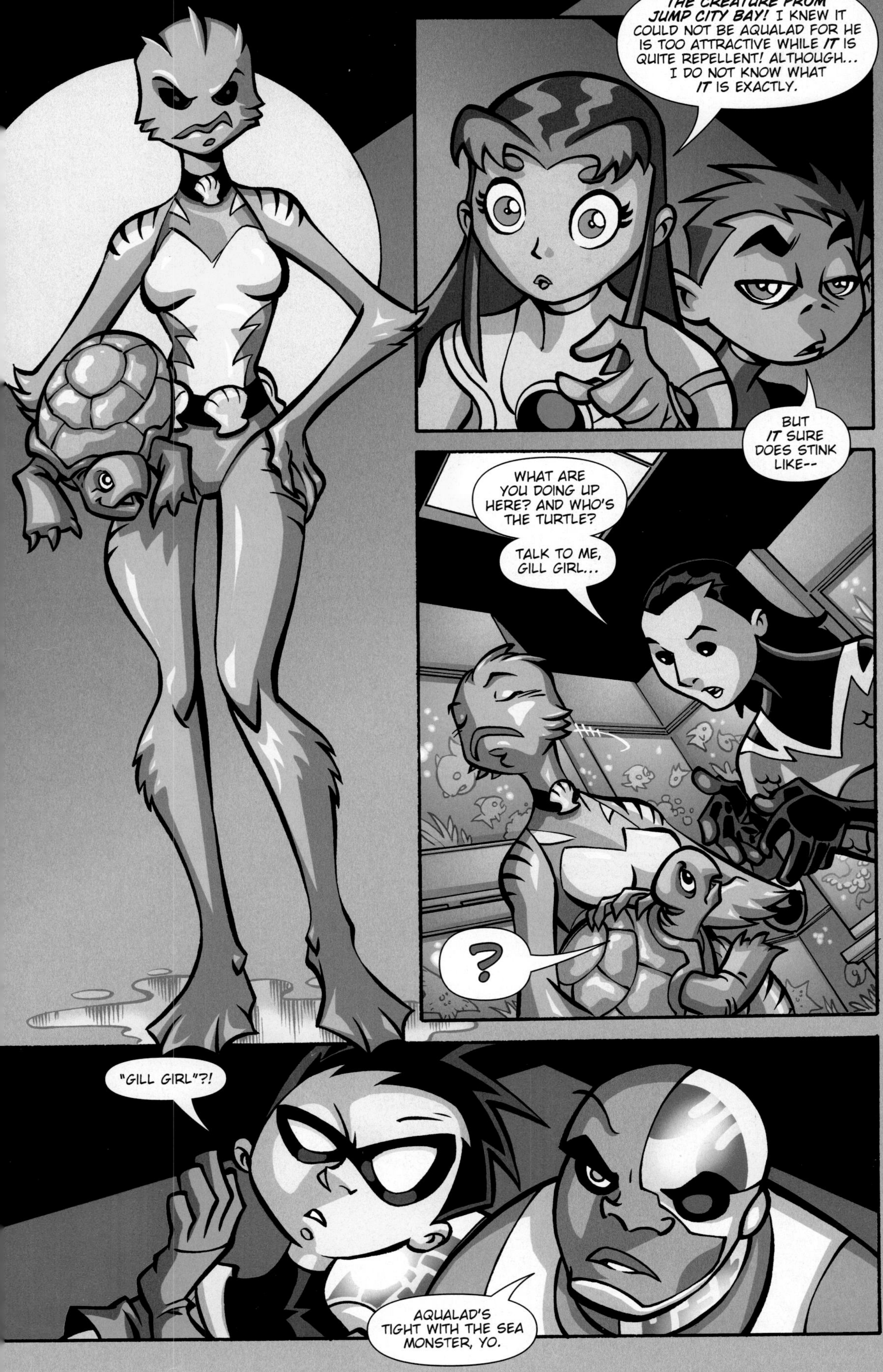
THE CREATURE FROM JUMP CITY BAY! I KNEW IT COULD NOT BE AQUALAD FOR HE IS TOO ATTRACTIVE WHILE IT IS QUITE REPELLENT! ALTHOUGH... I DO NOT KNOW WHAT IT IS EXACTLY.
BUT IT SURE DOES STINK LIKE--
WHAT ARE YOU DOING UP HERE? AND WHO'S THE TURTLE?
TALK TO ME, GILL GIRL...
?
"GILL GIRL"?!
AQUALAD'S TIGHT WITH THE SEA MONSTER, YO.

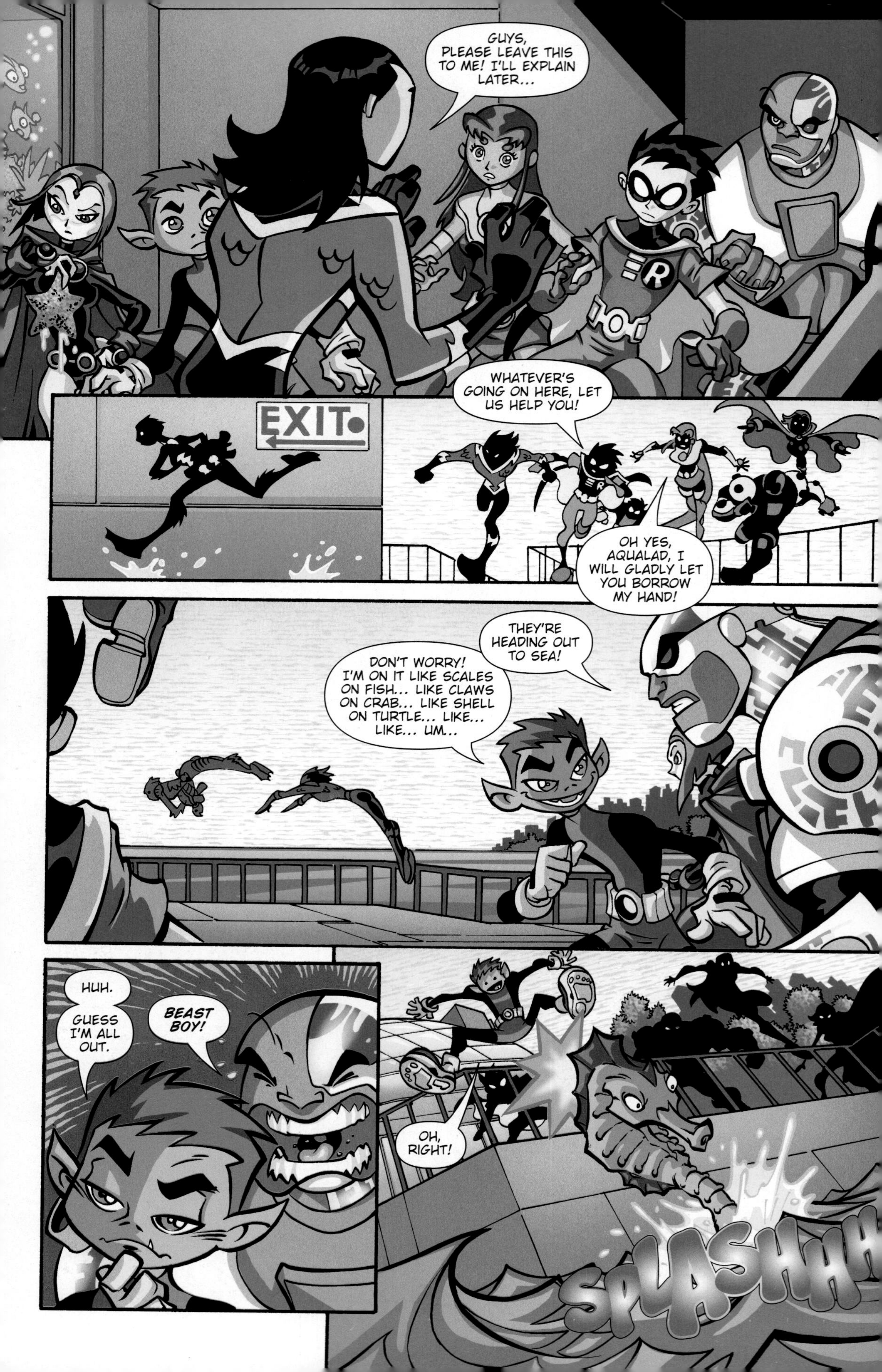
GUYS, PLEASE LEAVE THIS TO ME! I'LL EXPLAIN LATER...
EXIT
WHATEVER'S GOING ON HERE, LET US HELP YOU!
OH YES, AQUALAD, I WILL GLADLY LET YOU BORROW MY HAND!
THEY'RE HEADING OUT TO SEA!
DON'T WORRY! I'M ON IT LIKE SCALES ON FISH... LIKE CLAWS ON CRAB... LIKE SHELL ON TURTLE... LIKE... LIKE... UM...
HUH.
GUESS I'M ALL OUT.
BEAST BOY!
OH, RIGHT!
SPLASHHH

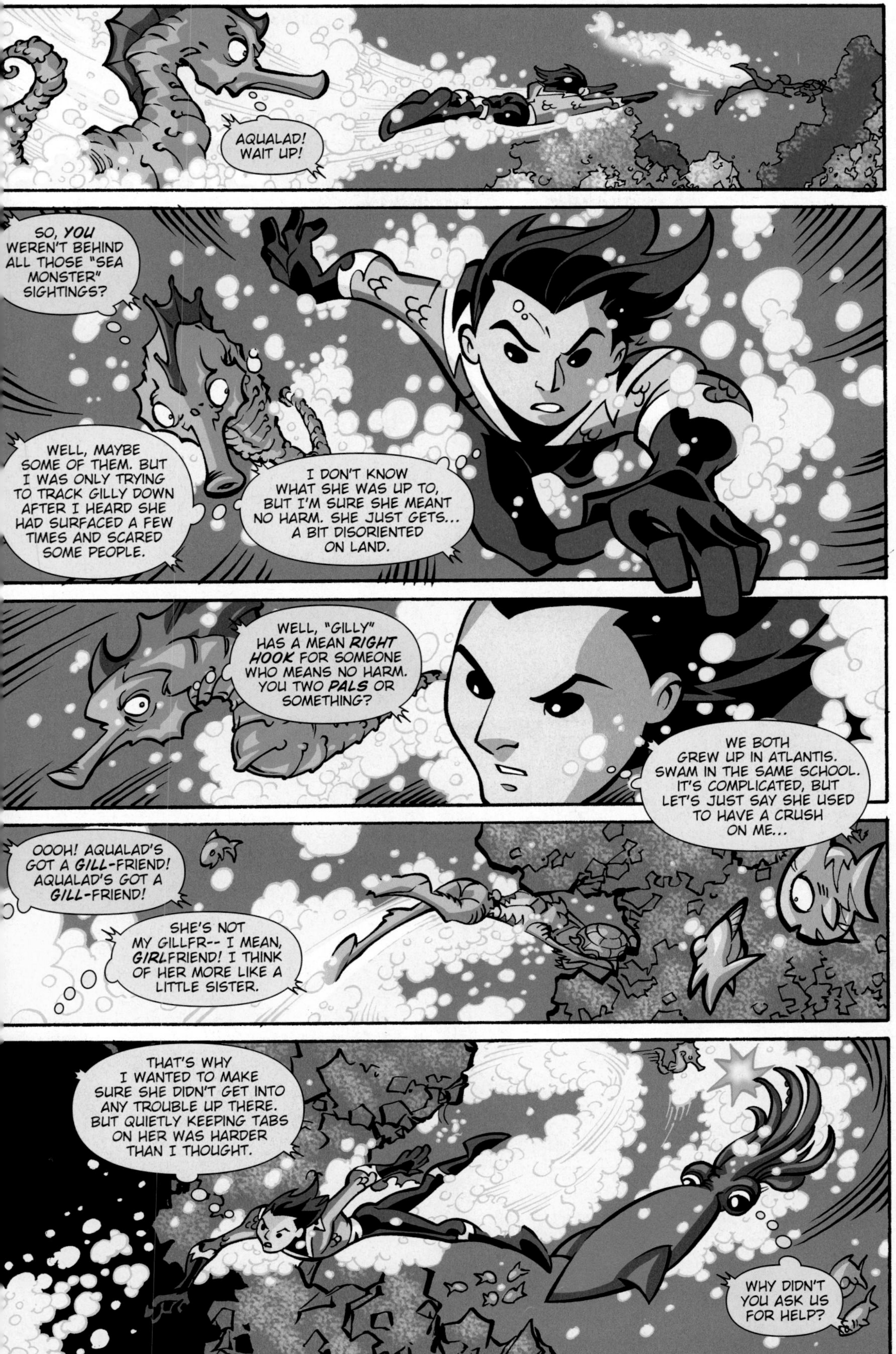
AQUALAD! WAIT UP!
SO, YOU WEREN'T BEHIND ALL THOSE "SEA MONSTER" SIGHTINGS?
WELL, MAYBE SOME OF THEM. BUT I WAS ONLY TRYING TO TRACK GILLY DOWN AFTER I HEARD SHE HAD SURFACED A FEW TIMES AND SCARED SOME PEOPLE.
I DON'T KNOW WHAT SHE WAS UP TO, BUT I'M SURE SHE MEANT NO HARM. SHE JUST GETS... A BIT DISORIENTED ON LAND.
WELL, "GILLY" HAS A MEAN RIGHT HOOK FOR SOMEONE WHO MEANS NO HARM. YOU TWO PALS OR SOMETHING?
WE BOTH GREW UP IN ATLANTIS. SWAM IN THE SAME SCHOOL. IT'S COMPLICATED, BUT LET'S JUST SAY SHE USED TO HAVE A CRUSH ON ME...
OOOH! AQUALAD'S GOT A GILL-FRIEND! AQUALAD'S GOT A GILL-FRIEND!
SHE'S NOT MY GILLFR-- I MEAN, GIRLFRIEND! I THINK OF HER MORE LIKE A LITTLE SISTER.
THAT'S WHY I WANTED TO MAKE SURE SHE DIDN'T GET INTO ANY TROUBLE UP THERE. BUT QUIETLY KEEPING TABS ON HER WAS HARDER THAN I THOUGHT.
WHY DIDN'T YOU ASK US FOR HELP?

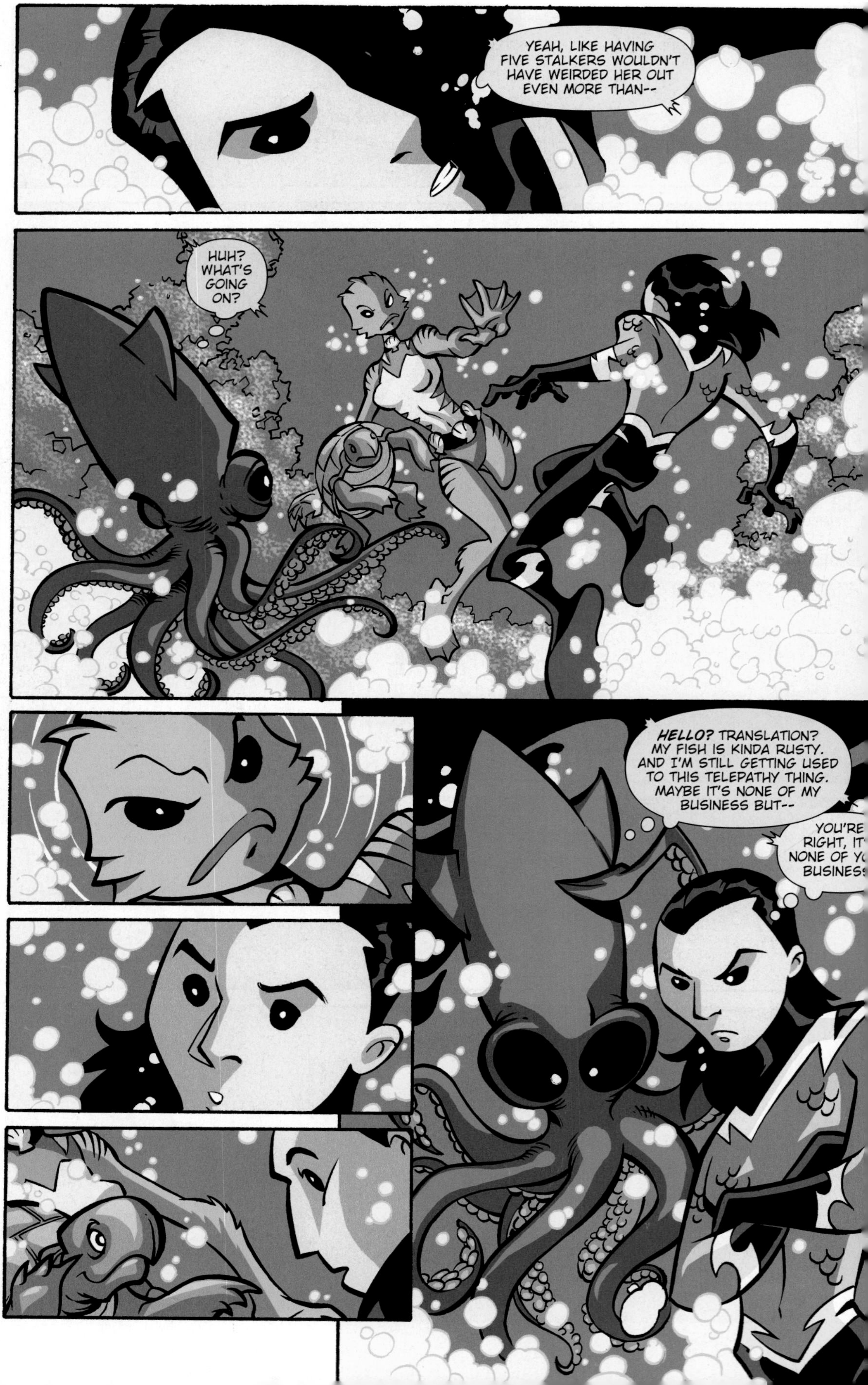
YEAH, LIKE HAVING FIVE STALKERS WOULDN'T HAVE WEIRDED HER OUT EVEN MORE THAN--
HUH? WHAT'S GOING ON?
HELLO? TRANSLATION? MY FISH IS KINDA RUSTY. AND I'M STILL GETTING USED TO THIS TELEPATHY THING. MAYBE IT'S NONE OF MY BUSINESS BUT--
YOU'RE RIGHT, IT' NONE OF YO BUSINES

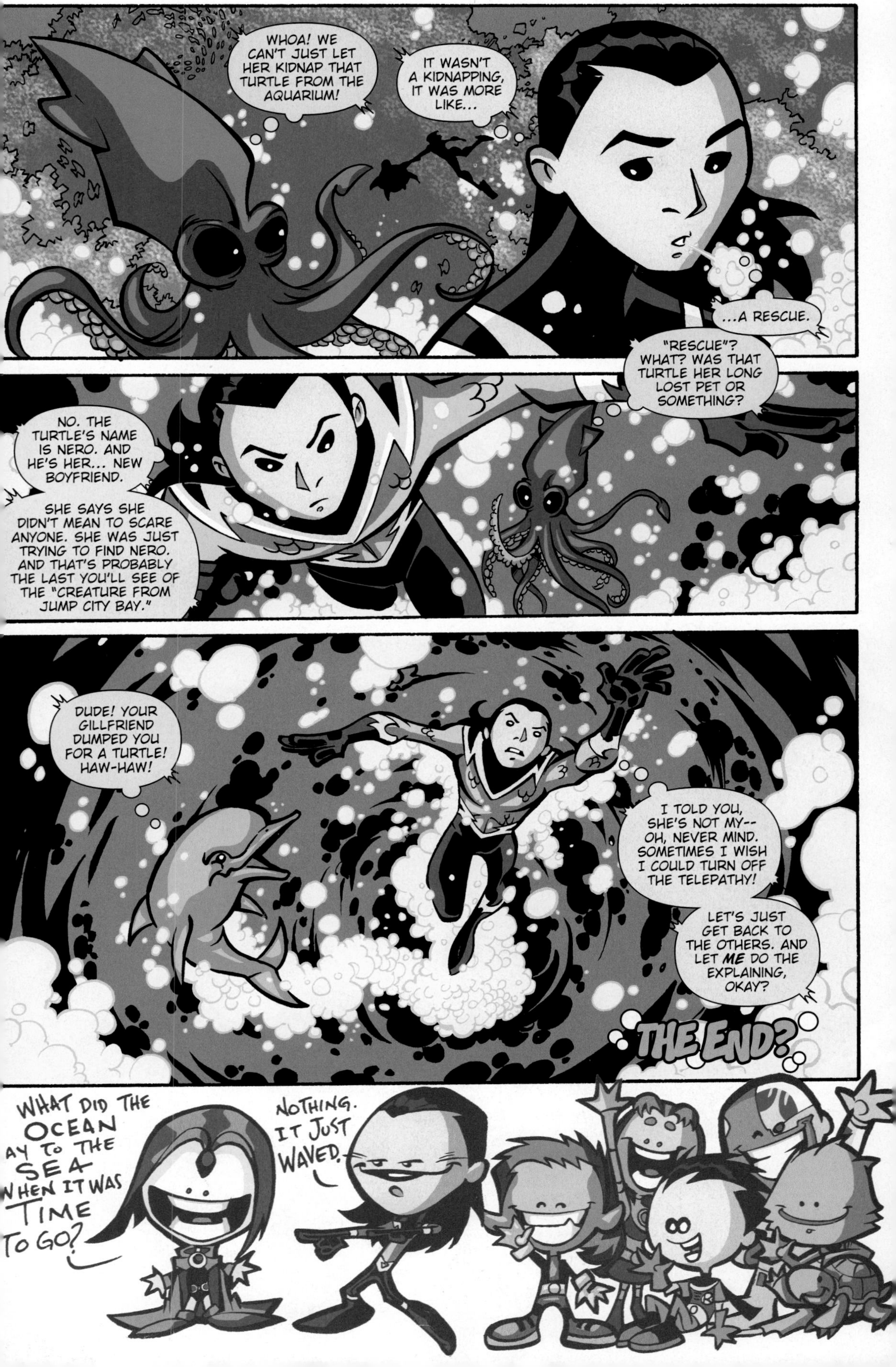
WHOA! WE CAN'T JUST LET HER KIDNAP THAT TURTLE FROM THE AQUARIUM!
IT WASN'T A KIDNAPPING, IT WAS MORE LIKE...
...A RESCUE.
"RESCUE"? WHAT? WAS THAT TURTLE HER LONG LOST PET OR SOMETHING?
NO. THE TURTLE'S NAME IS NERO. AND HE'S HER... NEW BOYFRIEND.
SHE SAYS SHE DIDN'T MEAN TO SCARE ANYONE. SHE WAS JUST TRYING TO FIND NERO. AND THAT'S PROBABLY THE LAST YOU'LL SEE OF THE "CREATURE FROM JUMP CITY BAY."
DUDE! YOUR GILLFRIEND DUMPED YOU FOR A TURTLE! HAW-HAW!
I TOLD YOU, SHE'S NOT MY-- OH, NEVER MIND. SOMETIMES I WISH I COULD TURN OFF THE TELEPATHY!
LET'S JUST GET BACK TO THE OTHERS. AND LET ME DO THE EXPLAINING, OKAY?
THE END?
WHAT DID THE OCEAN SAY TO THE SEA WHEN IT WAS TIME TO GO?
NOTHING. IT JUST WAVED.

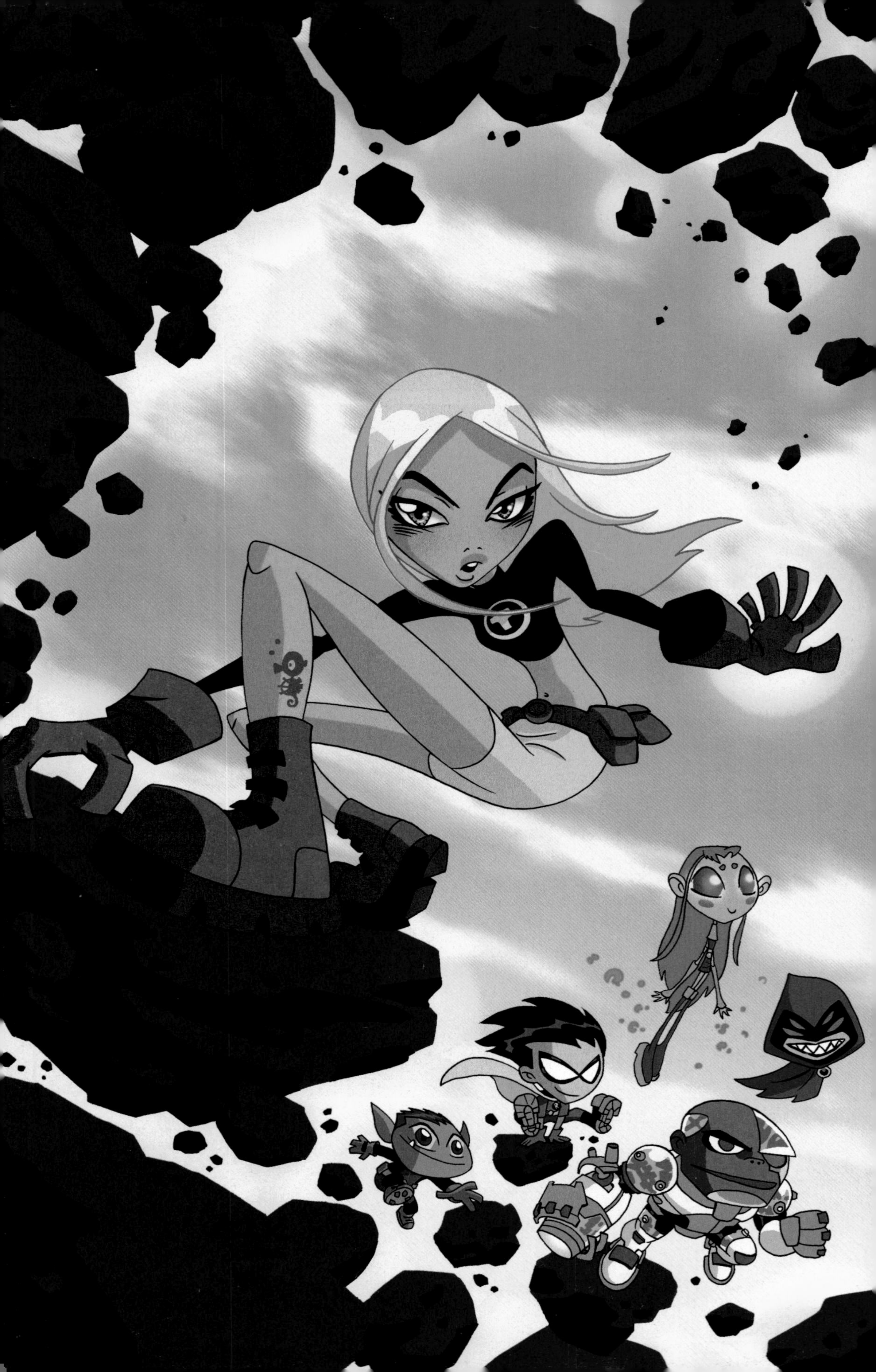

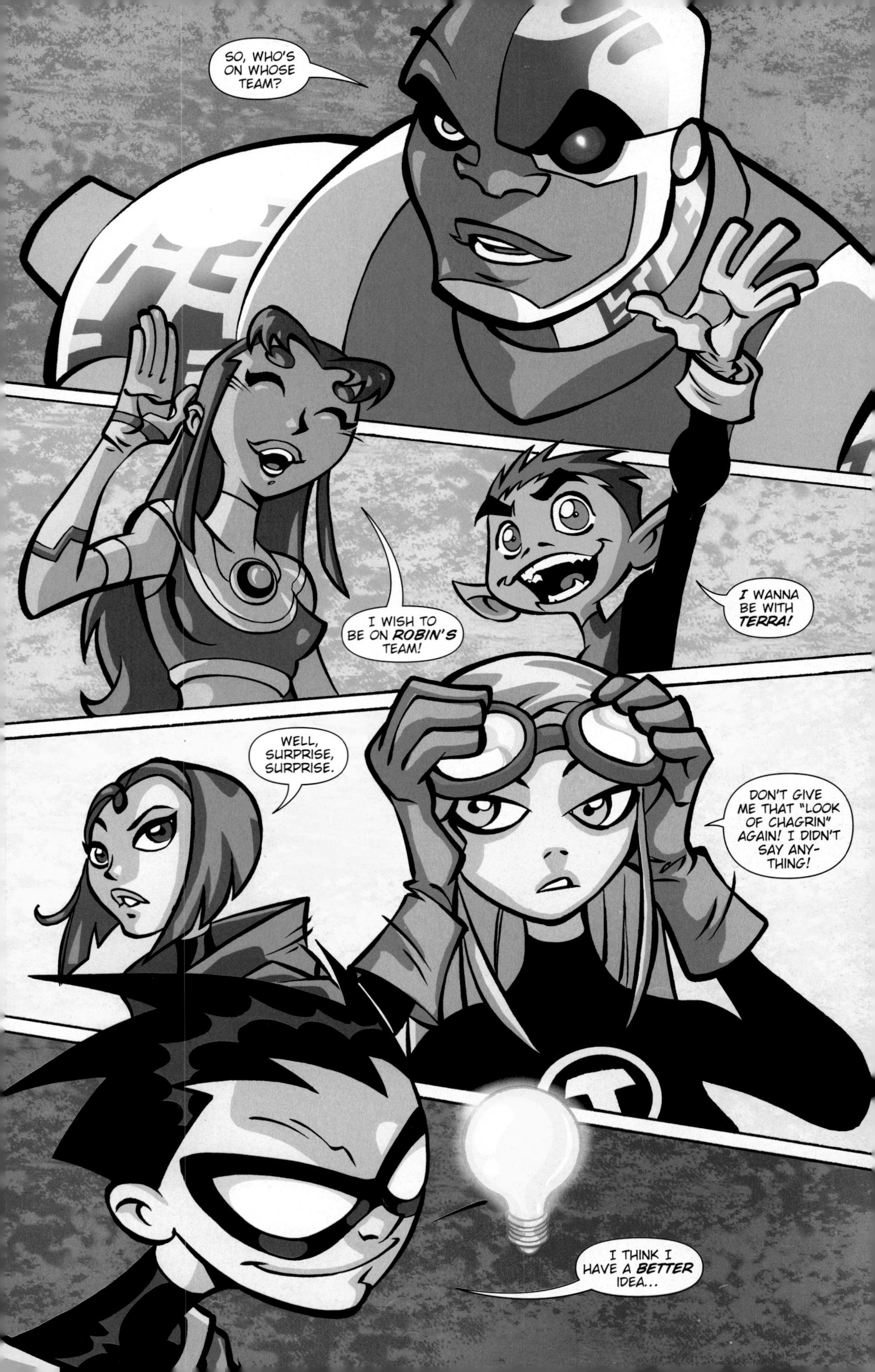
SO, WHO'S ON WHOSE TEAM?
I WISH TO BE ON ROBIN'S TEAM!
I WANNA BE WITH TERRA!
WELL, SURPRISE, SURPRISE.
DON'T GIVE ME THAT "LOOK OF CHAGRIN" AGAIN! I DIDN'T SAY ANY-THING!
I THINK I HAVE A BETTER IDEA...

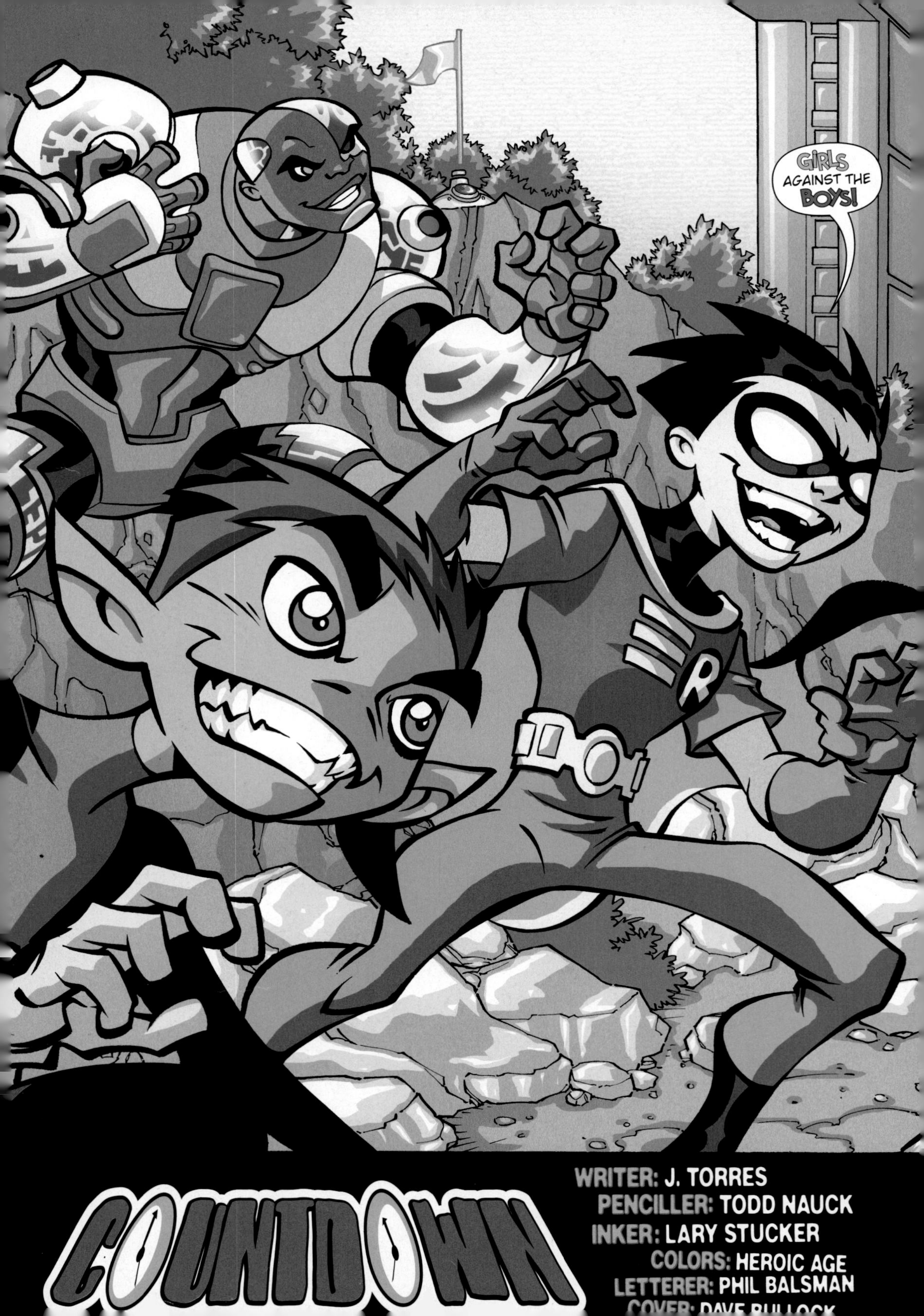
GIRLS AGAINST THE BOYS!
COUNTDOWN
WRITER: J. TORRES
PENCILLER: TODD NAUCK
INKER: LARY STUCKER
COLORS: HEROIC AGE
LETTERER: PHIL BALSMAN

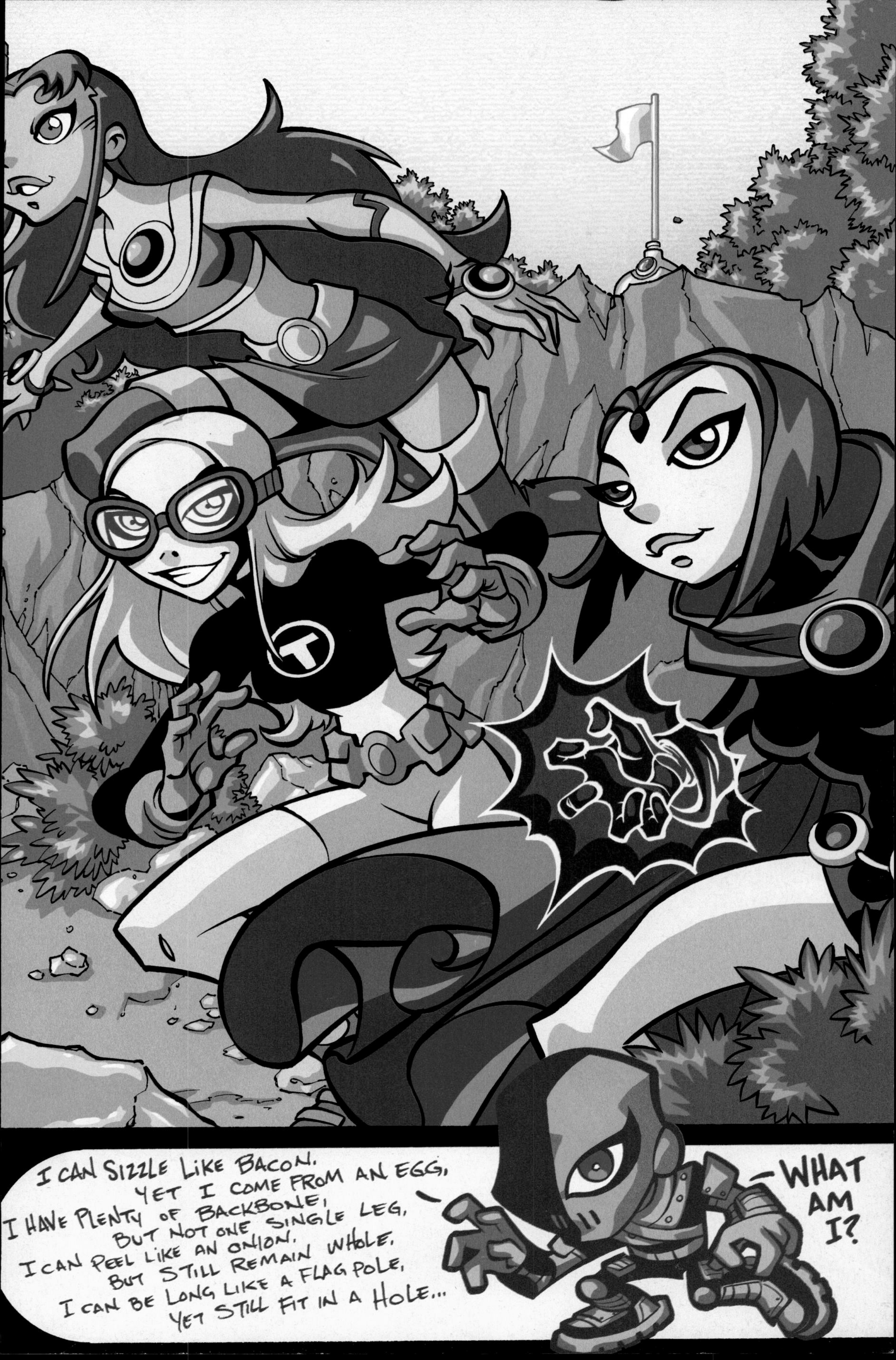

I CAN SIZZLE LIKE BACON, YET I COME FROM AN EGG, I HAVE PLENTY OF BACKBONE, BUT NOT ONE SINGLE LEG, I CAN PEEL LIKE AN ONION, BUT STILL REMAIN WHOLE, BUT I CAN BE LONG LIKE A FLAG POLE, I CAN BE LONG LIKE A FLAG POLE, YET STILL FIT IN A HOLE...
—WHAT AM I?

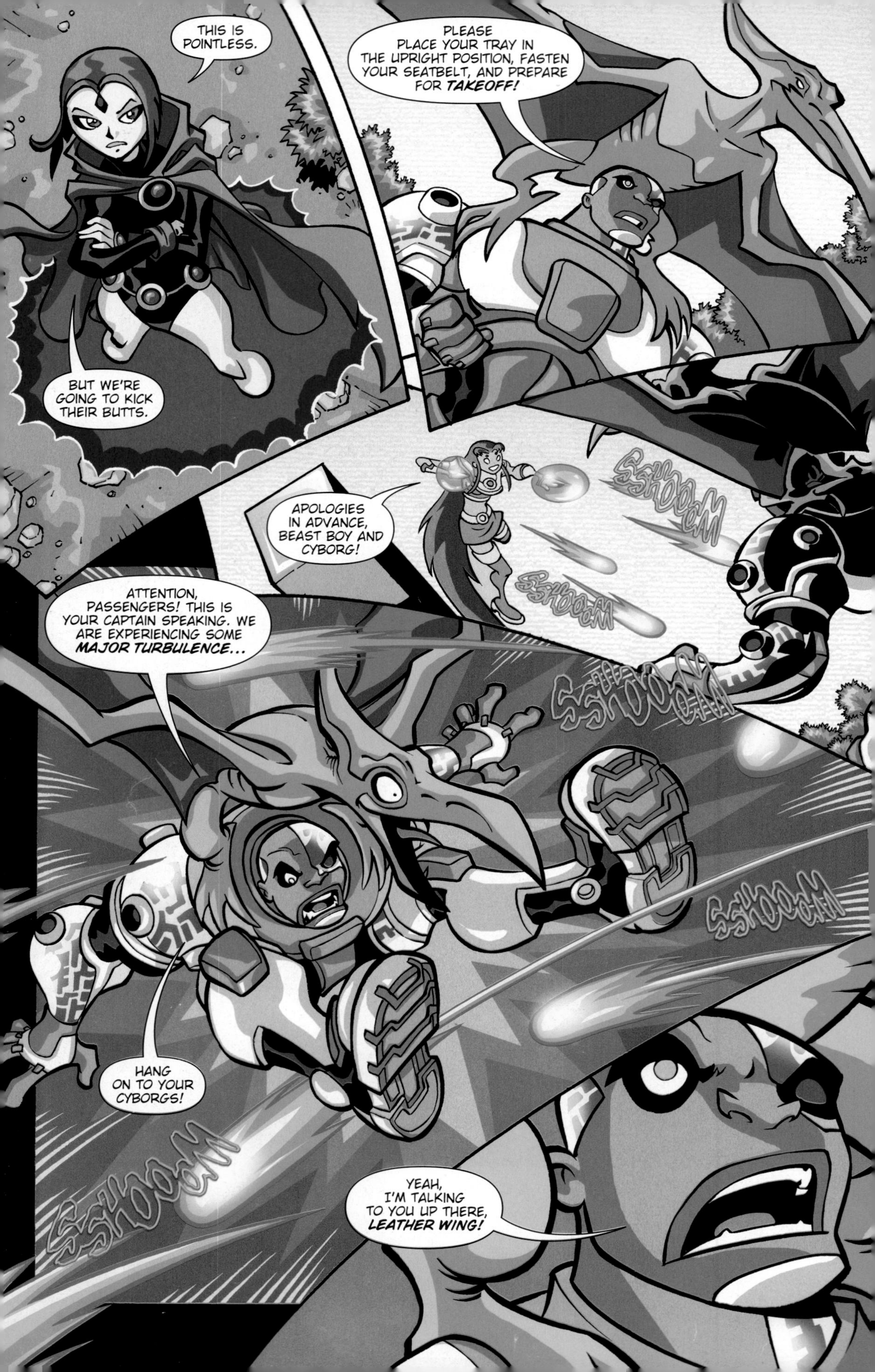
THIS IS POINTLESS.
BUT WE'RE GOING TO KICK THEIR BUTTS.
PLEASE PLACE YOUR TRAY IN THE UPRIGHT POSITION, FASTEN YOUR SEATBELT, AND PREPARE FOR TAKEOFF!
APOLOGIES IN ADVANCE, BEAST BOY AND CYBORG!
SSHOOOM
SSHOOOM
ATTENTION, PASSENGERS! THIS IS YOUR CAPTAIN SPEAKING. WE ARE EXPERIENCING SOME MAJOR TURBULENCE...
SSHOOOM
HANG ON TO YOUR CYBORGS!
SSHOOOM
SSHOOOM
YEAH, I'M TALKING TO YOU UP THERE, LEATHER WING!

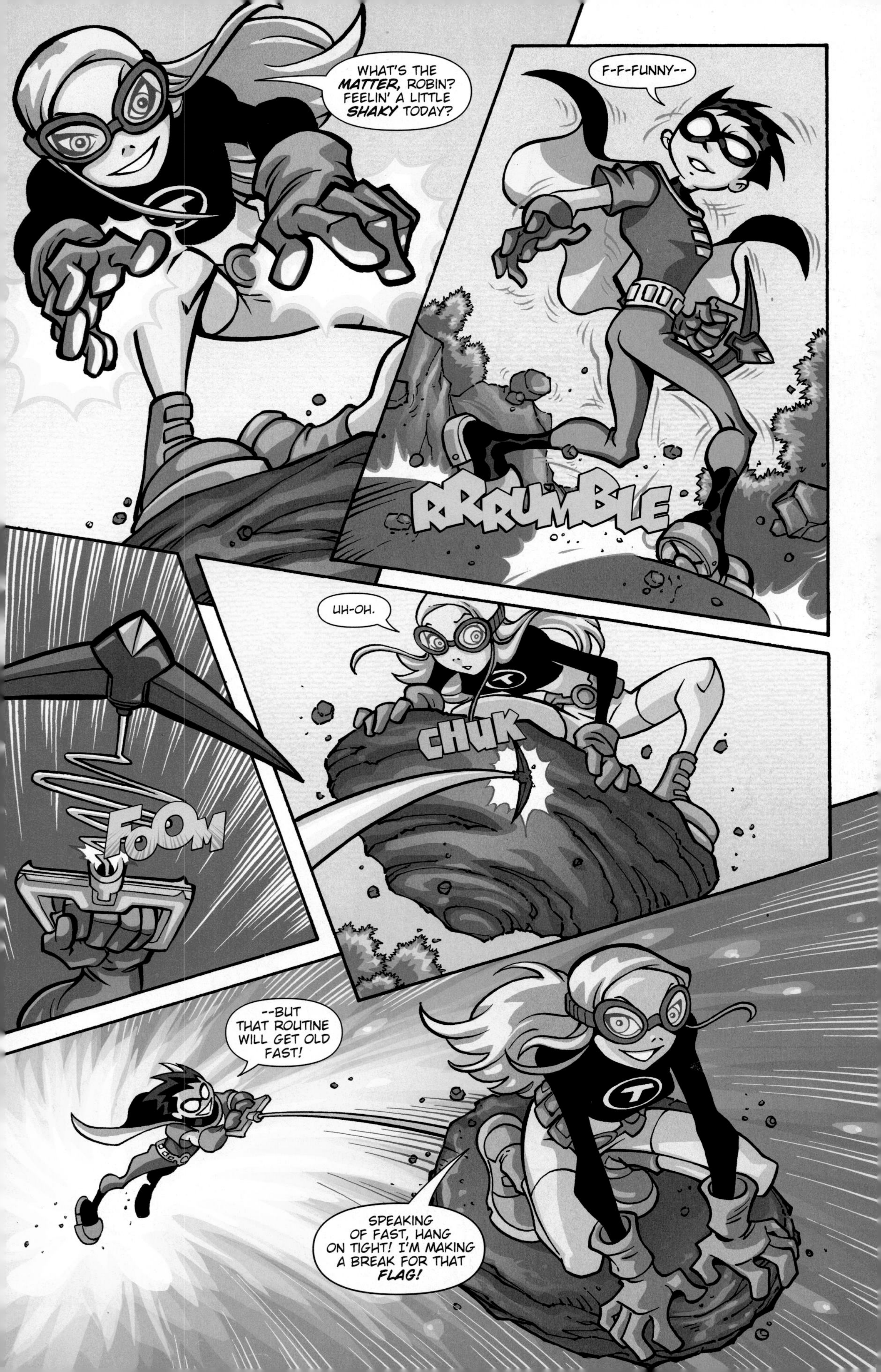
WHAT'S THE MATTER, ROBIN? FEELIN' A LITTLE SHAKY TODAY?
F-F-FUNNY--
RRRUMBLE
UH-OH.
CHUK
FOOOM
--BUT THAT ROUTINE WILL GET OLD FAST!
SPEAKING OF FAST, HANG ON TIGHT! I'M MAKING A BREAK FOR THAT FLAG!

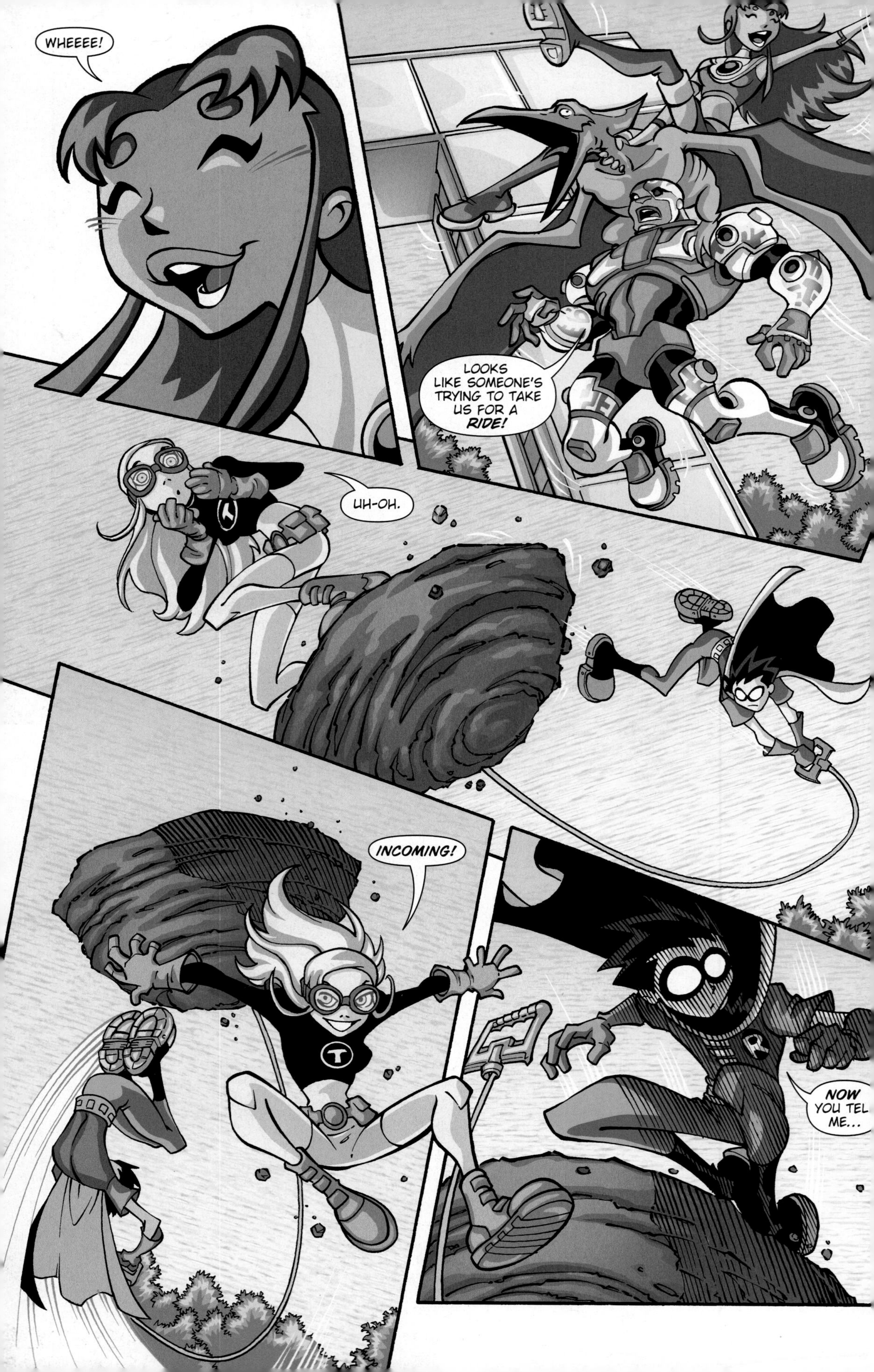
WHEEEE!
LOOKS LIKE SOMEONE'S TRYING TO TAKE US FOR A *RIDE!*
UH-OH.
INCOMING!
NOW YOU TEL ME...

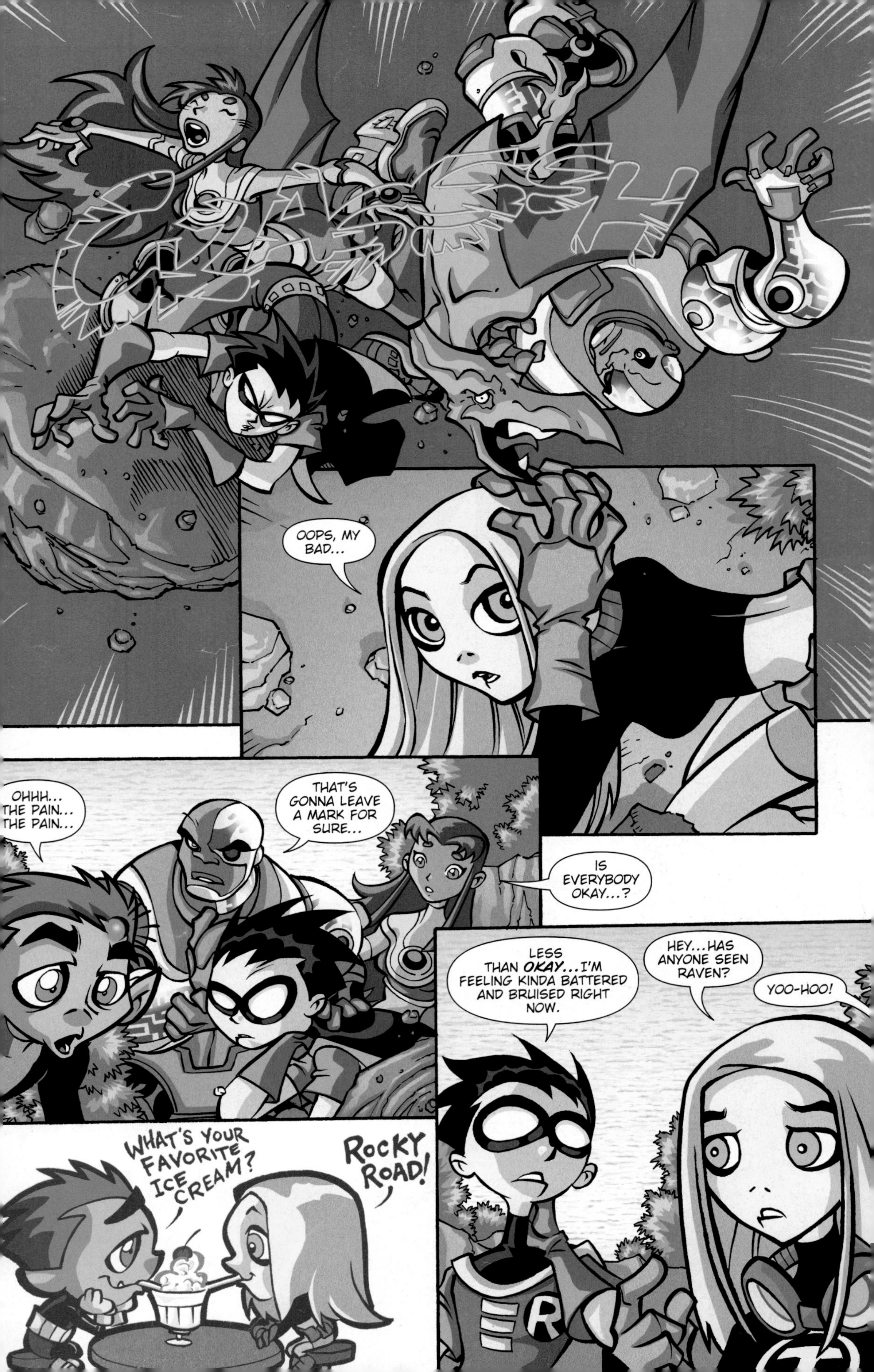
CRASH
OOPS, MY BAD...
OHHH... THE PAIN... THE PAIN...
THAT'S GONNA LEAVE A MARK FOR SURE...
IS EVERYBODY OKAY...?
LESS THAN *OKAY*... I'M FEELING KINDA BATTERED AND BRUISED RIGHT NOW.
HEY... HAS ANYONE SEEN RAVEN?
YOO-HOO!
WHAT'S YOUR FAVORITE ICE CREAM?
ROCKY ROAD!

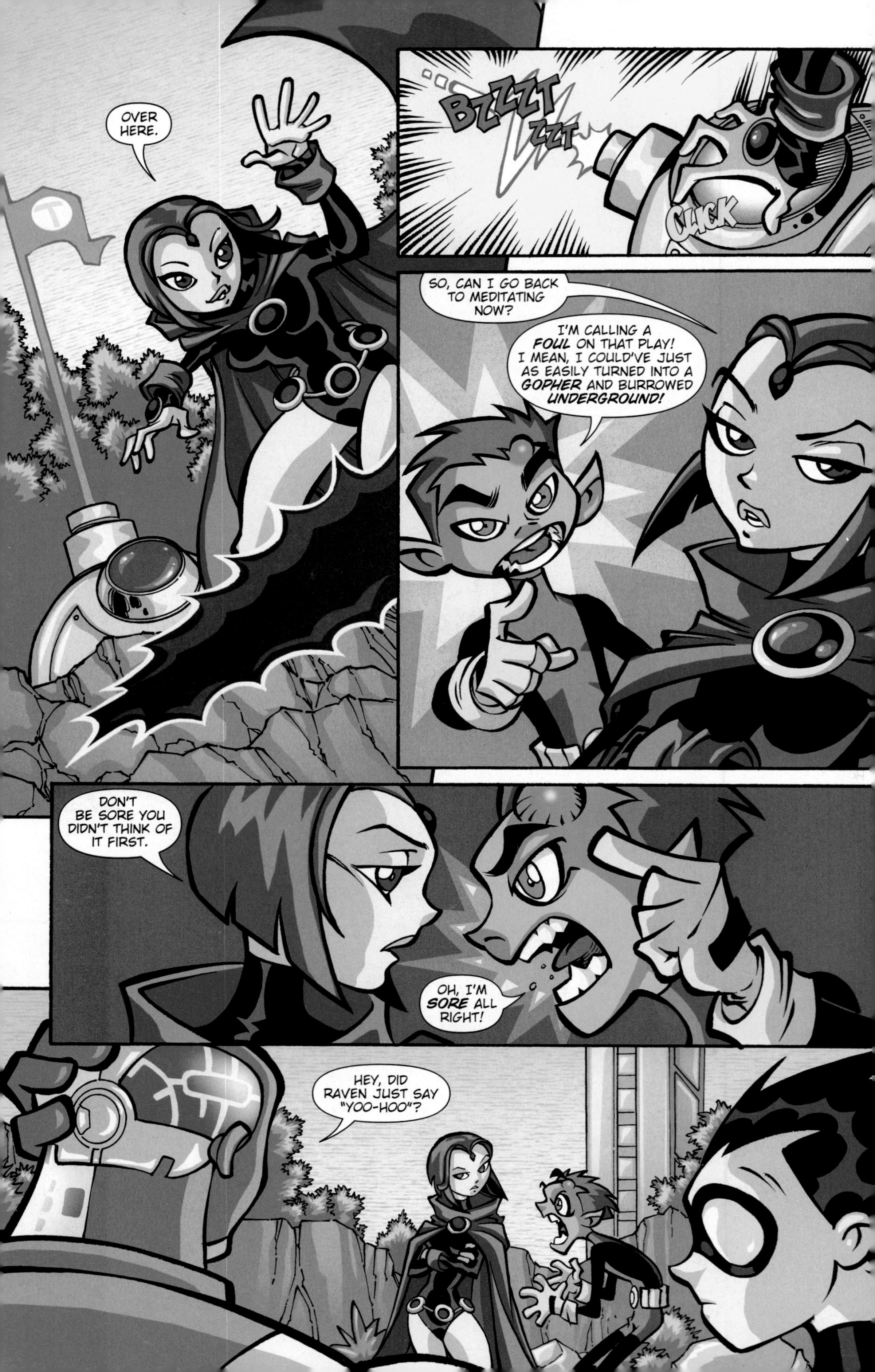
OVER HERE.
BZZZT ZZZT
CLICK
SO, CAN I GO BACK TO MEDITATING NOW?
I'M CALLING A **FOUL** ON THAT PLAY! I MEAN, I COULD'VE JUST AS EASILY TURNED INTO A **GOPHER** AND BURROWED **UNDERGROUND!**
DON'T BE SORE YOU DIDN'T THINK OF IT FIRST.
OH, I'M **SORE** ALL RIGHT!
HEY, DID RAVEN JUST SAY "YOO-HOO"?

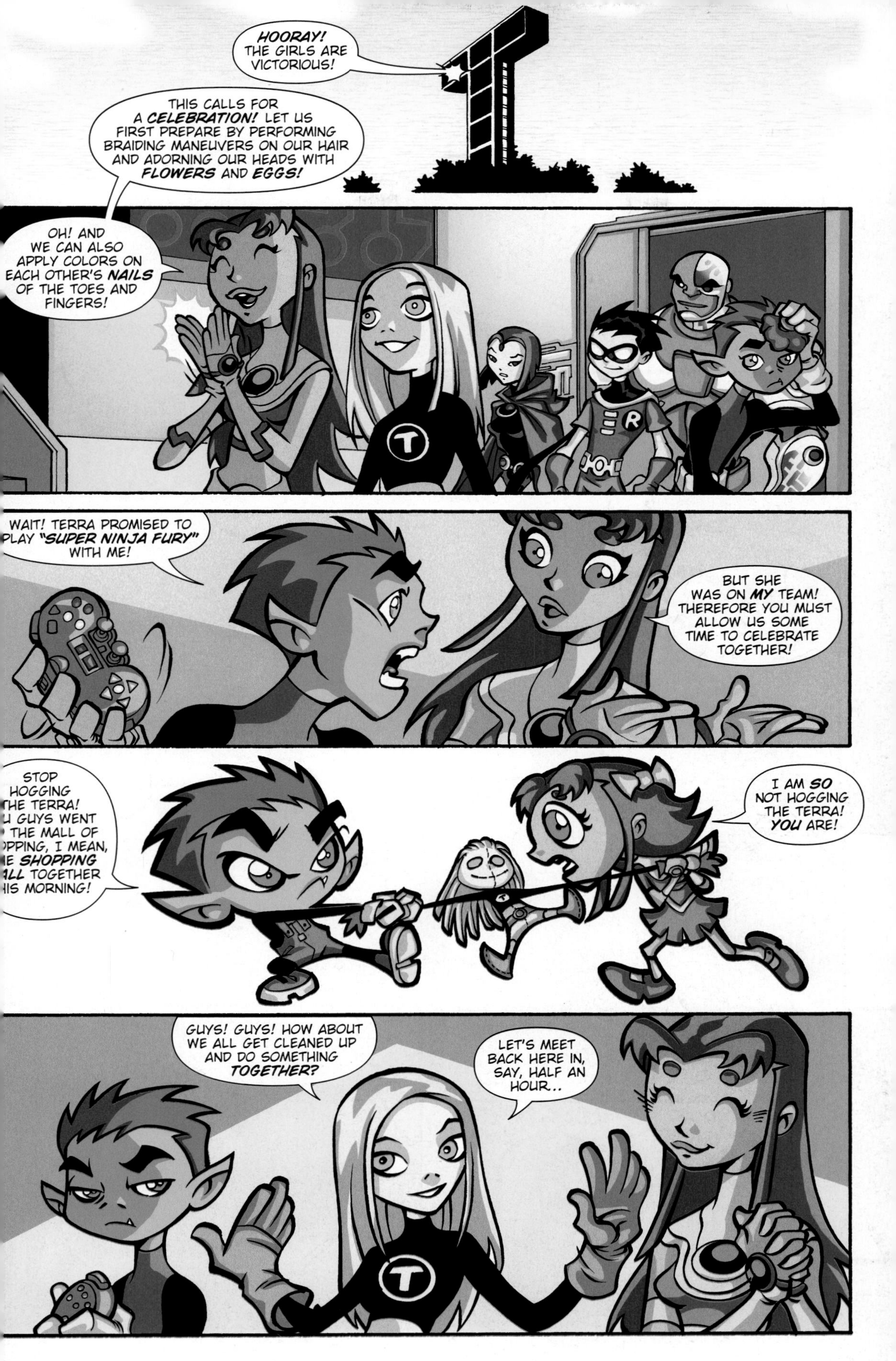
HOORAY! THE GIRLS ARE VICTORIOUS!
THIS CALLS FOR A CELEBRATION! LET US FIRST PREPARE BY PERFORMING BRAIDING MANEUVERS ON OUR HAIR AND ADORNING OUR HEADS WITH FLOWERS AND EGGS!
OH! AND WE CAN ALSO APPLY COLORS ON EACH OTHER'S NAILS OF THE TOES AND FINGERS!
WAIT! TERRA PROMISED TO PLAY "SUPER NINJA FURY" WITH ME!
BUT SHE WAS ON MY TEAM! THEREFORE YOU MUST ALLOW US SOME TIME TO CELEBRATE TOGETHER!
STOP HOGGING THE TERRA! U GUYS WENT THE MALL OF PPING, I MEAN, E SHOPPING ALL TOGETHER HIS MORNING!
I AM SO NOT HOGGING THE TERRA! YOU ARE!
GUYS! GUYS! HOW ABOUT WE ALL GET CLEANED UP AND DO SOMETHING TOGETHER?
LET'S MEET BACK HERE IN, SAY, HALF AN HOUR..

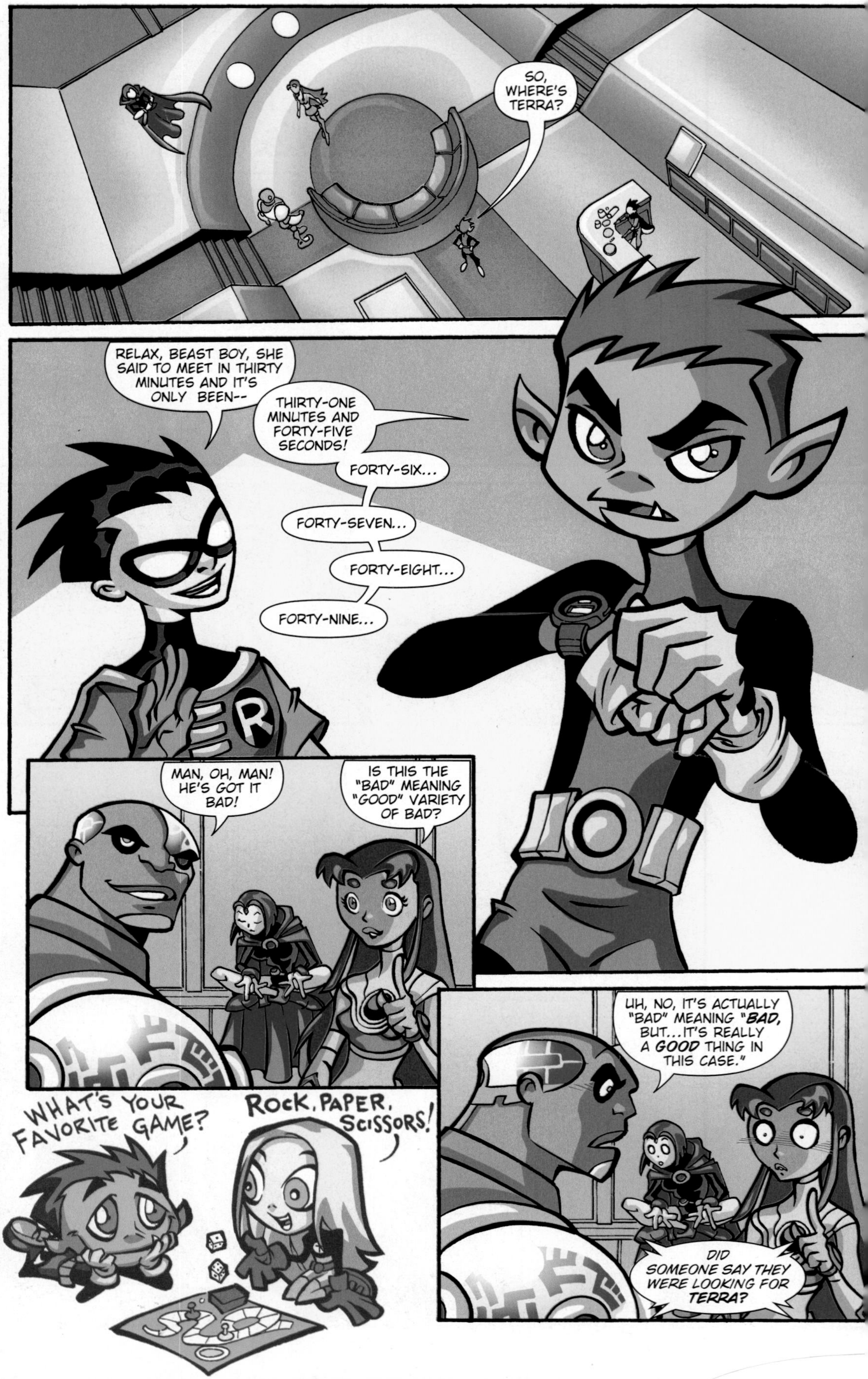
SO, WHERE'S TERRA?
RELAX, BEAST BOY, SHE SAID TO MEET IN THIRTY MINUTES AND IT'S ONLY BEEN--
THIRTY-ONE MINUTES AND FORTY-FIVE SECONDS!
FORTY-SIX...
FORTY-SEVEN...
FORTY-EIGHT...
FORTY-NINE...
MAN, OH, MAN! HE'S GOT IT BAD!
IS THIS THE "BAD" MEANING "GOOD" VARIETY OF BAD?
UH, NO, IT'S ACTUALLY "BAD" MEANING "BAD, BUT...IT'S REALLY A GOOD THING IN THIS CASE."
DID SOMEONE SAY THEY WERE LOOKING FOR TERRA?
WHAT'S YOUR FAVORITE GAME?
ROCK, PAPER, SCISSORS!

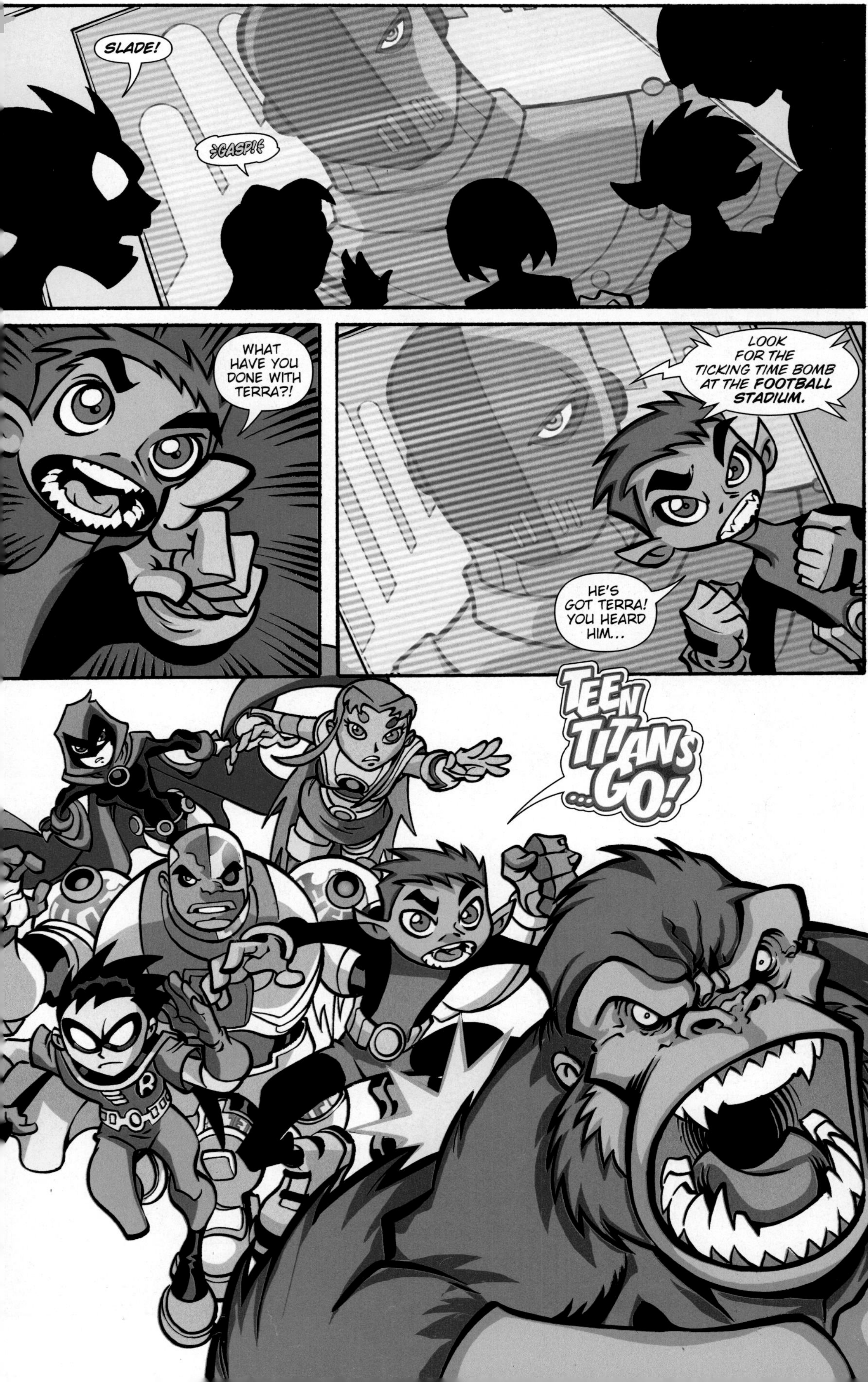
SLADE!
GASP!
WHAT HAVE YOU DONE WITH TERRA?!
LOOK FOR THE TICKING TIME BOMB AT THE FOOTBALL STADIUM.
HE'S GOT TERRA! YOU HEARD HIM...
TEEN TITANS ...GO!

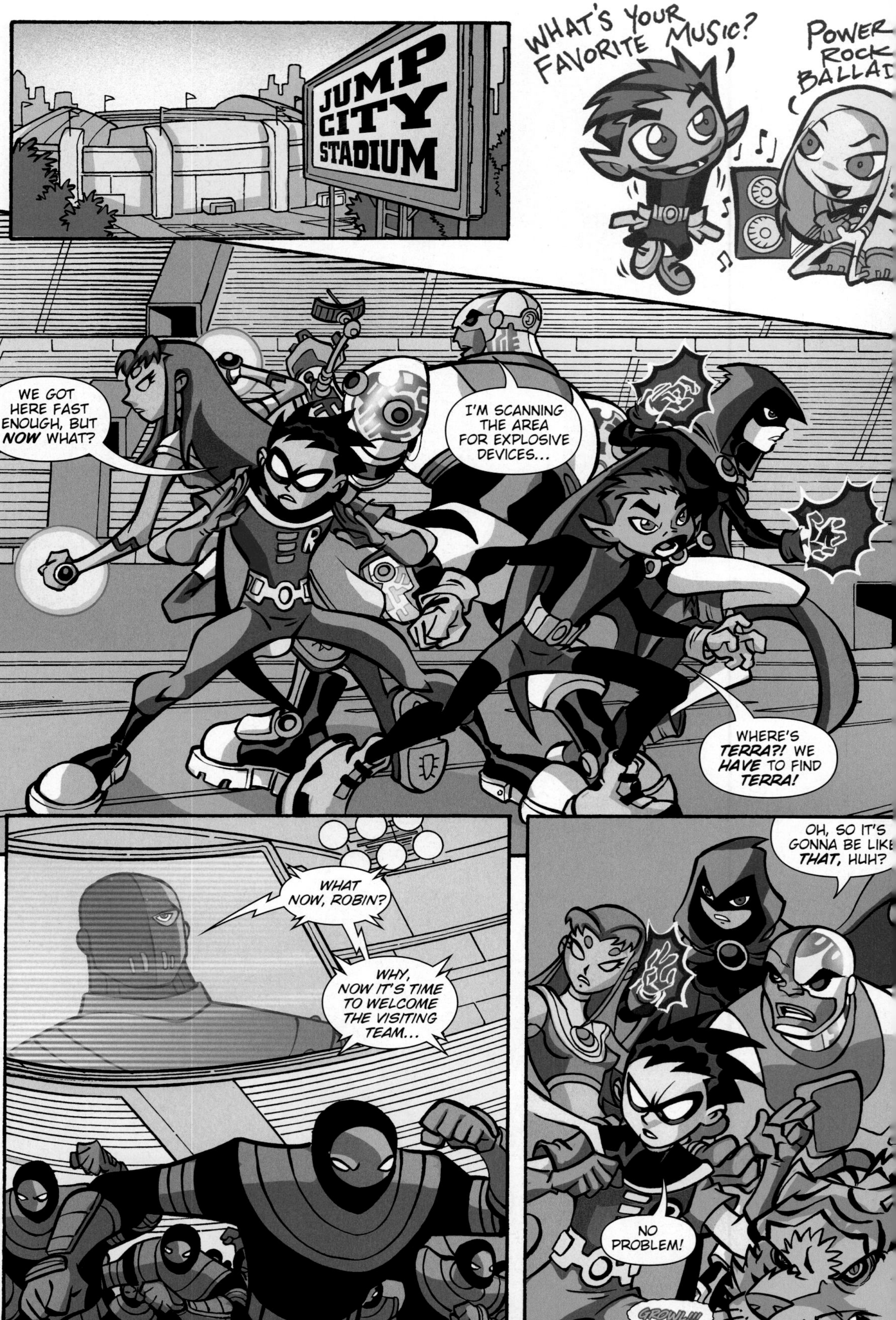
JUMP CITY STADIUM
WHAT'S YOUR FAVORITE MUSIC?
POWER ROCK BALLA
WE GOT HERE FAST ENOUGH, BUT NOW WHAT?
I'M SCANNING THE AREA FOR EXPLOSIVE DEVICES...
WHERE'S TERRA?! WE HAVE TO FIND TERRA!
WHAT NOW, ROBIN?
WHY, NOW IT'S TIME TO WELCOME THE VISITING TEAM...
OH, SO IT'S GONNA BE LIKE THAT, HUH?
NO PROBLEM!
GROWL!!!

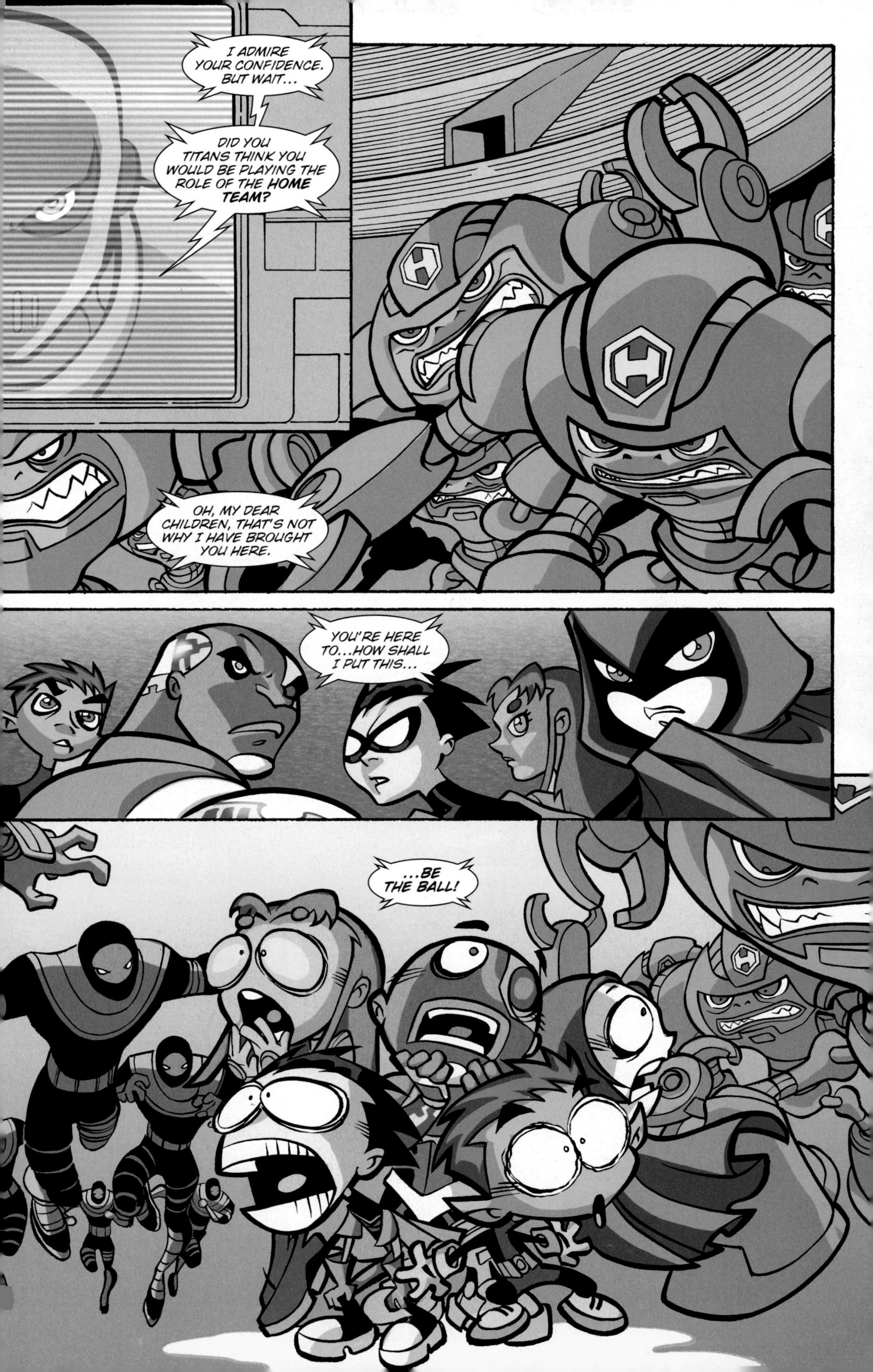
I ADMIRE YOUR CONFIDENCE. BUT WAIT...
DID YOU TITANS THINK YOU WOULD BE PLAYING THE ROLE OF THE **HOME TEAM?**
OH, MY DEAR CHILDREN, THAT'S NOT WHY I HAVE BROUGHT YOU HERE.
YOU'RE HERE TO...HOW SHALL I PUT THIS...
...BE THE BALL!

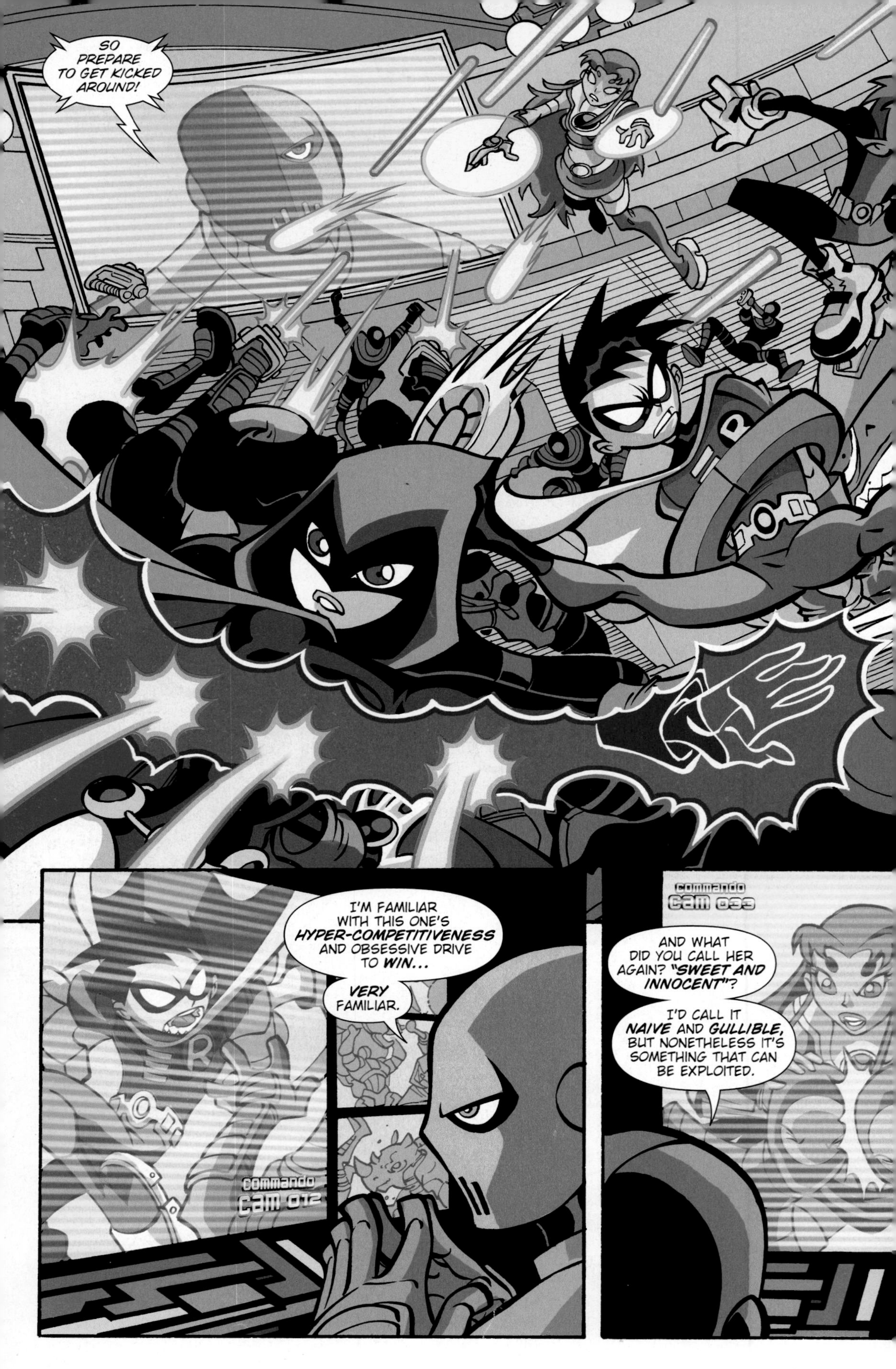
SO PREPARE TO GET KICKED AROUND!
I'M FAMILIAR WITH THIS ONE'S HYPER-COMPETITIVENESS AND OBSESSIVE DRIVE TO WIN...
VERY FAMILIAR.
COMMANDO CAM 012
COMMANDO CAM 033
AND WHAT DID YOU CALL HER AGAIN? "SWEET AND INNOCENT"?
I'D CALL IT NAIVE AND GULLIBLE, BUT NONETHELESS IT'S SOMETHING THAT CAN BE EXPLOITED.

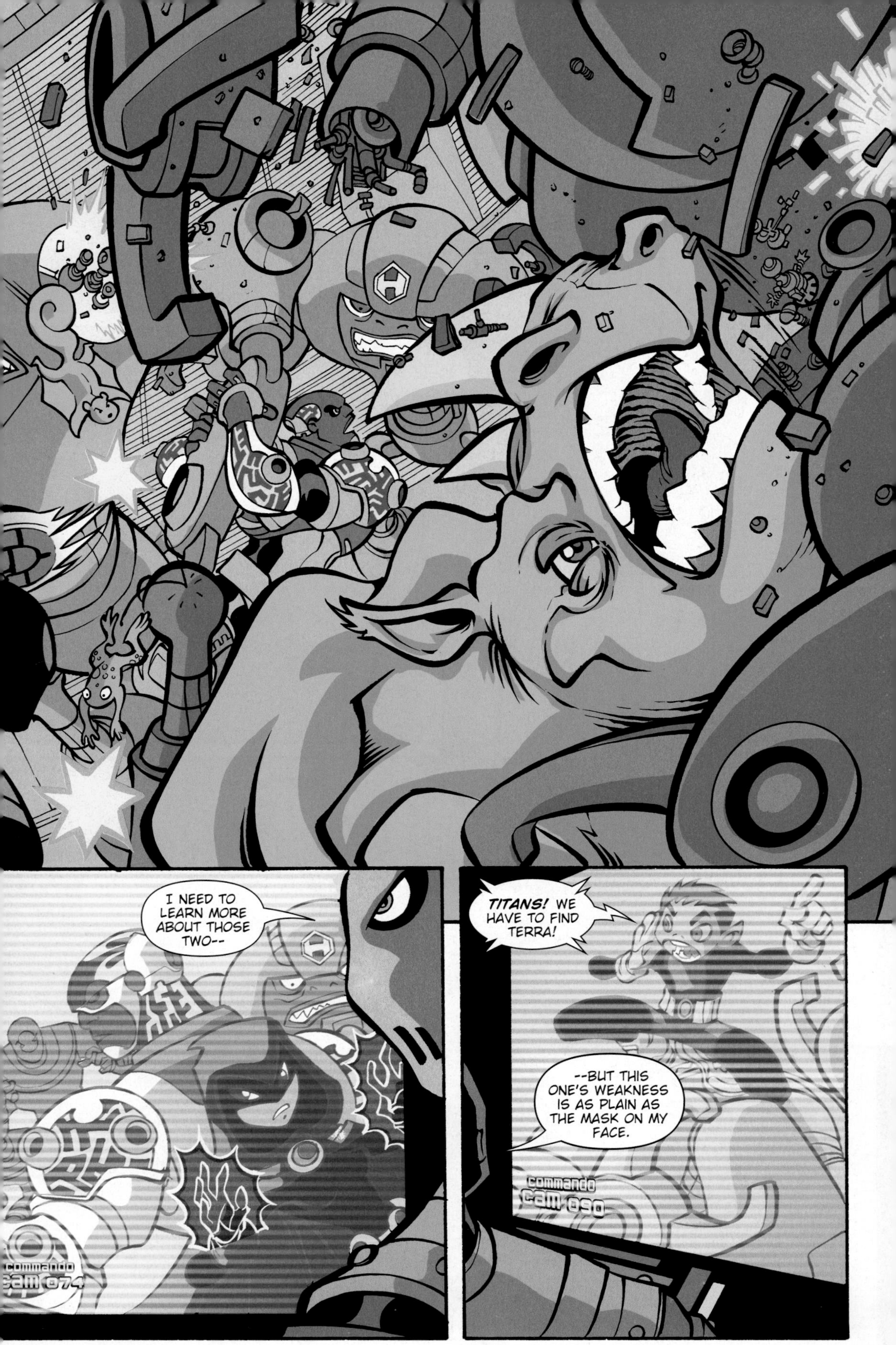
I NEED TO LEARN MORE ABOUT THOSE TWO--
commando cam 074
TITANS! WE HAVE TO FIND TERRA!
--BUT THIS ONE'S WEAKNESS IS AS PLAIN AS THE MASK ON MY FACE.
commando cam 090

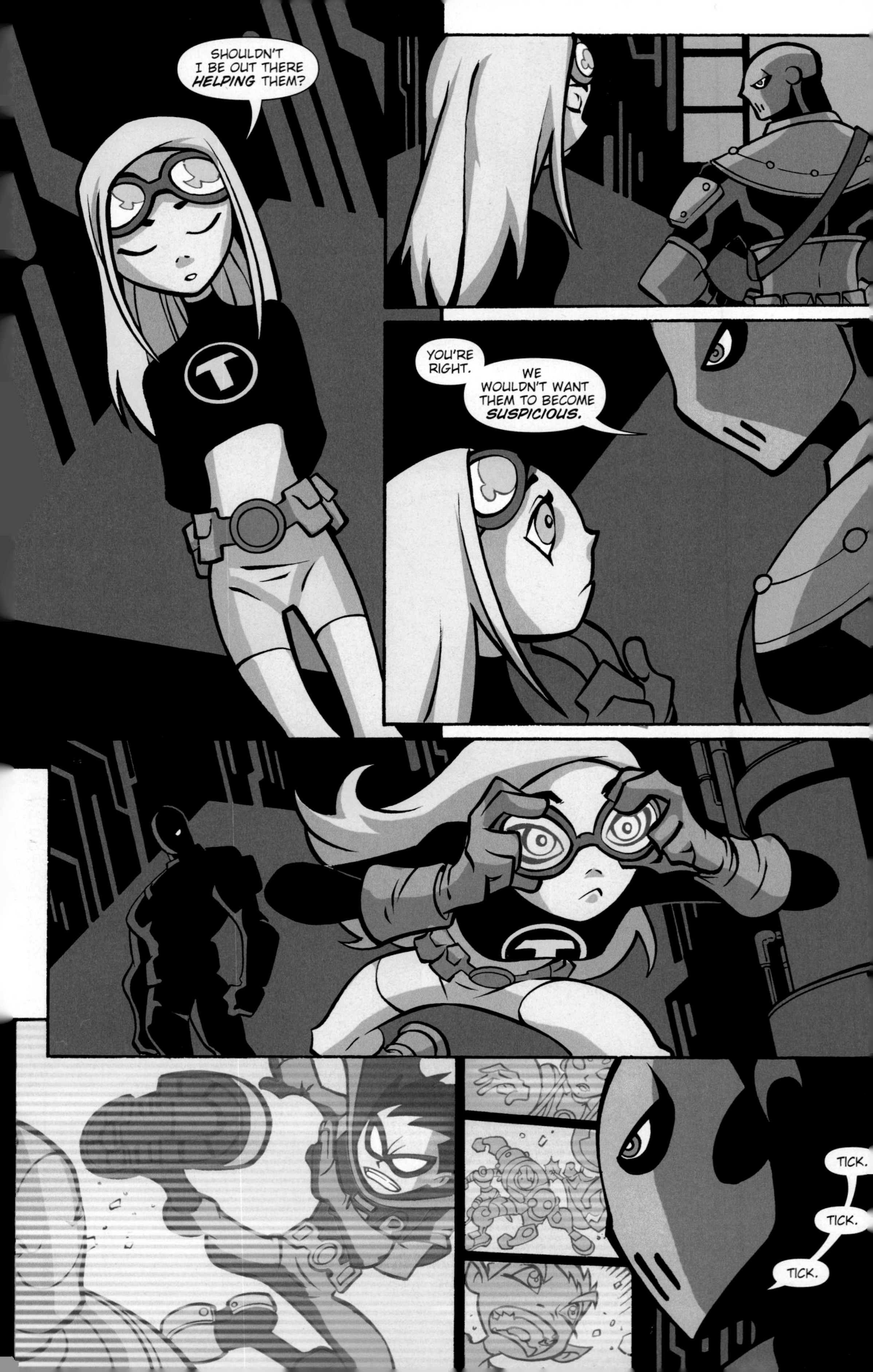
SHOULDN'T I BE OUT THERE HELPING THEM?
YOU'RE RIGHT.
WE WOULDN'T WANT THEM TO BECOME SUSPICIOUS.
TICK.
TICK.
TICK.

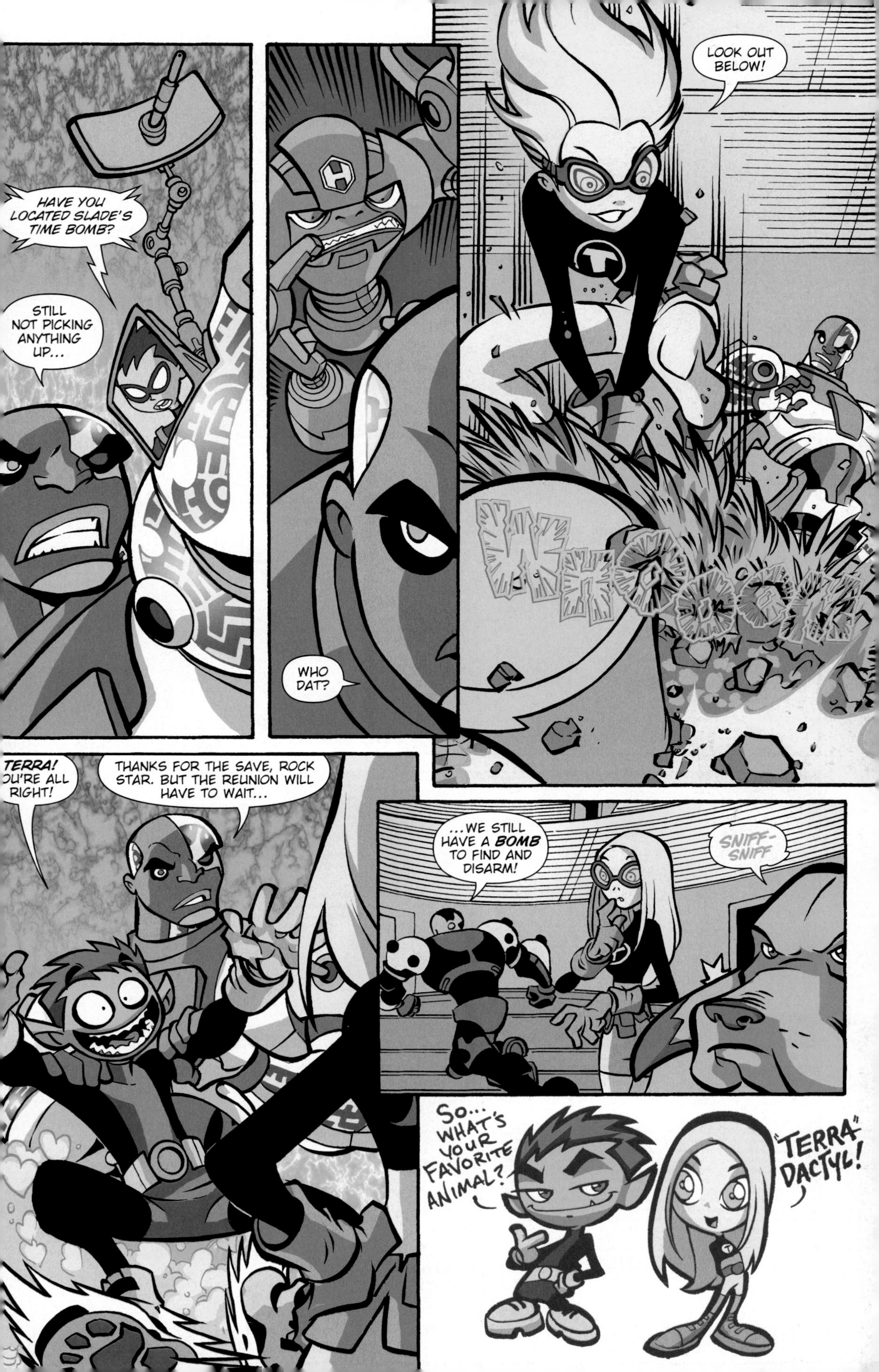
HAVE YOU LOCATED SLADE'S TIME BOMB?
STILL NOT PICKING ANYTHING UP...
WHO DAT?
LOOK OUT BELOW!
TERRA! YOU'RE ALL RIGHT!
THANKS FOR THE SAVE, ROCK STAR. BUT THE REUNION WILL HAVE TO WAIT...
...WE STILL HAVE A BOMB TO FIND AND DISARM!
SNIFF-SNIFF
SO... WHAT'S YOUR FAVORITE ANIMAL?
"TERRA" DACTYL!

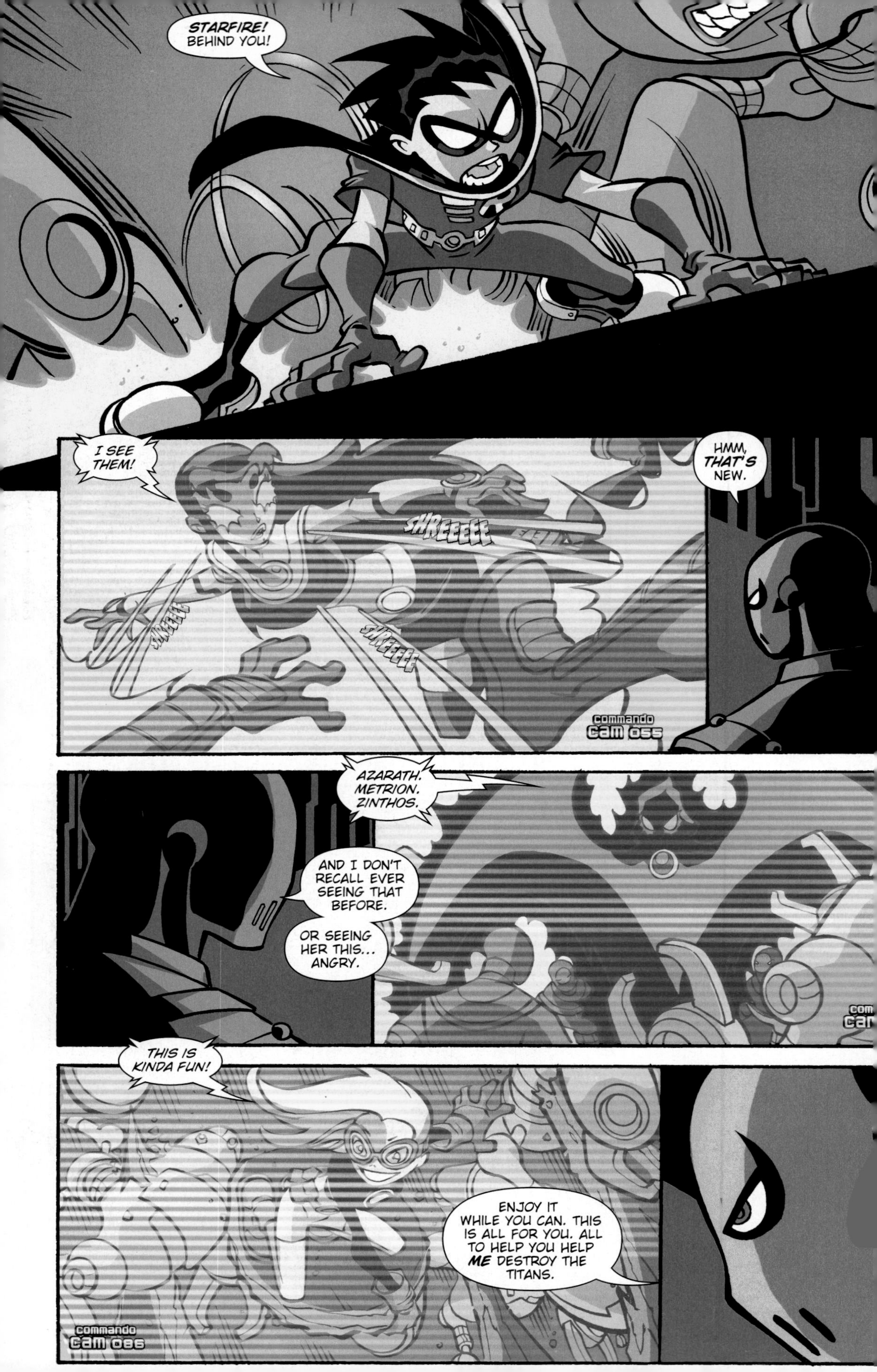
STARFIRE! BEHIND YOU!
I SEE THEM!
HMM, THAT'S NEW.
SHREEEEE
SHREEEEE
SHREEEEE
commando CAM 055
AZARATH. METRION. ZINTHOS.
AND I DON'T RECALL EVER SEEING THAT BEFORE.
OR SEEING HER THIS... ANGRY.
THIS IS KINDA FUN!
ENJOY IT WHILE YOU CAN. THIS IS ALL FOR YOU. ALL TO HELP YOU HELP ME DESTROY THE TITANS.
commando CAM 086

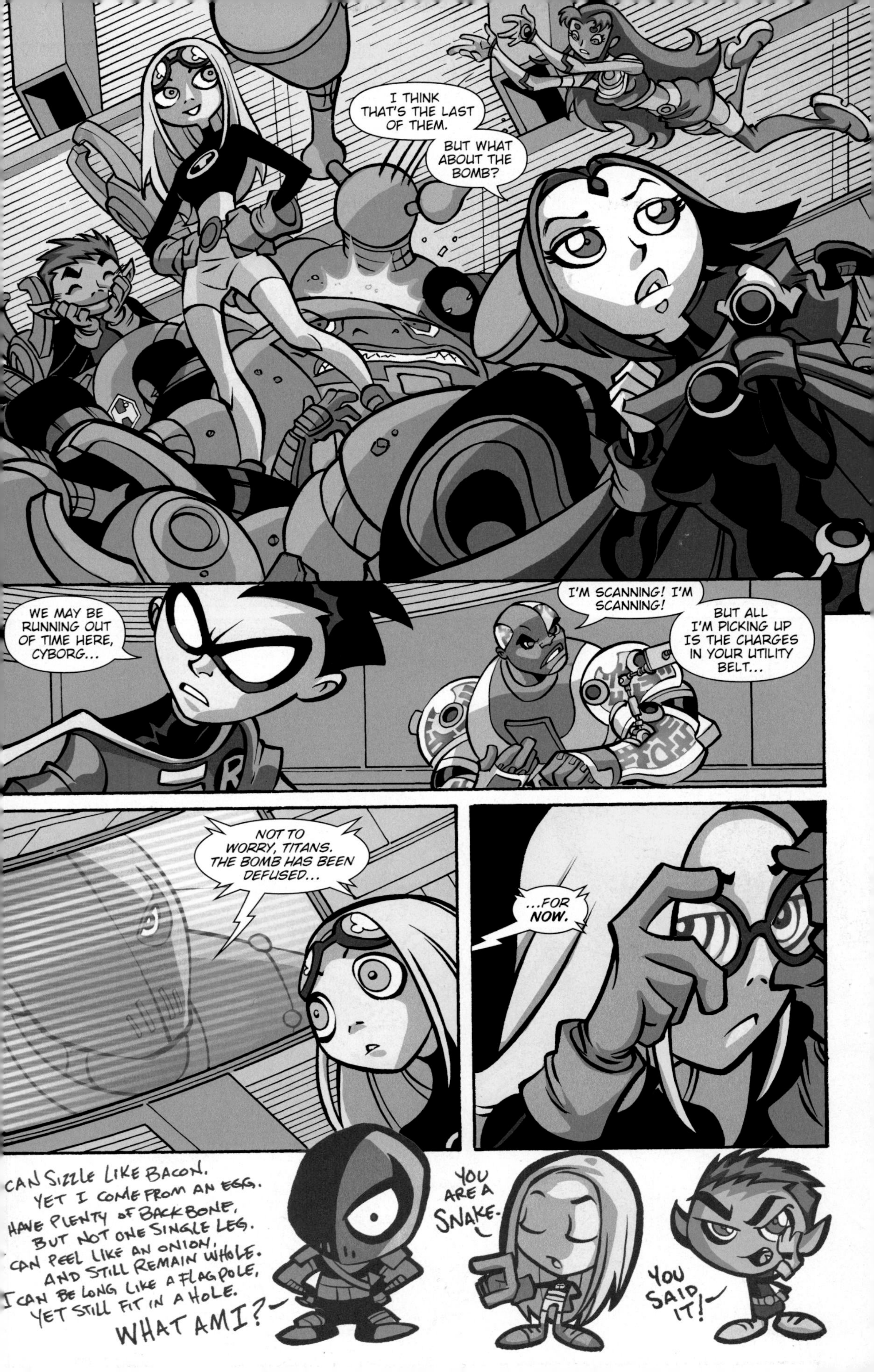

I THINK THAT'S THE LAST OF THEM.
BUT WHAT ABOUT THE BOMB?
WE MAY BE RUNNING OUT OF TIME HERE, CYBORG...
I'M SCANNING! I'M SCANNING!
BUT ALL I'M PICKING UP IS THE CHARGES IN YOUR UTILITY BELT...
NOT TO WORRY, TITANS. THE BOMB HAS BEEN DEFUSED...
...FOR NOW.
I CAN SIZZLE LIKE BACON, YET I COME FROM AN EGG. I HAVE PLENTY OF BACKBONE, BUT NOT ONE SINGLE LEG. I CAN PEEL LIKE AN ONION, AND STILL REMAIN WHOLE. I CAN BE LONG LIKE A FLAGPOLE, YET STILL FIT IN A HOLE. WHAT AM I?
YOU ARE A SNAKE.
YOU SAID IT!

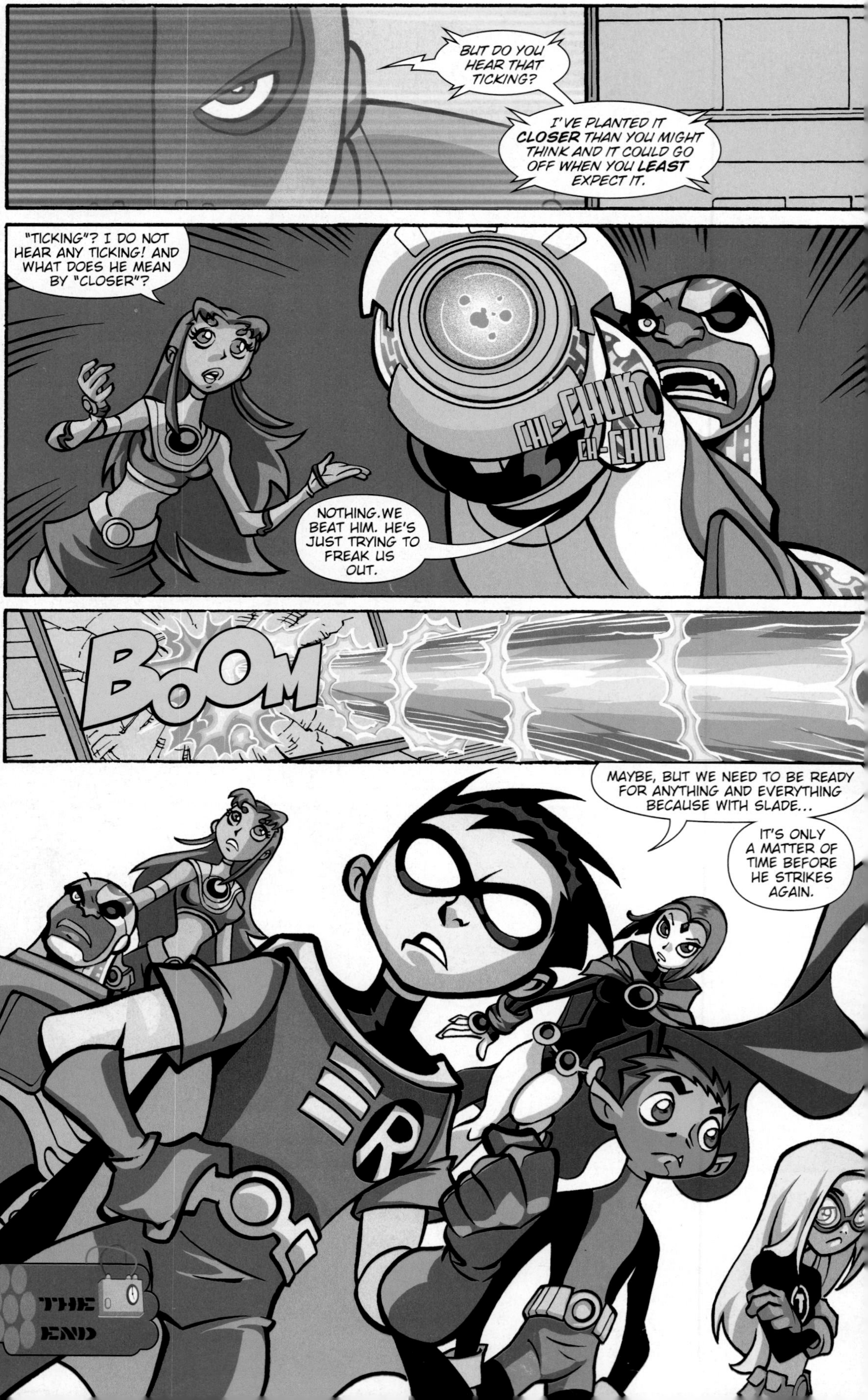
BUT DO YOU HEAR THAT TICKING?
I'VE PLANTED IT **CLOSER** THAN YOU MIGHT THINK AND IT COULD GO OFF **WHEN** YOU **LEAST** EXPECT IT.
"TICKING"? I DO NOT HEAR ANY TICKING! AND WHAT DOES HE MEAN BY "CLOSER"?
CH-CHUK
CH-CHIK
NOTHING. WE BEAT HIM. HE'S JUST TRYING TO FREAK US OUT.
BOOM
MAYBE, BUT WE NEED TO BE READY FOR ANYTHING AND EVERYTHING BECAUSE WITH SLADE...
IT'S ONLY A MATTER OF TIME BEFORE HE STRIKES AGAIN.
THE END

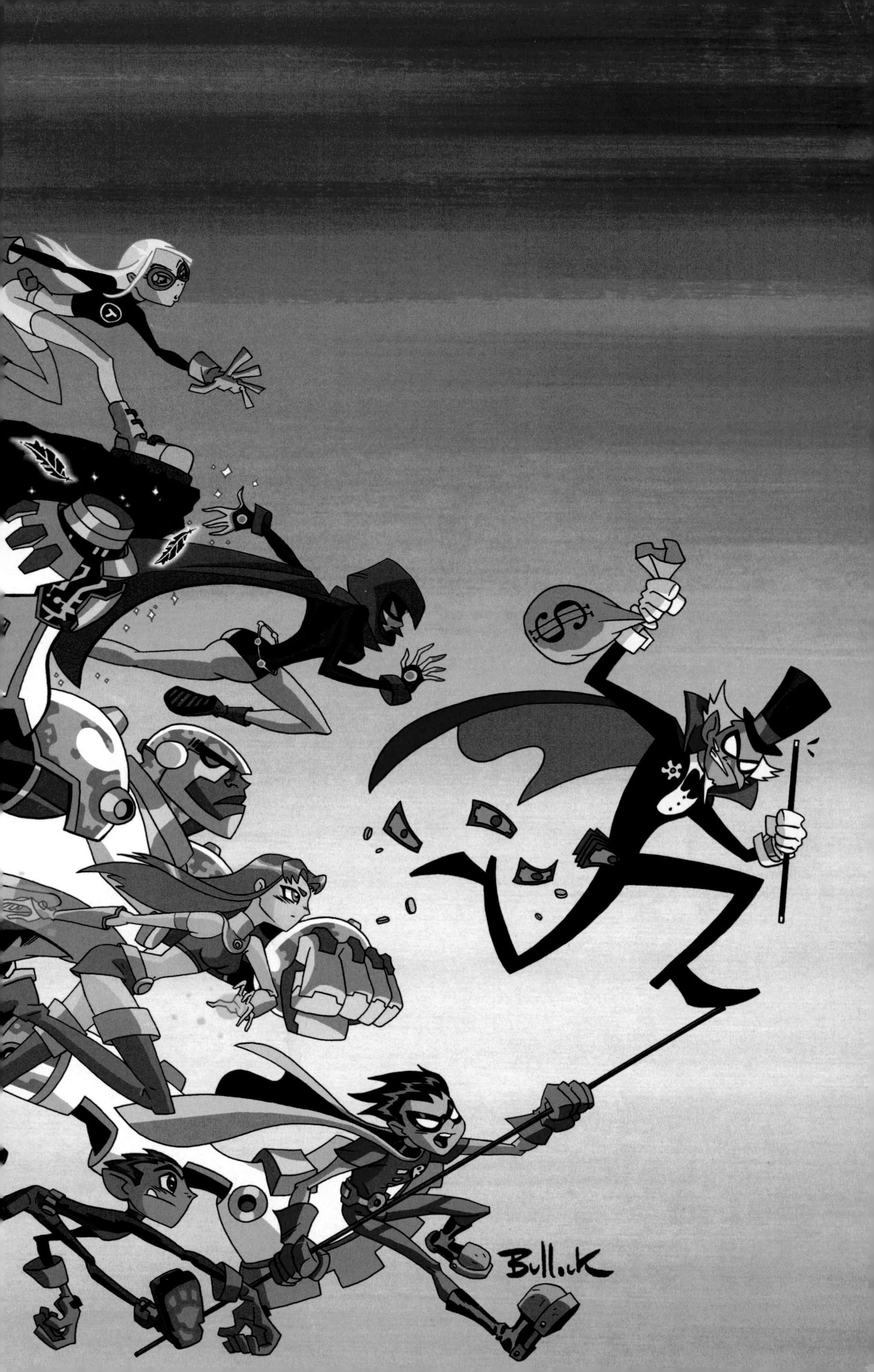
BULLOCK

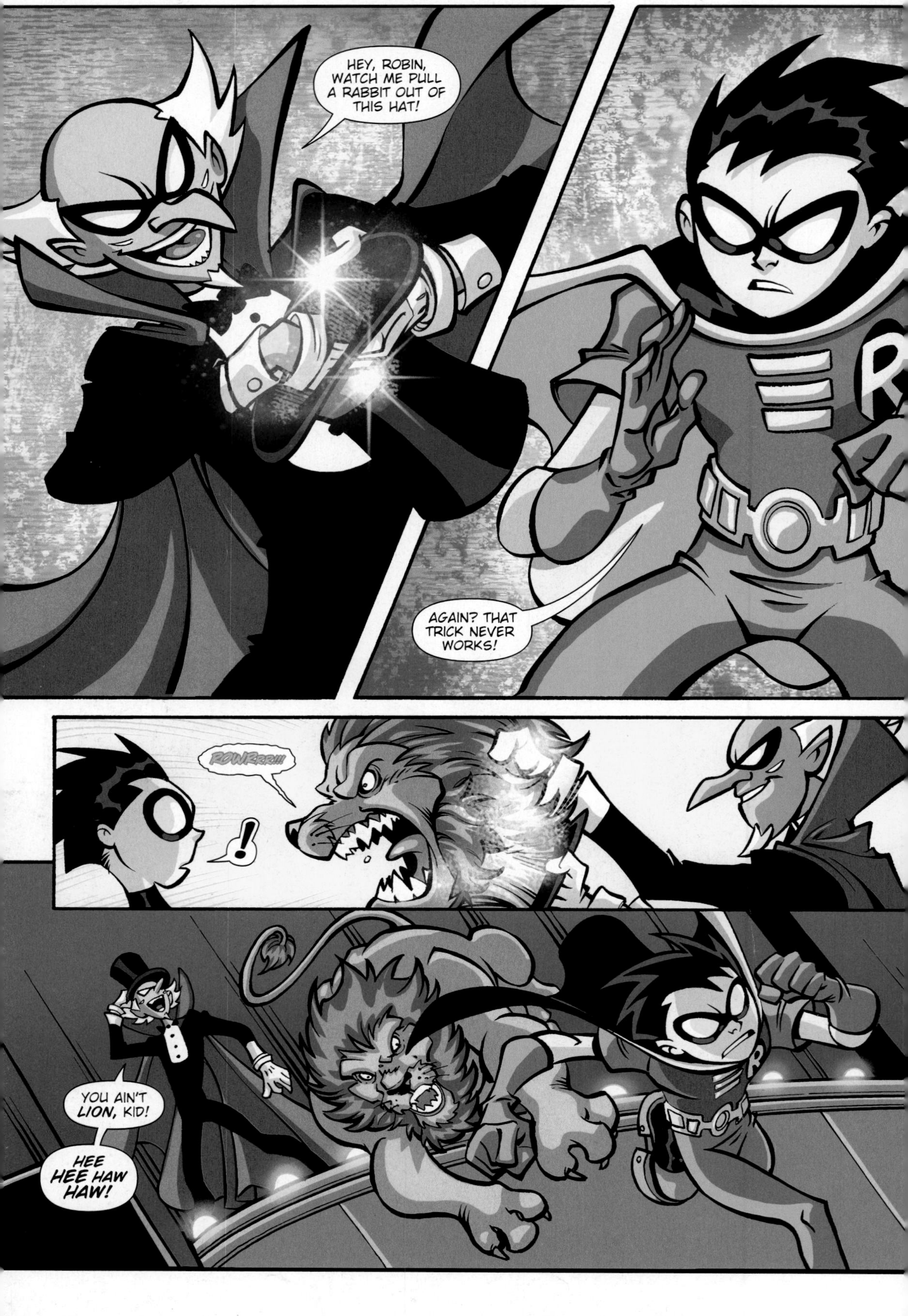
HEY, ROBIN, WATCH ME PULL A RABBIT OUT OF THIS HAT!
AGAIN? THAT TRICK NEVER WORKS!
ROWRrr!!!
!
YOU AIN'T LION, KID!
HEE HEE HAW HAW!

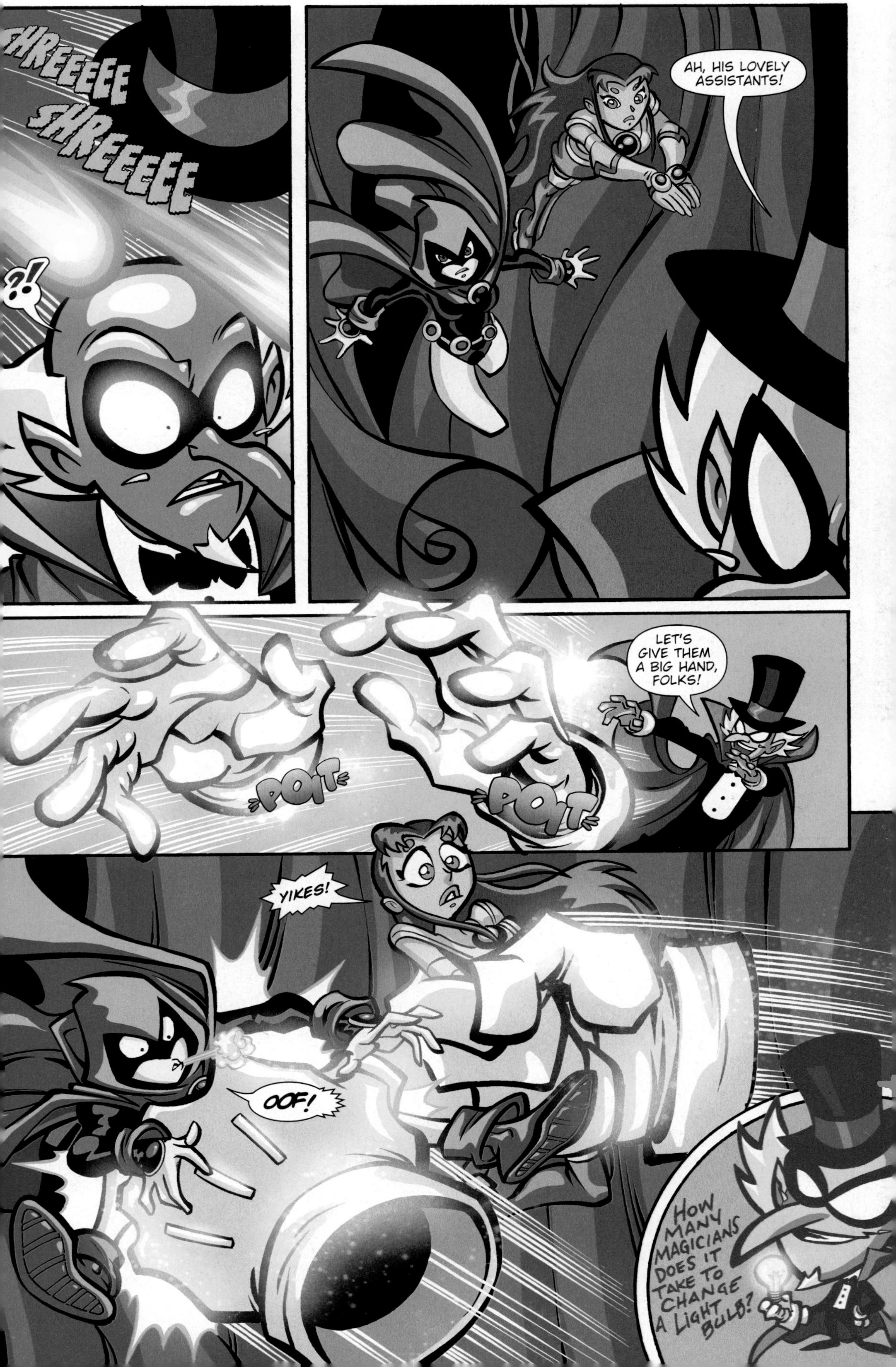
SHREEEEEE
SHREEEEEE
?!
AH, HIS LOVELY ASSISTANTS!
LET'S GIVE THEM A BIG HAND, FOLKS!
POIT
POIT
YIKES!
OOF!
HOW MANY MAGICIANS DOES IT TAKE TO CHANGE A LIGHT BULB?

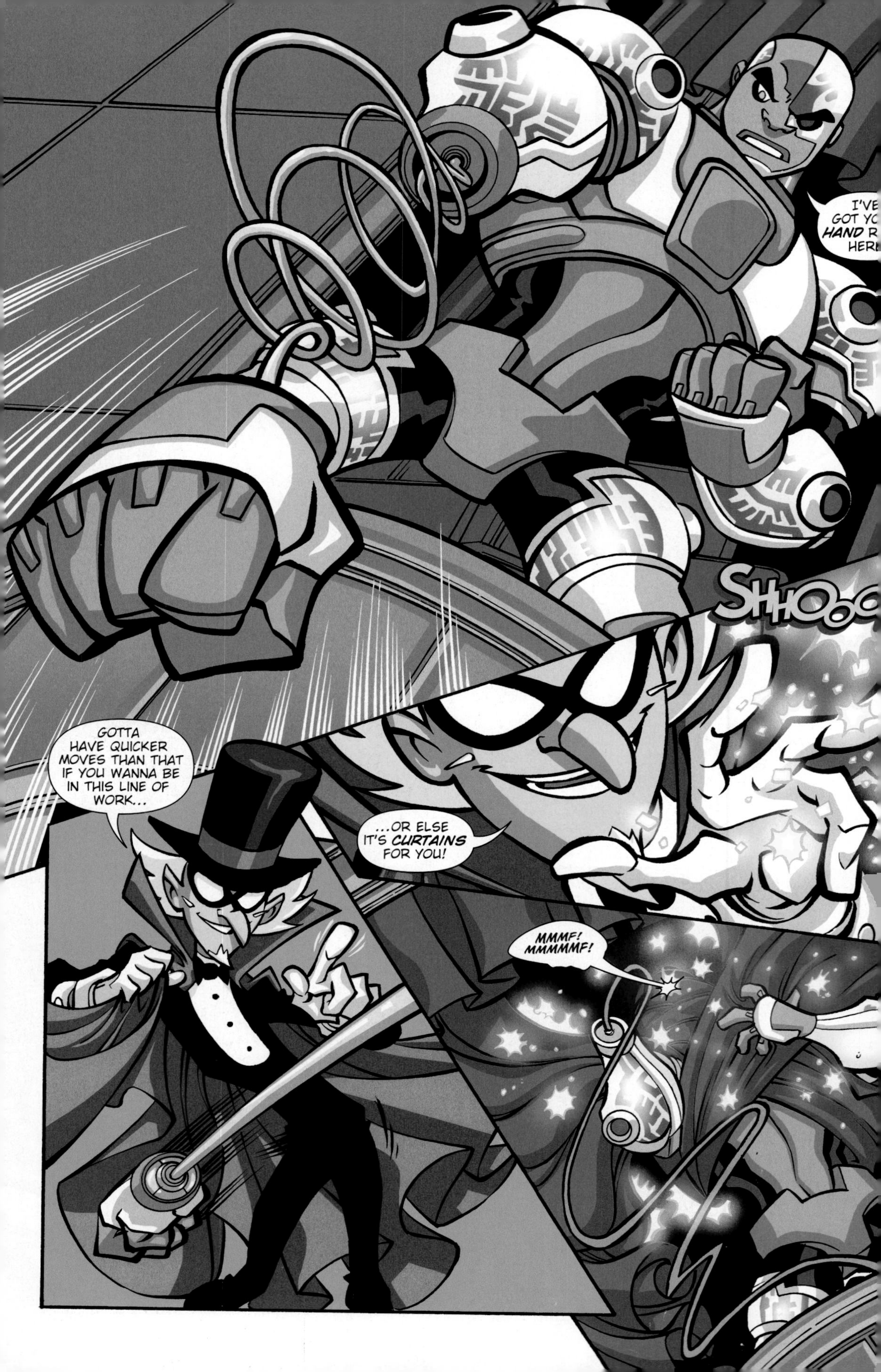
GOTTA HAVE QUICKER MOVES THAN THAT IF YOU WANNA BE IN THIS LINE OF WORK...
...OR ELSE IT'S *CURTAINS* FOR YOU!
MMMF! MMMMMF!

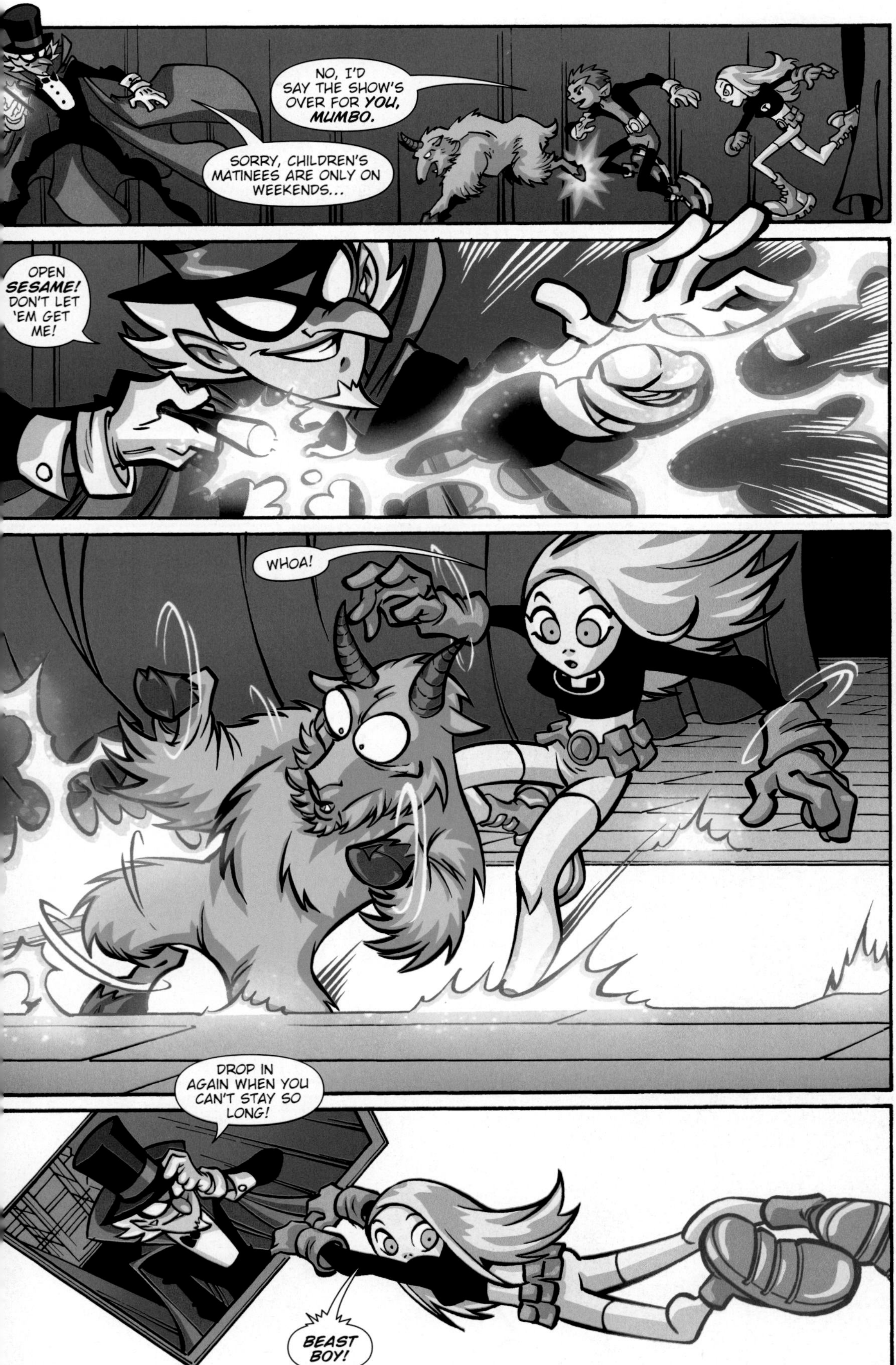

NO, I'D SAY THE SHOW'S OVER FOR YOU, MUMBO.
SORRY, CHILDREN'S MATINEES ARE ONLY ON WEEKENDS...
OPEN SESAME! DON'T LET 'EM GET ME!
WHOA!
DROP IN AGAIN WHEN YOU CAN'T STAY SO LONG!
BEAST BOY!

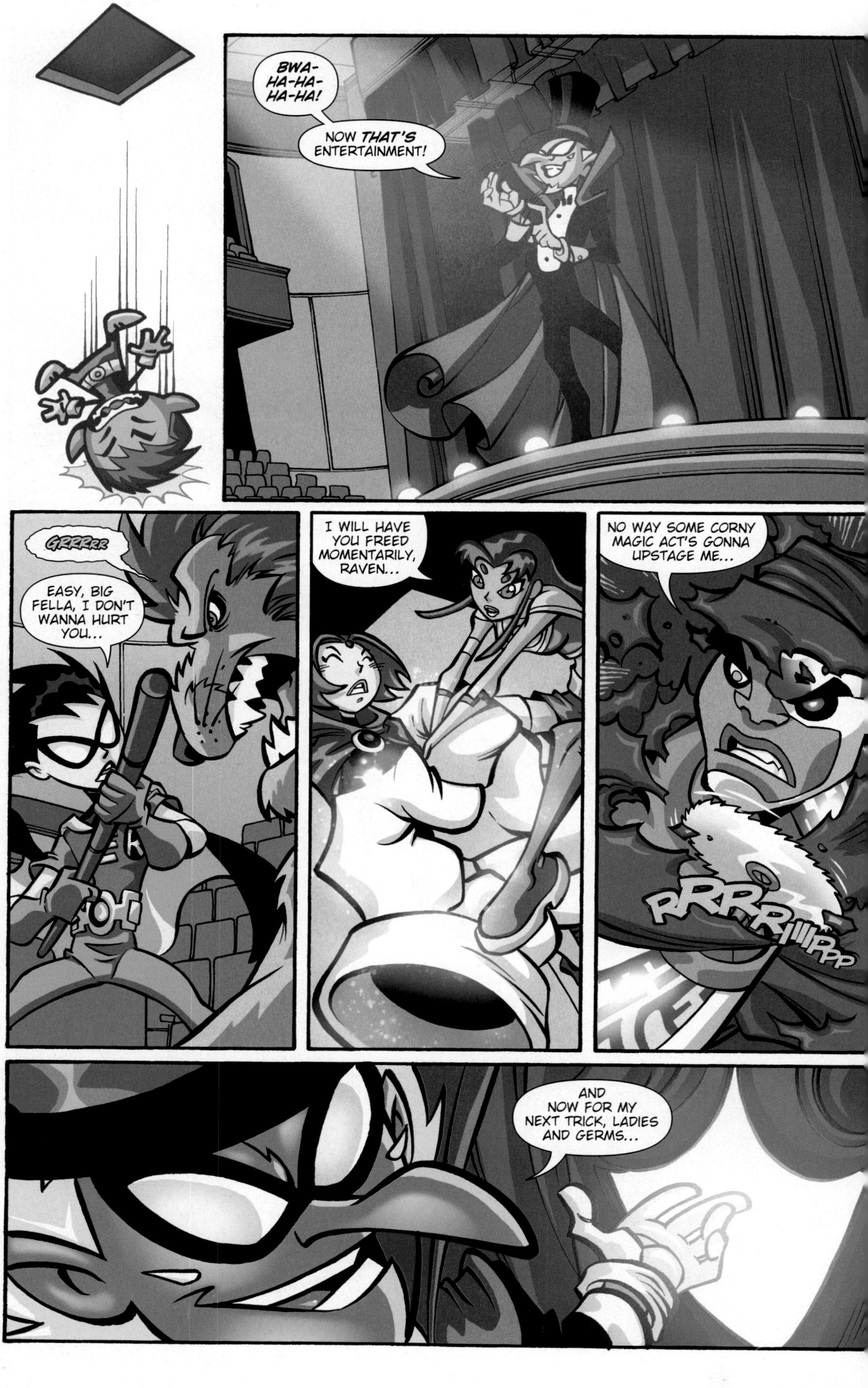
BWA-HA-HA-HA-HA!
NOW THAT'S ENTERTAINMENT!
GRRRRR
EASY, BIG FELLA, I DON'T WANNA HURT YOU...
I WILL HAVE YOU FREED MOMENTARILY, RAVEN...
NO WAY SOME CORNY MAGIC ACT'S GONNA UPSTAGE ME...
RRRRRIIIIRPP
AND NOW FOR MY NEXT TRICK, LADIES AND GERMS...

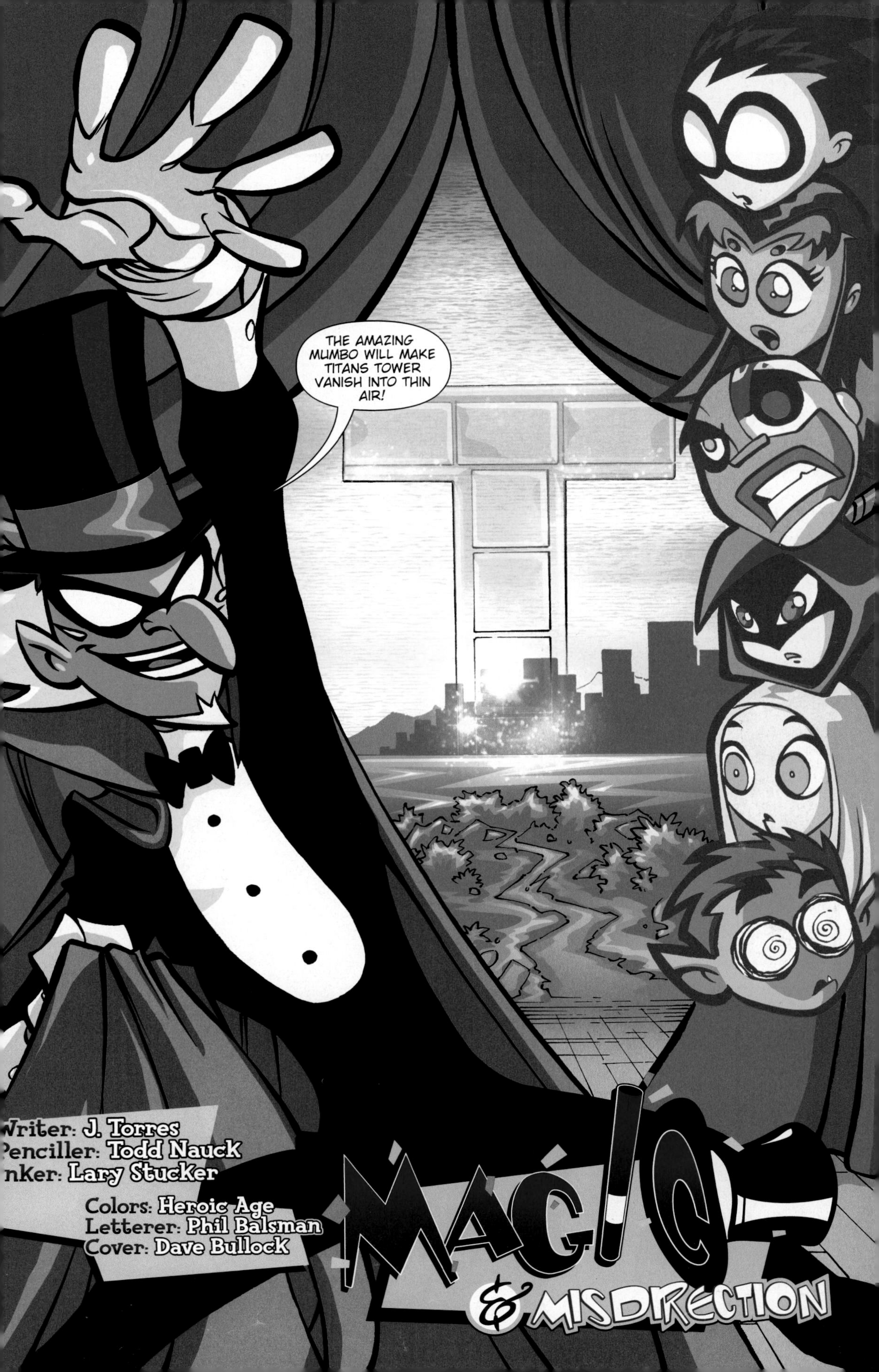
THE AMAZING MUMBO WILL MAKE TITANS TOWER VANISH INTO THIN AIR!
Writer: J. Torres
Penciller: Todd Nauck
Inker: Lary Stucker
Colors: Heroic Age
Letterer: Phil Balsman
Cover: Dave Bullock
MAGIC & MISDIRECTION

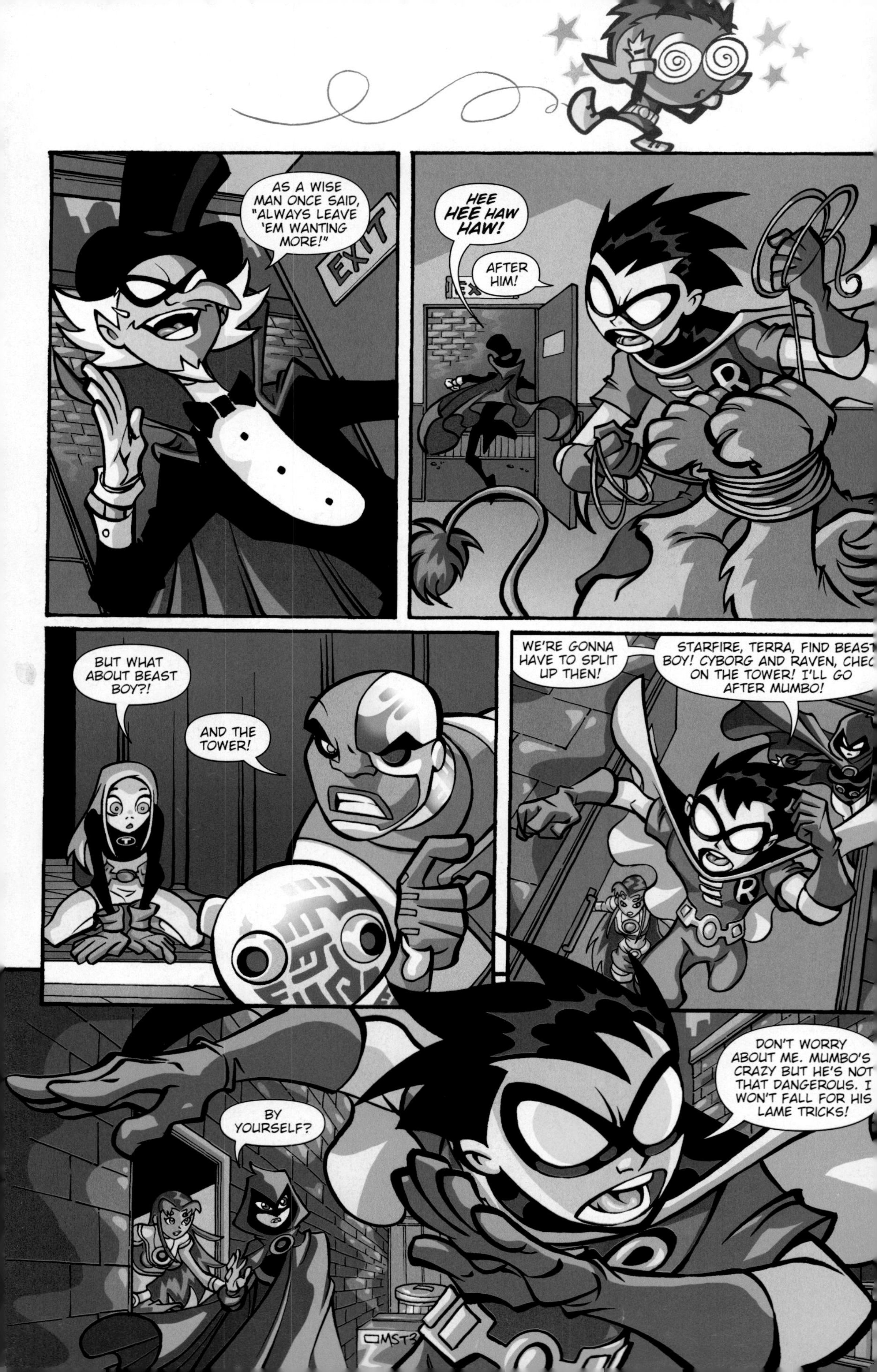
AS A WISE MAN ONCE SAID, "ALWAYS LEAVE 'EM WANTING MORE!"
EXIT
HEE HEE HAW HAW!
AFTER HIM!
BUT WHAT ABOUT BEAST BOY?!
AND THE TOWER!
WE'RE GONNA HAVE TO SPLIT UP THEN!
STARFIRE, TERRA, FIND BEAST BOY! CYBORG AND RAVEN, CHEC ON THE TOWER! I'LL GO AFTER MUMBO!
BY YOURSELF?
DON'T WORRY ABOUT ME. MUMBO'S CRAZY BUT HE'S NOT THAT DANGEROUS. I WON'T FALL FOR HIS LAME TRICKS!

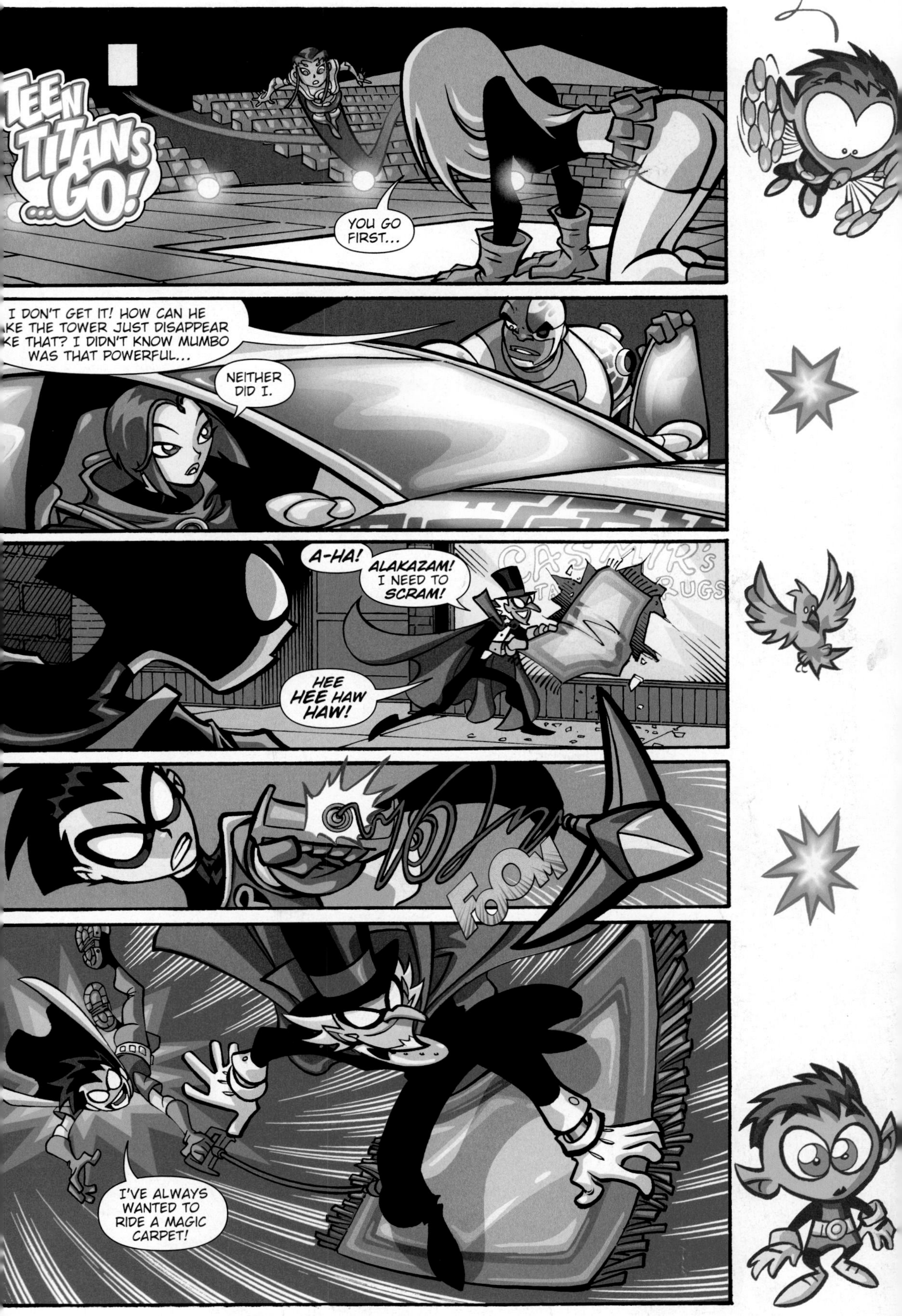

TEEN TITANS ...GO!
YOU GO FIRST...
I DON'T GET IT! HOW CAN HE ...KE THE TOWER JUST DISAPPEAR ...KE THAT? I DIDN'T KNOW MUMBO WAS THAT POWERFUL...
NEITHER DID I.
A-HA!
ALAKAZAM! I NEED TO SCRAM!
CASMIR'S
RUGS
HEE HEE HAW HAW!
FOOM
I'VE ALWAYS WANTED TO RIDE A MAGIC CARPET!

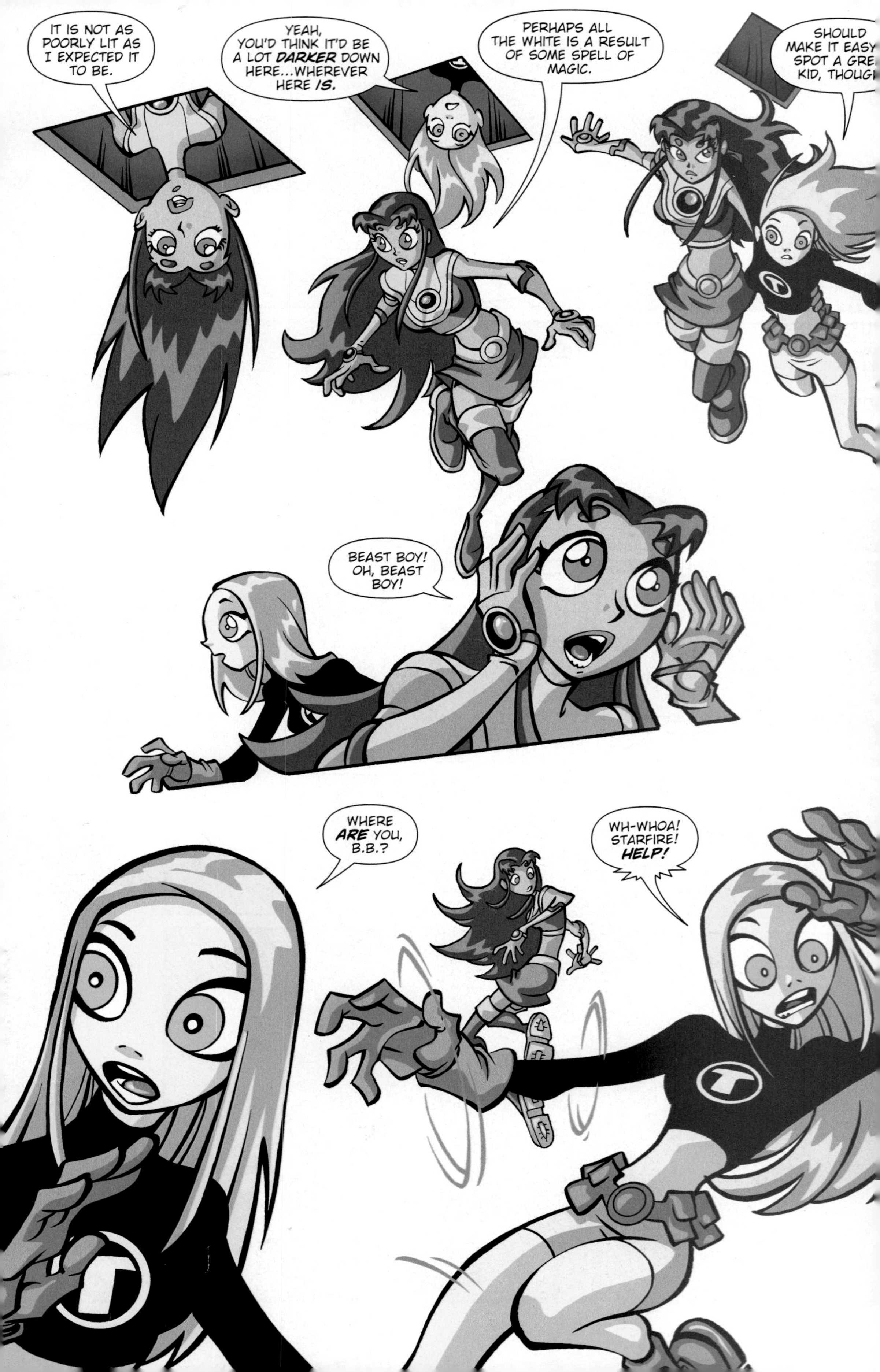

IT IS NOT AS POORLY LIT AS I EXPECTED IT TO BE.
YEAH, YOU'D THINK IT'D BE A LOT DARKER DOWN HERE...WHEREVER HERE IS.
PERHAPS ALL THE WHITE IS A RESULT OF SOME SPELL OF MAGIC.
SHOULD MAKE IT EASY SPOT A GRE KID, THOUG
BEAST BOY! OH, BEAST BOY!
WHERE ARE YOU, B.B.?
WH-WHOA! STARFIRE! HELP!

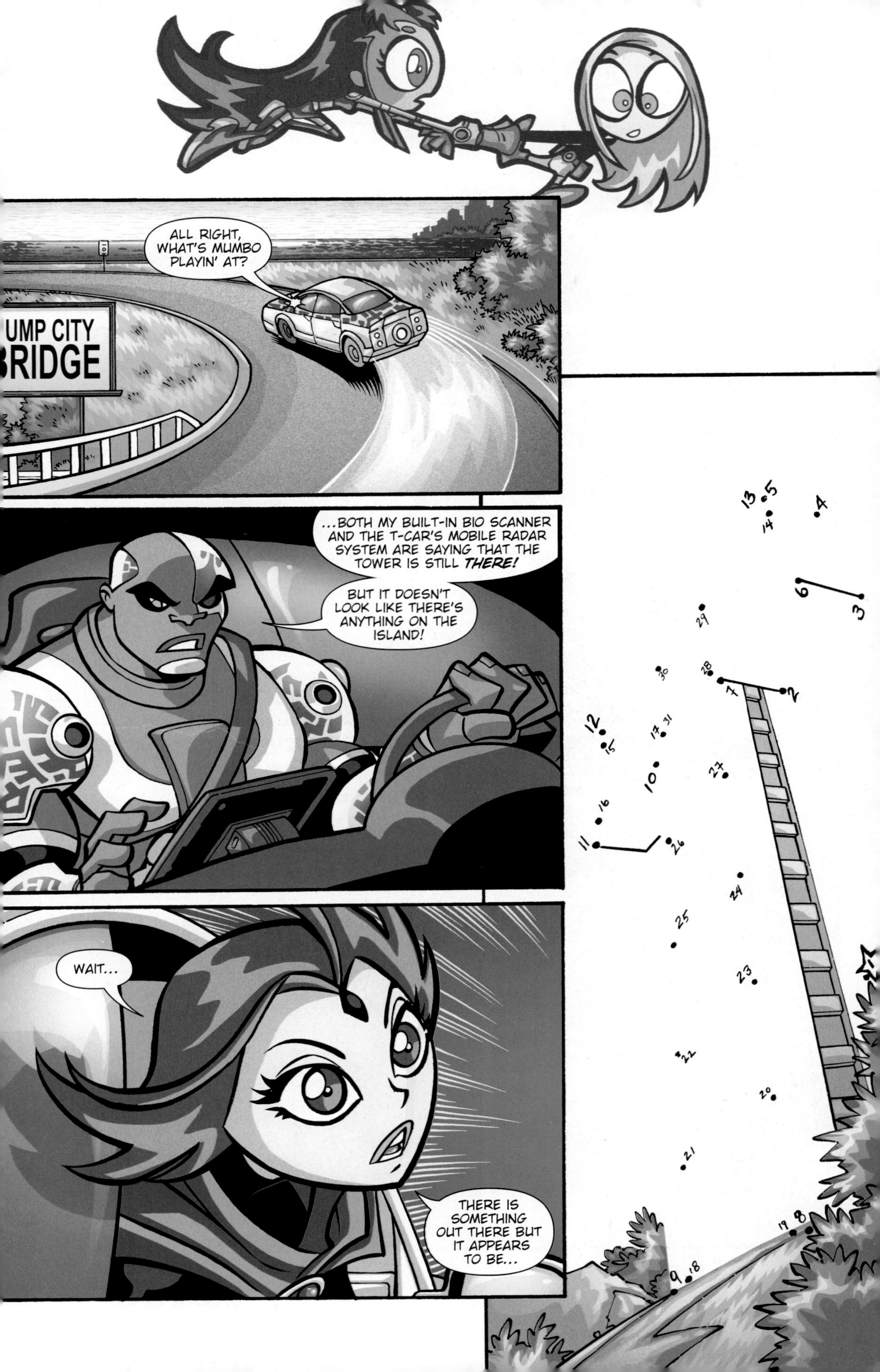
ALL RIGHT, WHAT'S MUMBO PLAYIN' AT?
UMP CITY
BRIDGE
...BOTH MY BUILT-IN BIO SCANNER AND THE T-CAR'S MOBILE RADAR SYSTEM ARE SAYING THAT THE TOWER IS STILL *THERE!*
BUT IT DOESN'T LOOK LIKE THERE'S ANYTHING ON THE ISLAND!
WAIT...
THERE IS SOMETHING OUT THERE BUT IT APPEARS TO BE...

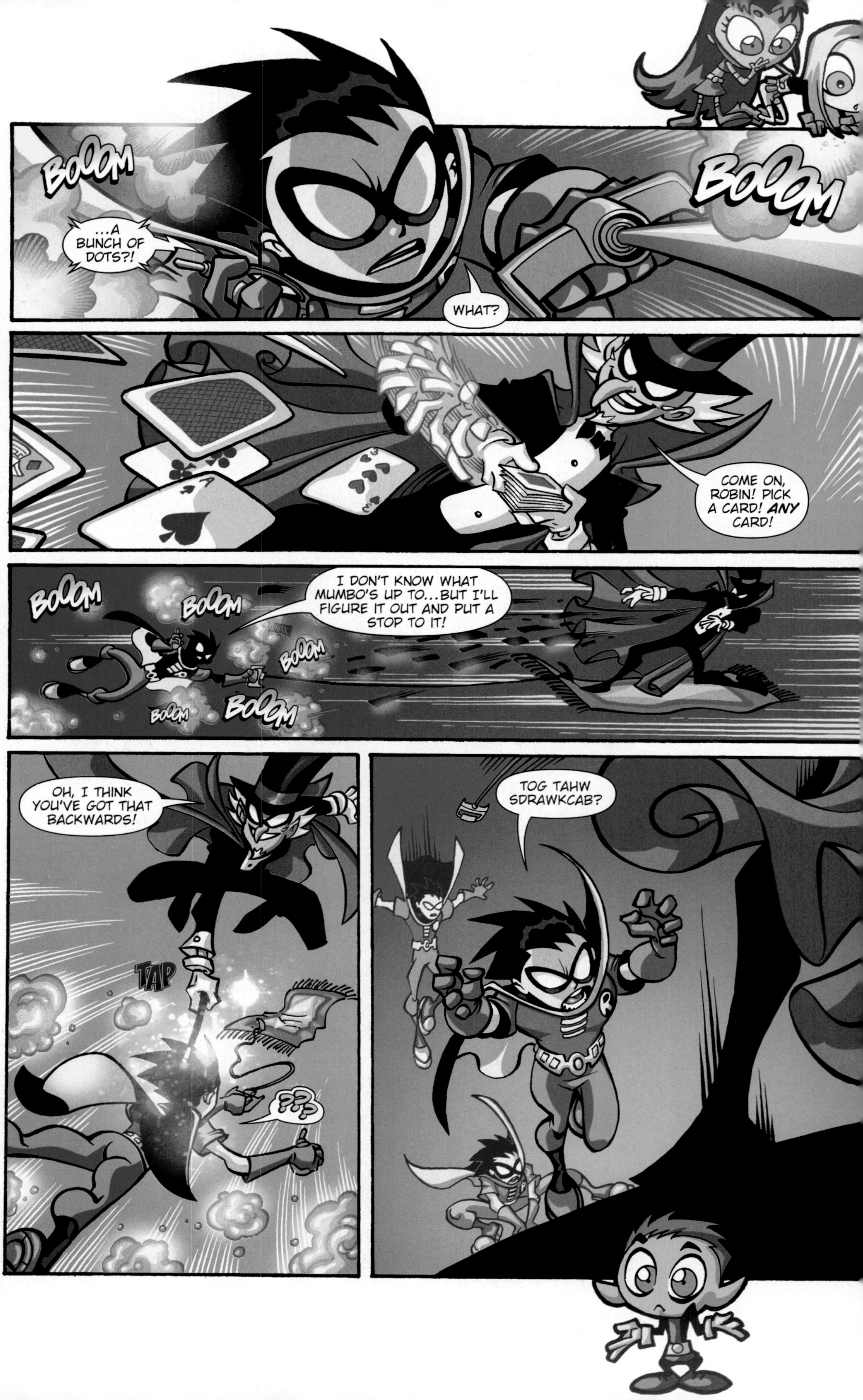
BOOOM
...A BUNCH OF DOTS?!
BOOOM
WHAT?
COME ON, ROBIN! PICK A CARD! ANY CARD!
BOOOM
BOOOM
I DON'T KNOW WHAT MUMBO'S UP TO...BUT I'LL FIGURE IT OUT AND PUT A STOP TO IT!
BOOOM
BOOOM
BOOOM
OH, I THINK YOU'VE GOT THAT BACKWARDS!
TAP
???
TOG TAHW SDRAWKCAB?

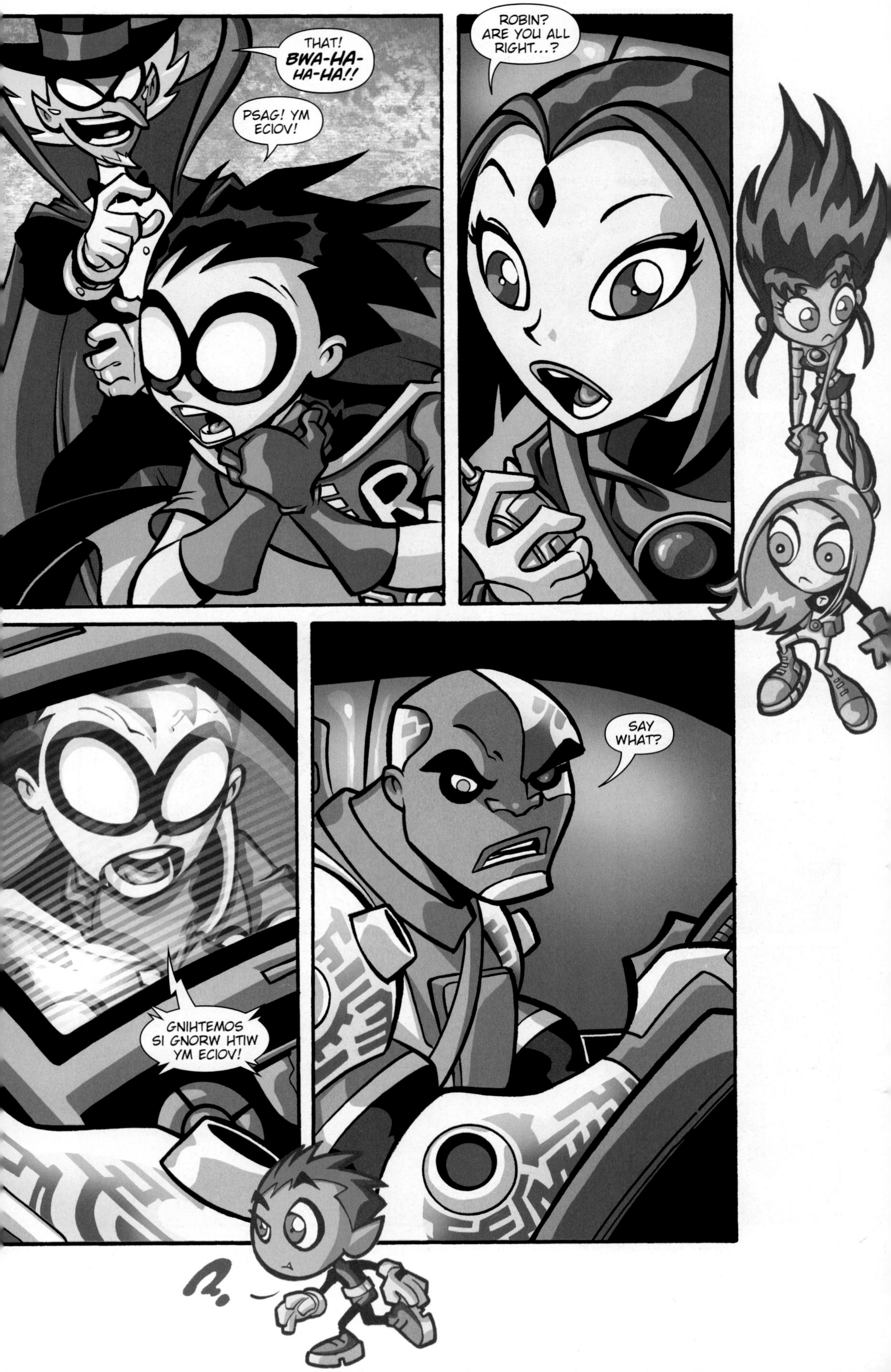
THAT! BWA-HA-HA-HA!!
PSAG! YM ECIOV!
ROBIN? ARE YOU ALL RIGHT...?
GNIHTEMOS SI GNORW HTIW YM ECIOV!
SAY WHAT?

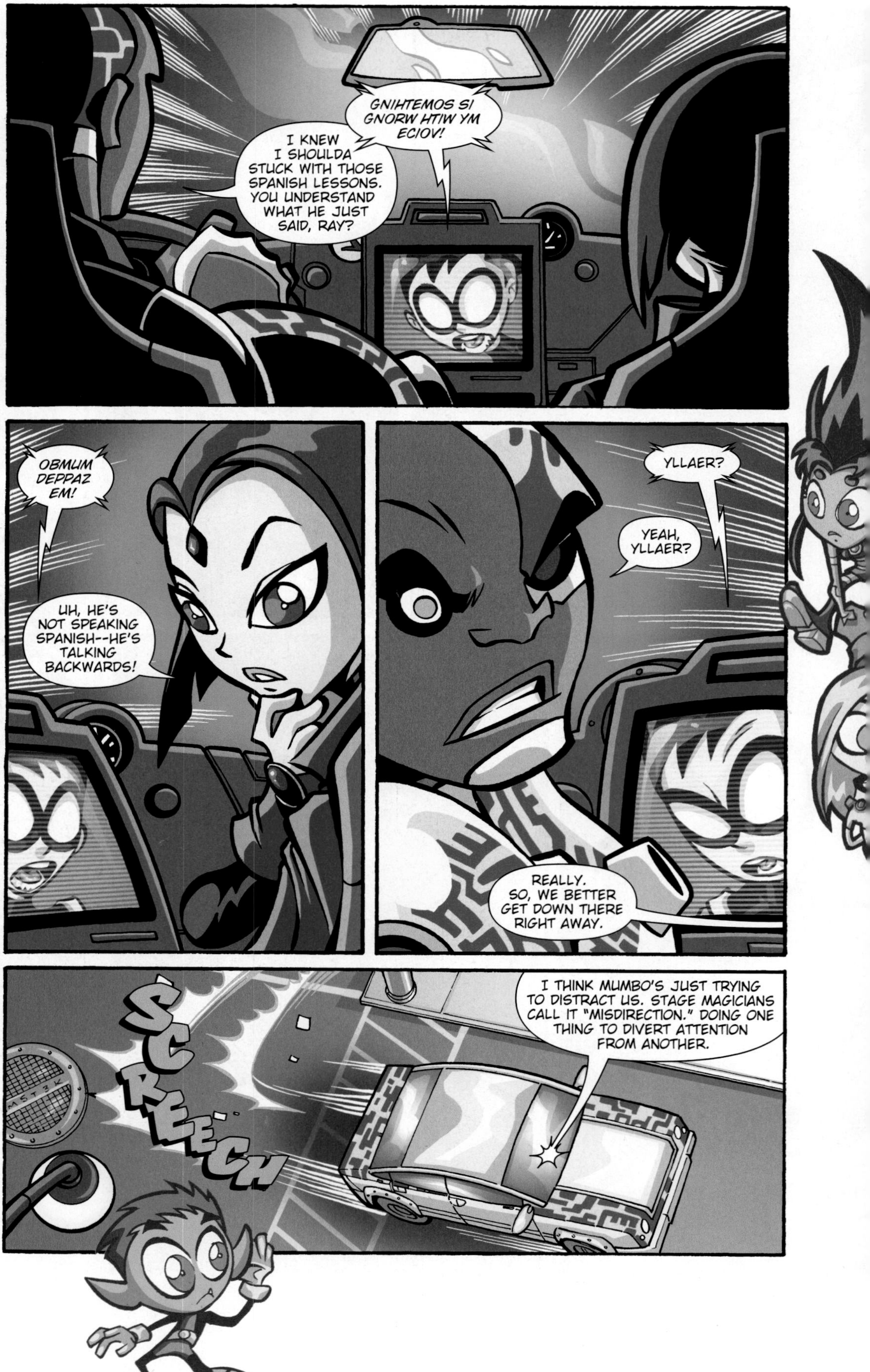
GNIHTEMOS SI GNORW HTIW YM ECIOV!
I KNEW I SHOULDA STUCK WITH THOSE SPANISH LESSONS. YOU UNDERSTAND WHAT HE JUST SAID, RAY?
OBMUM DEPPAZ EM!
UH, HE'S NOT SPEAKING SPANISH--HE'S TALKING BACKWARDS!
YLLAER?
YEAH, YLLAER?
REALLY. SO, WE BETTER GET DOWN THERE RIGHT AWAY.
SCREECH
I THINK MUMBO'S JUST TRYING TO DISTRACT US. STAGE MAGICIANS CALL IT "MISDIRECTION." DOING ONE THING TO DIVERT ATTENTION FROM ANOTHER.

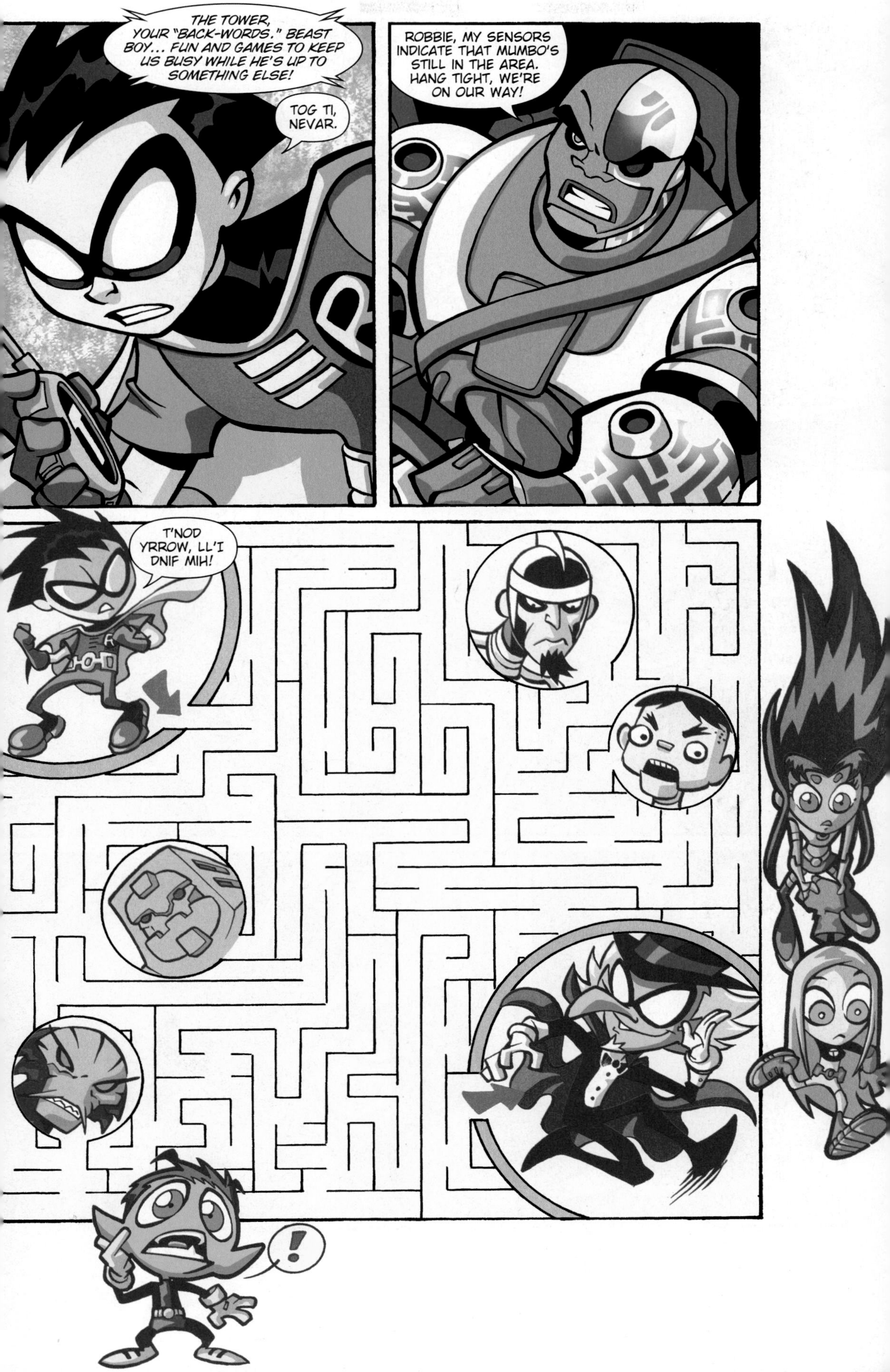
THE TOWER, YOUR "BACK-WORDS." BEAST BOY... FUN AND GAMES TO KEEP US BUSY WHILE HE'S UP TO SOMETHING ELSE!
TOG TI, NEVAR.
ROBBIE, MY SENSORS INDICATE THAT MUMBO'S STILL IN THE AREA. HANG TIGHT, WE'RE ON OUR WAY!
T'NOD YRROW, LL'I DNIF MIH!
!

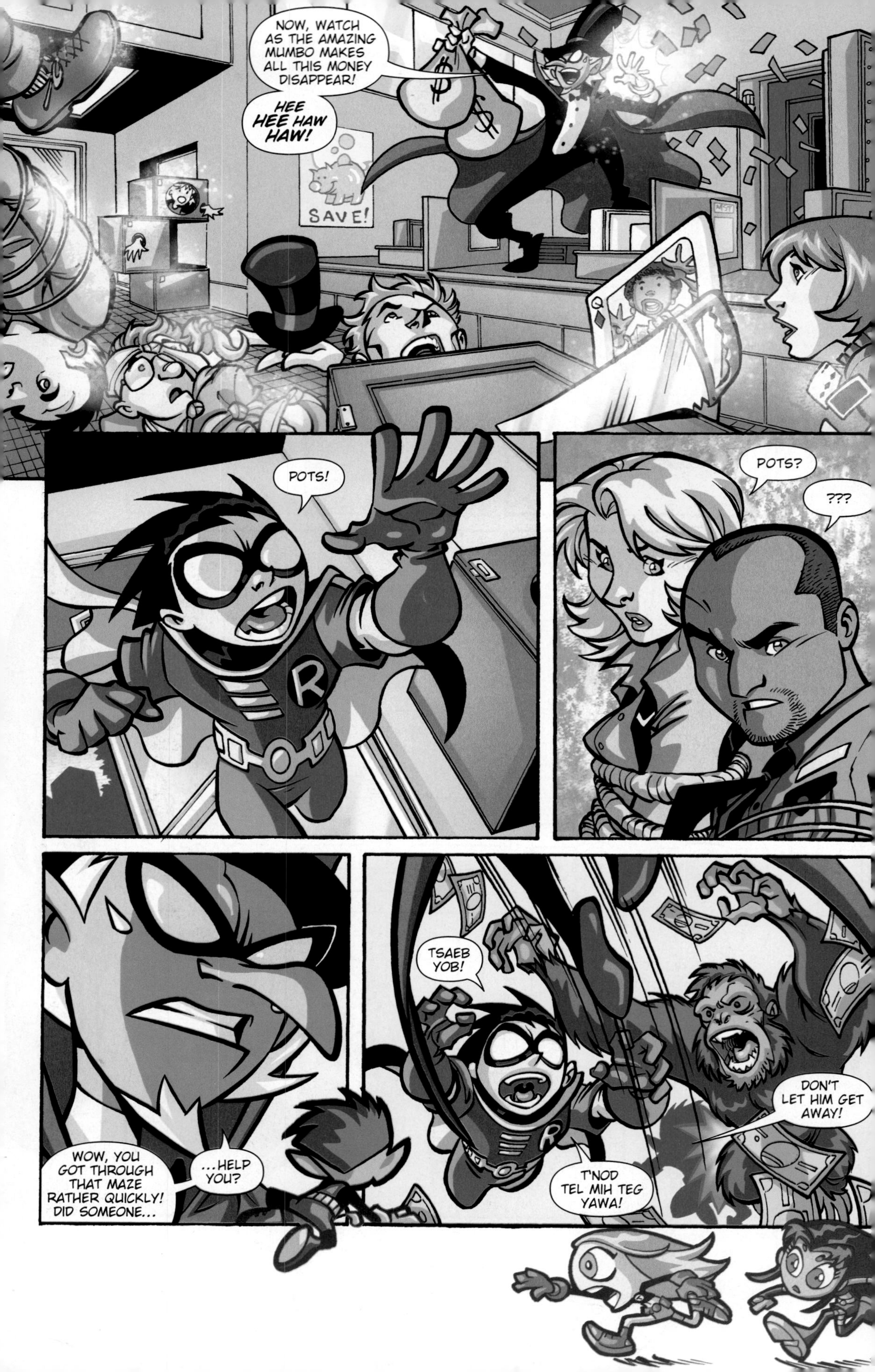
NOW, WATCH AS THE AMAZING MUMBO MAKES ALL THIS MONEY DISAPPEAR!
HEE HEE HAW HAW!
SAVE!
POTS!
POTS?
???
WOW, YOU GOT THROUGH THAT MAZE RATHER QUICKLY! DID SOMEONE...
...HELP YOU?
TSAEB YOB!
DON'T LET HIM GET AWAY!
T'NOD TEL MIH TEG YAWA!

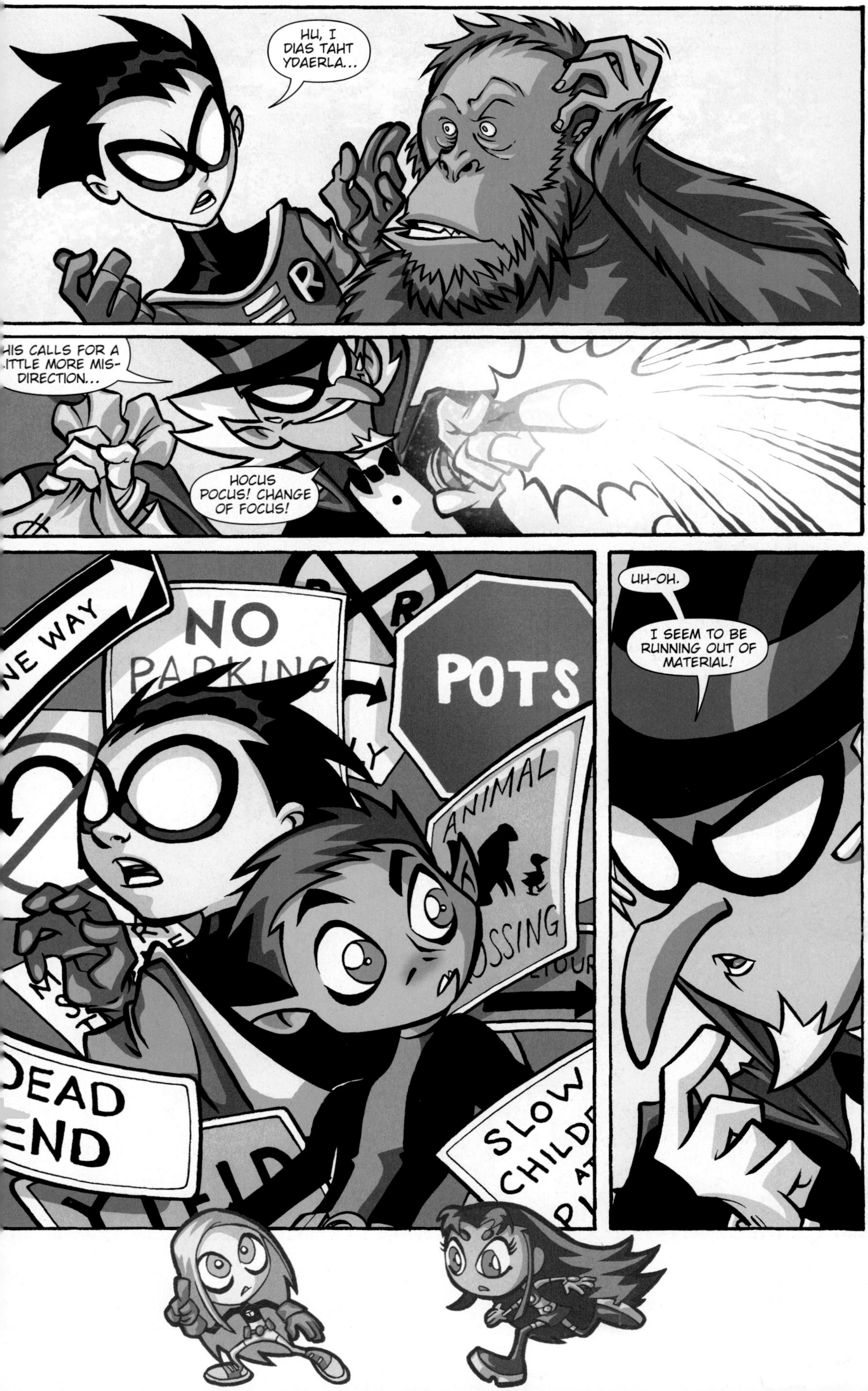
HU, I DIAS TAHT YDAERLA...
HIS CALLS FOR A LITTLE MORE MIS-DIRECTION...
HOCUS POCUS! CHANGE OF FOCUS!
NO PARKING
POTS
ANIMAL
SLOW
UH-OH.
I SEEM TO BE RUNNING OUT OF MATERIAL!

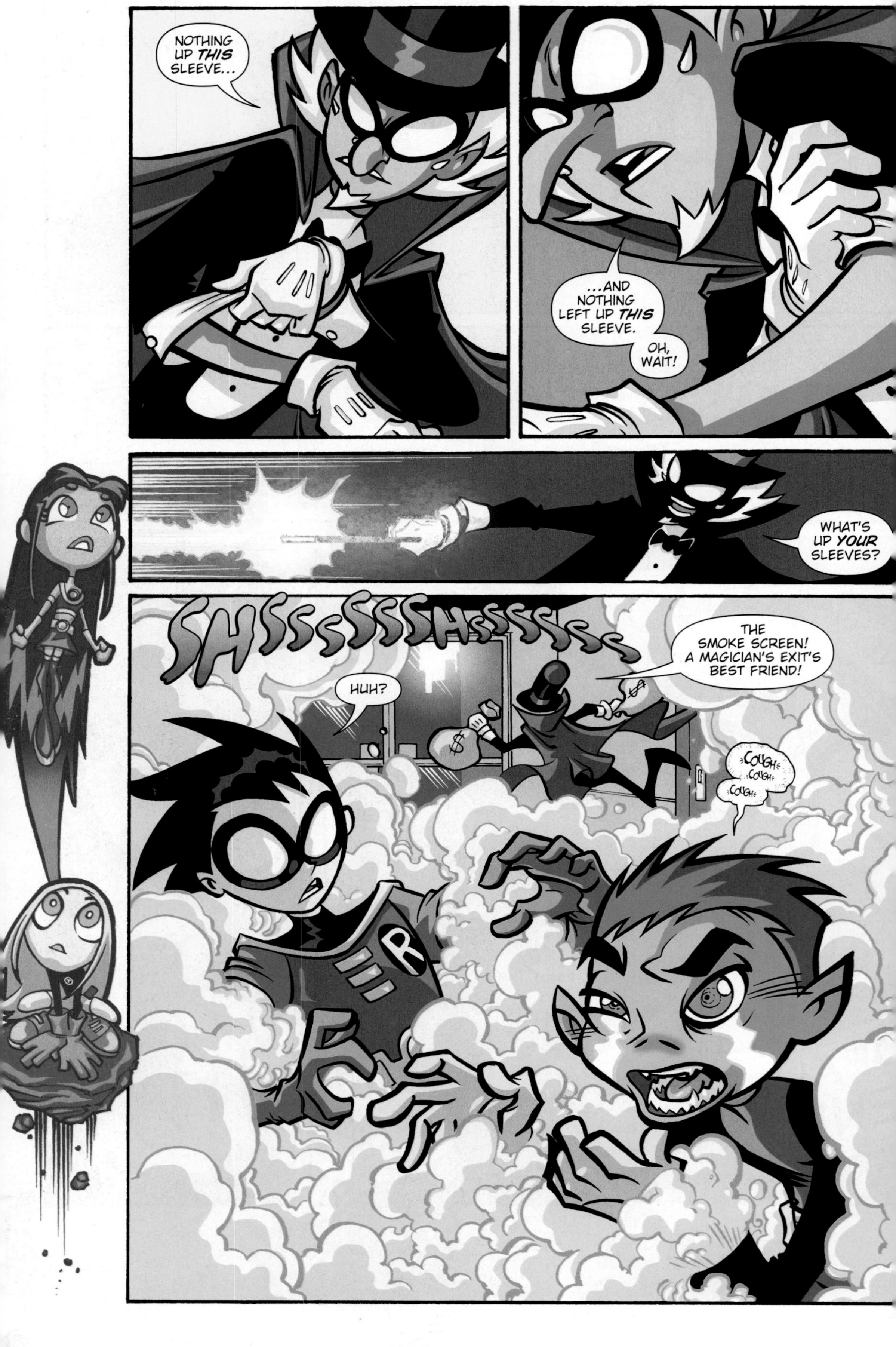
NOTHING UP THIS SLEEVE...
...AND NOTHING LEFT UP THIS SLEEVE.
OH, WAIT!
WHAT'S UP YOUR SLEEVES?
SHSssSSSShsSSSsss
THE SMOKE SCREEN! A MAGICIAN'S EXIT'S BEST FRIEND!
HUH?
COUGH COUGH COUGH

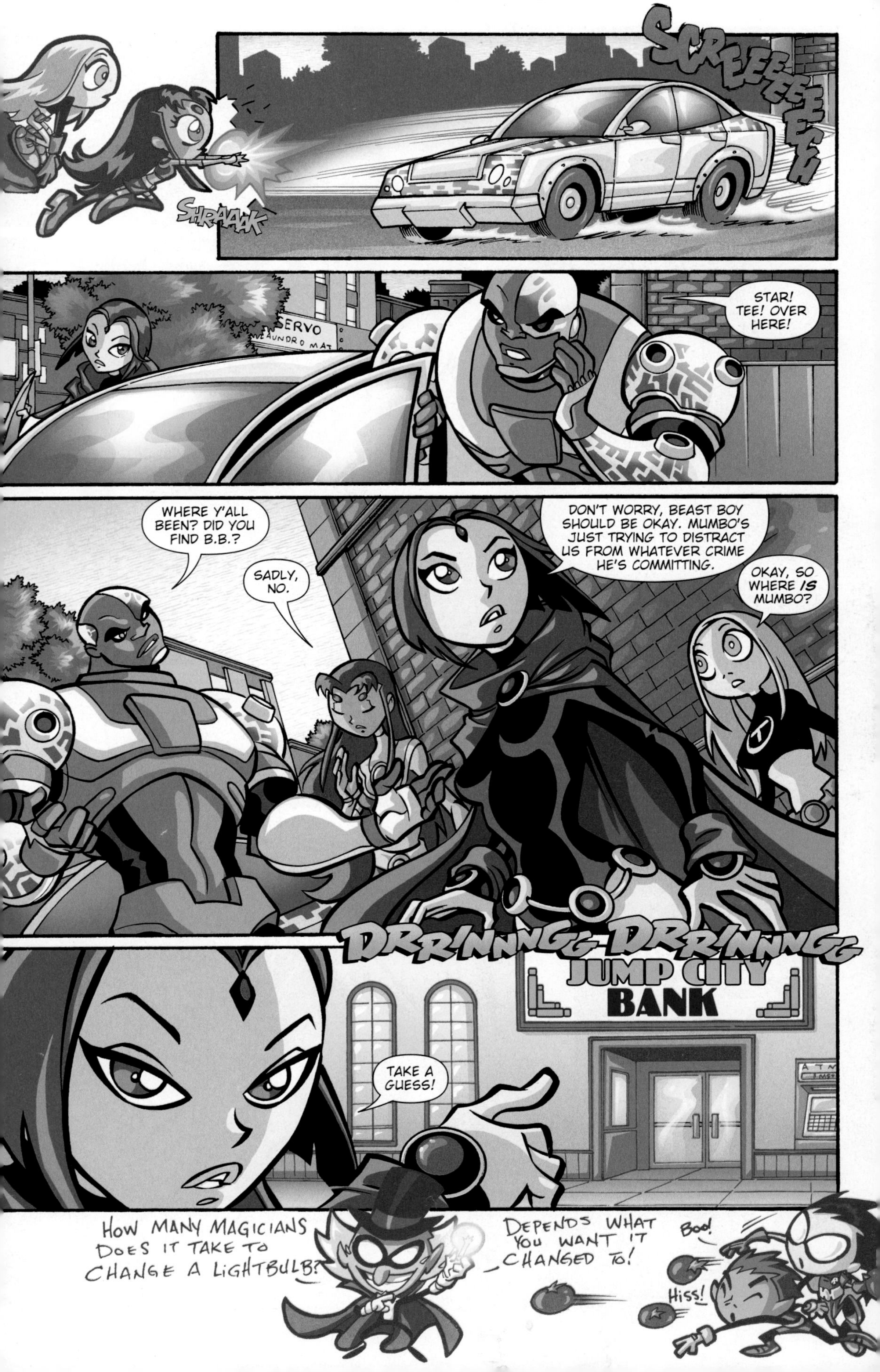
SCREEEEEEECH
SHRAAAK
SERVO LAUNDROMAT
STAR! TEE! OVER HERE!
WHERE Y'ALL BEEN? DID YOU FIND B.B.?
SADLY, NO.
DON'T WORRY, BEAST BOY SHOULD BE OKAY. MUMBO'S JUST TRYING TO DISTRACT US FROM WHATEVER CRIME HE'S COMMITTING.
OKAY, SO WHERE *IS* MUMBO?
DRRINNNGG DRRINNNGG
JUMP CITY BANK
TAKE A GUESS!
HOW MANY MAGICIANS DOES IT TAKE TO CHANGE A LIGHTBULB?
DEPENDS WHAT YOU WANT IT CHANGED TO!
Boo!
Hiss!

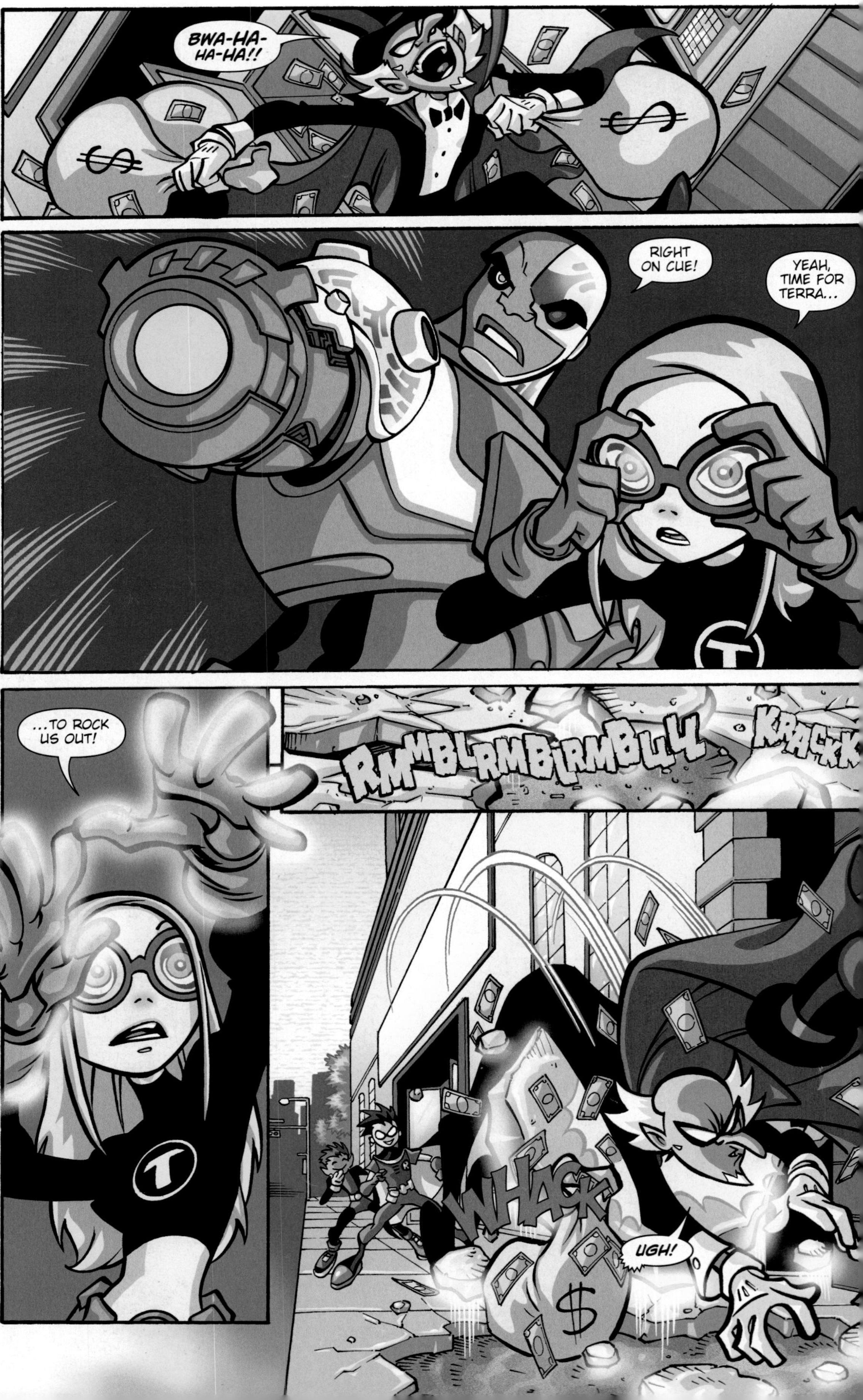
BWA-HA-HA-HA!!
RIGHT ON CUE!
YEAH, TIME FOR TERRA...
...TO ROCK US OUT!
RMMBLRMBLRMBLLL
KRACKK
WHACK
UGH!

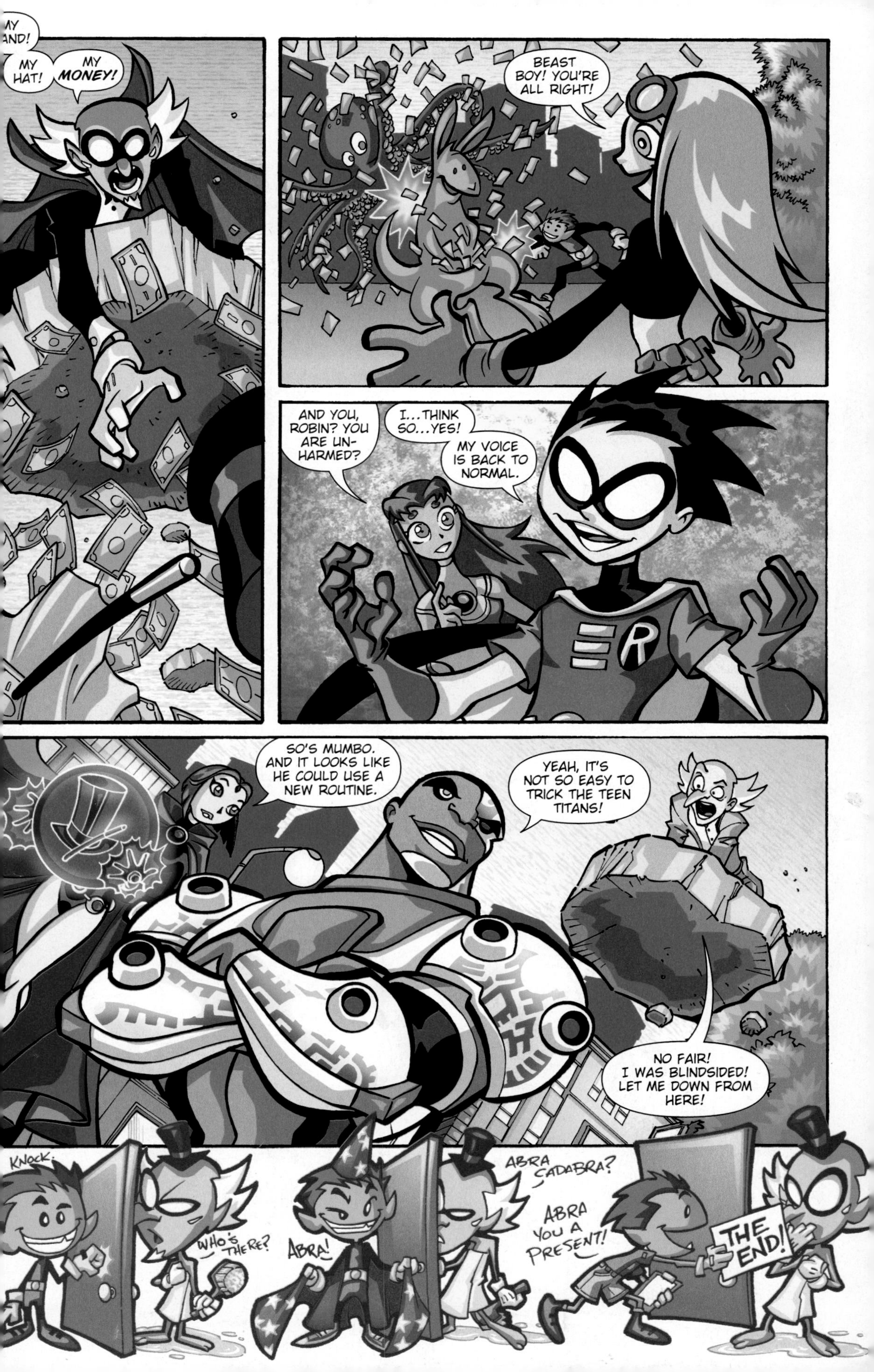

MY
AND!
MY HAT!
MY MONEY!
BEAST BOY! YOU'RE ALL RIGHT!
AND YOU, ROBIN? YOU ARE UN-HARMED?
I...THINK SO...YES!
MY VOICE IS BACK TO NORMAL.
SO'S MUMBO. AND IT LOOKS LIKE HE COULD USE A NEW ROUTINE.
YEAH, IT'S NOT SO EASY TO TRICK THE TEEN TITANS!
NO FAIR! I WAS BLINDSIDED! LET ME DOWN FROM HERE!
KNOCK.
WHO'S THERE?
ABRA!
ABRA CADABRA?
ABRA YOU A PRESENT!
THE END!

COLOR TEEN TITANS GO!

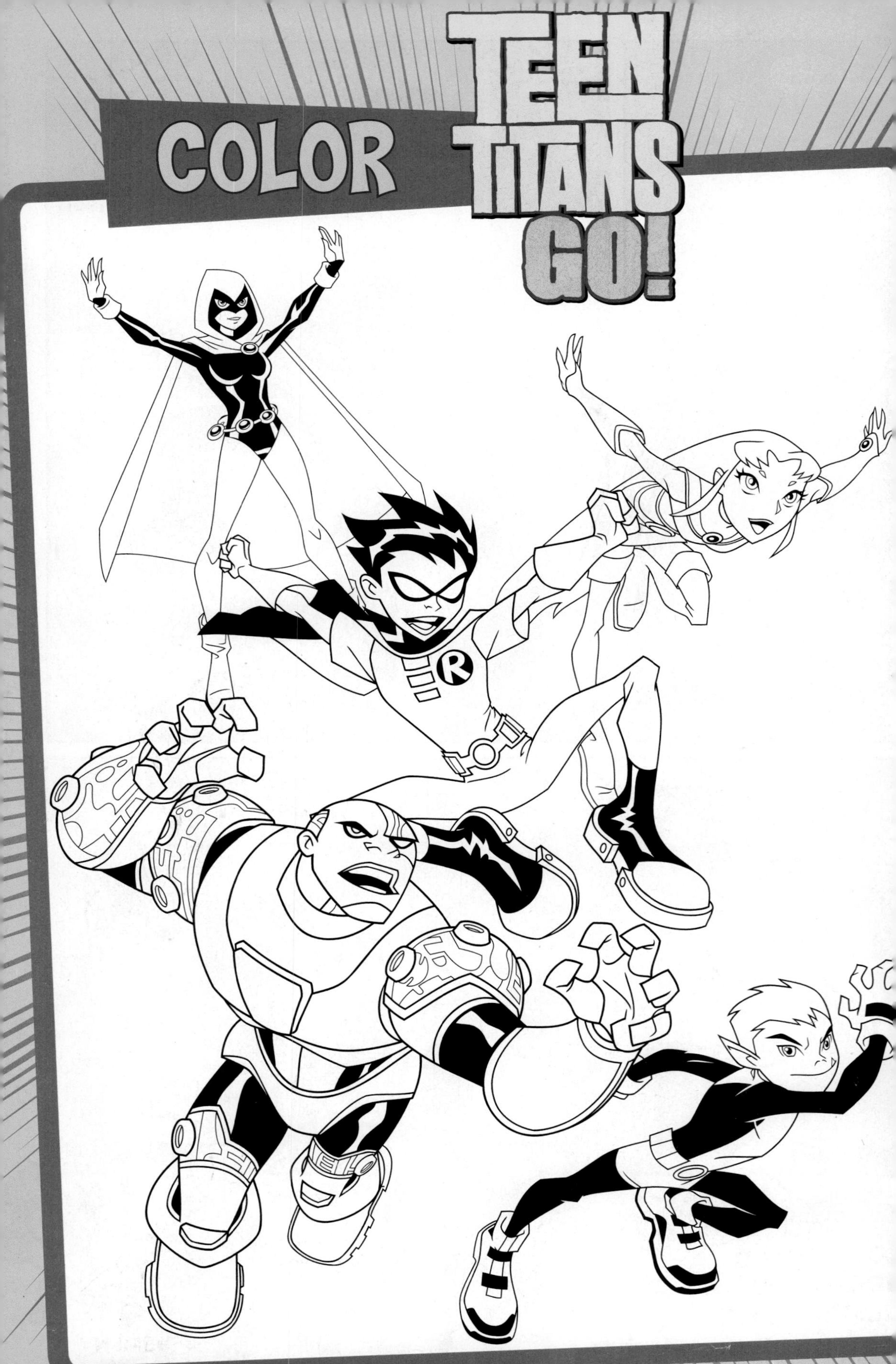

TEEN TITANS GO! SILHOUETTES

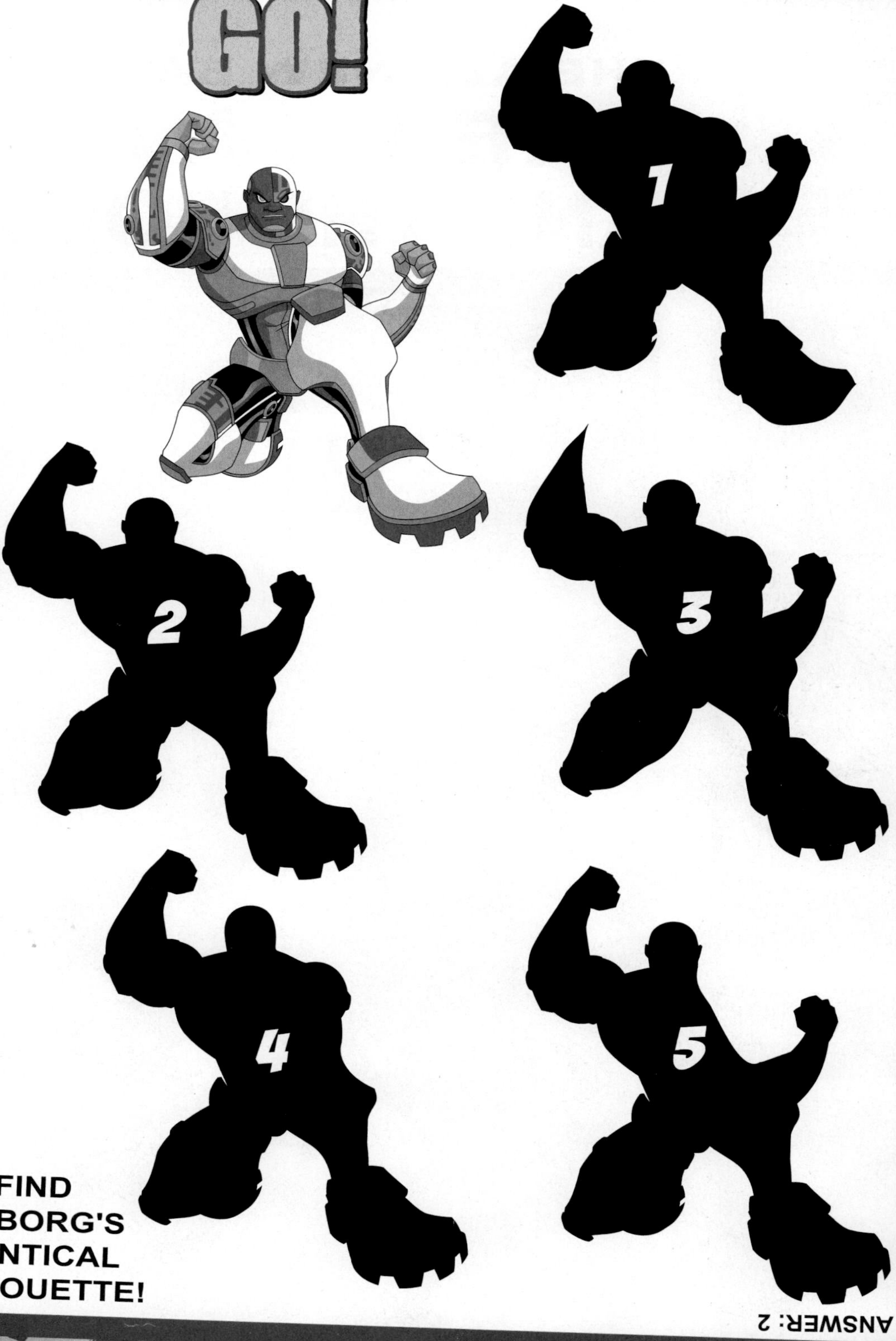
1
2
3
4
5

FIND CYBORG'S IDENTICAL SILHOUETTE!

ANSWER: 2

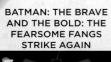

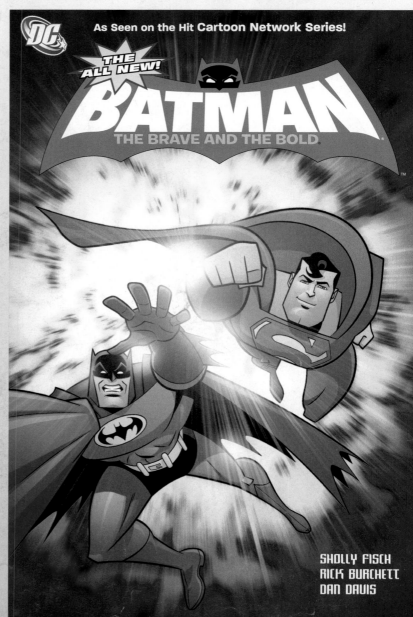

EISNER AWARD-WINNING GRAPHIC
NOVELS FOR READERS OF ANY AGE

TINY TITANS

BY ART BALTAZAR & FRANCO

TINY TITANS:
THE FIRST RULE OF
PET CLUB...

TINY TITANS:
ADVENTURES IN
AWESOMENESS

READ THE ENTIRE
SERIES!

TINY TITANS:
ADVENTURES IN
AWESOMENESS

TINY TITANS:
SIDEKICKIN' IT

TINY TITANS: THE FIRST
RULE OF PET CLUB...

TINY TITANS: FIELD
TRIPPIN'

TINY TITANS: THE TREE-
HOUSE AND BEYOND

TINY TITANS:
GROWING UP TINY

TINY TITANS:
AW YEAH TITANS!

DC COMICS™

START AT THE BEGINNING

TEEN TITANS
VOLUME 1: IT'S
OUR RIGHT TO FIGHT

LEGION OF SUPER-HEROES VOLUME 1: HOSTILE WORLD

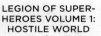

LEGION LOST VOLUME 1: RUN FROM TOMORROW

STATIC SHOCK VOLUME 1: SUPERCHARGED

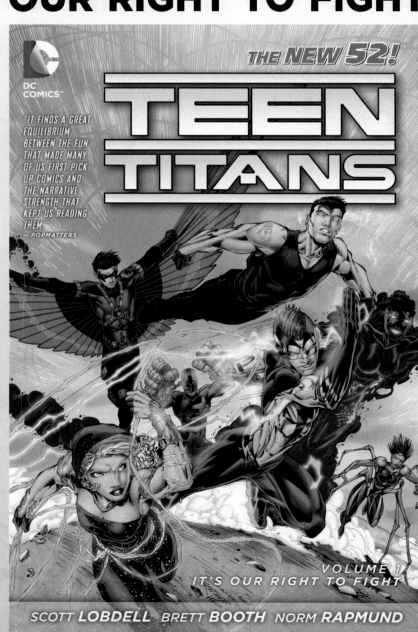

SCOTT **LOBDELL** BRETT **BOOTH** NORM **RAPMUND**